THE SEQUEL
TO
ALFRED CREEK

D. L. WATERHOUSE

CROSSBOOKS
PUBLISHING

CrossBooks™
A Division of LifeWay
1663 Liberty Drive
Bloomington, IN 47403
www.crossbooks.com
Phone: 1-866-879-0502

First published by CrossBooks 1/11/2012

ISBN: 978-1-4627-1311-0 (sc)
ISBN: 978-1-4627-1313-4 (hc)
ISBN: 978-1-4627-1312-7 (e)

Library of Congress Control Number: 2011963051

Printed in the United States of America

DEDICATION

This book I dedicate to my grandchildren: AJ, Walker, Tristan, Victoria, and Rhiannon, in the hope that it will contribute to their better judgment and decision making throughout their lives.

In addition, it is my hope that those who read this story will consider the deeper ramifications of every action and every behavior taken in life, for the sake of all affected.

Also, to those whose lives have been decimated by the effects of poor decisions throughout their lives and are on the verge of losing all hope, understand that to lose hope is also a decision.

dl waterhouse

ACKNOWLEDGMENTS

For the ambition to add my voice to the war against family dysfunction, I thank my firstborn daughter, Laney, to whom also I am forever indebted for the healing of my heart. I love you forever, my precious.

To my next born daughter Lori, I extend my congratulations and encouragement for the responsibility you have demonstrated for yourself and your family. I love you always and thank you for my grandchildren.

To my youngest daughter Nanci, the eternal student, thank you for your advice and encouragement in my writing endeavor, and I congratulate you for your untiring dedication to the advancement of your education and that of my grandchildren. From some secret place, you always manage to find the energy required to meet every demand and still find time to be the ideal mother, wife, and daughter.

Finally, to my wife, Florence. If not for you, this book would have never happened. When people ask me how we managed to stay married all these years, I always say it is because your love for me is greater than my dysfunction. Thank you for your support and encouragement. I love you always and forever.

INTRODUCTION

This is a fiction novel. For purposes of analogy, I have taken many literary liberties. All portions of the story are fictional with the exception of the spiritual connotations, references to the Authorized King James Version of the Christian Bible, and most geographical locations.

Credits include the alluding by the fictitious character Lou Worley to the literary work of Watchman Nee, the author of *The Normal Christian Life*, as well as reference to the popular phrase from the Allstate Insurance television commercial "in good hands."

From the perspective of humanity, there are as many character types in the world as there are people in the world, contributing of course to the individuality of each person. However, there is only one character permitted into the kingdom of God, the character of Jesus Christ. It is not difficult to understand the need for salvation when we witness a character wrecked by the effects of sin and dysfunction. The need for forgiveness through the blood of Jesus and the renewing ministry of the Holy Spirit is obvious.

Once in a while, however, along comes a man who appears to be the perfect husband, father, citizen, patriot, and all-around worthy person of all the good blessings God has to bestow. In fact, the cause-and-effect laws of the universe that the very same God created and made have given back a hundredfold in terms of providential good fortune for a life well lived; for a life disciplined by principle, right doing, and functional living.

So infrequently is that kind of piety found in this fallen and decadent age that societies often pay tribute and honor to such men, bestowing upon them its greatest recognitions. I often wonder if its purpose is to hold such men up as role models, or is it man's need to convince himself that all of humanity is inherently good?

Does a life of principle and decent living provide merit for man before God? Can he expect salvation and entrance into the kingdom of heaven by virtue of his uprightness? "By grace are ye saved through faith; and that not of yourselves: it is the *gift* of God" (Ephesians. 2:8, emphasis added).

The fictitious protagonist of this story has lived his life not realizing his spiritual lack or need. At the age of fifty-one, he embarks on an adventure that ultimately brings him to that realization.

It is like a man who carries no money in his pocket, not seeing the need for any until confronted with a necessity that can only be provided, if he has money. At that point, he becomes aware of something that was a fact all along, but a fact to which he was unconscious.

Lou Worley's character appears to be upstanding, but it is flawed. However, compared to the dysfunctional and criminally minded characters that he battles in defense of nation, community, and family, he—in the eyes of the world—is the ideal citizen. Yet, in the eyes of God, he is incomplete. What will it take for a man such as him to realize his need for the Savior? Where will Lou Worley encounter that epiphany that will reveal to him his helplessness apart from God?

Technically, this is a fiction novel about a fictional character. But is it really? Jesus described the gospel through many stories that were oftentimes parables he made up. Who is to say that those stories did not actually take place, somewhere, sometime, and to someone? *Maybe it is your story.*

Note From The Author

I am not going to bore you with my life story. I might save that for another time and format. However, I would like to tell you my purpose for writing this book.

My father was an alcoholic and professional gambler. In 1949, when I was four years old, we lived in a cabin next to a sawmill where my father worked part-time, if and when he was sober enough.

My earliest memories at that tender age were of the winter snow filtering through the cracks and gaps of the shake roof above my head, which then settled onto my bed covers without even melting. Also, I vividly remember the smell of bacon and eggs in the tiny kitchen where Mother tried in vain to please my perpetually angry father whose incessant yelling and cursing were the welcome my brother and I awoke to each morning.

It did not last long. Before my sixth birthday, our father who drank a fifth of liquor a day—robbing him of all will to live--committed suicide.

Instead of finishing high school, I joined the military in 1963 and spent the final year of a four-year enlistment in Vietnam.

The dysfunctional beginnings of my childhood formulated the dysfunction that followed me the rest of my life until the day the Lord Jesus Christ revealed Himself to me as God, Father, Savior and Redeemer.

Dysfunction has reaped a whirlwind of emotional pain and suffering in my life and the lives of my family members, as well as every person I have ever known. Its price can only be estimated in the trail of tears that are left as a legacy to their dysfunctional behavior. It has become to me a thing that I hate, a thing that I seek to overcome, and a thing that I war against.

I am now retired after forty-four years of driving trucks and intend to continue to write fiction stories that, hopefully, will inspire not only functional living but rest and confidence in the salvation of God for every man, woman, and child through Jesus Christ. As long as the Lord gives me time and opportunity on this earth, I shall work to inspire others to a higher calling of faith in God and motivation to functional living.

I am not a preacher or a minister. I can only give testimony to the revelations that the Holy Spirit of God has given to my mind and to the work of the Lord in recovering this sinner from the dysfunction that wreaked havoc in my own life.

The year of 2012 finds me living in Carnation, Washington, with my wife, Florence, to whom I have been married for thirty-three years and to whom I owe my life.

For more about this author and my passion for general aviation go to: www.ifli4fun.com

CHAPTER ONE

The town of Darington, located twenty-seven miles east of Arlington, Washington, and seventy-five miles northeast of Seattle, has been home to my wife Kati, myself, and our three daughters for the last thirty years.

It is a small town with a population of 1,405, close-knit and friendly.

1S2 is the FAA designation of our local airport, located adjacent to the north side of town. The 2,500-foot paved runway, situated somewhat east and west, sports a graveyard at the immediate west end of the airfield that can be a bit distracting when landing or departing.

My name is Lou Worley. I've made my living driving a logging truck for the past twenty-seven years which, in spite of the industry's economic vacillations, has supported our family reasonably well.

We are not rich but not poor either, due mostly to Kati's managerial skills. We are healthy, happy, and my wife and I are still in love, even after thirty-two years together.

At the time of our lives when this story began, our oldest daughter, Keera, and her husband, Rusty, lived in Spanaway down the Interstate 5 corridor just east of the Fort Lewis army base on the Mountain Highway. They have three-year-old twins, Manson and Michelle. Our middle daughter Kathy, with her husband, Richard and two-year-old son Randy, will soon be welcoming an addition to their growing family. Her name is already decided. Elaine. They lived in Auburn, Washington.

My youngest daughter, Kelly, with her husband, Mitchell, and their one-year-old triplets, Walker, Rhiannon, and Tristan, had moved to Missoula, Montana, three years earlier.

It was Memorial Day weekend, one year after their move to Missoula, that Kati and I loaded our overnight bags in the Cessna. Shortly after daylight that Saturday morning, we departed 1S2 and headed east to Montana.

Our weekend with the kids soon gave way to reality and Mitchell drove us to the airport, where I fueled the airplane for the return trip home. While the office girl was processing my credit card, I noticed several aviation publications in the glass case beneath the countertop. One in particular caught my eye. *I Flew the Alfred Creek Gold* was a fascinating tale of a pilot who flew for a group of Idaho cowboys in search of gold and finding with it grizzly bears and gangsters. I bought it.

During the next two years, I read the book five times. Each time, I would get a stirring inside me. There was something about that story and the adventure of flying to Alaska that gripped me like a pit bull on a pant leg, pulling, dragging, challenging me to pick up that pilot's story where he had left it twenty years before. Unable to put it off any longer, I put in for a long-overdue vacation.

I had just loaded my little airplane with enough camping supplies, food, and emergency gear to last at least a month, and there I was, waving good-bye to my precious Kati, who was rapidly deteriorating into a blubbering basket case. The pit bull was right. It was now or never, and for some reason, I actually felt my destiny was involved.

With my fingers crossed in the hope that I would clear the trees at the west end of the runway, thereby avoiding an untimely arrival at that disconcerting cemetery, I pushed the power forward. The little 1957 Cessna 172 straight tail obediently headed directly toward the trees.

At the time, I wasn't sure what I was looking for. Maybe my own adventure, or some time away from logging trucks, or even something more psychological or spiritual like the renewal of my inner self. Maybe I was going through a midlife crisis. At the time, the only thing I actually did know was that I *didn't* know. However, I did understand, and still do, that in life doors open and doors close, and he who hesitates never discovers what may be on the other side. I felt a bond with that pilot and his Cessna 206 Stationair. The adventures and challenges he faced and experienced appealed to me. Somehow, I had to find that place where his adventure took place, and that was where I was going. By the way, I cleared the trees.

It was the third week of June 1995. I had just turned fifty-one years old in the middle of March. Kati is two years younger than me, but every bit of ten years smarter.. We had just celebrated thirty-two years of married life a few weeks before, so we knew each other well. Still do.

The logging and dump truck industry that I worked in all those years had placed me in contact with hundreds of men whose lives were very dysfunctional, and I have been asked many times how my wife and I managed to stay married for so many years. "We don't try to change each other," I would say. I can't think of a thing I would ever want to change about her, and even though she may like to change a few things about me, she never has tried. We like each other just fine the way we are.

With the cemetery no longer a factor and my altitude approaching 4,500 feet msl (mean sea level), I leveled off, relaxed back against the seat, and watched an Navy A-6 Intruder pass below me on my right side. Flying low, just above the trees. Scooting along at about 300 knots, the navy pilot was obviously westbound, returning to the Whidbey Island Naval Air Station from a day of low-level practice maneuvers in the military operations area just east and a little north of Darington. We saw them frequently. They represented an angel of death to the enemies of our country, but on that day, to me, I saw it as an sign that a guardian had been sent to protect me on my adventure. I saluted and dipped my wings, knowing that unless he could see behind and above him, he would never know it. Then he did a barrel roll. I took that as a good luck sign of something. Don't get me wrong. I'm not superstitious, just optimistic.

After planning this trip for the last two years, I was finally on my way. The weather was cool and clear and forecast to remain the same for several days. I landed at Bellingham International for my last US fuel stop. There I filed an advise customs flight plan, or ADCUS, to Abbotsford, British Columbia, where I would clear customs into Canada, then proceed on to Watson Lake in the Yukon. By the time I departed Abbotsford, it was eight a.m., and with fuel stops at Williams Lake, Fort St. John, and Fort Nelson, I calculated that it would be near ten p.m. before I made Watson Lake, where I would spend my fist night before entering Alaska.

3

I love flying cross-country, and though I had driven to Alaska twice before in my car, that was my first time across British Columbia and the Yukon en route to Alaska in my airplane.

I made good time and landed at Watson Lake at 9:30 p.m., fueled the airplane, and paid a visit to the Flight Service Station (FSS) to close my flight plan and check the prognostication charts and weather forecast for the remainder of my trip.

The predicted weather for the next day was clear skies, and though in that part of the country it can change abruptly to something completely unexpected, at least I was able to sleep better anticipating favorable conditions.

With the airplane fueled and ready to go for the next morning, I taxied to the camping area, tied it down, and pitched my two-man dome tent. The mosquitoes were ferocious. I tried to get in the tent with my sleeping bag and mat before they all got in with me, but they got in anyway. While I was sleeping soundly, dreaming of fair skies and tailwinds, they ate me alive.

When I awoke, it was raining. I felt a sense of relief. It meant that I did not have to get out of bed so soon. My head and face; exposed while I slept had allowed the mosquitoes to have their uninterrupted way with me. I looked like I had crawled through a patch of poison oak. I noticed, however, that they were no longer buzzing around in my tent. I assumed they had all crashed from overloading themselves on my blood.

When the rain finally subsided, I peered outside to check the sky conditions. Obviously, the only mosquitoes that had actually crashed were the ones in my tent. I quickly zipped the tent fly closed long enough to conduct a frantic search for a mosquito head net that I was sure I had brought along.

Emerging from my nylon igloo looking like a Brit with the measles on African safari, I made my way once again to the Flight Service Station.

"What happened to all that clear sky you said I could expect today?" I asked, trying not to sound like the complaining type.

The Canadians are very cordial people and go out of their way to make us Americans feel welcome in their country. It's a good thing, too, because back in the States, a smart remark like that might have gotten me more bad weather, maybe even a couple of weeks of it. But because they are such pleasant people, the Flight Service Station attendant turned toward me and said, "Good morning. I'm sorry, were you expecting nice weather today?"

"I had my fingers crossed."

"That's about the only thing that works around here. Keep doing that and you might see some clearing in a couple of hours with some broken conditions by about 1700Z hours."

I looked at my watch. It was eight a.m., my time. "That's only a couple of hours. I can live with that. Where is the restaurant?"

Anywhere you go in Canada and Alaska that has fuel and a restaurant, you'll also find shower facilities.. By the time I had breakfast, got some sandwiches to go, took a shower, and packed up my igloo, the skies had returned to fair flying conditions. I then filed a flight plan to Northway, Alaska, which was my US Customs port of entry.

I was monitoring the navigation/communications (nav/com) radio tuned to the tower frequency when I heard the controller say to me, "Blue-and-white Cessna, on the condition that you have removed that ridiculous face mask and your eyes are not swelled completely shut, you are cleared for takeoff." (In an informal situation controllers often use color combinations as apposed to tail numbers)

"That's affirmative. Thanks. See you next time."

"Try eating garlic or sprinkling garlic powder on your skin," the controller added.

"You're kidding. Does that actually work?"

"It helps. Have a good flight, and thanks for visiting Canada."

Like I said, the Canadians are very nice and the controllers at times can be pleasantly informal.

In those days, cell phones and towers were still in the developmental stage, but I had purchased one of those fancy new portable satellite phones that I felt might be the thing to have in case of an emergency.

The FSS attendant had told me that I should call the customs office at Northway two hours before my arrival so they could have someone meet me at the airport ramp, which is a couple of miles past the border crossing. There is not a lot of activity at the airport, so it is primarily unattended. Well, I was a little distracted with the mosquitoes and forgot. By the time I remembered, it was a little too late.

I checked my sat-phone for coverage. There was none, so I decided to drop in low over the highway checkpoint to let them know they had an arrival, hoping I would not live to regret it.

Minutes later, after landing and taxiing to the customs inspection ramp, I once again checked the sat-phone and noticed it had picked up a couple of bars. I called the number the FSS attendant had given me.

A very authoritative voice answered the phone. "Border patrol, Northway."

"Is this customs?" I asked to be sure whom it was that I was talking to.

"Yes, can I help you?"

"Yes, sir. This is Cessna N..95b I would like to clear customs into Alaska. I just landed at the Northway airport."

There was a long pause, and I heard muffled voices in the background.

"Did you call to let anyone know you were coming?"

"No, sir, but I filed an ADCUS flight plan. I assumed Flight Service would do that for me, otherwise what would be the point of calling it—"

He interrupted. "Are you the one who buzzed the border crossing?"

"Yes, sir. I was going to call on my satellite phone, but I didn't have any—"

He interrupted again. "What is your name?"

"Lou Worley. I flew in from—"

"Where did your flight originate?"

"I cleared customs at Abbotsford yesterday morning."

"That's not what I asked you. Where did your flight originate?" His voice had gotten much sterner. I knew he wasn't happy with my arrival, especially the buzz job.

"Darington, Washington."

"Where are you calling from now?"

"My satellite phone. I picked up a couple of—"

He interrupted again. "Are you still in your airplane, or have you gotten out of your aircraft at anytime since you landed?"

"Yes, sir, no, sir."

"Is anyone with you, do you have any passengers, and if so, have anyone of them exited the aircraft at anytime since you landed?"

"No, sir."

"Is there anyone waiting for you at the airport or anyone nearby where you are parked?"

"No, sir."

"What is your business in Alaska?"

"I'm on vacation, and this is my first time flying my own plane to Alaska, so it is all about touring the country and seeing the sights."

"Have you ever been to Alaska before?"

"Yes, sir, twice by car."

"Do you have any drugs, alcohol or firearms, or any kind of plant life on board?"

"No drugs, no alcohol, no plants, but I do have a ten-gage shotgun."

"How long will you be staying in Alaska?"

"About a month."

"Thank you, Mr. Worley. That's all I need. You can proceed. Enjoy your visit."

Well, that was a relief. I did feel a bit foolish, though. Should have taken that customs thing a little more seriously.

A short distance (maybe forty yards) from where I sat in the airplane, I noticed a building with one of those jobsite san-a-cans. Walking over to it, I noticed a U.S. Customs vehicle backing away from the rear of the building and turning toward the main terminal that was obviously vacant. I chuckled, shook my head, and mumbled, "It isn't even cold out, and he couldn't come out of that building. Oh, well. I guess they got their reasons and their own way of doing things."

It was fifty more miles to Tok, Alaska. I had pre-rented a mailbox there and ten days before I left, I had mailed myself two packages. One was my favorite handgun, and the other was a generous supply of ammo for my favorite handgun.

I had stopped at Tok during both of my previous road trips to Alaska and really liked the town so on this trip I decided to stay an extra day. I needed to do some shopping and pick up a few things that I wasn't able to find at home, one of which was a product called bear bombs. I didn't know much about them but had heard they might come in handy if a guy ran out of ammo.

The morning I left Tok, I witnessed one of the most beautiful sunrises I had ever seen. It made me miss my wife, wishing she could have enjoyed it with me. I pointed the spinner southwest and a little more than an hour and a half later, I was turning final approach at the Gulkana airport.

Once again, full of fuel and feeling the excitement of being so close to my destination, which was now only twenty minutes away, I climbed to four thousand feet msl and entered Tahneta Pass. On the other side and several thousand feet below the Sheep Mountain airstrip gradually came into view.

Soon, I was in position to do a low flyby over the unpaved Sheep Mountain airstrip to check its surface conditions before I landed.

From only a hundred feet above the runway, I could see that the restaurant and inn were open and busy and that the turf conditions appeared excellent. A few minutes later, the tires softly kissed the ground in greeting. Three days and eighteen hundred miles since leaving home, I had arrived. A tingle of expectation traveled down my spine.

I taxied to the far west end of the runway and pushed the Cessna back into the trees. With the airplane parked as far off the runway as possible, I tied it down between two logs and set up my base camp.

It was at least a half-mile walk to the lodge from my camp, but the exercise felt good. Just past the end of the east threshold of the runway, the opening in the trees widened considerably, accommodating at least a dozen cabins, a large shop, smokehouse, bathhouse, and more importantly, the main lodge, which included in-house guest rooms and a restaurant.

As I ascended the staircase, I could not help but notice a sign above the door that read: "HOUSE RULES: DON'T MAKE MARGE MAD & THE CUSTOMER IS ALWAYS WRONG." I entered anyway.

"Howdy, stranger. I ain't never seen that bird in here before. Can that thing fly with all them extra wheels on it? Where ya from?" I turned and slowly made my way toward a large, husky woman (I think) who appeared to be addressing me. She wore an apron, so I assumed she must be the chief cook and bottle washer and was probably the one I was not suppose to make mad.

"I'm the new inspector for this district from the public health department. I just flew in from Fairbanks."

Abruptly, all noise stopped, and every eye in the place was now staring directly at me. The logger lady's cheery face turned to stone, and I do believe she was at a loss for words.

"Uh, oh. You're not Marge, are you?" I said, tongue-in-cheek.

The dining room full of patrons erupted in laughter as Marge's face went from stone to relief and then to red in rapid succession. She raised her hand and pointed her finger at me.

"I take it yer one of them fellers that can't follow the rules."

"They can be a little challenging sometimes. Especially if I think I can get a chuckle."

"Well, mister, you got yer chuckle, so do you have a name? And by the way, I was just kidding about yer airplane. It is actually kinda purty."

"Lou Worley. Glad to meet you." I extended my hand. "You must be Marge?"

"Likewise, Lou, and just for the record, it takes more than that to make me mad."

"You have no idea how glad I am to know that,"

Marge took my order of double cheeseburger, fries, and cherry pie, and I walked around the log-constructed lodge, looking at pictures and reading the history of the Sheep Mountain settlement.

Adjacent to the Richardson Highway, or Glenn highway so called by the locals, the Sheep Mountain airstrip was located 186 miles southwest of Tok Junction and fifteen miles south of the Alfred Creek mine where the Idaho boys' adventure had taken place. Although at the time, I did not know the exact location of the gold claim.

I prepaid for a weeks tie-down, intending on making the place my vacation home while I searched for the Idaho boys' mining camp and to where I would return every night from my aerial excursions to and from the camp once I located it. At least, that was the plan.

The next three days, I flew around the Tahneta Pass area, west and north of Gunsight, and the old Brandt's resort on the Richardson highway. From all that I could ascertain from the book of the Idaho boys and their prospecting adventure, I was still unable to pinpoint where precisely the gold claim had been located.

I had visualized as best I could the surrounding area as the author and pilot had described the approaches and departures, and with that vague picture, I spent those days zigzagging through canyons and gaps, sliding over ridges and streams, looking for any thing at all that might resemble their camp.

The first thing in the morning on the fourth day since I had arrived at Sheep Mountain, a patch of clearing caught my eye. At the confluence of the Alfred and Caribou Creeks, forming the headwaters of a drainage guarded by high terrain on both sides, lay a very short stretch of cleared ground that appeared to have long ago served as an airstrip. Maybe.

I circled above it several times, forming a mental picture of the best way to fly the approach, still not sure that I would be able to land. I would need to save that decision for when I was much closer and could get a better look at the surface conditions.

The drainage was one I had flown through just the day before, but somehow had overlooked this spot that more and more appeared to be just what I was looking for. I expected there would be more in the way of old mining paraphernalia lying around or some remnants of the prospecting operations that had gone on. Of course, all that activity took place back in the summer of 1975, so who knows what all had come and gone from there during the twenty-year interim until I arrived?

I turned northbound once again up the Caribou drainage that runs from north to south on its way to the Matanuska River. I had dropped in twenty degrees of flap and slowed the airplane to seventy on the airspeed indicator, calibrated in miles per hour. With a descent rate of five hundred feet per minute, keeping the turns to standard rate or less, I continued the descent deeper into the canyon.

My little straight tail was at that time powered by a 145 horsepower 0300 Continental engine and, in the kind of terrain I had entered into, was a wee bit shy on horsepower. However, the year before, in anticipation of making the trip, I had substantially improved the short field performance capability by installing a Horton STOL (short takeoff and landing) kit, which made it entirely possible to land in a place to short to depart from. I knew that would be a bad idea.

As I made the last turn to final, the big hill that earlier had been five hundred feet below me had quickly become four thousand feet above me. I was rapidly approaching the moment of decision.

I did not intend to land on the first pass anyway, as I always do a flyby at a strange landing spot, sometimes several of them if the approach is complicated. I needed time to evaluate the conditions and determine two extremely important things: Can I get in, without breaking the airplane or myself, and moreover, would I have enough runway length to takeoff once I landed?

The flyby went well. However, it was clear that any lower and at the slower air speed necessary on final approach, a go-around at that point would be out of the question due to the rapidly rising terrain on the climbing turn to the northwest and with the aforementioned power limitations.

The landing surface appeared to be a kind of sod, almost mossy-looking, substance. I guess I was expecting something along the line of hard surface dirt and rock. It also looked to be a little soft—something that could cost significant and much-needed takeoff speed when time to depart. Oh, well, It was turning into a perfectly executed approach to a landing. Everything was right on: airspeed, descent, and textbook landing configuration. The burm on the far end of the airstrip was almost a non-factor as the wheels kissed the carpeted surface. It was not until the nose gear made contact with the moss that I realized *I had made a serious mistake.*

Any concerns I had of getting stopped before charging into the burm at the far end were a moot point as the nose gear and main gear tires quickly sunk into a three-inch layer of gumbo beneath the thin blanket of moss. The aircraft was coming to a quick stop, and I had not even made it to the end of the runway. Instantly, I slammed full power and reefed back on the yoke. With just enough airspeed remaining and a little help from the prop-blast, the tail went down, bringing the nose gear back off the ground and out of the sponge. Directional control had all but disappeared, but I somehow managed, under full power, to make it to the far end of the strip.

Stopping just short of scratching the paint, I reduced the power, let the nose gear return to earth, and went through the shutdown procedures. As the propeller clattered to a stop, I sat listening to the sound of the creek and the ticking of the cooling engine while my heart rate slowly retreated to a mere level of panic.

I didn't move for at least twenty minutes as the realization of where I was and what had just happened sunk in. For a brief moment, I felt trapped and vulnerable. It was obvious that I wasn't going anywhere anytime soon until I could find something to scrape or shovel the gumbo from off the runway. I checked the time: It was a quarter to eight in the morning. I grabbed my jacket and stepped out of the airplane.

From the backseat area, I took both a fold-up military spade and my .44 magnum Desert Eagle handgun, a no-nonsense piece of survival equipment that I had pre-shipped from home via parcel post to that rented mailbox in Tok Junction.

As I retraced the tracks left by the tires in the gumbo, it did appear that beneath the three inches of sticky goo was a firm surface from which I would be able to takeoff, providing I could scrape away the gummy clay. In any case, it was certain that I was going to be there a few days and, if I were planning to fly out anytime soon, would need to get started on the clearing project right away.

My emergency pack, along with sleeping bag, (good to fifty below) included all the required items with some extras that I had collected over the years. Before I began the trip, I completely went though it, replacing batteries and other items that tend to become useless after a certain date. For food, I had granola bars, energy bars, dehydrated meals, fruit, soups, and instant coffee. But you guessed it—I had no stove.

By then, I was kicking myself for leaving the major part of my camping gear back at the Sheep Mountain airport. The tent, extra clothing, food, stove, coffee pot, and eating utensils. would have certainly come in handy in the unexpected predicament that I found myself in, though the extra weight might have been unwelcome when it was time to fly out due to the shortness of the runway. Another very significant issue yet to be resolved involving my future.

The landing strip lay at the base of a high mountain directly to the east rising a good 4,500 feet above the canyon floor. The creek ran parallel and somewhat north and south. There was a ten-foot-high burm on the north end, the other side of which, an area about the size of a football field appeared to have been dozed extensively with heavy equipment at one time. Beyond that, there was another mountain. Between those two hills, Alfred Creek wound its way down a narrow canyon to merge with Caribou Creek and ultimately, the Matanuska River that eventually flowed into the headwaters of the Knick Arm, seventy miles southwest and abeam Wasilla, Alaska.

For the next hour, I wandered around the site where the Idaho boys had lived their once-in–a-lifetime dream of prospecting for gold. I was satisfied that I had at least found the place. I had tried to imagine what it must have been like to find real gold. I could not really see myself going to all the work and trouble that they had. The logistics of such an endeavor made me tired even to contemplate.

From the other side of what I shall refer to as—for reasons previously stated--the football field, I made my way down to the creek. This was just below where Caribou and Alfred Creeks merge with each other. It is also clear that the two of them do not get along that well, as their place of convergence more resembled a perfect storm, creating a river too deep and too treacherous to attempt to cross. To get to the other side, one would need to go much farther downstream to cross the Caribou or much farther upstream before finding a suitable crossing to the other side of Alfred Creek.

There were remnants of a dilapidated shack or shelter lying about in the form of planks and boards that had been undetectable from the air. I knew I would be able to use some of that scrap lumber for a fire and maybe to fabricate a scraper with which I could clear the runway, one that would be more effective and less arduous then my military spade, which was only two feet long.

I found a barely visible trail heading up the east side of Alfred Creek. Working my way up this almost completely overgrown path, it took me to the northwest side of the big hill, residing on the east side of the runway. There was something eerie about the place. I couldn't put my finger on it, but I pulled the Desert Eagle from its holster and checked the clip and safety.

Designed by the Israeli's, the Desert Eagle—in the hands of a trained and practiced handler—is capable of making weak men strong, small men big, and grizzly bears either run or dead. It has interchangeable caliber barrels available in .357 magnum, .41 caliber, .44 Magnum, and .50 caliber, all, compatible with the same platform. It is an extremely reliable semi-automatic handgun that includes an eight round clip—nine if you keep one in the pipe, which I always do. In addition, designed with a dual safety feature, it is virtually impossible to accidently shoot your foot off, theoretically speaking, of course.

About a quarter of a mile upstream, the trail took a sharp left and hooked back down toward the creek where it appeared to suddenly end. As I stepped around to the other side of a boulder, the size of a three-quarter ton pickup truck, I saw in the sand next to the creek an old, rusted coffee pot, a fry pan, and remnants of a fire-ring of rocks, testifying to the once-occupied campsite. Just above the big rock and angling slightly back up the hill fifty yards was another short trail terminating at a sunken indentation in the ground approximately three-foot in diameter and covered with an old, dilapidated plywood box that appeared to have once been the camp pit-toilet. Expecting that the old "one-holer" might come in handy sooner rather than later, I unfolded my military spade and proceeded to reinvent it.

I had only removed five or six scoops of the fill—or whatever—when I noticed a shiny, yellow substance mixed with the soil that had stuck to the spade. I felt my heart rate immediately increase, and for a moment, my breathing stopped. I reached toward the shiny material, my hand shaking in anticipation. With my thumb and forefinger, I examined the yellow colored substance. *It was pure gold.*

CHAPTER 2

After more than five hours of separating and cleaning the gold from the ... *dirt*, I had by then dug a hole at least four foot deep and four foot in diameter. The gold I had discovered had originally been stored in a piece of clear plastic that had long ago decomposed. Once separated from the dirt, there was easily enough to fill a five-gallon bucket. I took a break to return to the airplane for a duffle bag and some plastic garbage bags that I had included in my emergency pack.

The yellow metal was in a variety of shapes, sizes, and textures, twenty percent of which were in the form of marble-sized nuggets. There were a few that were larger, but three in particular were exceptional both in size and quality. In terms of mass, they were somewhat larger than golf balls, but elongated in shape and pitted with unique crevasses and craters. They were the most spectacular things I had ever seen. No one needed to tell me they were worth far more as collectibles than they were worth in terms of troy ounces. I put them in my pocket.

The majority of the gold was more the texture of course utility sand, which graduated in size from fine dust to small and large pea gravel. I had separated out what was large enough to pick with my fingers, placing it in garbage bags of approximately twenty-five pounds each.

I remembered the crushed fry pan lying by the huge rock just below the privy. Although a bit mangled, with the right modifications, I was able to use it for panning and washing the gold.

I returned to the airplane once again, not liking what I was seeing in the sky to the south and the west. Huge, dark clouds had been slowly building and moving in the direction of my gold mine. With chilly air preceding a very ominous looking cold front, it looked for sure like rain, possibly mixed with sleet or wet snow and, most certainly, wind; the kind of wind that could flip an improperly secured airplane upside down. I shook my head, exasperated at the bad luck, but was reluctant to complain to the universe too much about my misfortune, especially in the light of my recent *good* fortune. Count your blessings, I always say.

I turned the airplane in a downstream takeoff direction, facing the anticipated weather that would be coming up the canyon from the west. I then shoveled the gumbo from behind the landing gear and nose gear tires, and using rope from my stash of equipment in the baggage compartment, managed to winch the airplane backward onto the firm ground.

I found a couple of six-inch diameter logs approximately five feet long and buried them four feet deep into the ground with a rope attached to each of them that would reach the tie-down rings at the upper end of the wing struts. That completed and soaking wet from sweating, with no change of clothes available, I started a fire. While drying myself, I prepared one of the dehydrated dinners along with a cup of soup and hot coffee.

It was only the middle of the afternoon, but already I was feeling tired from all the shoveling. However, with so much of the day remaining, I knew I had no choice but to keep working. With my energy somewhat restored, I decided to go back to the job of retrieving the gold. I took with me a medium-sized backpack that I use for day hikes along with the ten-gage shotgun and began making my way toward the glory hole.

Canadian and Alaskan law includes a firearm in the list of required survival equipment carried on any cross-country flight. In Canada, it must be a rifle or shotgun, but under any circumstances, never carry a handgun while passing through Canada. I carry with me a Winchester ten-gage pump action. A wee bit too much gun for grouse or rabbits in the case of bagging food for the fork, but loaded with five in the magazine of alternating slugs and buckshot, a great comfort in Grizzly Land.

On the way back, I crossed the football field and again worked my way down to where the Alfred Creek trail began just about a quarter of a mile downstream from the golden privy. Once again, I felt that creepy feeling. I couldn't make it out, but there was definitely something about that place that made my spine tingle. I stopped and jacked a round into the chamber of the ten-gage, checked that the safety was on, and then reached into my pocket to replace the now missing round in the magazine. With two 400 grain slugs as the first introduction, followed by alternating number-eight buckshot and slug, I was satisfied that whatever was giving me that creepy feeling, short of a rouge elephant, I stood at least somewhat of a chance. With a few extra shotgun shells and two additional clips loaded with three hundred grain jacketed, hollow-point .44 magnum ammunition, my uneasiness was somewhat displaced. My thoughts once again returned to the task at hand.

I was trying to imagine how all that gold got into that hole in the ground. I remembered in the story of the Idaho boys that someone had been seen messing around in the night down by the sluice boxes on several occasions, but had run off when discovered by the dozer operator. Also, there were two brothers—nineteen and seventeen years old—who had been camped somewhere up Alfred Creek, supposedly working a separate claim and who had on several occasions been spotted in the same area. One time, one of them even wandered into the Idaho boys' camp, wet, cold, hungry, and begging for food. He turned out to be the younger of the two, but the biggest. A month later, someone saw him hitchhiking on the highway by Brandt's Resort. He evidently was trying to find his brother who had disappeared. No one ever saw him or his brother again.

By one o'clock in the morning, it had turned a lot colder. My hands had been numb for the last two hours. I had separated and bagged all the gold that I could pick by hand, including the sand and gravel that I had pan-cleaned down at the creek. There was still a third of it left to clean and sort, which I placed in the duffle bag. But it was getting late and the rain had began to fall, so it would have to wait until the next day, which already had arrived.

Using pieces of wood gathered from the remnants of the old, dilapidated shed, I fashioned a lid for the glory hole. Placing the plastic bags heavy with treasure back in the hole where it had just come from, I covered the area with a variety of branches and brush. With approximately fifty pounds of gold in the daypack, I returned to the airplane for some much-needed rest.

I had awakened to the sound of nasty wind and rain smashing against the airplane. Confident in my efforts of securing it the day before, it still felt as though at any second it would be torn away to tumble over backward and crash upside down in the middle of the football field behind where it, with me in it, was tied down. I am not sure what time it was when I awoke to all of that racket. Snuggled warm and dry in my mummy bag, I ignored the noise and returned to my dreams of pockets bulging with gold.

When I awoke the second time, I had become painfully aware of how hard the floor of an airplane can be when lying on only a half-inch thick foam mat, separating my bones from the aluminum floor of the airplane.

As I wriggled out of my nest, the memory of the previous day's events came flooding back. First, the overwhelmingly exhilarating realization that I had just won an unbelievable lottery, immediately tempered by the dreaded reality of my predicament.

Stiff and sore from a long day of shoveling, I managed to rise up enough to look out of the passenger window. The rain had stopped, but the evidence of its intensity was clear from the standing water that lay in a thousand puddles all over the runway. It appeared that the cold front had passed, leaving in its wake warmer temperatures and an eight-knot breeze out of the southwest—a perfect headwind gently blowing up the canyon. Too bad I was stuck in the mud.

My woeful groaning in pain as I emerged from the cabin of the airplane was an intrusion to the tranquility of the morning. For the first time, I paused and admired the beauty of the place. The morning sun pierced its way through the gradually breaking overcast and illuminated the receding valley fog to reveal the beautiful Caribou Creek valley hidden beneath. The scene would have challenged even the likes of Ansell Adams to replicate. Even the mad roar of the two swollen, merging creeks could not erase the innate silence that seemed just as impervious to the thundering rapids as it was to my moaning.

One leg at a time, I slowly stepped out onto the saturated ground. The surface was much softer, not nearly as gooey. The idea of having to do more shoveling was an agonizing thought. However, the time had definitely come to start scraping the runway. Back in the airplane, I searched in my flight bag for a bottle of ibuprofen. It was either kill some of the pain or go back to bed.

The military spade was way too short and my back way too sore to expect to accomplish the task with that little instrument. I really needed a square point shovel. Searching through the assortment of lumber, which was all that remained of what was probably the cook-shack and from which the day before I had gathered makings for a fire, I found a two-by-ten-inch plank about five feet long.

Using my imagination, I envisioned what modifications I could make for it to be actually usable. With my hunting knife, I scored a deep groove on both sides of one end until I was able to break it off into a square point. On the other end, I whittled a forty-five-degree angle undercut designed to make shoveling possible. Again, by scribing into the wood, I fashioned a hole about one-third of the way up from the angled end of the plank into which I could insert the toe of my boot.

I then cut a short length of rope and fed it through the hole to the bottom side. To that, I tied a six-inch piece of kindling-sized wood that would serve as a stop. I did the same on the top end of the rope and soon had a handle for lifting. With an overactive imagination at work, it was actually beginning to resemble a shovel. It wasn't pretty, but as long as it didn't break, I would be able to make it work.

The first shovel (or board) full of muck worked so well that I overloaded it. Fearing that it might break, I tried again with a more moderate amount. My ingenuity, though on the level of caveman, had proven successful. Now it was not a question of *how* but of *how long* it would take to finish the laborious and painful job.

I walked back to the place the wheels had touched the ground when I had landed just twenty-four hours earlier. On final approach, this mountain airstrip had looked frighteningly short and in terms of takeoff distance, even shorter. However, looking at all the slime that kept me from my freedom, it suddenly appeared much longer.

From the south end of the runway, I counted 354 paces to where the airplane sat facing in the takeoff direction. At six foot and assuming my stride was an average of three foot, the takeoff distance figured pretty close to 1,062 feet. There were some advantages: the airplane was light on fuel, light on load, and by the end of the day, I expected to be somewhat lighter as well. The other variables included air temperatures, wind (or the lack thereof), and just how clean, dry, and fast this surface would eventually turn out to be. Sooner or later, the question of weight and balance would demand the very best of my calculation skills. If I tried to take too much of the gold at one time, I could possibly die trying. It would be better to take too little and be safe.

Concentrating my initial shoveling on the tracks the wheels made during landing, I gradually began to see some light at the end of the tunnel. It was a long, arduous, and painful process.

By one o'clock in the afternoon, after eating only a couple of nutrition bars with the ibuprofen for breakfast, I took a break, made a fire, and prepared some coffee and soup. I was actually starting to like the place. I lay back on my mat, watching the thin overcast give way to blue sky. With a belly full of warm food and coffee and another pain pill, I was soon dreaming of smooth air, tailwinds, and buckets full of gold.

Thump-thump-thump-thump-thump. The hammering of helicopter blades against the cool mountain air suddenly intruded upon my slumbers. I sat up, bewildered, attempting to comprehend what had just happened to my paradise. What is a chopper doing flying this low up the Caribou drainage? I watched as it grew closer. It was apparent that not only was it going to land on my runway, it also just happened to be the very last person or persons I expected to encounter at this remote and seriously unattended airstrip. On the side of the door, it read, "ALASKA STATE POLICE." I was suddenly wide awake.

Stepping from the idling light-and-dark-blue Bell Jet Ranger, a man in a brownish-green uniform waved in a neighborly manner as he made his way toward me. I arose from my mat and walked toward him, returning the gesture.

"Good day, sir," he spoke, suspiciously. "I am Officer Calvin Trent with the Alaska State Fish and Wildlife Department. Are you having trouble or just camping?" He was looking around as if trying to put together his own version of the answer to his question.

"Just camping," I said, trying to conceal my accelerated heart rate, and not at all sure how I would or could explain the several million dollars in gold I had found if he were to discover it as easily as I had.

"Looked like you were taking a nap," he said.

"Yes, sir. I've been shoveling the runway all morning. I landed here yesterday and found myself in a mess of gumbo. Scraping it off with this contraption is going a little slow." I pointed to my improvised shoveling implement. "Would you happen to have a real shovel with you?"

I thought maybe he hadn't heard me and was about to repeat the question, not wanting to take a chance on letting a good shovel fly away.

He stepped over to my airplane and was looking it over, trying not to be too obvious about peering inside.

"Are you a resident of Alaska?"

"No, sir," I said, and I told him of my other camp at Sheep Mountain and my recent trip from the lower forty-eight, leaving out the knowledge of any mining history concerning the place.

"Are you hunting? Or have you seen any game animals?"

"No, sir. Not hunting, but I sure appreciate your stopping to check on me. I don't suppose you have a shovel I could borrow, do you?" This time he looked me straight in the eye.

"I do have one, but I want it back. How long will it be before you're able to takeoff?"

"Well, sir, probably by tomorrow some time. I am actually researching a book that I want to write, so I will be in and out from time to time."

He looked surprised and his demeanor changed to somewhat less suspicious as he returned to the still idling Bell Ranger. Removing a brand-new square point shovel from the bracing of the pontoon-equipped helicopter, he handed it to me. "Leave it with Marge at the restaurant, and from now on, I would suggest you give her a heads-up as to your comings and goings."

From that, I pretty much gathered that Officer Trent had not just stumbled onto me accidently. A couple of days before I left Sheep Mountain, while having one of her delicious cheeseburgers, I had asked Marge if she had any knowledge of this claim and described it to her. She had without hesitation said no. At least it was comforting to know that she had some concern for me in spite of my wisecrack.

"Well, it looks like your not lost or in any trouble, and this *is* public access land, but I would like to see some ID, if you don't mind."

I stepped over to the airplane and retrieved my passport and commercial pilot license.

"Okay then, Mr. Worley. Here is my card if you need to contact me for any reason." With that, he climbed back into his whirly bird, spooled up, and soon lifted into the air.

I stood fascinated, watching the Bell Ranger hammer itself off the ground, retracing its approach path as it grew smaller and quieter until all trace of the thumping chopper blades had disappeared, returning the valley to its original solitude.

I was still gripping the shovel Officer Trent had handed me like a kid with a new toy as if I were afraid he might return any moment to take it back. Then with renewed energy, I put to work that literal gift from heaven.

I used the time shoveling the runway to plan and formulate the logistics involving the retrieval of my newly discovered fortune in gold. It would need to be done as inconspicuously as possible. Number one, it was certainly clear that I was being watched. To what degree of scrutiny would probably depend on how believable my book writing story had been. In addition, before I could go anywhere, I would need to relocate all of the gold, not to mention finish the panning to separate the dust from the dirt. I knew I would need to leave that hole without a trace of what it had been hiding for no telling how many years. It certainly was obvious that someone had buried that gold, and there was no doubt that person or persons surely must have intended on coming back. But whoever it was, they had never made it back. I wondered why, but was not sure that I really wanted to know.

By 8:00 in the evening, the runway was over half completed. Needing to check the glory hole just to make sure it was still there, I had a bite to eat and again, well-heeled with both firearms, made my way over the football field to Alfred Creek.

Just as I neared the lower edge of the excavation site within twenty yards of the trail to the creek, I stopped dead in my tracks. Once again, my heart kicked into high gear. In the soft dirt recently dampened from the rain and less than a hundred yards from my airplane were the distinct, fresh tracks of a very, very large grizzly bear.

Immediately, I charged the empty chamber of the ten-gage while looking in every direction at once to see if I was still in fact the hunter or had inadvertently become the hunted. Even with all my firepower at the ready, I still was not entirely convinced that I stood alone at the top of the food chain. The familiar tingle in my spine returned along with an eerie chill that remained with me long after I left Alfred Creek.

All was well at the glory hole. I placed two more of the twenty-five-pound plastic bags of gold in my daypack. I had an idea where I could hide them close to the airplane where I would be able to retrieve them inconspicuously when I was finally ready to go. Satisfied that I finally had a plan for the evacuation of the treasure, I returned to the airstrip.

Afraid that apprehension about the bear and the hard floor of the airplane might keep me awake, I took another pill and retired for the night. It was 10:00 p.m.

CHAPTER 3

I had removed the front and rear passenger seats before leaving Sheep Mountain for two reasons: One, to eliminate as much excess weight as I could, and two, I intended to use that space for my sleeping quarters. I felt the airplane might give me slightly better security than a tent, at least from the mosquitoes.

In spite of my stiff muscles, the less-than-ideal accommodations, and exhausted from the endeavors of the last two days, I barely remembered fluffing my pillow when I lapsed into the soundest sleep I had enjoyed since before I left home.

I awoke to the familiar sound of Caribou Creek en route to the Matanuska River. It took several moments for me to remember what world I had left and was gradually returning to as I slowly emerged from what had turned into a ten-hour, fatigue-induced coma.

Then I remembered the grizzly tracks I had discovered the day before. Instantly, I was awake and out of the sack. With blurry eyes, I quickly scanned the wilderness surroundings of the mining camp. Convincing myself that the grizzly bear was just passing through and that Officer Trent's air-hammering arrival and departure had perhaps motivated him to keep moving, I relaxed a little and made some coffee.

The morning was clear without a cloud in the sky. I had worked steadily on the runway at a pace my aches and pains would allow, never far from the shotgun. The slime had dried considerably and was turning back into the sticky consistency it had been before the heavy rain, which of course made shoveling more difficult.

When I first landed on the stuff, it had surprised me because, as I said before, I was expecting a hard-packed surface. I also noticed that the football field was primarily rocky pit-run type of material. Upon investigation, however, I soon discovered that the bank on the east side of the runway had a two--foot deep layer of clay approximately five feet below the surface that during the spring break-up season seeped a constant stream of saturated clay silt that over time had covered the entire surface of the airstrip.

With food supplies beginning to run short, I was anxious at the prospect of leaving sooner rather than later, though I still had much to do. Only now, I was thinking more along the lines of hot food, a shower, and a soft bed than I was my newly acquired wealth.

With the runway nearing completion, I could soon return to the far more pleasant task of finishing the glory hole and the relocation of the gold.

By eight o'clock that evening, the runway project was completed, and I had extracted every trace of the gold dust using the fry pan to separate the precious metal from the dirt. I soon had twenty Glad bags loaded with approximately twenty-five pounds of gold each, ready for relocation to the staging area. With at least a hundred pounds already stashed by the airplane, my estimate was something close to six hundred pounds of gold all together.

I decided to wait for dark to make the transfer. I didn't want to get caught out in the open with a backpack full of gold if the shovel owner decided to come thumping his way back up the canyon to see how I was doing. Company for supper was the last thing I wanted.

I placed the bags loaded with my fortune out of the way and picked up the shovel Officer Trent had so generously lent me. If only he knew what else it had been used for in addition to the runway job. Carefully, I filled in the hole and restored it as far as possible to its original condition. With two Glad bags in my pack, I returned to the airplane ready for a fire, some food, and coffee.

Then it occurred to me that maybe it was the food I had been cooking that had attracted the bear. "Oh, jeez!" I said to myself. But surely he would be long gone by now. Besides, I was very near ready to leave and right then, I was starving.

Finished with the supper, I let the fire go out. I really didn't want any smoke attracting either bears or humans. What I needed to do next had to be done discreetly.

As dark settled in and armed only with the Desert Eagle, I picked up the backpack and headed for the stash of gold. It would take nine round trips over the now quite-familiar route. The twilight would contribute to my finding my way without the use of a flashlight, but I knew that by the time I finished this chore and succeeded in getting the bags of gold reburied, it would be well into the next day.

Two of the twenty-five-pound bags were all the little daypack would hold at a time. From the glory hole to the airplane was a distance of three-quarters of a mile round-trip. By three o'clock in the morning, I had hiked a total of six and three-quarter miles; fortunately, only half of those miles were with a fifty-pound pack. But the job was finally completed.

All the gold, except what I would take with me, was buried directly beneath the wings of the airplane in the same holes with the tie-down logs that had secured the airplane during the storm. I then readied the aircraft for departure and returned my emergency gear to its proper duffle bag. On board was approximately a hundred pounds of gold from dust to nuggets and fuel for at least an hour and a half— just enough to make it to Anchorage only an hour away, where I planned to rent a car and make a phone call.

It had occurred to me early on that I would need some help with the logistics involving the evacuation and marketing of the gold. The problem, of course, would be finding the right person that could be trusted with this kind of venture. When it comes to money, gold, or any other kind of fortune this size, men have proven themselves capable of the most despicable kind of human behavior. However, there was one person I knew I could trust.

After finishing law school at the University of Washington and passing the bar, Rusty German had joined the army and become a Ranger. Four years later, returning from some place in the Middle East he never talks about, he married one of the three sweetest, most beautiful and precious young ladies in the whole world, my firstborn daughter, Keera. If I could trust Rusty with that treasure, I certainly would have no trouble trusting him with a measly bucket of gold.

Deciding to take a short nap and wait for the full light of day, which would be arriving in less then an hour, I crawled into the back of the airplane and immediately slipped into a sound sleep.

My first conscious thought was that there had been an earthquake. As I continued to regain a vague grasp on reality, I realized my bedroom was still moving. Something or someone very large had bumped into the airplane. *GRIZZLY BEAR.* The realization sent a shot of adrenalin straight to my fifty-one-year- old heart. I do not even recollect picking up the Desert Eagle, clicking off the safety, or pulling back the hammer. I guess it was the automatic reaction that comes from hours upon hours of practice and frequent handling of it and many other firearms. The bear was less then a foot away from and was looking into the pilot-side window. We were eyeball to eyeball, separated by no more than two and a half feet and a Plexiglas window. I saw him raise his gigantic right paw as if to wave good morning, and as it touched the soft window, I squeezed the trigger.

The deafening noise sounded as if it were a hundred miles away. I faintly remember aiming just to the right of his face and below the wing. Even in that terrifying moment, I was conscious of the need to avoid hitting any part of the airplane, and I certainly did not want to hit the grizzly without first attempting to scare him off. After all, the last thing I needed was a wounded grizzly bear trying to get even with me for his pain and suffering.

I was out of that airplane so fast that I barely remember opening the passenger-side door. I knew I had to keep track of my intruder and continue to provide motivation for him to keep going. As soon as I cleared the umbrella of the wing, I sent two more .300 grain jacketed hollow points skyward while yelling at the top of my lungs, "BEAR! BEAR! BEAR!," creating just enough noise and commotion sufficient to hurry him on his way.

I watched as he ran out over the football field. He stopped and stood on his hind legs, looking back at me. Feeling a little safer and wild-eyed from my adrenaline rush, I fired the remaining six rounds from the .44 magnum just low enough over his head so that he would hear the zinging of the bullets, but not so low as to part his hair. The big grizz, deciding that I was way too unfriendly, made an about-face and in high-gear running, not walking, disappeared up Alfred Creek toward the glory hole. By now, it was sufficiently light, and I was quite awake.

My weight and balance calculations, which took into consideration the shortness of the runway and the 2,500 feet of altitude, indicated that I could in all probability achieve lift-off in about eight hundred feet on a standard temperature day of fifty-nine degrees Fahrenheit with at least 250 pounds of gold on board plus me and my gear. If I were gambling only with money, I suppose I would take the chance. However, because my life was at stake, I opted for the conservative side of caution and settled for the one hundred pounds that I had already stowed and concealed in the back of the baggage compartment. Besides, what difference would it make? I would be back in a few days anyway.

I buried the tie-down ropes and left no trace of their existence detectable from above- ground or any clue of what else lay buried with them.

The engine fired on the third revolution, and with one eye over my shoulder for the unlikely return of my furry friend, I proceeded with the warm-up and takeoff checklist. The gauges indicated all was in the normal range, and the prospect of finally getting into the air with what could be over a million dollars worth of gold on board was a rush in and of itself.

The surface of the runway had dried quite well, and I was not at all concerned about any roll-out complications. My plan was to hold off on the application of any flap until about two-thirds of the way down the runway, and then bring in twenty-five degrees all at once to pop the aircraft off the ground. By lowering the nose to remain in ground effect, the airspeed would increase to best rate of climb, and I could then reduce the excess flap to ten degrees, holding that during the initial climb-out. If all went well, I should be able to avoid hitting the four hundred foot hill directly off the departure end of the runway.

With the breaks applied, I increased to full power. With one last check of oil pressure, temperature, RPM, carburetor-heat-full-in, and mixture leaned for takeoff, I released the breaks, and the airplane surged ahead. Even after twenty-plus years of flying the same machine, I was still a little surprised at how eagerly it responded. By the time I passed the halfway point, I was already bringing in the second notch of flap. The craft leapt from the ground, and I lowered the nose slightly. Then reducing to ten degrees of flap the aircraft quickly achieved best rate of climb airspeed, at which time I entered a right-hand, standard-rate climbing turn to the southwest. At sixty-five miles per hour, the vertical speed was already showing an eight hundred foot per minute climb. I had safely cleared by at least two hundred feet the hill that had loomed so ominously off the end of the runway a moment before, I could have easily taken more gold, but what did it matter? I would soon be back for the rest.

The wind was whistling through the broken window that the bullet had demolished less then thirty minutes before on its way past the big grizzly's left ear. I was in too much of a hurry to take the time to patch it before I left, deciding to wait until I landed at Sheep Mountain.

I leveled off at 4,500 feet msl. The sound of the motor was music to my ears, and a feeling of elation began to creep over me as I thought about the ordeal that I had just survived. I was pleased with the little straight tail. Although it was limited as far as performance capability was concerned, for its age, it was right on top of its game as long as I stayed within the performance envelope. Oh, and yes, it felt good to be rich, too.

Sheep Mountain, just off to my left, rose to an elevation of over 6,500 feet. Parallel to the Caribou drainage, the mountain abruptly terminates where the Caribou drainage and Matanuska rivers converged. As I slid around the west end of the mountain, I watched a family of Dall sheep scampering along the slopes, reviving fond memories of a photography road trip I once made to Denali National Park many years before.

As the airstrip slowly came into view, my thoughts again shifted to hamburgers and cherry pie. I could almost smell the kitchen. The kiss of the tires on the smooth turf reconnected me to the real world. My ordeal already seemed surreal as I shut down next to my base camp that had patiently awaited my return.

Just one more thing to do and I could return the shovel and get a hot meal. I fished in the back for a roll of duct tape, and with a couple of pieces of cardboard pilfered from the back of a notebook, I patched the bullet hole in the side window. This would have to do until I could find a maintenance shop at Anchorage.

I locked the airplane and, taking one last glance in the back to make sure I had sufficiently concealed my cargo, grabbed the game warden's shovel and headed for the café.

Marge was excited to see me and listened intently as I told her of my experience. Of course, I left out the part about striking it rich. I explained the shovel story to her. She agreed to hold onto it and seemed not at all surprised that Officer Trent had miraculously stumbled upon me all the way up at the Alfred Creek mine.

I thanked Marge for saving me from starvation, and with a very happy tummy, I showered, shaved, and packed up my tent camp for my flight to Anchorage.

I had used Marge's phone to call Flight Service for a weather briefing and filed a VFR flight plan to Merrill Field. Although I had filed for a cruising altitude of 4,500 feet msl, I expected by the current and forecasted weather in the Anchorage area—which had been reported as one thousand overcast and four miles visibility in mist--that I would eventually be forced to fly a much lower altitude. Just the same, I decided against filing an IFR flight plan. It did not seem necessary, and I felt it was important to maintain a low profile.

Many years had passed since I had flown into the Anchorage area, and it was in a rented airplane from one of the FBOs (fixed base operations) on Merrill field. Because it is one of the busiest, Class "C" airspaces in the world, I had asked the Flight Service briefer the preferred procedures for entering Anchorage Approach Control's complicated airspace. I like to keep those guys happy. After all, making someone mad at me on my first day could possibly result in a ramp check. I wanted very much to avoid that if I could, what with the bullet hole and all.

Fifty-six miles to the west-southwest lay the city of Palmer. I planned my descent accordingly and slid in under the thirteen-hundred-foot-low stratus that began just a mile east of the headwaters of the Knick Arm. Turning southwest and parallel to the Chugach Mountains, I picked up the familiar Glenn highway at the town of Bridge. Pleased that the ceiling was higher than forecasted, I relaxed and confidently made my initial call to Approach Control, which assigned me a squawk code and instructions to maintain VFR (clear of clouds) and a minimum of three miles of visibility. Approach Control quickly handed me off to Merrill Tower. As instructed, I reported Moose Run Golf Course inbound, and while turning final to runway three four was cleared to land. I found a vacant tie-down next to the Aero Flight Center FBO, rented a car, and called Rusty.

"Hello, Rusty German"

"Rusty, this is Lou. I am in Anchorage and need your help. Can you get away and fly up here in the 206?"

"Sure, Dad, is anything wrong?" "No nothing wrong just need your help with something. I can't go into all of it on the phone, but when you get here, you will be glad you came and so will I. How soon can you get here?"

"Okay, Dad, whatever you say. Maybe a few days, I'll get away as soon as possible. Are you at Merrill Field?"

"Yeah. Meet me at Aero."

"Okay. See ya."

I was concerned that someone in the control tower or anywhere for that matter might inadvertently observe me transferring the heavy bags from my airplane to the trunk of the car. Merrill Field is a very active airport, and there are always people around. I called the FBO and asked if the fuel truck could come out to my tie-down and fuel the airplane for me. I knew the fuel truck driver would park directly in front of the airplane, which would block the view of anyone in the tower that may be interested in what I was doing. When he arrived, I quickly parked the car on the far side of where he was standing on a ladder fueling the left wing tank and proceeded to transfer my cargo and luggage from the rear of the airplane. I managed to get it done without the driver even noticing.

Fifteen minutes later, I was on my way to the hotel. The next item of business would be converting some of the gold into cash money.

CHAPTER 4

I rented a room at a rather upscale inn on Aviation Avenue next to Spenard Lake just east of Anchorage International Airport. Since leaving my home in Darington almost three weeks before, I had been camping out of an airplane and was more than ready for some plush accommodations and gourmet food, even if it were a little high-dollar. Of course, since my experience at Alfred Creek, I considered any food other than granola bars gourmet.

The rental car, a new Ford Taurus, was parked directly in front of the ground-floor hotel window, and I kept the curtains parted just enough to keep an eye on it. I had locked all of my camping gear, shotgun, flight bag, and the gold securely in the trunk, but I kept the Desert Eagle on my person at all times.

Since landing at Merrill Field two days earlier, I had returned to the airport and moved the airplane to a maintenance shop that was repairing the window I had shot out during my encounter with the big grizzly. I had given the service department manager my hotel room number, and he said he would call when the repairs were completed.

I then set out to test the waters, to see what kind of price I could get for the gold. I had separated eleven ounces of the pea gravel and sand-sized tailings, which I put into a zip-lock plastic bag and sealed in a small manila envelope. Rolling it like a newspaper, I placed it in the breast pocket of my flight jacket and began to cruise the sleazier section of old downtown Anchorage.

After visiting a couple of the gold coin shops and feeling uncomfortable with the rather condescending attitude of both dealers, a certain pawnshop on south King Street caught my eye. The marquee had a picture of a grizzled old miner panning in a stream that said, "WE BUY GOLD."

The bells above the door jingled as I entered the shop. I noticed at once the variety of gold nuggets and jewelry on display. As I moved in the direction of the showcases, the proprietor, an apparently well-fed, bald man in his mid-fifties covered in tattoos and sporting a .45 caliber Glock on his right hip, emerged from a curtain that separated the storefront from a back room.

"Can I help you?" he asked in a gravelly voice. From his voice and shortness of breath, I concluded that he still was, or at least had been, a heavy smoker and that his future was—as a consequence—somewhat uncertain.

I paused for a moment while staring at his display, not wanting to give the impression that I was new at my business. "Yes, sir. You might be able to," I said as I extended my hand. "My name is Lou Worley."

He shook my hand. "Grueder," he said. I was not sure if that was a first name or last.

"I have a small amount of gold tailings I would like to have analyzed. Can you do that for me?"

"Let me see what you got," he said.

I opened the manila envelope and placed it on the counter. He looked inside, gave the bag a couple of shakes, and then motioned for me to follow him as he headed through the curtain to the back room.

Keeping my eyes glued to both him and the envelope, I failed to notice that we were not alone. Seating himself on a four-legged stool with a spinning top in front of a long, narrow, cluttered workbench built against the wall, he proceeded to pour the contents of the envelope into a six-by-eight-inch weight and measure pan. Hearing the sound of slippers on the plank floor startled me as I suddenly became aware of movement at the far back of the long, narrow room.

With one eye on Grueder, I watched as a much older gentleman, who resembled Grueder, slowly ambled his way toward us from the darkened living quarters. Obviously lame from some ancient mishap, he glanced briefly at me on his way to Grueder's left side, as he sat facing the long wall to my right; intently inspecting the gold with an optical magnifier he had attached to his right eye.

"Mind if I ask where this came from?" Grueder asked.

"Well," I said, "the only thing I care to say is that I acquired it legally."

After examining the gold for what seemed like an unusually long time, Grueder placed the pan on his scale. "You have eleven ounces here, Mr. Worley. Do you know what you want for it?" He got up from the stool.

"Is that regular ounces or troy ounces?" I queried.

He paused for a moment before answering, "Pound-ounces."

"Then I need seven hundred an ounce," I said. Grueder, who was now returning the gold to the manila envelope, turned and looked at me with a *you must be crazy* expression on his face.

"I'll give you four hundred," he said, coarsely.

Not exactly sure how I should proceed and wondering if I had made a mistake starting with such a high figure, I found myself wishing I had waited for Rusty who I did not expect to arrive for at least three or four more days. I quickly tossed up a Hail Mary. "I have plenty more where this came from, and half of it is nuggets the size of marbles," I blurted out, aware that nuggets were far more valuable then the tailings and dust.

Grueder collapsed back onto his stool with the spinning top. The old man bumped him on the shoulder and gestured toward me with his thumb. As he turned to walk away, he said something to Grueder that I was unable to hear. Grueder nodded, and then turned to me. "I can do it this time, but I can't promise the same price for the rest until I see what you have."

"I understand," I answered.

It seemed like it took an hour, but in four or five minutes, the old man returned and, without saying a word, placed $7,700 cash in my hand.

"Do you know when you will be back and how much you will be bringing with you?" Grueder asked.

"I'm not sure yet. Maybe four or five days and possibly as much as one hundred pounds." Grueder look at me, his eyes wide but didn't say any thing. I walked out of the shop closing the door behind me.

I wanted to hop and skip my way across the street to the car. I restrained myself, though, sure that I was being watched. I was surprised and pleased at just how easily the whole transaction had gone. I could hardly wait to tell Rusty.

As I drove up Minnesota Drive on my way back to the hotel, for the first time I felt concerned about being away from Alfred Creek for so long. I reminded myself that it had only been two days since I had left the place. I was anxious to return to the mine as soon as possible to get the rest of the gold, but my better judgment told me that I should wait for Rusty to arrive.

I felt certain that the big 1966 Cessna T206 with the Robertson STOL kit and its Continental IO-550 fuel-injected turbo, even with Rusty and I both aboard, would have no trouble hauling out the remaining gold in one trip. If I tried to bring it out in my little Cessna, I would have to make three or four trips and that would mean re-digging the hole each time, increasing the chances of discovery. I also wanted Rusty with me whenever we returned to Grueder's pawnshop with the gold that was still in the back of the car. Assuming that we could get the same price, and with the large amount of high-grade nuggets, we would be walking out of there with close to a million dollars in cash. I felt it would not be wise to undertake that transaction alone.

I wondered if Grueder would even have access to that kind of coin, which was why I told him how much I would be bringing the next time. I saw his reaction when I told him a hundred pounds but interpreted it more as anticipation than anything else. However, just to make sure, I decided to ask him the next time we talked on the phone.

Back at the hotel, I called Kati to share with her the events of the last couple of weeks.

"Hello, Worley residence." Her voice was like honey on fresh cornbread.

"Hi, sweetheart," "Sorry I haven't called in awhile, but I have been stranded at an old mining airstrip and had to dig myself out, and oh! By the way, we're rich."

"Lou, are you all right? What do you mean, 'stranded'? Is the airplane … did you say that we are rich?"

"Sweetie, have I told you lately that I love you with all my heart and miss you horribly and terribly?"

"I love you, too, Lou baby. Now tell me more about this rich business." Suddenly, I got a picture of my cute little wife standing at the door when

I would come home from work on payday with her hand out, tapping the palm of one hand with the forefinger of the other. Which always meant that before I did anything else with my hard-earned money, she was first in line for her fair share. I immediately burst out laughing.

Beginning with the Jurassic Park mosquitoes at Watson Lake to buzzing the border crossing at Northway, Alaska, I told Kati every detail of the events that had transpired over the last week and a half. I could tell she was excited, but at the same time, she immediately began to worry. She was relieved, however, that Rusty was coming to watch my back, but would still rather I left the whole thing and get back home. I assured her that I was safe and that she was by far more important to me than a bucket of gold. However, I fully intended to have both.

After his discharge from the army, Rusty went to work for a law firm in Seattle. When he finally had enough of the minor pot possession cases and the gangbangers' plea bargain routine, he accepted an opportunity with a private investigating firm, and after a few years there, started his own practice. That was three years earlier, and with a man-and-wife team of investigators as well as a full-time secretary, he had done exceptionally well.

I first met Rusty German only six months after his discharge from the army. He was taking flying lessons at a local airport where I had just completed an annual inspection on my airplane and also where I had taken *my* first flight lesson over thirty years before. It was a rather windy day, and I decided to do some air work, practicing windy-weather landings. As I was opening the doors of the hangar, a young man in his mid- to late twenties approached me.

Full of questions that obviously hinted that he would enjoy going along, and apparently not intimidated by the wind, I took him with me. So began a friendship that in just over a year turned into a son-ship.

My daughter Keera was still in med school when she and Rusty were married, and then went on to become a pediatrician at a hospital in Tacoma, Washington. As soon as Rusty finished his flight training, he bought the Cessna 206. Of course, Keera wasted no time in joining him in completing her checkout in the big Cessna as well. The two of them share a love for flying and, over the years, have spent many hours flying the backcountry of Idaho and Montana, along with her mother and me.

Knowing Rusty the way I did, I was sure he would not abruptly drop everything and come scooting up to Alaska just because I had found a bucket of gold. Therefore, I was quite surprised when he said he could be here in only a few days. I wasn't too worried about the gold; I was confident that no one had a clue of its existence except, of course, the person or person's who put it there in the first place. I still wondered why whoever it was had never returned to retrieve it.

The big Cessna with its six hours of fuel capacity would have no problem flying from Friday Harbor, Washington in the San Juan Islands nonstop to Ketchikan, Alaska. With no need to land in Canada, clearing customs would not be an issue. Fueling at Ketchikan, where he would spend the night, Rusty would easily make it nonstop to Anchorage in not much over four hours. The entire flight time, not including layovers—a trip of over fifteen hundred miles—would total less than eleven hours from their home airport at Spanaway.

The maintenance shop had left a message that my little bird was ready. I drove to the airport and paid the bill, expecting some mention of how the window had been broken, but there was none. I relocated the plane back to the transient parking area and returned to the rental car a little nervous to be very far away from it. As I was unlocking the car door, I noticed two men sitting in a dark, smoky gray Crown Victoria who seemed to be watching me. At first glance, they resembled detectives or FBI, but on the other hand, too gangster-looking to be cops. Not wanting to appear as though I had noticed, I started the car and headed west on Fifth Street. Several blocks away, and failing to see any indication that they were following, I relaxed and focused on my next item of business.

The ten-gage shotgun and .44 magnum still in the trunk of the car was really too much gun for concealed-carry in a city environment. Anticipating the need for personal protection due to the nature of my upcoming business and the large amount of cash and gold I had with me, I found the nearest pawnshop and, with my Washington concealed pistol permit, made a same-day purchase of a .45 Glock semiautomatic handgun, just like the one Grueder had carried. I had no doubt that Rusty would be similarly prepared.

When my phone rang and it was not Kati's number, I knew it had to be my son-in-law. Rusty was on the ground in Ketchikan, fueling the plane and would be leaving first thing in the morning, planning his arrival at Merrill Field for eleven a.m.

I briefed him on my experience at Grueder's pawnshop. He congratulated me on my success and suggested that I call Grueder to try to set up a meeting for the next afternoon. He also felt it would be a good idea to pick up an ore scale from a prospector shop and separate the nuggets from the tailings, weighing each separately.

Grueder answered the phone on the first ring. Acting at first as if he could barely remember our business of only three days before, I asked him if one hundred pounds of gold was more than he could deal with or did I need to look elsewhere. His feigned disinterest immediately vanished. He assured me that he would be ready with enough cash for the transaction and that the next afternoon would be just fine. I hung up.

Returning to the pawnshop where I purchased the Glock, I inquired where I might find a prospector shop. Within an hour, I was back in the hotel room, separating and weighing the gold. It totaled ninety-eight pounds. Fifty-two pounds was the sand tailings and dust. The remaining forty-six were a variety of pea gravel and marble-sized nuggets that came in many shapes and sizes.

Placing a pound of the nuggets in a plastic bag and sealing it in a manila envelope, I took a black marker and wrote on it, "For Keera." Repeating the process for my two other daughters, I then set the three envelopes aside to send home with Rusty. I am in the habit of doing things like that because I want my daughters to know that I am always thinking about them.

I waited in the pilot lounge of the FBO, listening to the Merrill Tower frequency. I heard the call sign of Rusty's big Cessna reporting Providence Hospital inbound and the tower clearing him to land. I was anxious to see him. He really was the son I never had. Emerging from the pilot-side door, I watched as the familiar, six foot one, 220 pound, muscular ex-Ranger walked toward me. His big grin, broad shoulders, and narrow waist reminded me of the Caucasian version of the Allstate Insurance guy in the television commercials. I, too, felt like I was 'in good hands,' and my confidence level soared like an empty Super Cub on a cold winter day.

CHAPTER 5

On the way to the hotel, I brought Rusty up to speed on a few of the details associated with the Alfred Creek mine: a description of the runway environment, the conditions of the airstrip, its approximate length, and elevation, and my recommendations for the approach. Important information he would find useful flying into that very marginal environment.

I had no doubt concerning Rusty's ability or skill in flying into or out of the Alfred Creek airstrip. As I have already mentioned, he and I have flown together in the backcountry of Idaho and Montana for a number of years. Nor did I have any reservation with the performance capability of the Cessna T206. The IO 550 Continental was capable of producing more than enough power and thrust to lift that big Cessna fully loaded up and away from airstrips even more challenging than Alfred Creek.

With our combined weight including survival gear of only slightly less then five hundred pounds and the still questionable weight of the remaining gold, also estimated at five hundred pounds, I was still well aware of how close we would be to maximum gross weight during departure. Therefore, I recommended we go with only fuel enough for there and back plus the legal reserves, or about three hours of fuel.

Rusty had left Ketchikan without breakfast, so after stowing his gear in the room, we headed straight for the hotel restaurant. Requesting a private booth in a corner, we followed the waiter. I must have turned another color or something because as Rusty was seating himself against the wall, he noticed immediately that something was wrong.

"Did you want to sit here, Dad?"

"No, your fine right there," I motioned with my thumb over my shoulder at the booth behind me. Seated in the next booth were the two characters I had seen the day before in the Crown Victoria. We ate our meal in silence, expecting that anything we said could be overheard. Finally, the two goons left.

"Rusty, I have three envelopes for you to take home when you go," I said. "One for each of my daughters."

"Letters?"

"Yes, that too, but I'm sending a pound of nuggets for each of them as a memento. Just so they know I'm always thinking of them."

"I can do that, Dad. Have you called Grueder yet?"

"I'll do that now."

"Who *were* those guys?"

"They have been trying to follow me, but they are not very good at it," I replied. "I figure they are associated with Grueder. Probably hired protection or something. I'm no longer concerned about them now that you're here."

Rusty grinned. "Aw, shoot, Dad. You could handle them on your own without any trouble."

"I'm sure I could, but they would probably get blood all over everything, too, and that could draw a lot of attention." Rusty chuckled again.

I left Rusty to finish his meal while I went back to the room to call Grueder, who again answered on the first ring.

"Yeh!"

"Grueder, this is Worley. The total comes to ninety-five pounds. We are ready whenever you are."

"Let me call you back,"

It was another half-hour before Grueder returned my call.

"This is Worley"

"Worley, this is Grueder. We're ready."

"We're on the way, I'm bringing my son along."

While I checked the .45 Glock and positioned it in the small of my back under my belt, I couldn't help but notice the .45 Smith & Wesson belted to Rusty's right side, which was concealed under his long Carhartt winter coat.

We drove out of the parking area onto Aviation Avenue. Glancing in the rearview mirror, I noticed the Crown Victoria following us. We decided to ditch them on the way.

I knew I would not be able to outrun the big Ford with the little Ford, so I would have to use some deviation. Turning south on Spenard from Aviation Avenue, I purposely turned west instead of east on International Boulevard. The Crown Victoria was no longer behind us. Back on International Boulevard going east, we continued to C-Street and south to Diamond Boulevard. A few minutes later, we were turning north on King Street where I parked in front of the pawnshop. The Crown Victoria sat across the street, unoccupied.

"Rusty?"

"Yeah?"

"I'm thinking seven hundred an ounce for the tailings, and let's go for nine hundred for the nuggets."

"Sounds good."

"You want to handle it or should I?"

"You go ahead. I'll back you up," We stepped out of the car and retrieved our luggage from the trunk. Rusty took the nugget case, and with the other case of gold tailings in my left hand, we entered the pawnshop.

Grueder and the Crown Victoria goons were on the far side of the counter over by the curtain, apparently having a serious discussion. As Rusty and I walked in, the discussion ended abruptly. Grueder turned to me and, without saying a word, motioned for us to come into the back. I extended my hand toward the shorter of the two goons.

"I'm Lou Worley, and this is Rusty, my son," I said as a matter of courtesy.

"Deano," he said, grasping only my fingertips in a useless imitation of a handshake. "That's, Judo." He nodded toward his partner who had stepped over to the front window but did not acknowledge the introduction.

Deano, at five foot ten and 170 pounds soaking wet, wearing a black polo shirt under a light North Face windbreaker, appeared to be the leader of the two. Following close behind Grueder, he stepped into the back room on the far side of Grueder's four-legged stool with the spinning top. I stepped near Grueder and his bench and glanced back to see where

Rusty had lined himself up on this little chessboard. He stood just inside the curtain and to the left about four feet.

"Judo, lock the door." Deano spoke directly to the big man.

Judo, six foot and every bit of three hundred pounds, wearing a white T-shirt under a knee-length, black leather coat with an obvious bulge on one side, shuffled his way to the entry door and locked it. After switching the Open sign to Closed, he returned to stand just inside the curtain barely three feet from Rusty and the case of gold nuggets, which put him directly behind me.

I sat the case on the workbench. "There are forty-nine pounds of tailings and dust in this case and forty-six pounds of nuggets in the other one," I said as Grueder turned to look at me.

Looking past me to Rusty and pointing at the other case, Grueder said, "Let me see the nuggets."

Rusty stepped forward and handed me the case, which I placed on the bench in front of Grueder. Deano stepped closer to Grueder's left side as he opened the lid on the case. The gold was contained in a black plastic garbage bag, the top of which I had cut down and tied with a twist wire. As Grueder opened the bag, Deano reached his hand into the sack of small gold nuggets, letting them sift through his fingers. Looking up at me, he said, "Where'd you boys git this?"

"At the gittin' place," I retorted, finally realizing who in fact we were doing business with. It was now clear that Grueder had called in black-market buyers for the gold. I immediately began to worry about how this was going to go down.

"Are you boys here to buy or look?" I asked, a little annoyed that Deano was sticking his nose into my business with Grueder.

Deano straightened up and stepped back from Grueder, looking at Judo who I knew was barely five-feet directly behind me. Confident that Rusty had my back, I let on that I was unconcerned.

"I never buy without looking. You want top dollar, don't you?"

Grueder pushed the nugget case aside and opened the case of tailings. Shoveling it around with a small garden-type scoop, he looked up at Deano and said, "It's the same stuff I got from him the other day." Then he added, "Very high-grade. Looks like Alfred Creek gold to me."

I was stunned. Trying not to let on as though there could be any possible truth to that, I said, "So, if y'all are ready to deal? I'm looking for a K an ounce for the whole lot."

"Not today," Deano sneered. "I'll do eight hundred for the nuggets and five for the sand." The look in his face told me he wanted this gold and was not above dickering one more time.

"Nine for the rocks, seven for the rest of it, or we go elsewhere," I said, replacing the twist wire on the plastic bag.

Before Deano could respond, Grueder interrupted. "I get a fifteen percent broker fee."

"You will have to get it from him." I said, gesturing toward Deano.

"You get five, and that's it," Deano said as he shut the lid on the nugget case. Grueder said no more, and Deano reached behind him for a large satchel he had brought with him. "What's that come to, Grueder?"

Rusty and I watched carefully as Grueder weighed the gold and did his figuring. Having already done the math at the hotel, I needed only to be sure that the cash count would be accurate and that they were not going to try to pass counterfeit money our way. For that, I motioned for Rusty to step up and use his detective skills in the protection of our interest.

Deano handed Grueder his fee of $60,560 and placing $1,211,200 in hundred-dollar bills back into the case, handed it off to Rusty. Grueder stepped over to a large steel safe in the corner where he secured his profits of only twenty minutes' work.

We waited as Grueder went to the front of the shop and peered out of the window before unlocking the door. Motioning to us that all was clear, Rusty handed me the case and followed me out to the car. With the cash locked in the trunk, we returned to the hotel.

I had discussed with Rusty what we would do with the remaining five hundred pounds of gold we would soon be retrieving from the mine, which we now felt much more anxious about since the bombshell Grueder laid on us when he clearly recognized the source of the gold as Alfred Creek. I wondered if he or maybe his father might have been the same people the Idaho boys had dealt with. Rusty had suggested we buy a safe and rent a storage unit in Wasilla for the time being, giving us a somewhat secure place to put the gold when we returned from the mine.

"Rusty, I'm not sure I want to show up at Grueder's with five hundred pounds of gold all at one time, and I certainly don't feel comfortable making five or six more trips to and from there, carrying large amounts of gold in and cash out." I looked at Rusty, waiting for his response.

"I was thinking about that, Dad. I suggest that you just keep it in the safe for now at a storage facility, and I will look for some other options. Unless you think you might blow through that first million before then," he said with a silly grin.

Checking out of the hotel, we went directly to a used car lot on the north end of town. Paying cash for a two-year-old Toyota Land Cruiser, we drove to the airport and returned the rental car. We then found a lock and key shop that had a variety of security safes and purchased the largest one they had that would fit into the back of the Land Cruiser.

We would soon be on our way to Wasilla, and in the event of a very unlikely accident involving Rusty in his 206 or me in the Land Cruiser, we did not want to have all our eggs in one basket, so we divided the money. With exactly $605,300 apiece, we headed to Wasilla with Rusty in the big Cessna and I in the Land Cruiser.

In barely over an hour, I was turning off the George Parks highway and into the airport parking area at Wasilla, Alaska. I found Rusty in one of the FBO hangars, talking with a local pilot. He had already located a nearby storage facility.

The twelve-by-twenty-four-foot storage unit was the perfect size. It was not only adequate for the safe, but also the Land Cruiser. With the money in the safe and the safe locked in the storage unit, we checked into a motel and found a diner that served Alaska-style meat and potatoes and homemade cherry pie.

The next morning, with exactly three hours fuel on board, Rusty secured a shovel in the baggage compartment of the big Cessna. Having recently spent three days at Alfred Creek, I had filled Rusty in on what we could expect in terms of fog in the early mornings. The crummy weather of the past week had given way to higher overcasts and dryer air, so it didn't seem likely that the fog would still be around, although we expected that the runway could be a little slick depending on when it had last rained. Finally, the time had come to return to the buried treasure. I began to feel the familiar excitement of the first day that I had found the gold in the old privy.

Rusty's big Cessna climbed to 7,500 feet in less time than it would have taken my little Cessna to climb two thousand feet. I pointed out the

Caribou drainage as we approached its confluence with the Matanuska River. Remaining at this cruising altitude, Rusty flew well above the ridgeline of Sheep Mountain as he followed the drainage straight to Alfred Creek. Entering a counterclockwise standard rate turn just to the east of the Alfred Creek runway, he let the Cessna begin its descent.

After first doing a slow flyby, he set up a perfectly executed approach to final and let the 206 touch the threshold. The ground speed, though much faster than my little Cessna, dissipated quickly, and the big Cessna came to a stop exactly where I had parked just the week before. We turned the airplane in a take-off direction and pushed it back as close to the burm as possible. Removing the shovel, I located the tie-downs where I had buried the gold and began to dig.

"Dad," Rusty said. "Did you have on different boots when you were here before? These tracks look a lot more recent then a week old to me." Already halfway down to the stash, I paused and walked over to see what he was looking at.

"Those are not my footprints. Someone else has been here. In fact, it looks like maybe several people," I said, somewhat puzzled. Sensing an urgency to complete our mission, I quickly finished digging the hole, and we loaded the gold into the plane.

As soon as Rusty had positioned, secured, and covered the load, he locked the doors, and we followed the fresh tracks down to the Alfred Creek trailhead and straight up to the golden privy. As we approached the big boulder, I could see that, up the path where the glory hole had been, yellow tape completely encircled the ancient pit toilet. In bold, black lettering, the tape read, "CRIME SCENE INVESTIGATION AREA. DO NOT CROSS."

Once again, my heart went into double time as I carefully worked my way around the tape until I was able to peer into the hole. Obviously, someone had not only removed what I had filled in, but over twice as much. I had only dug a hole four-foot deep; the thing was now seven- or eight-foot deep and at least five foot across.

I looked at Rusty. "It looks like the law has been here, but I'm not sure what they were looking for unless they thought I poached something while I was here."

"Better cover your tracks, Dad, and let's back out of here."

As Rusty and I returned to the airplane, I described to him the events of the three days I had recently spent in the place. He was amazed that I had shoveled that whole runway. Rusty walked to the far end of the strip, inspecting the surface, while I told him the story of the big grizzly. Immediately, his inspection was finished, and he was ready to go.

Not certain just how heavy we were, I asked Rusty if we needed to unload any of the gold just to ensure that we could get airborne.

"I'll let you know in a minute," he said as he shoved the throttle forward.

The big Cessna screamed under the full load and staggered into the air just as Rusty ran out of airport. Lowering the nose slightly, he reduced to ten degrees of flap, comfortably maintaining a five hundred foot per minute rate-of-climb, even fully loaded. I sat back and pondered, *What could have possibly turned that glory hole into a crime scene?*

Back in Wasilla, and the last of the fortune in gold secured in the safe along with the cash, we settled into a comfortable booth at the diner and, over a pot of hot coffee, tried to make sense of this new twist to my vacation adventure.

Suddenly, the door of the diner opened. In walked an Alaska State Trooper and with him, Officer Calvin Trent.

CHAPTER 6

I said to Rusty. "It just keeps getting better, doesn't it?"

"Who is that?"

"The shorter one would be Officer Calvin Trent, in the flesh. He is the game warden who flew into Alfred Creek to bring me a shovel. I don't know who the trooper is."

"Nice guy! Do you think those two are the ones who put up the crime tape?"

"I'm sure of it."

The trooper and Officer Trent exchanged greetings with the waitresses as they made their way to a table in the back corner of the dining area, one that would take them past where Rusty and I were seated. On the way, the game warden, who was looking directly at me, initially indicated no sign of recognition. Then as he neared our table, he pointed at me and said, "Worley, right?"

"Yes, sir, Did you get your shovel back? I left it with Marge on my way out."

"I did, and I appreciate that."

"Well, I very much appreciate your helping me with that predicament I was in,"

Handing me another of his business cards, Trent said, "Mr. Worley, this is Detective Daily." The detective and I shook hands. "Nice to meet you Sir." "Nice to meet you too." Then Trent added. "I need you to stop by my office. Could you do that sometime tomorrow?" "Sure no problem," I replied.

Although I agreed I was still a little perplexed but, under the circumstances, not entirely surprised at the request.

Officer Trent and detective Daily took a seat in the adjacent booth and Rusty and I finished our lunch. As we were leaving the diner, I turned to Officers Trent and Daily, nodded, and bid them a good day.

After we left the diner, I said to Rusty, "I was kind of expecting that."

"Actually, you would have more to be concerned about it you hadn't gotten that invitation."

"Why do you say that?" I asked.

"Because that would have indicated that you were more of a suspect than a curiosity."

"What is a curiosity?"

"A piece of the puzzle that doesn't fit."

"I like being a curiosity. Can curiosities be arrested?"

"Only if one starts leaning more toward being a material witness who may be in danger, or is a suspect. Even then, they couldn't hold you more than seventy-two hours. Besides, if Trent or Daily had suspected either of us of anything criminal, Trent certainly would not have let us walk away."

I expected that Rusty might be getting anxious to get back home, never wanting to be far from his family for too long, so I was glad when he said he would stay to see what the investigators wanted to talk about.

We returned to the storage unit to weigh and separate the gold. I attempted to convince Rusty to take an equal share. After all, there was plenty of wealth for the both of us, and I most likely would not have been able to retrieve it all without him. Rusty did not want half, as he was never the type of person to be greedy.

The gold we had brought out of Alfred Creek totaled 486 pounds, close to what I had estimated; no wonder the big Cessna had struggled getting into the air when we departed. When the nuggets and tailings were finally separated, the gold weighed in at 331 pounds of nuggets and 155 pounds of tailings. Sold over the same counter for the same price, we were looking at $6,502,400.00.

With the $1.2 million in cash already in the safe plus the $7,000 still in the breast pocket of my flight jacket, I was no longer concerned with my vacation time that expired in only four more days. Back at the motel, I called my employer. I felt bad about not giving at least a two-week notice, but told them they could keep my vacation pay that normally would be waiting for me upon my return. They seemed good with that.

I told Rusty that I thought it would be best if he took off first thing in the morning and take all of the gold with him. Without stopping in Canada, there would be no requirement to clear customs, and the gold would be safe at home in case it was somehow involved in the investigation. Rusty, on the other hand, felt that if the gold was connected in some way, we would both be making ourselves suspect by his leaving. I had to agree; after all, he was the lawyer, not me. We also decided that unless the investigators were already aware of the presence of gold in that hole, we certainly were not going to mention its existence.

The next morning, after a late breakfast, we went to see the game warden. The Department of Public Safety Office was less then a half-mile from the diner. When we arrived, the receptionist pointed us in the direction of Trent's small office at the end of a long hallway. As we approached the office door, we saw that the game warden was on the phone, so we waited in the hall.

With Alaska State Trooper investigators and detectives all over the place, I almost felt like I had broken some law in finding and keeping that bucket of gold. I glanced at Rusty; he was looking at pictures on the wall, obviously oblivious to the intimidation I was feeling.

Trent hung up the phone and motioned for us to come in. As we entered the office, Trent, rising from his seat, reached across his desk to Rusty. "I'm Cal Trent."

"Rusty German, sir. Nice to meet you. I'm his son-in-law," Rusty gestured toward me as they shook hands. Trent and I also greeted each other with a handshake.

"Have a seat, gentlemen," Trent said. "I appreciate your coming in."

"Not a problem. What's on your mind?" I asked.

"I'll get right to the point. Mr. Worley, have you been back up to Alfred Creek in the past few days?" I glanced at Rusty. He was looking at pictures on Trent's wall.

"Yes, sir. Rusty and I were up there yesterday morning. We saw where someone had dug a big hole up the creek by the rock. What's up with all the crime-scene tape?" I looked Trent straight in the eyes. Rusty stopped looking at pictures and for the first time appeared interested. Trent ignored my question. He was good at that.

"I need to know what you were doing when I found you up there, and why did you dig that hole in the first place?" Trent demanded.

"Well," I replied. "I was looking for something that I could use to shovel the runway and happened on the old privy. I had set about restoring it to usability, thinking that it may come in handy when I found this ..." I pulled from my pocket the smallest of the three gold nuggets I had found at Alfred Creek and still kept with me, handing it to Trent. He took the nugget, examined it briefly, and getting up from his desk, made his way to the door.

"Just a minute. I'll be right back." Trent left the office. Rusty looked at me.

"You might not get that back, you know that, don't you?" he said, grinning.

"I'll sic my attorney on him," I replied. Rusty laughed.

Shortly, Trent returned with detective Daily who had been with him in the diner the day before. But instead of his state police uniform, he was dressed in jeans, a plaid wool shirt, and hiking boots. I was ready to bet my gold nuggets that those boots had contributed to some of the footprints we had seen at Alfred Creek.

"You remember Sergeant Daily," Trent said. "He is in charge of this investigation and would like to ask you a couple of questions." I stood up from my chair and shook his hand, as did Rusty.

"Cal tells me you were digging a hole to use for an outhouse, is that correct?" Daily asked.

"Yes, sir," I said, "until I found that nugget. I then kept digging to see if there were any more. When I got to four foot or so, I gave it up because I had bigger fish to fry. I needed to do something about the predicament I was in, which is precisely what I was doing when Officer Trent came along and was generous enough to lend me his shovel." Daily glanced at Trent, who was still holding my gold nugget.

"If you needed to borrow a shovel from Officer Trent to clear the runway, what did you use to dig the hole with?" Daily asked.

"I had a fold-up military spade that I keep in the airplane along with my survival gear."

"Why did you go back there yesterday?"

"I wanted to show the place to Rusty. Finding that nugget got me to thinking that maybe the Alfred Creek mine might still have some potential as a workable claim, so I asked my son-in-law, who is a private investigator, to help me look into the possibility of acquiring the rights to it. You wouldn't know who holds those rights, would you?" Daily and Trent looked at each other. Their expressions suggested that they had no further reason to suspect either of us in their investigation.

"You will have to research the land records at the county court house," Daily said.

Both Officers Trent and Daily seemed satisfied with my explanation. Thanking us for our time and returning the nugget to me, Trent closed the door behind us as we left.

Rusty and I were still baffled as to what Trent and Daily had discovered that suddenly turned the glory hole into a crime scene. However, under the circumstances, we felt it best not to press the issue. Rusty said he would have one of his investigators look into it.

"Dad, did you make up that part about the claim?" Rusty asked.

"Not really. It's just that there has been so much going on, I haven't had time to mention it to you till now. Why? Do you think you'd be interested in looking into it?"

"How much gold do you think is still in that hill?" Rusty asked.

I thought a minute before answering. "At least another bucket." As we got into the Land Cruiser. The thought of finding more gold must have sparked Rusty's curiosity. He decided to stay a few more days to do some research.

So that Rusty would have his own transportation, we found a used car lot in Wasilla where I purchased a three-year-old Toyota 4Runner, giving the Land Cruiser to my personal private detective. I decided that when Rusty left, I would drive the Four Runner to Anchorage when I returned to Merrill Field to pick up my little Cessna. I planned to leave it there, eliminating the need to rent a car whenever I flew into Merrill Field.

I also needed a hangar for my airplane, and there were none available at the Wasilla airport. I inquired at the FBO and learned of an older gentleman, living five miles west of town, who no longer owned an airplane but who still had a hangar and turf runway on his ninety acres of flat land. I decided to have a look.

Finding my way to Hollywood Boulevard from Goose Bay Drive, I turned west to a fork in the road. Staying left for another three miles, I arrived at an east/west grass airstrip, which looked to be approximately twenty-seven or twenty-eight hundred feet in length. Adjoining the east end of the runway was a lone building that appeared to be either a hangar or a shop. As I parked, I noticed a walk-in man-door that was open. Thinking that someone might be inside, I entered.

The building was well constructed and had indeed originally been designed as a hangar. Since then, it had become a storage barn, cluttered with everything from old furniture to lumber, airplane parts and pieces, even farm implements. Mesmerized by the many old but well-preserved antiques, I forgot for a moment that I was an intruder.

"HEY!" the older gentleman said. "Whaterya doin' in here?"

I spun around, looking like I had just been caught with my hand in the proverbial cookie jar.

"Howdy. Looking for the owner of this place,"

A figure stood silhouetted in the doorway. Medium height, about five foot eight or so, his appearance was rugged and sturdy. But as he stepped into the dim light of the hangar, I could see that he was well past retirement age. "Yer lookin' at him. What d'ya need?" he demanded.

"My name is Lou Worley. I'm looking for a hangar to rent and was told you might be interested in some extra income."

"How d'ya do," he said. His voice had become slightly friendlier. He offered his weather-worn hand and a very firm, almost crushing, handshake.

"I'm Arthur Bold. Well, I could sure use extra income, that is a fact, but I'm too old and tired to be movin' all this stuff. Besides, I'm more interested in sellin' the whole place, land, hangar, and everything in it, just like it sits."

"How much you figure you need for the whole deal?" I asked, somewhat distracted by the many ideas racing through my mind of all I could do with the place.

"Well, it's ninety acres all together, with the airstrip and the hangar. I'd take a thousand an acre and fifteen for the building. Do ya want it?" he asked, somewhat impatiently.

"Will you take cash? And you can keep anything you want."

"Cash will be just right, and there ain't nothin' here I want anymore," he said. "It's all yours. When do ya want to do this?"

"Mr. Bold, if you know where there is an escrow office in town, we can get it done right now," I said, wondering if all my newly acquired wealth had already gone to my head.

I gave Arthur my cell phone number, and he said he would call me with our appointment time at the title company.

I immediately called Rusty, and he met me at the storage unit where I picked up the cash.

"What are you planning on doing with the place?" Rusty asked.

"I'm tired of staying in motels. Besides, if we aquire rights to a claim we will need a place to live while were up here."

The next morning, I was well on my way to being a property owner and an official resident of Alaska. I found a labor force agency in Wasilla and hired five of the huskiest, most sober-looking, and somewhat willing individuals available, and we headed for Bold's. All I needed was enough room in the hanger for my little Cessna. As I went through and selected what would go outside and what would remain inside, the workers made it happen. Anticipating the future need for their services, I rewarded them generously.

Arthur lived in a large, two-story log house that was only a quarter-mile north of the runway up a long gravel drive. The lodge-style home and four-car garage sat on its own twenty acres of land. Although adjacent, it was separate property from the ninety acres. He wanted a $125,000 for it. I quickly made another trip to the storage room. I told Arthur that the name of the airport would remain for as long as I had control over it and that anything he wanted from the place was his anytime.

Arthur Bold was over eighty years old and had raised a family, buried a wife, lost a son in Desert Storm to a roadside bomb, and was ready to move back to the lower forty-eight where his only daughter lived in Sikeston, Missouri, with her husband and their three children.

Rusty and I spent several evenings with Arthur, helping him pack some personal effects he wanted to take with him and just talking while relaxing over coffee. He told us many intriguing stories of his life in Alaska and much of the history of the place he had just sold to me.

Bold's one-man airline career had provided air transportation and service to the native people and villages of Alaska's interior for almost sixty years, during which time he amassed close to thirty thousand hours of flight time. All from his little grass runway known throughout Alaska as simply "Bold's."

With the exception of closing, which would not take place for another thirty days or more, the sale of the house and property was complete. Arthur planned to be with his daughter by that time, so would handle all that through a notary public signing the papers and faxing them back to the escrow office in Wasilla. I, too, would be home by then, but would return with Kati to sign the papers in person.

The men from the labor force fully loaded a fourteen-foot moving van, containing all that Arthur cared to keep from his lifetime in Alaska—the memories of the past, fit only in his mind.

A week later, we were waving good-bye to Arthur Bold as he began his journey to Sikeston, Missouri. His attempt to appear impervious to the emotional connection he had to the place that had been his home for so many years failed miserably. As Arthur climbed into the rented moving truck, the tears were already blurring his vision.

Rusty was also ready to go home. He had done some investigating into the claim at Alfred Creek and anticipated favorable results, but still had more people he wanted to locate. So the next day, taking only the three pounds of gold I had bagged separately for each of my girls and a hundred grand in cash, he loaded his gear into the Cessna-206 Stationair.

"Tell Keera and my grandkids I love them with all my heart." Rusty took the zip-lock plastic bags with my daughters names on them, and with a big grin on his face, almost squished me with his bear hug. "So, long, Dad. Don't spend all that money in one place." I watched for several minutes as the big Cessna melted into the gray sky.

CHAPTER 7

It was time to bring the little Cessna back from Merrill Field. I loaded my flight bag in the Toyota 4Runner and set out for Anchorage. After the window repair and picking up the airplane from the shop, I had returned it to the tie-down that I originally rented upon my arrival from Sheep Mountain.

I was amazed at what all had transpired since I first landed at Tok Junction, Alaska. I had gone from being a truck driver on vacation to becoming a multimillionaire in less than three weeks. Until Rusty had left, I had barely had a chance to wrap my mind around it all.

Merging onto the Palmer freeway, I relaxed and reflected. For the first time, I wondered why I had purchased Arthur's place. I wasn't even sure. Was it because I needed to spend some of that money just to prove to myself it was real? Or had I subconsciously decided to move to Alaska and retire without even realizing it, or for that matter, consulting with Kati? Reaching for my sat phone and selecting *Home* from the call list, I mashed on the green button.

"Hello, Worley residence."

"Hi sweetie."

"Lou, when are you coming home?"

As I stated before, I had been a truck driver for the last twenty-seven years. Kati and I had been married thirty-two years. Nothing I could do would be much of a surprise to her. She knew me better than I knew myself and had adapted long ago to my spontaneous and adventurous ways. She was a country girl whose roots went back to the blue grass hills of Kentucky. I was nineteen and she was only seventeen when we were married in a chapel in Memphis, Tennessee, because the only one she ever loved more than me was Elvis.

"I have a better idea. Why don't you come here and see our new home?"

"Oh my God, Lou Worley "…what have you done now?"

I drove directly to the Cessna still parked in the transient parking area. After loading my gear and completing a pre-flight inspection, I then went to the airport manager's office. There I rented a more permanent tie-down space on the airport where I would be able to keep either the car or the airplane (or both) as long as I faithfully paid the rent.

Wasilla lies only twenty-eight and a half miles from Merrill Field by air. Depending, of course, on how direct or indirect the route, a direct flight in my little Cessna would only take about sixteen minutes. Driving by car is roughly an hour from Anchorage to Wasilla, a route that would take you east by northeast around the end of the Knick Arm, a very wide channel of half seawater and half freshwater forming the mouth of the Matanuska River, which spills into the Cook Inlet.

Cleared for the Chester Creek VFR departure, I pushed the power forward, leveling off at seven hundred feet until the north side of the Knick Arm. Within a few minutes, I was turning final at my very own private airstrip. It still felt surreal, like it was all a dream. I pushed the airplane into the hangar and closed the door. Climbing into the Land Cruiser, I drove to the cabin. When I had called my wife earlier, Kati was somewhere between shocked and awed and could not wait to see the place. She immediately booked a flight from Seattle to Anchorage for the next day where I agreed to pick her up at noon.

The cabin needed a lot of cleaning and rearranging. I knew Kati would want to supervise the rearranging part, so I set about to clean up as much as I could in preparation for her arrival. It was three in the morning by the time I got to sleep.

At eleven o'clock the next morning, I again was in the air, heading back to Merrill Field.

Securing the airplane, I climbed into the Toyota and drove to the international airport. Kati's flight had just landed, and she was waiting at the baggage claim when I arrived. With one suitcase and a carry-on in the back of the 4Runner, I took my sweetie on the grand tour of the big town. She had never been to Alaska and was amazed that Anchorage was not that different from most other cities. Of course, I did not mention the part about winter.

We departed Merrill Field and flew directly to our new Alaska retreat. I circled the cabin and the airstrip a couple of times to let Kati see it from the air and then headed east to show her the Alfred Creek mine, all the while describing the three incredible days I had spent surviving the place and its grizzly resident. From there, we landed at Sheep Mountain, where I treated her to one of Marge's famous meals and a piece of cherry pie.

Marge was excited to meet her, and they became so involved in conversation that I thought I would have to cook our own food. Then I remembered the sign on the door and decided not to push my luck.

In the air once again, pointing the spinner toward Bold's, I reached across to my wife and grasped her hand as we let the magic of the moment and the awesome beauty of Alaska convince us that this truly would be a great place to live.

This time, when the wheels touched the turf, I got the feeling that very soon this place would become our home.

With the little Cessna put away, I took Kati on a tour of the cabin. It was love at first sight. She immediately wanted to go shopping for groceries, curtains, sheets, and bedspreads. For the next week, I did nothing but take her here and there. She suggested that I buy another car that she could use for shopping so I wouldn't be bored, but I had been away from her so long I was enjoying our time together, although I admit that the shopping part was a little boring. Of course, if we had been shopping for airplanes, I probably would not have been nearly as bored.

A week was all that Kati could stay away from our two cats, as they can't get by alone much longer than that. The day her plane was to leave, the weather made a turn for the worse. With ceilings and visibilities of five hundred feet and two miles, I filed IFR and flew the instrument approach into Merrill Field.

She always cries, so I stayed with her until she boarded her plane. I told her that I would be home in a month.

Upon returning to Merrill Field, I noticed a man over by the pedestrian access gate to the general aviation parking area, waving at someone. I glanced around, not completely sure that he was waving at *me*. Seeing no one else in the area, I parked by the little Cessna and headed his way. As I got closer, I realized it was Deano, the goon from Grueder's. Somewhat surprised, I looked around for Judo, but didn't see him. Nor did I see the Crown Victoria.

"Deano," I said, glancing around as if someone could be listening.

"Hey! Worley, My boss wants you to call him." Deano extended his arm over the belly-high fence to hand me a business card that read "GINO PASTELLI & ASSOCIATES."

"Who's your boss?" I asked.

"It's all on the card, don't keep him waitin, he don't like to wait." He added, walking away.

Not quit sure what this was all about, I returned to the car and headed to the closest off-airport pay phone. I noticed that the number had a Chicago prefix, so I called collect

"Yea!" a man rudely answered.

"Will you accept a collect call from Mr. Lou Worley?" The operator asked.

There was a long pause, with voices in the background.

"Will you accept—?"

"Yea! Yea! Operator, I will," another voice answered.

"Is dis da Lou Worley in Anchorage, Alaska?" Another man asked.

"Yes, this is Lou Worley. Who's this?" I asked without the slightest clue of where this was going.

"I'm-eh, Gino Pastelli. I wantz to do some more bizness, jush yuz an' me." He said in a wise-guy slur. "Do you remember the bizness you did with my boyz, Deano and Judo?"

Now I knew who I was talking to. What I did not know was what made him think I had any more of that kind of "bizness" still to do?

"Nice meeting you, Mr. Pastelli. What kind of business was that again? I forget."

"Thatz okay, Worley. I understand, after all itz been a whole two weeks. Let me say it thiz way, how much more of that Alfred Creek gold dooz you have?"

"Oh, *that* business. Well, I might still have some. How much do you want?"

"Listen, Mr. Worley. Don't yank me 'round. I wontz to deal with you direct so's I don't looze any to Grueder and his broker feez. I'm ready to pay the zame as I did the last time. Fair 'nough? And I can take as much of that gold as you got."

"That's clear enough for me, Mr. Pastelli. I have 486 pounds ready to deal any time you are. Three-hundred-thirty-one pounds in gravel nuggets and 155 of the tailings."

"I'll give you seven extra large for the holla ting," Pastelli said.

I was shocked. That was almost $500,000 more than I expected. *Why is this guy giving money away? But then again, what do I care as long as its real money?* All of a sudden, I was ready to get this done before Mr. Gino Pastelli changed his mind.

Gino said he wanted to do business somewhere isolated. I told him where my airstrip was located in relation to the Wasilla airport, and he said he would send someone in an airplane with the money, right to my door. Gino said he would get back with me and let me know when to expect his "boyz." I assumed that he was referring to Deano and Judo.

This was huge. I called Rusty to tell him I needed him to come back and bring a friend

I parked the car and fired up the little Cessna. The weather conditions had deteriorated even more. The ceilings had dropped to below minimums, but forward visibilities had remained better than three miles, so, requesting a special VFR departure clearance, I stayed low over the Arm and scooted into my new home field, barely three hundred feet above the bushes.

I don't know if it was good, bad, stupid, or smart, but I had given Gino my sat phone number. In addition, he now knew where I lived, at least in Alaska. I was crossing my fingers that it would not come back to bite me in the butt.

The next morning the phone rang. I was in such a hurry to answer that I spilled my coffee. It was only Rusty. He wanted to know if I had heard from Gino. Rusty was planning to leave by noon his time. Kevin Gaither and his wife, Brenda, the man and wife investigator team who worked for Rusty's firm, would accompany him.

I was at the hangar the next day when the big Cessna turned onto final and touched down on the 2,800-foot turf runway. I felt a huge sense of relief. Seven million in cash for 486 pounds of gold was no small potatoes, and I was very thankful for the company.

Kati and I had known Kevin and Brenda Gaither since the first day they came to work for Rusty. They had become a part of our family and had invested a significant amount of their savings in Rusty's business. Their association was more a partnership than an employer-employee relationship.

Kevin was shorter then his wife by about three quarters of an inch. Brenda was five foot seven, and if you put a little gold dust in her pocket, she might weigh 125 pounds. Kevin, though shorter, was solid muscle and 175. Both were in their late forties and had been with Rusty a little over two years. Prior to that, Kevin had worked for the CIA and Brenda the FBI, both retiring five years earlier. They had been married eighteen years.

With the connections they had from their years of experience in investigation, there was not much the two of them were unable to discover about a person. In addition, Brenda was quite familiar with the smalltime Mafioso Gino Pastelli and the questionable nature of his import-export businesses. According to her, Gino was reliable, but whenever doing business with him, it would be wise to, faithfully keep any agreements.

I asked Brenda what he would do with the gold. I felt we were getting a great price for it compared to market value and had wondered how he would make his profit on it. She said he would at the very least double his money, selling the gold to jewelry manufacturers around the world who wanted only the highest grade of metal. Now I better understood Gino's fascination for the Alfred Creek gold and wondered if I should pursue other options for marketing if, or when, there was a next time.

With Kati gone back home, we piled into the Land Cruiser, and I took us all to dinner at the finest restaurant in Wasilla, Las Margareta's. We had no more then finished our meal when the sat phone began to blink.

"Hello!" I answered.

"Mr. Worley, thiz is Gino Pastelli. Is your runway the one with the hangar at the eazt end?"

"Yes, it is."

"We iz on the ground." He said and hung up.

I looked at Rusty. "They have landed and are at the hangar."

Rusty looked up at me and said thoughtfully, "Go ahead with your deal. We'll watch your back."

"Who's going to check the cash?" I asked. "I don't want to get stuck with homemade money."

"I will," Brenda said.

We stopped by the storage shed and picked up the gold that I had already prepared for transport. When we arrived at the airstrip, a brand-new turbocharged Stationair sat parked in front of the hangar. Emerging from the car, we saw two men walking down the driveway from the cabin toward us. The first man called my name as if he were asking a question.

"Worley?" he said in a familiar voice

"That would be me." I extended my hand in greeting.

"I'm-eh, Gino Pastelli, I think you already knowz Deano, my zon, am I right?"

"Yes, we have met." Deano made no eye contact, so I did not offer to shake his hand.

I was surprised, both at the news that Deano was Gino's son and I had expected someone in a five-thousand-dollar suit with a sharkskin fedora and black-and-white wing tip shoes. Gino was wearing jeans, a goose down coat from REI, and no hat. He did have the typical Italian—or maybe it was Sicilian—mafia face and slicked back hair, but then again, maybe it was just my imagination doing overtime.

I introduced Rusty as my son-in-law and Kevin and Brenda as business associates in our mining operations. What did it matter that our mining operations as far as a business had not yet begun, or that the prospecting that had produced the gold he was buying had happened long ago at someone else's expense, if not their life? Or, that I had only recently retrieved it out of an out-house hole.

I will say that with just Gino and Deano, I felt much more at ease with the whole transaction. I was glad Judo was not involved. Something about him made me feel cold inside, and without anyone telling me, I knew he was a very dangerous man.

"Are you ready to do thiz thing?" Gino asked.

"We are!" I said. "It has already been weighed, but I have a scale if you want to reweigh it."

"I truzt you, Worley! I see you are a zmart guy, so I have no doubt that itz all there. "I could sense that his comment was more of a warning than a statement of confidence.

Rusty backed the Land Cruiser up to the passenger side of the Stationair, and he and Kevin began transferring the gold. Deano unloaded seven medium-sized, silver, metal cases from the baggage compartment of the C-206, and Brenda and I placed them in the car. I had no idea how much was there, but assumed that there must be a million in each case. Brenda looked them all over and nodded her head, indicating that it was all good.

I extended my hand first to Gino, shaking his hand, and then to Deano, who ignored it. "How did you know where that gold came from?" I asked Gino.

"There ain't no other gold like it," he said. "I can take all of it you can find."

"Good!" I said. "Maybe we'll have some more for you next year. I'll keep your card."

Gino turned toward the Stationair and then paused. Turning halfway around, he looked back at me. "I like you, Worley, but whatever you duz, don't deal with anyone elze but me until I zay itz okay. *Capisce?*"

"Why would I look anywhere else, Gino? Could it ever get any better then this?"

I was surprised to see Deano climb into the pilot seat and fire up the new Cessna with its sophisticated IFR equipped panal. He had not struck me as being that intelligent. It just goes to prove that anyone can learn to fly.

I returned Gino's wave as Deano pitched the propeller to climb. The big Cessna easily lifted the heavy load into the air, disappearing into the western twilight.

CHAPTER 8

The living conditions in the cabin had much improved from what they were when Rusty was last there. With Kati as my supervisor, before she left, we had restored the log cabin from a bachelor's cluttered bunkhouse, into a beautiful home that was actually livable.

With the money from the gold transaction locked in the safe, and with Kevin and Brenda's help, Rusty and I moved it to a secured room in the basement of the cabin. I was much relieved yet still concerned about having over eight million dollars cash in one place. Rusty suggested that we divide it between several banks, putting it into safe deposit boxes.

Kevin and Brenda bunked at the cabin while they spent the next three days researching the Alfred Creek claim. During that time, Rusty and I flew around Alaska to twelve different banks, renting safe deposit boxes into which we placed a half-million dollars in cash, equally.

Rusty planned to take a million back home with him, and I still had slightly under a million from the original transactions at Grueder's pawnshop.

It would be at least another two and a half weeks before the title closing when Kati and I would sign the papers and the two properties we had purchased from Arthur would finally be in our name. I had moved in a little prematurely, but had signed a rental agreement with Arthur for the interim.

The time had come for me to find another airplane more conducive for the challenging Alaskan climate and terrain. I anticipated that I would be in and out of the Alfred Creek airstrip on a regular basis and would need something stronger than the little Cessna 172 that I had initially flown to Alaska. I liked Gino's Stationair, but I was really looking for a Cessna 180, built with the same rugged design yet much lighter in weight and capable of carrying a payload only slightly less than the C-185 or the C-206 and with much better short-field performance capability.

Before he left, Arthur had told me the Cessna 180 was the airplane he had primarily used during his years of flying the Alaska bush country, and he highly recommended it. He had also given me the name of an airplane dealer in Anchorage who I could trust to find whatever I was looking for. His name was Ray Sumner.

I had first contacted Ray after Rusty left for home the first time— shortly after we had brought the gold out of Alfred Creek—explaining to him what I was looking for and who had referred him to me. Ray had called the day before Rusty and the Gaithers were to leave, informing me that he had found a 180 that I might want to look at.

Kevin and Brenda would continue their investigation from Spanaway. Taking $150,000 in cash with me, I hitched a ride in the big Cessna as far as the Lake Hood hard surface, where I thanked them for all their help and promised I would be home in a week.

Ray's office was located on the west end of Lake Hood. He looked up as I walked in.

"Are you Mr. Sumner?" I asked.

"I am. You must be Lou Worley," he said as we shook hands. "How did you know Arthur?"

"I bought him out, he wanted to go back to Missouri where his daughter lives and spend the rest of his life with her."

"Really!" Ray exclaimed. "I didn't even know he had a daughter. Well, that's good. I'm very glad for him. So did you already live in Alaska, or are you just moving here, if you don't mind my asking?"

"I'm just moving here. I have a home in Darington, Washington, and am actually working on the idea of transplanting my family up here."

"Well, Alaska is lucky to have you, Lou Worley. Come with me, and let's see if you're going to like this airplane I found for you." Ray rose from his desk and headed for the back door of his office.

Ray Sumner was no spring chicken. A tall, slender man, he was at least thirty-years older than I was with a full head of hair that, for his age, had resisted turning gray quite well. He seemed to be a friendly, genuine person, not the phony friendly one would normally expect from a salesperson. I felt sure that I could trust him.

I followed Ray through the back door to a parking lot hosting at least fifty different aircraft ranging from various models of Cessna's, DeHavilland Beavers and Otters, to old military surplus C-47's, DC-3's, even a 1949 Norseman.

Ray pointed to a recently painted, dark, beet-red Cessna 180 Skywagon with black trim and undercarriage. I was immediately impressed with its sinister appearance. The 180 was equipped with a Horton STOL kit, dual navigation communication radios, and a full IFR complement of instrumentation, including GPS radio navigation (RNAV). The 285 horsepower I-0470 Continental engine and constant-speed, three-blade propeller topped off the instrument panel. Ray watched quietly until I completed inspecting every nook and corner for cracks or corrosion before he began his sales pitch.

"It's a 1966, with only 3,300 hours total time on the airframe. The engine is an STC retrofit with fifty hours, and the aircraft has no damage history. It has long-range, retrofitted wing tanks, with a total capacity of eighty-eight gallons and a range of seven hours, or approximately 1,056 miles." Ray paused, taking a breath. "I need 95K for the airplane, and if you want the floats and skis that go with it, that will take another twenty-five," he added.

"I'll take it all," I said. "By the way, who was the original owner?"

Ray paused for a moment before answering, "Well, that guy you bought out? Now you own his last airplane."

Ray and I finalized the deal and the paperwork. He called a flight instructor friend of his by the name of Phillip Later, who would check me out in the Skywagon.

Phillip was short, maybe five foot four with a medium build, and had to sit on a pillow to see over the instrument panel. I am usually careful about prejudging someone without plenty to go on, which was a good thing in Philips case, because I don't think I have ever been with a finer instructor and pilot.

We departed the Lake Hood hard surface runway, a stone's throw from Anchorage International, and flew to Campbell's field about twelve miles to the southeast, a five-thousand-foot, dirt runway where I would have plenty of room to practice three-point landings.

When landing at Campbell's had ceased being a challenge, Phillip took me way to the other end of the 'Turn Again Arm' an extension of the Bering Sea that you could boat on if the tide was in but not if it was out. Beyond where the inlet ended on the other side of Portage Pass lay a grass mountain airstrip called Whittier's.

The fifteen-hundred-foot strip would ordinarily be quite long enough for the 180 were it not for the intimidating terrain and high trees that hampered both approaches. That, along with wind blowing from four different directions at the same time, provided a challenging training environment.

After thirty-five practice landings and an exhausting amount of air work including stalls, slow flight at minimum controllable air speeds, unusual attitude recovery, and then more stalls and slow flight, we headed back to the Lake Hood hard surface.

As Phillip signed my logbook, he commented, "*Now* you can say you fly a *real* airplane."

I thanked him, paid him, and departed for home.

I realize that tail-draggers are a bit more challenging to land than a tricycle gear like my little straight tail, but to say that they are not a real airplane is a little demeaning to someone who owns one of those sweet flying machines. I think a real airplane is one that gets you there and back in one piece. If a tail-dragger pilot is the only kind of pilot who qualifies as a *real* pilot and suddenly finds himself in a tricycle gear due to financial limitations, is he no longer a real pilot because he now drives a tri-gear? Sounds like a big ego trip to me.

By the time I finished the check-out, I knew for certain that my new Skywagon was not only a keeper but that all my dreams of the day I would actually own one had fallen way short of the actual moment when it became a reality. On the ground at Bold's, I spun the tail a 180 degrees and shut it down in front of the hangar, facing to the west. As I sat there listening to the ticking of the cooling engine, I gently ran my fingers over the beautiful mahogany instrument panel. "Now this is a *real* airplane." I was somewhat shocked to hear the words actually come out of my mouth, but now I knew what Phillip had meant.

It was time to load the Skywagon and prepare for the trip home. Kati and I would fly back commercially when it was time to sign the papers, but with winter fast approaching, the time had come for me to head south, down the inland passage.

I had winterized and secured the log cabin, locked the Land Cruiser in the hangar with the little Cessna, and with 200k in cash stowed in the baggage compartment of the Skywagon, departed for Merrill Field to top off with fuel and pick up a sack full of sandwiches to go.

With the long-range tanks, I expected no fuel quantity issues. From Merrill Field, I would file IFR to Juneau where I would spend the night and the next morning continue nonstop to our home in Darington, Washington.

The first half of the trip was a bit challenging due to inclement weather. I was on the gauges from Anchorage to Juneau, where Approach Control issued me a clearance for the LDA/X approach. Emerging from the bottom of a twenty-five-hundred-foot, solid overcast with Juneau International gradually appearing in the windshield, I received my clearance from the tower and landed runway zero-eight-right.

By the next morning, the weather had turned severe clear. I filed a VFR flight plan straight through Canada and was home by noon, local time. I had gone fifteen hundred miles in nine and a half hours of flight time.

The next morning, after breakfast with my lovely wife, I called Keera, who I knew could not wait another minute to see me. Climbing into the Skywagon, Kati and I scooted down to Spanaway where our daughter and grandkids mauled me half to death. Rusty was also there and said he had plenty of information to share with me. We excused ourselves and retreated to Rusty's office along with Kevin and Brenda.

"Dad," Rusty began, "Kevin and Brenda have put together the details involving the Idaho boys and the Alfred Creek mine. I have asked them to share that with you." He turned toward Brenda and nodded for her to begin.

"Well, Lou, it seems that about twenty years ago the Idaho boys had leased the claim at Alfred Creek for the summer from an Alaska resident named Clark Ramsey. The claim had been in his name for over twenty years, during which time he had not only worked it himself off and on, but also sold temporary subleases to out-of-state, wannabee prospectors. Along with the sub-leases he sold them specially designed sluice equipment that were not designed to extract all of the gold. When the crew finished for the season Clark would bring in his own sluices the next season and re-work the material extracting as much or more gold than his customers without near the expense. That probably was where a portion of your gold came from. He also held mining rights to two other claims adjacent to the one where you found your gold. Clark Ramsey died within a year after the Idaho boys worked the claim, leaving the mining rights to his son Rodger. It took some time to find Rodger, but as it turned out he was living in the Washington State Penitentiary, doing a fifteen year sentence for armed robbery."

"So was Rodger one of the two brothers stealing from the Idaho boys?" I asked.

"No!" Kevin quickly responded. "Actually, Clark Ramsey had a brother named Henry. Frank and Shawn Ramsey were Henry's two sons, which obviously made them Rodger's cousins. As far as we know, Rodger never worked any of the claims."

"So which one of the two brothers that was up there stealing from the Idaho boys made it home?" I asked.

"Shawn." Rusty said. "The Idaho boys had suspected for some time that the two brothers were stealing from their sluice boxes, but they could never catch them in the act. In addition, as you just pointed out, only one of the brothers came home from the adventure, and no one knew what happened to the other one, which was Frank, the older of the two. Shawn said Frank had left him there alone, so he returned home, claiming he had not seen him since."

"So where is Shawn now?" I asked.

"He is in the Washington State Penitentiary," Brenda answered, "along with his cousin Rodger, except Shawn is doing twenty-five-to-life on an unrelated charge due to a three-strike law in the state of Washington. The two cousins, Shawn and Rodger had together been busted robbing a filling station, which resulted in Shawn's third felony conviction, landing him life in prison." Brenda paused for a sip of tea before continuing. "I was able to discover from sources I am not at liberty to disclose what the two officers, Trent and Daily, found in the pit toilet that turned it into a crime scene."

"After you finished with your chore of scraping the runway and finally left Alfred Creek, Officer Trent, the game warden, overcome with curiosity and wondering if you had possibly poached something illegally, reopened the glory hole where you had found that bucket of gold. Digging slightly deeper than where you had stopped, he soon encountered human remains.

Trent then turned the investigation over to Officer Daily, who sent the remains to their crime lab in Fairbanks for dental testing. The remains were subsequently identified as that of Frank Ramsey."

"So, Rusty, do you think that Trent and Daily actually suspected me of the murder of Frank Ramsey?"

"I really have my doubts about that; the crime scene was obviously many years old. Besides, it was obvious where the newly disturbed earth and the old undisturbed earth began and ended. I think they were more curious about why you dug the hole in the first place and if you found or removed any thing that might have been related to the crime. At that time, they were not aware of the existence of the gold. Isn't that right, Kevin?"

"That's right. By the time they figured out that your newfound wealth— which didn't remain a secret to the public very long once you bought Bold's place—probably came from that old pit toilet, they had already paid a visit to Shawn Ramsey in the Walla Walla State Penitentiary. Daily and another detective interviewed the younger brother who ultimately confessed to the killing of his older brother, Frank. He claimed it was an accident, and he had buried him down by the big rock. Furthermore, he had no idea how the body ended up in the bottom of the pit toilet. Brenda can fill you in on the rest of the story."

"Lou, we believe that the following spring after the Idaho boys were long gone, Clark Ramsey returned to Alfred Creek to work his own claim. No one knew exactly when, but sometime during that summer, he died of a heart attack. His body lay on his bunk in the old cook-shack for a year until finally discovered. We are convinced that it was Clark who found and buried Frank in the pit toilet, and the gold that he had placed on top of him was a combination of what the boys had stolen from the Idaho crew and what Clark himself had gleaned while working his own claim after they left and before his death."

"So who holds the rights to the claims now?" I asked. Rusty's hand went up.

"Dad, I have something for you to sign. It seems that the mining laws of the state of Alaska clearly state that if a claim remains un-worked for a period of five years, it becomes available to the public for re-filing. I have the paperwork for all three claims."

I was so excited I could hardly write my name, but I managed to get it done just in time to celebrate.

Everyone was impressed with the Skywagon and congratulated me on a great find. I told them it was Ray who had found it for me and that it was the last airplane Arthur Bold had used in his long career of flying the bush.

We packed everyone into both airplanes and winged our way north up the Puget Sound past Seattle to Darington, where Kati prepared a welcome-home meal and had invited everyone over, including Kevin and Brenda.

On our way back to Darington, Keera, Manson, and Michelle rode with me in the Skywagon while Kevin and Brenda rode with Rusty. We partied way into the night on fruit smoothies and popcorn.

On our way back to Spanaway the next morning with Keera and the kids, I reached in my pocket and took out the largest of the three nuggets I had been carrying with me since I first discovered the gold at Alfred Creek. Handing it to my daughter, I said, "This is for you, sweetie, because you are more precious to me then gold."

"I love you, Daddy," she said and laid her head on my shoulder, hanging onto my arm with both hands the rest of the way to Spanaway. I love it when she does that. I guess you could refer to it as a Hallmark moment.

Three weeks later, Kati and I received the call we had been waiting for. Carol, the woman at the title company, informed us the papers were ready to sign. We immediately booked a flight.

After arriving at Anchorage International, we took a taxi to Merrill Field, picked up the Toyota 4Runner, and headed to Carol's office in Wasilla. On the way, we talked about what life in Alaska would be like. Kati was growing fonder of the idea with every day she spent there.

I handed the signed papers and the titles over to Kati as we drove to the cabin. I watched her from the corner of my eye as she kept re-reading the documents. I could tell she felt the same as me.

Our plane would not be leaving for another week, during which time we worked, played, and planned. It appeared that our new life in Alaska had already begun.

A week later, we returned to Darington and started packing. By the end of the following spring we would be permanent residents of Alaska.

CHAPTER 9

My long-anticipated vacation adventure had become a turning point in my life and, I might add, the lives of my whole family. I am not sure it had fully sunk in that we were rich beyond anything we could ever have imagined and that never again did we need to be concerned about the basic necessities, such as education, medical expenses, etc. For one thing, I hadn't had time for any of that. I am a project-focused personality, and the project had only just begun.

I was convinced that the Alfred Creek mine was still hiding a significant amount of gold somewhere under that huge landslide of cascading pit-run making up the southwest face of Syncline Mountain. As far as I was concerned, neither the Idaho boys nor Clark Ramsey had so much as scratched the surface in terms of the amount of wealth that lay hidden in its hills. The possibility of finding a mother lode had also crossed my mind as more than just a notion.

The winter prior to moving to our new home, I had made several trips to visit our other two daughters and their families. My middle daughter, Kathy, and her husband, Richard Fortner, lived in Renton, Washington, with their two children, Randy, who was three, and Elaine, who was finally out of the oven and would soon be one year old. My youngest daughter, Kelly, and her husband, Mitchell Wilson, lived in Missoula, Montana, with their two-year-old triplets, Walker, Rhiannon, and Tristan. (By the way, this does not mean you can get away with buying an all-for-one birthday card.)

With financial concerns no longer an issue, I easily persuaded both Richard and Mitchell to join us in the move. Neither of my two youngest daughters needed any persuasion to be close to their parents. Rusty was the only hold-out due to his private investigation business obligations. I purchased separate homes in Wasilla for each family. It would be only a matter of moving in and setting up housekeeping.

The winter passed quickly as we all prepared for our move to Alaska. I continued to monitor the weather conditions and stayed in touch with the movers until the day came when the vans finally showed up and they started loading our belongings.

It took a tractor-trailer rig with a fifty-three-foot trailer to move the two families. Kati and I packed our personal effects along with the kids' belongings into the big van and left the furniture in the house at Darington, which we had decided to rent out. Everything else—tools, lumber, equipment, etc.—filled a second moving van of the same size.

One month later, with Mitchell and Richards families finally settled in Wasilla, Rusty, Keera, and the kids came up for the housewarming. While we were all together, Rusty and I decided we should take Mitchell and Richard to Alfred Creek to have a look around and let them see the place. Before climbing into Rusty's big Cessna, I grabbed a shovel from the tool shed, just in case. Since my first experience at Alfred Creek, I seldom went anywhere without a shovel.

Circling a couple of times before beginning his approach to let Mitchell and Richard get a bird's-eye view of the area before we landed, Rusty skillfully set the 206 firmly on the ground. We spent the rest of the day hiking and exploring.

Mitchell, while taking pictures, was interested in the rock formations and the possible source of the gold discovered there. He was sure the sliding mixture of dirt and gravel had been grinding away at some concentrated source that was giving birth to the nuggets and tailings that continually showed up at the base of the hill side.

Rusty stayed with Mitchell, and I took Richard up the Alfred Creek trail and showed him the ancient privy. The only evidence of the investigation that had taken place was a couple pieces of yellow crime-scene tape that lay nearby.

We returned to the airstrip to find Rusty and Mitchell ready to go.

Back at the cabin, with Kati giddy over serving as host to her whole family all together in our new Alaska home, we men folk retired to the living room to discuss the logistics of getting more gold out of Alfred Creek.

We decided that Mitchell would be the mining boss, and Richard would operate the equipment. I would be the pilot/gopher, while Rusty would provide our legal counsel. It would remain a family matter, no outside partners. If we couldn't dig it and carry it, it would have to stay there. We all agreed and toasted our partnership with another of Kati's delicious fruit smoothies.

It was still early in the season, only the middle of May. Snow still lay in the shaded pockets and crevasses of the mining area. I had been to Fairbanks and purchased a D-9 Caterpillar. It was delivered on a low-boy to the old Brandt's Resort at Tahneta Pass where Richard climbed aboard and crawled his way west down Squaw Creek and north up the Caribou on the west end of Syncline Mountain to Alfred Creek, a trek of eleven miles. Additional equipment on the way included two more Caterpillars a D-8 and D-6, with a flatbed equipment trailer with which we brought in the two sluice systems complete with shakers and wash plants. A one-thousand-gallon rubber diesel-fuel bladder permanently mounted on a four-wheeled tongue trailer came in behind the D-6 and last but not least, an Hitachi 400 excavator.

After about two dozen roundtrip flights into the airstrip in the 180 with everything from a stockpile of airplane fuel to food and camp supplies, I was finally able to pause long enough for Richard to begin some runway improvements. Improvements, that included a longer and wider landing strip plus parking areas that would accommodate two airplanes, one on each end of the runway. By the end of July, we had a very sturdy combination cook-shack/bunkhouse and a cozy wood stove.

We did our best to keep the dozer moving at least sixteen hours a day. Mitchell staked out the perimeters and traded off eight-hour shifts with Richard, pushing the rich gravel barrow down the hill to the sluice boxes. I also relieved Richard occasionally when he needed to take the D-6 and trailer to bring in more diesel fuel in the huge rubber bladder. It was an enormous amount of work for only the three of us to keep up with, and we were tempted at times to hire help, but decided against it.

Mitchell kept the excavator feeding the sluice boxes, and we cleaned the cages each night. As the season grew shorter, the hours grew longer until the time came to button it all up for the season. All the equipment accept the two wash plants were stored at home for the winter.

It was the middle of October by the time we had that all accomplished with the equipment winterized and staged not far from the hangar. We had taken almost eleven hundred pounds of gold out of Alfred Creek in just five months. At last year's prices and last year's sources, we would be looking at $14,080,000.00, but Gino's cell phone was no longer in service, and Grueder's Pawnshop had gone out of business.

The word was out about our little family enterprise, but no one had a clue if we were having any success. However, the Alfred Creek claim had a reputation of yielding high-grade metal, and we suspected that soon enough we would have visitors sniffing around. So far, thankfully, there was no indication that anyone had been up there during our first season.

I called Rusty to let him know that I had been unable to make contact with Gino or Grueder. He said he would put his people on it and try to find other options for marketing the gold.

With my Cessna 180 becoming a frequent flyer in the central and southwest skies of Alaska, occasionally I would get calls to join in search-and-rescue efforts to locate downed aircraft. Earlier, around the middle of August, Kati received a call from SAR (search and rescue), inviting me to join in a search for a downed missionary pilot who worked and flew out of Venetie, Alaska. Venetie—a village with a population of 260 souls—lies 394 miles north by northeast of Wasilla and 160 miles due north of Fairbanks.

Pastor William Shearer and his wife, Sharon, had lived among and ministered to the native peoples of Alaska for thirty-five years. On a routine flight returning to Venetie from Fairbanks in his 1949 Piper Clipper, Pastor Bill had gone missing. I dropped what I was doing and joined in the search.

Ordinarily, there would have been a huge turnout of volunteer search planes looking for any downed pilot, whoever it was. However, as Providence would have it, there had been as of late a rash of airplane emergencies at the time Bill decided to have his turn at it. I joined two other local pilots to fly an eight-thousand-square-mile grid that spanned a one-hundred-fifty by fifty-mile search area between Fairbanks and Venetie.

After three days of low flying to and from the departure and destination points, there was talk of giving up the search. While having lunch and fueling at the Fairbanks Metro airport Café, I managed to persuade one of the other two pilots to continue for at least another day.

The middle of the next afternoon found me seventy-two miles north of Fairbanks, flying northbound up the meandering mile-wide Yukon River barely two hundred feet above the ground and under a solid, four-hundred-foot overcast. Suddenly, I saw smoke coming from the chimney of an old abandoned and dilapidated cabin.

I dropped in a notch of flap and slowed the airplane as I circled to see who was home. Amazingly, by the time I had completed only half of the counter clockwise turn, someone wearing an orange vest was already out of the cabin furiously waving his hand. It appeared to be the downed pilot, Bill Shearer, and he was pointing to the west. I presumed that meant there would be a place to land in that direction.

As I maneuvered the Skywagon, I soon saw a short patch of ground surrounded by creeks and inlets from the nearby Yukon River. On the south end of the short patch of sand and gravel lay the upside down, mangled remains of Bill's Clipper. Whatever problem Mr. Shearer had encountered, it left him just a wee bit short of making the old riverbed runway. Fortunately, he only ran out of airspeed and not luck, or grace depending on the point of view.

Pastor Bill was not hurt and showed no concern over his predicament or the slightest surprise that someone had found him. It seems the tired old Clipper developed a fuel leak, which went unnoticed until Bill was almost out of options. Remembering the old cabin and the long-time abandoned landing strip by the river, Bill did the only thing left to do—keep flying the airplane all the way to the ground, where he almost made it over the last bush, but not quite. Out of both power and airspeed, the nose-low Clipper snagged the underbrush with its main gear and nosed over, landing Bill on his noggin.

I loaded Pastor Bill Shearer with his suitcase and Bible into the Skywagon and took him home to Venetie, where his very lovely and extremely relieved wife of forty-five years insisted I spend the night.

During my evening with Bill and Sharon, while she filled my belly with fine food and homemade cherry pie, I was fully briefed on the need their village and many other villages had for Bill and his ministry. It was obvious that their ministry, along with the people it served, would suffer as long as Bill was without an airplane. The next day, Bill and I flew to Anchorage to pay Ray Sumner a visit.

Ray put Bill into a very nice, 1976 Cessna 185 that had just been completely refurbished. Bill was very thankful and signed over the title of the Clipper to me.

I had examined the Clipper carefully when I landed to pick up Bill. The damage was not that bad, mostly torn fabric and one broken wing spar, all of which were repairable. I mentioned to Ray that I would like to have it restored. He said he would make arraignments for the retrieval and the restoration of the little Piper. As soon as that project was finished, the Clipper would join the little Cessna in the old hangar at my place, waiting for my two youngest daughters to learn to fly.

During the winter months, Mitchell studied the notes and pictures he had taken of the Alfred Creek geological landscape and pondered the question, "Where's the mother lode?" Richard and I were not in the least disappointed in the last season, but it had come in somewhat below Mitchell's expectations. "Dad," he would say, "that gold didn't just fall out of the sky one day, and there isn't any sign of volcanic action that would have left it on top of the ground. The fact that the greatest concentration is at the lower end of the slope indicates that it has originated from higher up the hill and deeper into the ground, and that's the source I want to find."

"Mitchell," I said, "we have plenty of money and are not going to starve for a very long time. We can just play in that dirt every summer for the rest of our lives as long as it keeps giving us a bucket of gold occasionally. I could probably live with that."

Mitchell didn't say anymore, but I somehow knew that, for reasons only he could explain, he wouldn't quit until he found what he was looking for.

Kathy and Kelly were settling into Alaska life. The older kids were in school, and Kelly, who had been a schoolteacher in Missoula, was enjoying being an at-home mom to her children. Kathy, who was a licensed practical nurse, had completed her training as an operating room technician and was nearing the completion of her RN certification. She did not relish the one and a quarter hour commute to and from Anchorage everyday where she worked at the hospital, but would not let that keep her from achieving her goals.

I told Kathy that if she would get her private pilot license and instrument certificate, I would give her the little Cessna for commuting. At first she didn't seem that interested, but after the first winter, she decided to do it after all. I went with her to the Wasilla FBO as she enrolled in the private pilot training course.

Finally the day came for Kathy's first solo flight, and the entire family turned out to cheer her on. Kelly was so impressed that she could barely contain herself. When Kathy finished her third perfect landing, we all cheered as the instructor recorded the event and signed her logbook. Kelly could take no more; I knew when she walked over to me that she was ready to follow suit. Eventually, all three of my daughters would be pilots. I was beaming with pride.

Brenda had found a variety of sources for marketing the gold, most of which were jewelry manufacturers and a few gold collectors. The collectors wanted only large nuggets. They paid better than the jewelers who would take anything, but they, too, had their preferences. Either way, we would be getting half of what we had gotten from Gino, who, by the way, had been convicted of tax evasion and was doing hard time in a the federal prison at Leavenworth, Kansas.

With over twenty-one million dollars from last season's work and now having to market through a variety of sources, we formed a corporation called Alfred Creek Mining Enterprises, Inc. Due to Gino's new standard of living, Rusty felt this would be in our best interest.

Spring thaw lay just around the corner, and work would soon begin on a new and much larger hangar at Bold's, which would include a heated shop, office, and an underground walk-in vault located next to the existing hangar at the east end of the runway. With a full-time diesel and A&P mechanic, the aircraft and heavy equipment were being prepared for another season in search of the mother lode.

CHAPTER 10

S pring break-up came late. The past winter had arrived early and set in hard and long, stubbornly remaining well past the time we had planned to be back to work at Alfred Creek.

I had initially filed the claim as a private citizen. There were environmental restrictions in place that did not allow disturbing or diverting the creek's course or contaminating its environment. Any drilling or the use of explosives would require a permit and that only after inspections by government geologist. In addition we were required to document and report the recovery of any precious metal.

The boys and I discussed these and many other issues over the course of the long winter. Rusty and, of course, Mitchell wanted to go for it. Get the permits and dig all the way to China. Richard and I were satisfied to sluice the area out and retire fishing and flying or just fly-fishing.

I had started to see a change in Mitchell. I'm not so sure it was gold fever exactly; I think it was the potential of a super-geological exploration that held his fascination. He really was not that taken with money and the things that money could buy as he was the idea of discovery.

By the middle of June, we were finally up and running in Alfred Creek. We used the D-6, the smallest of the three dozers for the arduous treks to and from the old Brandt's resort at Tahneta Pass. We had also added to our fleet of equipment a lowboy heavy hauler to transport the heavy equipment to and from Bolds and the un-loading area at the Tahneta Pass landing. This kept the operation going whenever maintenance and repairs to the equipment became necessary.

The level of yield had dramatically declined. Mitchell was searching for an area of better production. He moved the operation first to the high ground and then to the low. At times, we would begin to see an increase of yield only to watch it fizzle out. Once again, he would relocate.

By September 1, we had collected only 150 pounds of gold, which, turned into cash, would equal about 3.3 million dollars. Only three short years before that would have been like winning the lottery. Instead, we were all moping around as if someone had swiped our lunches.

I had just finished restocking the camp with enough provisions for two to three more weeks and was refueling the Skywagon at the hangar in Wasilla, when I got a call from Mitchell.

"Dad, you better come up here," he said in a low voice, "and call the cops." Then he hung up the phone.

Something was not right. That was totally unlike Mitchell. I knew there was a serious reason he had not taken time to explain. I had not completed re-fueling the airplane but had more than enough fuel to get to the mine and back. Sensing the urgency, I quickly twisted on the fuel caps, fired up the 180, and took off for Alfred Creek. On the way I called Calvin Trent.

I approached the camp lower and faster than normal, looking for anything unusual. As the airstrip came into view, I quickly made a head count, realizing immediately there were four extra people, and no one was working the equipment.

Mitchell was talking to someone over by the 400 and Richard was down at the main wash-plant, apparently cleaning out the cage. A strange man was standing about ten feet away with a rifle pointed at them. Two other men had just come out of the cook-shack and were watching me as I flew over, setting up for my approach.

Slamming the 180 on the ground like an F-18 Eagle on a carrier deck, I spun the tail dragger 180 degrees, simultaneously killing the engine and popped open the door. Stuffing the .45 Glock under my belt and grabbing the shotgun, I bailed out of the airplane.

I had just punched the safety to fire-when-ready when I heard a voice not fifteen feet behind me from the bank above call out, "I'll take that scatter-gun." I spun around. At the same instant that I saw the hunting rifle leveled at me, I touched the trigger of the ten-gage. For one brief instant, the would-be shooter stood silhouetted on the hillside above me with half his head missing. Then, in slow motion, he fell over backward where he lay lifeless on the ground.

I ran in the direction of the football field, watching for anyone I did not recognize, when suddenly something smacked me in the face, very hard. I struggled to turn away from it until I realized it was the ground. I staggered to my feet, not immediately aware that someone had shot me in the head. Then I heard a gunshot, and something that felt like a white-hot branding iron ripped a hole in my right side just below the bottom rib. Turning toward the sound, which came from behind me, I saw a strange man re-aiming a handgun at me. Realizing my time had apparently come, my only remaining hope was that I could get one more of them to even the odds a bit for my boys. I let go with the second of the four-hundred-grain slugs that I had prepared and thought I would only ever use against a charging grizzly bear. This time, my advancing assailant kept his head but lost half his rib cage all over the cook-shack door behind him. The combination of running backward and the recoil of the ten-gage shotgun landed me on the back of my head, and everything went black.

I faintly recollect seeing dim lights and ghostly shadows, hearing muffled sounds, and then it all returned to darkness. Out in the distance, very far away, I thought I could hear Kati.

"Lou, baby, I'm here. I'm here, sweetie. I love you."

As I opened my eyes, I tried to comprehend what was happening. I wanted to go back to sleep. Then I remembered that someone was trying to kill us all. I tried to get up, but something held me down. Again, I heard Kati.

"Its okay, baby, its okay. I'm here. Just lay back." Her soft voice made me feel safe, and I again drifted back into the security of my coma.

The next time I awoke, I was alone. For the first time, I realized that I was in a hospital. Then I remembered the boys. *What happened to the boys?* I started to cry. I sobbed uncontrollably as my subconscious attempted to deal with the reality that we had surely lost both Mitchell and Richard. Suddenly, Kati walked in the door, and with her was my entire family.

I had survived something terrible, the details of which I did not fully comprehend. In fact, I was not even sure what all had happened. Kati collapsed on top me, along with my three daughters and seven grandkids, almost finishing the job the gunmen had unsuccessfully attempted.

By the next day, I was sitting up in bed. I had a bandage around my head that looked like a white turban where a nine-millimeter slug had cut a four-inch-long trough just above my left ear. An additional speeding bullet from the same weapon had taken out part of my love handle on the right side and left me with another bandage that wrapped completely around my midsection.

I tried to get someone to explain to me what happened after I passed out, but, so far, everyone just changed the subject whenever I mentioned it. Suddenly, into the hospital room walked officers Daily and Trent.

My family all stepped out of the room as the detective and the game warden stepped forward, one on each side of my hospital bed. Daily spoke first. "Are you feeling strong enough to talk?"

"Well, I'm a little more awake than I was yesterday, so I guess so,"

"When you're on your feet and out of here, we'd like you to drop by the office and help us with some details. Don't worry about the paperwork. I have all that handled."

Officer Trent moved closer, placing his hand on my shoulder. "Don't worry about your plane, I brought it out of there myself. It's in your hangar, and by the way, that is the sweetest 180 I ever flew."

"Well," I said, "don't get too attached to it, 'cause I'm walking out of here real soon, and I'll be right back into it. But all kidding aside, thanks for bringing it out for me."

Trent and Daily chuckled on their way out of the room. Pausing at the door, Daily pointed at me and said, "Nice shooting." I knew he meant well, and I tried to smile, but I don't think he noticed.

Rusty, Keera and the twins had come up as soon as they heard what happened, but could only stay a short time. The twins would be starting the first grade soon so Keera could only stay for a week or so.

A week later I was discharged from the hospital and Kati and Keera brought me home. I was still very sore but had already quit taking the pain medication. Three days later Keera and the twins returned home. To keep the whole thing from ending the season for us, Rusty agreed to stay and help us get the operation up and running again.

Since the gunfight, neither Mitchell or Richard had said a word to anyone about what happened nor had they returned to work. Rusty finally got them to talk about it.

According to Rusty, Mitchell had relocated to a spot lower then he had previously worked, just above the banks of Alfred Creek where it merged with the Caribou. He had removed three or four bucket scoops of the pit-run with the excavator when he noticed several gold nuggets in the gravel. Climbing down from the track-hoe to investigate, he heard strange voices. As he looked around, he saw four men approaching from the hill above, making their way toward the wash-plant. Two of them had handguns, another, a rifle, and the fourth man was unarmed. It was then he called me on his cell phone.

It was at least thirty minutes before I arrived, during which time the four men asked a hundred questions about how much gold they had found. Mitchell could tell the gravity of the situation was escalating and tried to stall the potentially ugly outcome as long as he could.

One of the men, who appeared to be the leader, told his partner to make Richard clean out the cage on the sluice. Richard had tried to buy some more time by pretending that he couldn't find the key to the padlock. The one with the rifle shot the padlock off.

Mitchell expected that it would rapidly go sideways from there. He knew he had to buy some more time. While two of the thieves made their way toward the cook-shack, Mitchell told the leader that he had just found something he thought might be gold. That was when I came over the hill.

The two from the cook-shack were waiting for me as soon as I landed. One of the men--the one who was formerly unarmed—was carrying Richards .300 Winchester Magnum that he had stolen from the cook-shack. It was he that was waiting for me on the bank above the airstrip when I landed.

When I let go the first shot from the ten-gage, dispatching the first gunman, it distracted the leader long enough for Mitchell to tag him with a good left jab. On his way to the ground, he dropped his .45 auto. Mitchell picked it up and, turning toward the sluice boxes, put one into the head of the fellow still pointing his rifle at Richard.

As soon as I popped the first gunman, the other guy who had just emerged from the cook-shack slipped in behind me as I ran toward the football field. Having failed to practice enough at the local shooting range, his first shot only grazed my head, knocking me to the ground. I had no sooner staggered back to my feet and he shot me again. The second shot was just wide enough to the right that, though he did hit me, I still managed to spin around in time to end his miserable existence only a moment before I stumbled backward onto the ground where I started my nap. When Mitchell realized I was still alive, he called 911 who sent in a Medivac helicopter.

It was over in a half an hour, but to Mitchell, it felt like all day. Within ten minutes, Trent and Daily arrived in the Bell Ranger. After placing the leader of the gang under arrest and taking statements from Mitchell and Richard, Daily flew the Bell Ranger out with the one suspect left alive. Officer Trent flew my two boys in the 180 to my place, where he put the Skywagon away and closed the doors on the hangar.

Kati said that after Trent had completed his part of the paperwork, he came to the hospital, where he remained in the waiting room until I was out of surgery and in stable condition.

A few days later, Kati and I drove to the public safety building in Wasilla to have a chat with officers Daily and Trent. There were at least seven or eight troopers crammed into Daily's office as I gave him a statement of the facts and sequence of events right up to the point I lost consciousness. That completed, Kati and I thanked them both for helping our boys and returning the Skywagon. As we stood to go, one by one the troopers shook both Kati's and my hand. We asked who the would-be robbers were. It turned out that the four men were escaped felons from the state penitentiary in Fairbanks. They had stolen the rifle and two hand guns from a pair of prospectors the day before who were later found dead. Daily told us that I had arrived on the scene not a minute too soon. All the officers agreed that those boys had murder on their minds as well as robbery.

Two weeks had gone by since my discharge from the hospital. Rusty flew Mitchell and Richard back to camp in the 206, and I followed behind in the 180. Mitchell immediately went back to the place where he had seen the gold nuggets. They were gone. Firing up the Hitachi 400, he continued searching where he had left off before the gunfight.

We gasped at what was coming from the hole he was digging: nuggets the size of golf balls. Dozens of them. Mitchell was ecstatic. Rusty immediately came down with a case of gold fever. I watched as the boys ran the gravel through the sluice. It seemed that the farther down he dug, the greater concentration of gold there was.

The hole was filling with water as fast as Mitchell scooped out the gravel. The permit did not allow us to dig any closer to the creek or to divert it in anyway, as there would be no way to stop the water if we did dig too close. But, water or no water, Mitchell kept digging as far down as the track-hoe could reach.

Rusty and I both stayed with the boys in camp. I wasn't good for much except guard duty, so that's what I did. The word was out that we were here and that we had found gold. Every day a dozen planes or more would fly over low and slow, looking and taking pictures. We packed our handguns and kept a watchful eye everywhere we went.

Winter was a little late in coming, which helped us make up for some of the time we had lost. I was getting stronger everyday and could do a little light duty. In the last three weeks of the season, we had taken over thirteen hundred pounds of gold out of Mitchell's gravel hole. If our marketing sources remained consistent, we were looking at another $29,120,000. With the other $3,360,000, we had an incredibly profitable season.

We knew the mother lode was somewhere right under our nose. Mitchell had a plan that could very feasibly put it in the bank.

CHAPTER 11

During the winter, we applied for a drilling permit. Expecting that it would be sometime after spring break-up before an environmental inspection would take place and the application approved, we were pleasantly surprised when the permit arrived in the mail within thirty days.

Mitchell immediately contacted a drilling company in Fairbanks. They would supply, set up, and operate a platform capable of auguring to fifteen hundred feet and up to forty-five degrees in any direction from the platform. The price would be $675,000 for the season, which included a five-man crew.

Rusty and Keera decided they wanted to be a part of the project. Tired of being so far away from family, Rusty turned the private-eye business over to Kevin and Brenda Gaither and moved his family to Wasilla.

After the gunfight the previous season, we decided to take some extra security precautions. I didn't want my boys packing pistols and worried about who might show up in camp at any moment. We gave the responsibility of providing our security to Rusty. So much for the no-outside-help clause we had all initially agreed to.

One morning, in January of 1998 while having breakfast with my beautiful wife, Bill Shearer called.

"Lou, I could use your help. Can you and Kati get away for a couple of days?" Bill's booming preacher voice could be heard through the phone halfway across any room. Kati nodded her head in excited anticipation of visiting Sharon.

Kati and Sharon had been phone pals since the Piper Clipper accident. Kati had kept me updated on all of Pastor Bill's ministry projects, and I was well aware that funds were always an issue. We, of course, had contributed substantially on several occasions without hesitation. After all, it wasn't like we couldn't afford it, and they never used any contributed funds for their own use. Bill and Sharon's salary came from a ministerial society based in Juneau.

"Absolutely, Bill," I said, "we're on our way."

Kati packed lunch, I packed the overnight bags, and together we packed the airplane. I was still a little sore but was getting around much better and no longer needed help moving the airplane out of the hangar. I checked the emergency gear and secured our bags for the four-hour trip to Venetie, nearly five hundred miles away.

The two-thousand-foot overcast was stable with current and forecast conditions for the route expected to remain the same. We pointed the nose of the Skywagon northbound, leveling off at fifteen hundred feet AGL (above ground level). It had been three and a half years since I purchased the 180 from Ray Sumner, this my third winter flying with the skis attached. I was looking forward to the additional ski time.

Conditions had deteriorated to one half-mile in fog as we crossed midfield over the Venetie runway. Turning a tight closed pattern to keep from losing sight of the airport in the reduced visibility, I set the skis on the freshly fallen snow. The landing was so smooth that neither my passenger nor I could feel them touch. Bill and Sharon were waiting and greeted us with enthusiasm and gracious hospitality.

With the airplane covered and sitting on blocks to prevent the skis from freezing to the ice, we climbed into Bill's Ford Excursion and drove to their home.

William Shearer was a strong bull of a man who barely cleared most doorways by more than two inches. Born and raised in Aberdeen Washington, Bill, along with his five brothers, learned the value of hard work and little pay alongside their father in the sawmill not far from their home. It was obvious that the lessons learned there prepared Bill for the thankless life of service he and Sharon had devoted themselves to for the last thirty-five years.

Bill and his wife had lived modestly, and sometimes poorly, their entire married lives. Sharon, a petite five foot three and 120 pounds, wore her waist-length, flowing red hair—now generously accented with gray—banded behind her head. She had come from a wealthy family. Her mother had died giving birth to her, the last of five children. Her father, a real estate tycoon, singlehandedly raised her and her siblings in the upper-income suburbs of Chicago.

Bill entered the born-again Christian experience at the age of eighteen and enrolled in a ministerial college near Chicago where he and Sharon met at a wedding reception and were married the following year.

Forty-five years had passed since then, and the legacy of small churches and private schools in dozens of villages throughout the interior of Alaska remain as a testimony to the fruit of their lives and ministry.

The couple of days turned into a week as the four of us, strapped into Bill's 185 Skywagon, visited fifteen different villages where Bill and Sharon had started small churches and home schools. Observing the people in the villages, I could not help noticing there was a problem.

"Bill," I said. "Why are these people so lifeless? What is it that they need?"

Bill pondered a minute before answering. "Heart," he said, "they need heart and hope. They have no reason to get up in the morning, no reason to stay sober or off drugs. If they complete an education, they would need to leave their home villages to pursue any occupation. They feel they would be deserting their families and ancestral honor if they were to do that. Drugs are more available to them than food, and boredom has become a worse enemy than the alcohol and drugs they use to escape it. Their lives are maladjusted and counterproductive. They have no vision for change. We have reached many with the gospel, but the majority still see no way out, leaving them hopelessly stuck in their dysfunctional lethargy."

Bill continued by saying that the work he and Sharon had been building for thirty-five years would soon come to naught because both he and Sharon were having health issues. Though their ministry had resulted in far more functional lifestyles for hundreds of the native people, there was no guarantee that any of it would remain once they were gone. Bill wanted us to take over.

"Bill, I'm not a preacher!" I said.

"You don't have to be. Just put the people to work building their own schools and clinics, provide doctors and nurses that can train them to take care of themselves. Teach them to live productive lives. Build vocational tech schools, complete with dormitories where they can stay while learning the trades essential for supporting their families. Also facilities where I can train pastors and ministers to take over our work after we're gone. If they could just have a chance at life on their terms, you would be amazed at what they could accomplish. Remember what Proverbs 29:18 says, 'For lack of a vision, the people perish.' Implicit in that statement is another one: *With* a vision, the people shall not perish."

"I think I see," I said. "I'll look into it."

Kati and I were subdued on the way home from Venetie. I was not sure where to begin, but I supposed I would need to find an architect.

I have never been the church-going type. Other than Easter Sundays and weddings, I seldom go. On the other hand, Kati and our daughters are very involved in church, especially ministries that help the less fortunate and children. I admire them for that.

Normally, I shy away from religious types. So many of them are either fanatical and legalistic or smooth-talking con men looking for people who are stupid enough to give them there hard-earned money in exchange for the assurance that they have a place in the great hereafter by virtue of their monetary contribution. Although I hadn't known Bill that long, I had gained a high level of respect for the man and could tell up front that he didn't fall into either of those categories. No one lives a life of sacrifice and ministry for other people for thirty-five years if their motive is selfish. If they were all like Bill Shearer, I wouldn't even have to agree with all of their theology to be more than willing to help in their ministry in any way I could.

I'm not sure why my family and I fell into all of the wealth that we discovered, but I could plainly see that it came with the responsibility to help other people. Because the gold had come from Alaska, it seemed only right that I should invest it back into Alaska. I decided that if money could buy whatever Bill wanted for his ministry, he was going to get it.

Keera had picked up our mail for us and left it on the kitchen table. To one side was an official-looking letter from the Office of the Superintendent of Public Safety. Kati opened it and read aloud, "To Mr. and Mrs. Lou Worley, your presence is requested on 14 January 1998 at seventeen-hundred hours (5:00 p.m.) in the Office of Arnold Bradley, Superintendant of Public Safety, Wasilla Alaska."

I looked at Kati and exclaimed, "That's tomorrow!"

Neither of us had a clue why the Superintendant wanted to see us. I admit I felt a little apprehensive, wondering if it had anything to do with our mining operation. Maybe we needed another permit of some kind.

The next morning, our curiosity went up another notch when Rusty, Mitchell, Richard, and all their families simultaneously arrived as Kati and I were parking in front of the public safety building. Kati, who hadn't seen them in over a month, was so excited it didn't even occur to her that there was apparently more going on with this then we first thought.

With Rusty and Keera directly behind us, Kati and I entered the building. As I stepped inside the two-way, double-glass doors behind Kati, a roar of cheers and applause erupted from both sides of the entry and down the long hallway in both directions. From around the corner, flanked by Officers Trent and Daily, came the Superintendent of Public Safety, Arnold Bradley.

With a dozen state troopers, another fifteen office personnel, and our own family, there was barely room to breath. With his hand extended toward us, Bradley approached Kati and introduced himself to us both. Then holding his hand in the air to quiet the noise, he turned to Officer Daily, who stepped forward to speak. Suddenly realizing where this was all going, I looked around for a rock to crawl under. Daily immediately started speaking. "…Without regard for his own safety …" Yada, yada, yada. I just tuned him out. Finally, he stepped back and Officer Trent stepped forward, adding his version of how we "need more citizens with his kind of mettle …"

By now, I was so embarrassed that I closely resembled the color of my Cessna 180.

Kati was beaming from her left foot up to the top of her head and back down to her right foot, as was my whole family. I glanced at Keera just in time to see her wink at me.

Then Bradley stepped up to the podium, holding a medallion with a blue-braided cord in one hand and an Alaska State Trooper badge in the other. I knew it was about to get worse.

"In appreciation of your bravery in defense of our community, the people of Alaska and its law enforcement agencies would like to present you, Mr. Lou Worley, the department's highest Civilian Commendation Award, along with this Alaska State Trooper badge, inducting you into the law enforcement community of Alaska."

My knees went weak as Kati gave me a shove forward. I fumbled around for some words that would express my appreciation. However, it didn't matter if I got it right or not because the roaring returned along with handshakes and back slaps. Now I knew why we got that permit so fast.

I turned to Mr. Bradley and said a few personal words of thanks as a preliminary to asking where I could find the office of rural development. He immediately introduced me to Mr. Gilbert Riley. When I finished a very productive conversation with Gilbert, I had the name of the top architect in the country, Leonard Gerard, whose office was just up the road in Palmer.

At the conclusion of the ceremony, as things returned to business as usual, Trent approached Kati and me, informing us that they had planned a dinner in our honor at the Mexican restaurant and would like our whole family to attend. Of course, we accepted. It was there that we finally met the game warden's wife.

"Lou and Kati, I would like you to meet my wife, Nanci." Calvin beamed with pride as he respectfully ushered her toward us.

Kati was speechless, and if I had false teeth, they would have fallen out of my wide-open and paralyzed mouth. Keera stabbed us both in the back with her thumb as I managed to regain my composure in time to return the handshake extended to me by the governor of Alaska.

Again stumbling around for words that might make some sense, I said, "So nice to meet you, madam ... uh, Nanci ... or uh, Mrs. Trent. I mean, uh, Governor."

At least I said something. Kati stood staring at her, still in shock.

The governor took the initiative and approached my wife, breaking the spell.

"Hi, Kati," she said as she extended her hand. "I'm Nanci Trent, and I am so glad to meet you. Would you and your husband join Calvin and me at our table for the evening?"

"Oh, my goodness! What an honor! We would be delighted!" Kati answered.

During the evening, I had the opportunity to share with the governor some of the plans Bill and I were formulating for building schools and training facilities around the interior of Alaska. She already knew of the incident involving Pastor Bill and his Piper Clipper and was aware of his years of work and service to the native people.

"Mr. Worley, I find it commendable that you want to invest in the people of Alaska. Whatever you need from our agencies, I will see to it that you have it, I give you my word."

I felt like she had just handed me unrestricted authority to do whatever I wanted. At the time, I had no idea that soon enough authority was exactly what I would need.

Officer Daily introduced us to his girlfriend, a very lovely creature by the name of Priscilla Vasquez, the Superintendant of Public Instruction for the State of Alaska. She had overheard my conversation with the governor and volunteered her assistance.

The first thing Monday morning, I placed a call to Leonard Gerard's office, requesting an appointment to meet with him. A very professional-sounding secretary answered the phone. "Gerard's Architectural. This is Hilda. May I help you?"

"Good morning Hilda. My name is Lou Worley, May I speak to Mr. Gerard?"

"I'm sorry, but Mr. Gerard is in a meeting." There was a short pause, and then she said, "What was your name again?"

"Worley. Lou Worley," I repeated

"One moment, please."

A few seconds later, a professionally confident but not overly assertive voice answered. "This is Gerard."

"Mr. Gerard, my name is Lou Worley. I would like to talk to you about drawing some plans for a number of school buildings, medical clinics, and training facilities that I plan to build. Can you help me with that?"

There was a long pause. I think he was trying to decide if I was for real. "How soon do you want to do this?"

"As soon as I can get plans and approvals. Of course, we still need to choose property for building sites. I'd like your help with that as well."

"Can you come by the office sometime this week? I would like to know more about what you want to do."

"I can get in there today if that will work," I said.

"I'll move my one o'clock to tomorrow and see you this afternoon," Gerard said and hung up.

It was one o'clock sharp when Mr. Gerard emerged from a rather large conference room where he had been in a meeting, greeted me with an exceptionally firm handshake, and invited me into his office. It was three o'clock when we walked out of his office, and he again was shaking my hand, this time on retainer as my architect.

Gerard was indeed the man for the job. He had architectural designs already drawn that would be more than adequate for what we were planning to do. We made plans to fly to Venetie after spring breakup where he could meet Bill and the three of us could examine potential building sites. With those preliminaries taken care of, it was time to return my attention to my family.

By the first of spring, my two youngest girls, Kelly and Kathy, had finished their private pilot training. Kelly, having also completed her tail wheel instruction, began the instrument course. Kathy decided to wait until the following summer to begin her instrument training.

Ray Sumner had called, and the Piper Clipper was ready for pick-up. Completely restored with a full stack of new IFR avionics adorning the beautiful mahogany panel, I tucked it away in the old hangar covered with a soft drop cloth, waiting for Kelly's birthday. Next to it, sat the little Cessna also rewired, reupholstered, and retrofitted with a brand-new 180 horse Lycoming engine and variable speed prop. With a new paint job, interior, and avionics package, it, too, awaited the day Kathy would complete her IFR training.

Kati had supervised a few home additions and modifications to our cabin that included two spare bedrooms, another full bath and huge recreation room, which along with the new hangar/shop project, were completely finished by the winter of '97'.

When Kati decides she wants something done, she doesn't let any grass grow under it that's for sure. During the longer daylight hours of the summer, she scheduled around-the-clock work. Three eight-hour crews worked nonstop, finishing in just three months what otherwise could have taken more than a year to do.

Spring of '98' had arrived and the snow had receded enough to begin to move the equipment back into Alfred Creek. The drilling company wanted to inspect the area, so with Mitchell, we headed to Fairbanks to pick up the superintendent and his foreman in charge of the operation.

On the way, we made a stop at Alfred Creek to check the conditions of the airstrip.

The surface was still a bit soft but in good enough condition for the very capable Skywagon. While we were there, we walked the perimeters of the claim. The footprints in the soft earth and remaining snow were indication that the curiosity seekers had found the claim. Not too concerned about it, we continued on to Fairbanks to pickup our passengers.

Three and a half hours later, we were back at the mine. Mitchell and the drilling supervisors spent at least two hours looking over the site. They decided that in addition to the main platform, they would also bring in a rubber-tire portable, a smaller drill rig that could sink test holes remotely from the main platform. With the site evaluations completed, we returned our passengers to Fairbanks in time for Mitchell and me to be home before dark.

The drillers would be on the road within a couple of days. Mitchell was the most excited I had ever seen him. We met with Rusty, informed him of the evidence of trespassers we had observed, and he briefed us on his security plans.

Everything was coming together. Kati threw another party, with fruit smoothies and popcorn.

CHAPTER 12

I was flying the socks off the 180. With the additional people in camp, we needed everything from a larger cooking facility to eating and sleeping accommodations, not to mention warm and friendly outhouses.

I flew in a half-dozen carpenters and their tools, and Richard brought in several more piles of lumber with the D-6, towing the equipment trailer. We hired a cook and, as per his request, brought in a long list of things that cooks can't live without, and of course, we were obliged to provide if we wanted to be well fed.

Rusty had hired nine security men with background training in special opps armed with M-14 semi-auto assault rifles and nine-millimeter semi-auto side arms. Rusty then positioned his men in strategic locations out of sight but in range of the mining operations. With three guards working three separate eight-hour shifts, we had twenty-four-hour security on duty. However, on duty or off, the deal was that nobody could leave the camp. Anyone needing to leave would get replaced and not be allowed to return. We had separated the mining areas from the living area, and material and men were already on-site, installing a temporary security fence completely encircling the active mining area.

Rusty's big Cessna, parked at the far northeast end of the strip and my tail dragger at the other end tucked into a wide spot Richard had cut for me with the D-8, occupied the only two tie-down areas. Rusty and I arranged our schedules in such a way that one of us was always in camp in case of an emergency.

I could see that my plans to take Gerard to Venetie might need to be altered due to the demanding schedule of the mining operations. I called him and requested that he go without me to meet with Bill. Whatever plans or projects the preacher had in mind would be fine with me.

I had hired three more equipment operators and brought in another Hitachi 600 excavator with a five-yard bucket. Mitchell worked with the drilling crew as the helicopters began bringing in the drill rig a piece at a time.

Richard had prepared a one-hundred square foot pad about four hundred yards uphill from the creek where Mitchell had last been working and where we had extracted the last twenty-nine million in gold. It was Mitchell's theory that a very large vein lay under that hill on an east to west line, extending from the platform down to the creek, hopefully, within drilling reach. From below, the rubber-tire portable would drill numerous exploratory holes in search of the lower end of the vein and then determine the course and direction it took on its way into the mountains side. All, of course, was speculation and theory, but one that Mitchell felt was very feasible.

The portable was capable of depths of eighty feet if no hard rock were encountered. The main rig, capable of depths of up to twelve-hundred feet, could also drill through hard rock. We could use explosives if we needed them, but so far we didn't have permits for that. I felt we would be able to get them if we had to. The drill rigs were just for finding the gold; they were not capable of extraction. For that, we would have to either dig open holes or mine shafts, depending on the location of the vein.

The work had begun, and I kept busy flying. Everything I could possibly cram in the airplane came in by air. If it couldn't fit in an airplane, it had to come in on the trailer behind the D-6, which was extremely time-consuming.

With the help of the additional operators, the big dozer kept moving twenty-four-seven, except for maintenance and fueling. We had a huge generator providing power to a lighting system that lit up the entire area, which by now had grown to the size of three football fields. We even had five refrigerators and two huge freezers. Alfred Creek had become a city.

The portable had only just begun when I heard hollering. They had sunk a shaft not more than thirty feet deep on a forty-five degree slant in the direction of the hill and had encountered gold. This was actually no surprise since it was the same hole Mitchell had been playing in at the end of the last season.

Mitchell had prepared a grid and made a note of the placement of each test hole and its depth, angles, and findings. From there, the portable moved twenty feet south and setup to drill another test hole. Again, Mitchell would record the findings.

Test hole after test hole was drilled, each one documented, flagged for safety, and the portable would again move on. It was clear there was still a lot of gold waiting to be harvested from the lower end.

Suddenly I heard yelling from up above. I saw Mitchell wildly waving his arms. "Dad! Dad come up here!"

My first thought was that someone had been hurt, but I soon realized he had found something he wanted me to see. I ran up the hill, heart pounding and gasping for air by the time I reached them. Rusty and Mitchell were both staring at the four-inch augur bit that the operator had just brought up from a sixty-foot shaft. On the end, stuck to the drill bit like clay, was the most beautiful pure gold shavings I had ever seen. The auger had hit solid gold.

Mitchell had already hollered down for the portable to come up top. Rusty just stood there, staring at it and feeling it with his fingers. I turned to Charlie, the supervisor of the drill crew, to ask him if he could drill straight through the mass of gold to see how deep it went. He said he could, but would need to change to a smaller bit.

Mitchell ordered the portable to set up only twenty feet to one side of the main drill rig. The object was to establish where the edges of the vein were and how deep it went. "Just go till you hit solid, and then bring it back up," Mitchell told the operator.

With a smaller bit installed on the main drill rig, the drill again descended into the hole. At sixty-feet deep, again hitting the solid mass, it slowly penetrated its way into the gold vein. The gold shavings no sooner began appearing at the top end when it broke through the bottom of the vein and back into the gravel barrow. Our hearts sunk for a moment as we wondered if it was the main vein or just a very large gold nugget. Whatever it was, it had only been about a foot deep.

The drill turned freely now as it was back into the pit-run. Suddenly, once again it hit solid. Back up to the top appeared the gold shavings. Mitchell, Rusty, and I were carefully collecting the shavings from the auguring. Expecting the augur to once again break through into the gravel, we watched in astonishment as the pure gold kept pouring up from the shaft. Down and down it went, fifteen feet, twenty feet. Finally, at twenty-eight feet, the shaft finally broke through into the barrow. Mitchell stopped the drill.

"Bring it up," he told Charlie. It would now be up to the portable to try to determine the edges and upper extent of the vein. We were sure it went all the way to the creek, possibly beyond.

The main rig had sunk a vertical shaft. The first encounter was at sixty feet, the second at sixty-five feet. That put the bottom of the vein at ninety-three feet. With any luck, the portable, which could only go to eighty feet, would at least be able to identify the outer perimeters.

Mitchell ordered the main rig platform to relocate to a position 150 feet lower. Rusty and I discussed the situation for a minute and motioned for Mitchell to join us.

"What's up?" Mitchell asked.

"Mitchell, how large a vein is too much for us to handle?"

Mitchell did not answer, but Rusty did. "I think we need to talk to some experts."

"I agree with that," I said. "I think you should go ahead and locate the perimeters of the vein as best you can, carefully document all the information, and then hold off. I will find some attorneys that specialize in mineral rights."

On my way to the airplane, I stopped by the cook-shack for a bite to eat and a sack lunch for the road. I had just stepped out of the dining room when I heard an airplane overhead. I looked up and saw a Cessna Cardinal 177 RG (retractable gear) circle low over the camp. Whoever was flying that plane did not appear to be in very good control, for it was dangerously low and slow. I paused as it continued its turn, setting up an approach to landing. As I watched the Cardinal continue inbound, I realized his airplane ride was not going to end well. The pilot certainly had no clue how to fly a mountain approach to a short airstrip. In the first place, he was never going to touch down in time to get stopped, and Rusty's 206 sat right in the way at the far end.

I frantically flailed my arms in an attempt to wave him off. It did not work, and he was at the midway point of the runway when he finally touched down, still doing close to seventy miles per hour. I put my hands over my ears and dove to the ground as the Cardinal slammed into Rusty's Cessna 206. Both airplanes instantly exploded in a ball of fire.

I must have looked like a salamander on steroids as I dove to the ground, scrambling on my belly to get back into the cook-shack. The sky was raining burning aluminum, and black smoke filled the canyon.

As the flames and heat subsided, I ran along with everyone else in the camp to the smoldering remains of the two airplanes. Looking for but not expecting there to be any survivors, I turned from the crash site and headed for the 180 to check it for damage. Halfway down the runway on the uphill side of the airstrip, I saw something move. It was an injured man.

I was not sure if someone had jumped from the Cardinal and actually survived or if he was one of the workers from the camp who happened to be nearby. I screamed for help. Richard and Rusty were the first to reach me, and we carefully rolled him over.

He was torn and scratched and had huge patches of hide and flesh missing, but he was alive. His clothing and body were in shreds from jumping out of the airplane onto the gravel surface of the runway at such a high speed. None of us recognized him.

As Rusty and the others tended to our survivor, I called 911. I then proceeded in the direction of the 180. Bits and pieces of debris along with dirt, gravel, and black soot covered the wings and empennage. There were some scratches on the paint from the falling metal, but other than that, it was undamaged. I breathed a sigh of relief, thankful that it was still airworthy.

As the black smoke finally dissipated and visibility returned to the area, my anxiety soon changed to relief as I heard the familiar sound of the State Police helicopter thumping its way up the canyon, reminiscent of my first week at Alfred Creek.

Two troopers, whom I recognized from the ceremony Kati and I had attended earlier in the year, piloted the helicopter. Redistributing the silt from the fire lying on the surface of the runway, the chopper settled into ground effect and came to rest within a few feet of the 180, blowing away the crap left on my airplane from the explosion. Two emergency response personnel climbed from the cargo section with their aid cases and headed straight to the injured man.

The medical aid team quickly stabilized and field dressed the man's wounds, loading him into the helicopter, departed, leaving one of the troopers at the scene of the accident. The pilot of the State Police helicopter had notified the FAA (Federal Aviation Administration) and an NTSB (National Transportation Safety Board) investigation team was already on the way.

With all that had happened that day, I was beginning to feel a little overwhelmed. I called Kati and told her of the crash, but did not say anything about the discovery of the mother lode. I asked her to find an attorney who specialized in mineral rights and claims and to call me with a phone number.

I told Rusty and Mitchell to put the whole operation on hold until the NTSB were finished and to tell the men to keep quiet about the mining interest if anyone were to ask them any questions.

Two hours later, another helicopter arrived, and two NTSB investigators immediately cordoned off the crash-scene area with yellow tape. By then, it was mid-afternoon. Expecting that they would not be interested in spending the night, I became optimistic that the investigation might be short. Boy, was I wrong.

Fortunately, Rusty was able to persuade the investigators to allow us access and usage of the remaining runway so that we could resume our flights. They proceeded to take all of our statements and seemed satisfied that the accident had nothing to do with our operations.

The next day, three more investigators showed up, two of which were wearing blue jackets that said DEA (drug enforcement agency), who spent another day searching through the remains of the airplanes as well as boxing and bagging the burned, charred, and stinking remains of the cargo that was onboard the RG.

With the investigation work taking place behind the cordoned-off area of the crash site, the mining work, including the flight operations, were allowed to continue. Richard and Rusty worked with the D-9 and Hitachi 600, feeding the gold-rich barrow into the large sluice. Mitchell documented and supervised the progress of the rubber-tire portable as the drilling crew resumed their work of searching out the perimeters of the huge vein.

Kati had called our pre-paid legal provider who assigned to us a law firm from Fairbanks that specialized in mining claims and all issues related to mineral rights. As soon as the NTSB and DEA teams finished, I flew to Fairbanks to retain their services, explaining the dilemma we were facing due to our fantastic discovery. After all, we had just found what could possibly be as much as a billion dollars in gold. We were open to suggestions.

I called Bill to see how things were going on his end. He said Gerard would be arriving the next day. When I completed my business with the attorneys in Fairbanks, I scooted up to Venetie and enjoyed a quiet evening with him and Sharon. What a relief.

Pastor Bill, Gerard, and I spent most of the next day looking at several building sites and blueprints. It was a very productive meeting. Gerard went away with a far more complete picture of what we intended to do, not just in Venetie, but in many other villages scattered throughout the interior of Alaska.

CHAPTER 13

I had no idea who the man was that had jumped from the speeding Cardinal only a moment before it collided with Rusty's 206. The resulting explosion killed the pilot and destroyed both airplanes. I decided to stop by the hospital in Anchorage to see how the survivor had fared, which happened to be the same hospital where my daughter Kathy worked. I was surprised to find a state trooper guarding the injured man's room. The trooper recognized me and filled me in on some of the details.

The survivor's name was Beltray Gibbons, a twenty-one-year-old, smalltime drug user and street dealer, whose rap sheet began at the age of ten years old. His injuries, though no longer life-threatening, would scar him for life.

The pilot, a major player in the history of drug organizations by the name of Simon Clemons, had suddenly become sick and was attempting to get the airplane on the ground before he passed out. The NTSB presumed that he lost consciousness about the same time the airplane touched down due to the lack of evidence of any braking prior to the impact.

The investigators believed that Clemons and Gibbons were on their way to the interior of Alaska with the intention of delivering a load of drugs when the pilot became extremely dizzy and short of breath, probably suffering a heart attack. Within a week, the autopsy confirmed that speculation.

Bill had mentioned that drugs in the interior villages were a growing problem and was responsible for the ruination of hundreds of native families and their young people. I felt I somehow needed to join this fight, especially after the druggies had just brought their business in such close proximity to my family, endangering our lives, not to mention scratching the paint on my 180.

While in Anchorage, I paid Ray Sumner a visit. He had heard about the crash, and I told him we were looking for three more airplanes. Rusty wanted a brand new 206 Stationair, and the Alfred Creek Mining Corporation needed a couple of Helio Courier's to keep up with the heavy workload The Helio Courier, with its G-0480 295-horse, fuel-injected power plant and three-blade, constant-speed propeller, was capable of lifting fifteen hundred pounds of payload into the air in less than six hundred feet at sea level. I didn't want to use my Skywagon for the mining work anymore.

Ray ordered the Stationair and said he would call when he found a couple Helios that would measure up to the work demands of the mining operation.

The installation of the twelve-foot fence was completed and included a security gate that was manned at all times. We were not concerned with theft so much as the security of the workers while on duty. No one had time to be looking over their shoulder for intruders, be they two-legged or four-legged. Security was top priority.

The mineral rights attorneys from Fairbanks had assembled a team of three geological survey gurus, specializing in mining operations. They wanted to conduct an on-site study of the documentations and findings Mitchell had recorded, which convinced us we had found the so-called mother lode. It seems the claims we made were a little too fantastic for them to believe, and because we needed their input on how to go about excavating this humungous vein of gold, I flew to Fairbanks to pick them up along with one of the attorneys.

It was becoming increasingly clear to me that this whole operation was not only getting way too complicated, but, at this stage of my life, was also more than I wanted to commit myself to on a long-term basis. I had already spent the majority of my adult life working twelve to fifteen hours a day six days a week, scratching out a living for my family. I felt it was time for me to turn this whole deal over to Mitchell, Rusty, and Richard. They were young, enthusiastic, and capable, with a lot more years ahead of them than I had. On the other hand, I was ready to enjoy the American dream that had come true for my Kati and me. In the back of my mind, I also knew that I wanted to help Bill realize his dream as well. Of course, to do that, I would need to finish this last project—the excavation of the mother lode. With the survey team buckled comfortably in the 180, I pointed the spinner toward Alfred Creek.

I took a back seat to the discussions that went on between the inspectors and Mitchell. I was glad to see Richard getting more involved, who normally was the one watching from the sidelines. Rusty, always the gentle giant, intelligently listened and said little. I watched my three sons and beamed with pride, thankful for the wisdom my daughters had shown in choosing their husbands. I could not have been more pleased.

With the security measures completely in place, Rusty and I took time away to pick up the two Helios that Ray had found for the corporation. Now I just needed to find a pilot who could take my place keeping the camp supplied. Searching through my list of phone numbers, I scrolled up the name of Arthur Bold's daughter in Sikeston Missouri, and mashed on the green button.

"Hello?" a very lovely-sounding, middle-aged woman answered the phone with a strong Missouri accent.

"Yes, ma'am," I said. "May I speak with Arthur Bold, please?"

"I'm sorry," she said. "Arthur Bold passed away two months ago. I'm Genneta Williams, his daughter. Can I help you?" The inflection in her voice hinted of her recent emotional distress.

"I'm terribly sorry. My name is Lou Worley, calling from Wasilla, Alaska. My wife and I purchased Arthur's home from him a few years ago. I am sorry for your loss, and I apologize for intruding."

"No, not at all," she said, her voice taking on a more enthusiastic tone. "My daddy spoke of you often. How can I help you?"

"Well, I know Arthur flew many years in Alaska, and I need a pilot to fly a Helio Courier for our mining operation. I was going to ask him if he could suggest someone."

"My husband could do that," Genneta offered without the slightest hesitation.

"Really!"

"We both fly," she said. "I am a CFII (certified flight instructor/ instrument) at the local FBO, and he has been flying crop dusters in this area for the last thirteen years. I know he is tired of it and both of us have discussed how we would dearly love to live in Alaska."

"What is your husband's name?"

"Jeffery," she said, "Jeffery Williams."

I gave Genneta my number, told her to discuss the proposition with Jeffery, and if he wanted the job, he could have it. Just let me know, and I would pay for all the moving expenses. Jeffery called me an hour later.

Genneta had been born in Wasilla and lived the first fifteen years of her life there, but Jeffery had never been nor had he given much thought to ever going to Alaska until Arthur had come to live with them the last three years. Arthur had ignited a passion for the North Country that Jeffery never thought he would ever have the opportunity to realize.

Jeffery and Genneta began packing and preparing for their new future. I gave him the phone numbers of the moving specialist and continued flying for the camp until their arrival.

Kati found a nice little house in Palmer that she was sure Genneta would love, paid cash for it, and put it in their name. Within a month, they moved in.

Jeffery at thirty-seven was the serious type, much like Richard. At five foot ten inches tall, he was medium build and strong from many years of handling fifty-five gallon drums of chemicals at his crop dusting job. Genneta was thirty-three, brunette, a hundred thirty five pounds, full-figured, and looked just like Arthur when he was younger. Her mother and Arthur had separated but never divorced. She had grown weary of the lonely life in Alaska and, taking her fifteen-year-old daughter with her, returned to Sikeston, Missouri, where she had been born and raised.

The next weekend was Kelly's birthday. We had a special occasion planned for the entire family, which now included Jeffery, Genneta, and their three children Mickey, twelve, Chelsea, ten, and Lucy, seven. Kati immediately fell in love with them all.

Kelly was turning twenty-six years old. I had a surprise for her in the hangar that I was sure she would really like. The little Piper Clipper was just recently restored, and I had it painted her favorite colors, powder blue with a pale yellow sunbursts topping the wings.

I had planned to wait until Kathy finished her instrument rating to give her the recently refurbished little Cessna straight tail that I had first flown to Alaska. However, I just couldn't wait, and I could not think of a reason why she should not be able to have it to do the rating in. Therefore, I decided I would give them both their airplanes at the same time.

The big day came, and Kati had a houseful. The boys and I talked mining and caught Jeffery up on the history of the mine all the way back to when the Idaho boys first worked the claim they had leased from Clark Ramsey. I pretended to be so engrossed in the conversations that I think Kelly was wondering if maybe I had forgotten her present.

After a huge display of food had all but disappeared, I invited everyone to the hangar for a family portrait. As I opened the doors, the *oohs* and *aahs* started up. Kelly looked in the door and screamed in delight, with Kathy right behind her. There on a big sign on each aircraft were the names of the birthday girl and her sister, the new proud owners of their very own airplanes. I love it when a plan comes together. I am never in a hurry when my girls are lavishing their hugs and kisses on their daddy. I am content to stay and put up with it as long as they can dish it out. There is no greater joy in the world.

Jeffery took to the Helio Courier like a beaver to a tree. In no time at all, he was coming and going from the Alfred Creek strip as if it were a soybean crop in Missouri.

I had paid Gilbert Riley a visit at the Office of Rural Development. We needed a permit to build a road from Tahneta Pass at the old Brandt's Resort down across Squaw Creek to the west end of Syncline Mountain and then North up the east side of Caribou Creek to the Alfred Creek camp, terminating at the airstrip. By now, everyone and his uncle had heard a hundred different rumors related to our gold discovery, so Mr. Riley, expecting that financing would be no problem, was more then eager to issue a permit for the building of the road, if for no other reason than it would put some Alaskans to work. At first, he indicated the following summer would be the soonest that it he could finish the environmental impact study until I made it clear that I wanted to get it done before the winter set in and was ready to put together a crew if I could just get the permit. Indicating the permit would not be a problem, he told me to go ahead with the construction.

After recovering from their shock, awe, and stupefaction, the geological survey boys returned to Fairbanks. The geologist had told Mitchell there could be as much as one hundred to a 150 tons of gold in that vein that could very well be worth as much as 6 or 7 billion dollars. They said they would do a feasibility study and send a recommendation for its excavation. It probably would not be until the winter some time, so Mitchell and Rusty decided to send the drill rigs home and concentrate on sluicing the entire bottom end where there was still plenty of gold waiting for extraction. There certainly was no point in uncovering the vein and leaving it exposed during the winter. It would have to wait one more year.

Kati and I paid Bill and Sharon another visit, spending a week going over plans for the building of clinics and schools for at least ten different villages. Bill wanted to get construction started as soon as we could get permits. In light of the recent discovery of the mother lode and in anticipation of a completely new level of unimaginable wealth, I had been considering another option. I decided then would be a good time to share my idea with Bill and Sharon.

I suggested that we build a central facility located in the interior within reasonable flying distance of the largest percentage of the villages—a combination of an accredited grade school, high school, and trade school, complete with clinic and hospital where students all over the interior of Alaska could come for education and training. The trade schools could teach everything from auto mechanics to the building trades, and the students would receive on-the-job training by building and improving living conditions, and repairing and servicing vehicles in their own villages.

We could even include an FAA-accredited flight school. We could buy as many training airplanes as the flight school needed and even apply for an air taxi operators certificate that could provide not only the transportation for the students from their villages to the learning center, but serve other transportation needs of the villages as well. In addition, we could include an A&P mechanics school where the pilots could also learn to be aircraft mechanics. The students would stay in dormitories during the week and have the option of going home to their villages on weekends. Once it was up and running, it would eventually become entirely self-supporting.

Pastor Bill looked at me with a blank stare. "Were you born in Bethlehem in another life and time?" he asked. I tossed my head back and laughed.

"I don't think so, Bill. Don't even go there, look Bill, we have just located what could possibly be six to seven billion dollars in gold at the Alfred Creek mine. It is my belief that that resource really belongs to the people of Alaska. Kati and our families are fixed for life and wouldn't know what else to do with all that money anyway. So I say let's use it to turn these dysfunctional villages and people into productive communities, contributing to their own economies and setting a standard of functional living for the rest of their society."

"What about the drug problem?" Bill asked. "How will this get them off drugs?"

"We will build a rehabilitation unit for those who are already using. By providing a place of learning and security, it will eliminate the customer base of the drug dealers, and they will have to peddle their poison somewhere else. It will take time, but I am convinced it will make a difference."

Bill looked at Sharon. "What do think about all of that, my dear?"

"I am not sure the drug dealers will just quietly give up their hold on the interior. I think we could be in for a battle."

"I believe you may be right," Kati said.

"Kati," I said, "we will need a foundation through which we can funnel the monies that fund the learning center. Would you and Sharon make that happen for us?"

Kati and Sharon looked at each other then both nodded their heads in agreement. By the time we left for home, Kati and Sharon had decided on a name for the foundation, it would be called: The William Shearer Center of Learning.

The boys continued to work the sluices well up against the encroachment of the winter weather. I had hired a road construction contractor to build the road from Tahneta Pass over land to the mine. It was nowhere near completed but was well on its way and expected to be finished by the middle of the next season.

With a finished road down to the mine, the huge Cat-wagons would haul out the pit-run and make a stockpile on the site of the old Brandt's resort. With the pit-run covering the lower extremity of the gold vein removed, the work of extraction could then begin.

The day we were certain we had discovered the main vein of the mother load, I had immediately arranged for the construction and installation of another one-hundred-by-one-hundred foot underground vault next to the new hangar, with an additional hangar constructed on the top of the new vault with access from inside the building. The quantity of gold that would be coming from that vein would be more than we would even be able to market and would need to be safely stored in a large, secure place and gradually introduced into the world economy.

With another cold winter of more darkness than light separating the last mining season from the next, I concentrated on the planning and initial proposals of the learning center. Bill and I had found a location four miles square and within a mile southwest of the airport at Bettles, Alaska. We then met with Gerard, who set about revising the drawings.

The next step was putting together a team of leaders. We held a meeting at our home. Those we invited, besides Bill and Sharon, included all of our family as well as Priscilla Vasquez, Officer Daily, Jeffery and Genneta, Arnold Bradley, Gilbert Riley, and Leonard Gerard, who brought an attorney he introduced as Gerald Connors and whose attorney group he recommended that we retain to form the Shearer/Worley Foundation. I actually already knew Mr. Connors; he had recently helped me finalize a purchase of land that I made involving nearly 330,000 acres and a huge lodge that we often used as a resort.

Amazingly, they all actually showed up. Bill and I laid out the proposal. The boys and I had agreed to fund the cost no matter what it came to. The meeting and refreshments lasted three hours, during which time the first members of the learning center faculty volunteered for primary leadership positions.

Priscilla Vasquez would take charge of the educational design and curriculum. Kelly said she would like to be one of the schoolteachers. Keera accepted the nomination to head up the design and development of the medical center, including operating rooms, emergency rooms, and clinics, as well as all the staffing.

We needed a drug rehabilitation center and someone who could take that position. Arnold Bradley said he would find someone who could fill that need. I asked Leonard Gerard if he would take the responsibility of superintendant over the entire project and all of its development. He could hire any assistant management he felt he needed. He accepted.

Genneta Williams accepted the responsibility for establishing a flight school with an accredited FAA curriculum. Included in all of that would be the construction of a private paved runway for the Learning Center along with adequate hangar space for the schools fleet of aircraft.

According to Gilbert Riley, who was the man in charge of all rural development in Alaska's sparsely populated areas, the four-square-mile piece of real estate southwest of Bettles was available through the little-known and very old homesteaders act, which meant that it was available for us only on the condition that we lived on it. We all agreed that it would all be in Bill and Sharon's name. They would live there, and the official name for the center was ratified as, The William Shearer Center of Learning.

CHAPTER 14

I belted myself into the 180 and, through the open window, hollered, "CLEAR PROP" as I flipped on the fuel pump and fired up the big Continental. Next to me, Kati sat dressed in black, as was I, along with the twins, Manson and Michelle, seated in the rear.

It had been four years since work on the learning center began. The educational department opened its doors in less than three years of the groundbreaking. In just over a year, the number of students of all ages enrolled from one hundred towns and villages all over Alaska were already reflecting the initial success of the project.

Their education had been prepaid and all transportation needs provided by a fleet of Cessna Caravans and pilots assigned to any village or town where five or more students were enrolled in the learning center. During the week, the villages were almost ghost towns with so many of the residents, young and old alike, staying in the dormitories provided at the Center.

With the drug rehabilitation wing and clinic, the first of the medical facilities to open, a large number of drug addicts had sought help in kicking their debilitating habits. The market for drugs had already declined dramatically, and the drug dealers, livid over their diminishing profits, had responded by drawing first blood.

Pastor Bill Shearer was dead. With his wife, Sharon, he had been visiting the many native villages, towns, and communities from the interior to the coast over the last four years, offering free scholastic education and trade school training, including room and board, with enrollment in the William Shearer Center of Learning.

As he was stepping from his aircraft, having just landed at one of the coastal communities heavily saturated with drug activity, a shot rang out from a nearby wooded area. Pastor Bill died instantly from a rifle bullet in the back. When the local police arrived, they found Sharon sitting on the ground, holding her husband's head in her lap and reading her Bible.

The learning center's main auditorium was standing room only, and there was not a dry eye as a half-dozen speakers contributed to the eulogy. Even the governor of the State of Alaska had come to give the final presentation.

"Alaska has suffered a great loss," she began. "However, Alaskans are made of a precious mettle. William Shearer, this great man we are laying to rest today, was made of that mettle. William Shearer dedicated his entire life to the higher calling of humanity, particularly to the native people of Alaska. His life stands as a standard to which all Alaskans and humanity must endeavor to reach. In our lives, our communities, and our societies all over the world, Alaskans salute you, Bill Shearer, and GOD BLESS the WILLIAM SHEARER CENTER OF LEARNING!"

Applause erupted as the governor retreated from the podium.

I knew it was a time of mourning, but with so many influential people present, I knew Bill would want me to take advantage of the time and opportunity to begin my retribution against the people or organization responsible for his murder. Mingling and asking a few questions, I was soon shaking hands with the attorney general of the State of Alaska, Carl Brightwater.

Mr. Brightwater had heard of me, but he seemed more interested in the gunfight at Alfred Creek than what I was saying. I tried to get him to commit additional manpower and investigative resources into learning who killed Bill and give me some assurance that this sort of thing was not going to happen again, but I didn't get either one. It was clear to me that we would have to take care of the matter ourselves.

I found Rusty and pulled him aside. "Do you think Kevin could come up here and help us find out who did this?" I asked.

"I can give him a call. Where do you want him to start?"

"Right where it happened," I said, "then work backward all the way to the top of the organization that ordered the hit."

"You think it was a hit? Like an organized crime hit?" Rusty asked.

"I certainly do, I believe there is an organization involved here that probably involves organized crime people which could include someone on the political ladder.

I know that in some circles that might sound preposterous, but it seems entirely possible to me that someone high up the political pole might be getting re-election contributions in exchange for protection."

"You might be onto something, Dad. I'll call Kevin."

The Alfred Creek mother lode had long ago been excavated and securely hidden in seven different places throughout Alaska with a billion dollars worth of gold at each location. At least, that was what we told the newspapers. Only Rusty, Mitchell, Richard, and I actually knew where it was. There were four combination locks on the vault, and each of us only new the combination of one of the locks. For us to remove any gold from the vault, all four of us had to be present. Included in the legal jargon was the granting of Power of Attorney to the surviving principles in the event of death or comatose condition of one or more of the principles, in which case the issuing of the combination currently sealed and in a safety deposit box could take place for the newly appointed principle or principles.

The Alfred Creek mine had played out. The total weight of the humungous gold vein had come to two hundred tons. Valued at the time at approximately $1,100 per ounce, the vein represented just over seven billion dollars worth of gold. The boys continued for the next three years sluicing and drilling every inch and corner of Alfred Creek until there was no longer any yellow metal showing up in the traps, accumulating an additional $11.7 million worth of the remaining gold. At that time, we closed down the operation, with the exception of the required working of the claim every five years to maintain active claim status, which basically consisted of walking around the place for an hour or so with a shovel in hand.

For the last four years before Bill's murder, Kati and I had shifted all our energy and resources toward the building of the learning center. Though not entirely finished, the effect on the community was already apparent. We had watched as the drug dealers' power over the people and communities gradually diminished. The native Alaskans were taking their lives back, and the drug lords did not like it. We all expected this was not the end of it.

With the mining operations briefly taking a backseat, Jeffery turned his attention to helping his wife, Genneta, who had taken responsibility for the design, construction, and development of an on-campus airstrip and flight school. With single-engine Cessna's from 170Bs to 185s, the fleet also included a 206, a 207, four 208 Caravans, and a Helio-Courier.

Jeffery became his wife's first instrument student in Alaska and went on to acquire the certified flight instructor and instrument instructor ratings as well. Keera gave Rusty's 206 back to him and now flew her own Stationair to and from their home to the institution's medical facility. With the grandkids enrolled in school at the institute and practically the whole family staying and teaching or working in one capacity or the other at the learning center, the log home at Bold's seemed a bit lonely at times. So I decided that the time was right for me to start my investigation into who killed Bill.

It had already been close to six years since I had landed on that gravel bar on the Yukon River to pick up the downed missionary pilot, Bill Shearer. When I looked into his eyes and shook his hand for the first time that day, I knew even then that our chance meeting was not chance at all. I had never met a man like him before and immediately recognized a power attending him that was not of this world. His life was tangible evidence of the truth that was in his preaching. We became more than fast friends; he was like a brother to me.

Bill never preached to me about becoming a Christian or joining a church. He just continually praised God for sending me in answer to his prayers concerning his ministry.

I did not see myself sent by anybody, especially God. To me, God was intangible and impossible to know or understand. The Bible had nice things to say, but I really could not see how they related to me. As far as I was concerned, Jesus Christ was just a good man that lived his life as an example of unselfishness, humility, and brotherly love. I really did not see what the big deal was other than that I felt that I did the same thing for the most part.

I knew that Bill would have not wanted me to go after his murderers. Revenge just was not in his nature. However, it was in mine, and the murderers of the best friend I had ever had in my life were not going to get away with it as long as I had legs to chase them and shotgun shells for my ten-gage.

Two months had already passed since Bill's murder, and Rusty and I were anxious to follow up on some of the information we had acquired from people Kevin and Rusty had interviewed during that time.

Kevin had arrived and was staying in a spare room at the cabin, and with Rusty, Richard, and me, the four of us formulated a plan that might possibly flush out a drug dealer from whom we may be able to get more information.

So far, Kevin had discovered that the primary demand on the streets was for methamphetamines, probably produced in some remote facility somewhere in the middle of nowhere, but still likely to be dependent on air support for the import of chemicals and the export and distribution of the finished product. We wanted to find that facility. If we could find it and destroy it, maybe the little cowards would get mad and do something stupid, like pick a fight or something, in which case they would have to come out of their hole.

Kevin's wife, Brenda, had discovered through a DEA (Drug Enforcement Agency) source that the methamphetamine lab was actually a known location to the DEA, but they had left it alone for reasons they described as "critical to the ongoing investigation." Brenda said she would continue trying to get more information on its specific location.

The ambush had taken place in a little town by the name of Eli, located on the coast ninety-three miles east of Nome and a mile west of Norton Bay. I would take Richard in the 180, and Rusty and Kevin would follow in one of the Helios. It had already been determined that there was an unusually high volume of drug activity in the coastal areas. Therefore, we felt confident the source might be in relative close proximity. Our plan was to try to purchase some meth to see where that might lead us.

The solid, four-thousand-foot overcast suggested we could expect a smooth ride but could also spell marginal conditions through the Denali Reserve and the Shellbarger Pass located just south of the "Big One." (Mt. McKinley) The aircraft were each equipped with plenty of survival gear and provisions for three weeks and fifty-below temperatures in the event of an unplanned, forced landing.

Expecting more then just passive resistance, we prepared ourselves with a sack full of surplus grenades and other weaponry that Rusty and Kevin imagined we might need. I, of course, had the ten-gage shotgun, two

Glock .45s in shoulder holsters, and a backpack full of clips and ammo for both, into which I had also included two of those grenades.

Eli lay five hundred miles to the west by northwest. Rusty and Kevin would follow Richard and me, as I was more familiar with the route through the Alaska Range. With the ceilings that low, one wrong turn through the pass could result in an unwelcome encounter with a rock wall.

We would need at least 4,500 feet of altitude through the Shellbarger Pass. The highest ridge to cross would be Dillinger Ridge just east of the headwaters of the Dillinger River some two-thousand feet below the pass. I would need to determine, prior to entering the Shellbarger canyon, if we would indeed be sure to clear the Dillinger ridge. Once past the gateway, there would be no room to execute a 180-degree turn if we needed to get out of there. Due to the fact that the narrow canyon walls rising to nine and ten thousand feet above sea level on both sides and disappearing into the clouds as if they no longer existed, made a U-turn impossible.

The Sky wagon's triple-blade fan clawed its way into the late spring air as we left the home turf behind. Passing through one thousand feet msl, I drifted a bit to the right, establishing a heading of 285 degrees magnetic and settled back for the ninety-four-mile ride to the gateway of Shellbarger Pass.

Level at four thousand feet msl and barely five hundred feet below the cloud cover, we watched the village of Skwentna pass below on our left. It seemed that the ceilings were rising with the terrain, indicating a consistent barometric pressure, temperature, and dew-point. I felt confident that as long as it all remained the same, we would have no trouble.

The problem with flying around mountain ranges is that nothing is ever consistent for more than five minutes. The closer you get to them the colder the air gets. The colder the air, the less moisture it can contain and support. Therefore, the clouds usually increase and get lower. With the differential in temperatures, the air starts to move, warmer air rises and cools off, and cooled-off air descends and warms, creating turbulence that can be anywhere from benign to fatal. The first question a flyer learns to ask himself when approaching a mountain range is, "Are you *sure* you want to do this?"

Mount Shellbarger slid by on our left completely indifferent to our dilemma. At an altitude of 4,300 feet msl and pressed tightly against the bottom of the solid overcast ceiling, I knew our margin of safety would be slim, but with my experienced cautious judgment now replaced with fearless jaw-clenching determination and adrenalin, we entered the narrow canyon.

The antennas wrote scripts in the bottom of the cloud layer and the breeze from the prop kicked up dust from the top of Dillinger Ridge as I slid between the dirt and the overcast. We could see the valley broaden as the Dillinger River squirmed its way south and then west toward Farewell Lake.

We had made it, with several inches to spare. It was encouraging to think that the force was with us; maybe it was because our cause was just. Over the radio, Rusty said, "Hey, Dad, I think I just did a touch-n-go on Dillinger Ridge."

"That's better than doing a touch and *not* going, isn't it?" I replied.

The Skywagon carried enough fuel for better then eleven hundred miles in light wind conditions, but the Helio only held enough for about eight hundred. We decided to make a fuel stop at McGrath, top off and have some lunch in the event we may need to do some diversionary flying on the way back home. With full fuel and bellies, we returned to our aircraft. I was unlocking the driver's-side door when I noticed a familiar looking Stationair that had just landed and was exiting the active runway to the general aviation parking. I paused for a moment and watched. The doors opened, and emerging from the pilot side of the aircraft was none other than Deano Pastelli.

Another man exiting the airplane from the passenger side appeared familiar, but I could not for the moment place him. Two more goons emerged from the backseat who I had never seen before. I kept the Skywagon between Deano and me, hoping he would not recognize it, not so sure that he had even seen it before. Motioning to Rusty and pointing in the direction of the Stationair, I managed to call his attention to the four men. Rusty immediately recognized the first passenger. It was Beltray Gibbons, the survivor from the deadly crash at Alfred Creek almost six-years before.

We retreated as inconspicuously as possible, hoping Deano and Beltray had not noticed. We decided to wait and see if they would be staying or continuing on their way. Either way, we all agreed they would be worth following and that Kevin would be the perfect follower.

Rusty and Richard waited at the airport. While Deano and Beltray had lunch at the airport café, I signed for and Kevin and I waited in the courtesy car provided by the FBO in the event we would need to follow them on the ground, as we were not sure what their intentions were.

Deano and Beltray finished their lunch and headed back to the Stationair. Kevin rejoined Rusty in the Helio and began taxiing out for take-off behind the big Cessna. Richard and I returned the courtesy car and quickly followed in the Skywagon.

I knew that neither the Helio nor the Skywagon would be able to match the speed of the Stationair, but as long as I knew their general direction, I was sure I could outdistance them. Leaving the McGrath airport, they turned west towards Norton Bay and Nome.

CHAPTER 15

There was no evidence that either Deano or Beltray Gibbons had recognized us back at McGrath or were aware that we were following them. Actually, attempting to keep up would be more accurate. The Cessna 206 Stationair Deano was flying had run off and left both the Helio Courier and my Skywagon.

I called Rusty on the cell phone, suggesting that at Norton Bay if we did not see Deano's Cessna on the ground either at Moses or Eli, we should split up. Rusty volunteered to continue west to check the airport at Nome. Richard and I, ten miles behind in the Skywagon, would turn north at Norton Bay to investigate the area around the desolate and deserted Granite Mine airstrip.

Passing by Norton Bay and Eli, with no sign of Deano's big Cessna, Rusty and Kevin continued to Nome, Alaska, another ninety-five miles west.

Twenty-five miles north of Norton Bay, the long narrow outline of the Granite Mine airstrip began to come into view. I let the Skywagon descend to twenty-five hundred feet, putting us at twelve hundred feet above the ground. Reducing the power setting to nineteen inches of manifold pressure and bringing in a notch of flap, I slowed the 180 as we studied the canyons, draws, and ridges for any sign of an airplane. Directly straight ahead lay the long dirt runway. Setting up for a low approach and flyby, we continued to scan the area for any sign of activity.

Suddenly, I began hearing multiple ticking sounds like gravel hitting the metal skin of the airplane. Instantly realizing that someone was shooting at us, I stuffed hard left rudder, banking the airplane in a steep fifty-degree left turn when a heavy spray of oil splattered the windscreen. I searched in every direction for a survivable landing place as I quickly cut the power to idle and shutdown the engine while there was yet enough oil to keep the big Continental from seizing.

"Dad! Dad! They're shooting at us!" Richard screamed.

"Look for a place to land!" I hollered back.

As the Skywagon rapidly exchanged the remaining altitude for its trade-off in lateral distance, I headed for the rutted remnants of an old jeep trail not more then three-hundred yards from the runway, which had rapidly become our only remaining option. Yanking in the last notch of flap, I bounced the tail dragger to a stop, miraculously arriving in one piece and, more importantly, without scratching the paint.

We knew it would only be seconds before the bullets would again be coming our way. I hollered at Richard to find some cover and keep his head down as I bailed from the airplane, backpack in one hand and shotgun in the other. I knew that Richard had a nine-millimeter handgun, but was not sure if he had brought his .300 Winchester Magnum. Therefore, I wanted to keep track of him. I also expected that whoever was doing the shooting would try to separate us from the airplane and our survival gear.

"Richard," I called out just above a whisper, attempting to determine his position.

Hunkered down in a hollow, I was about fifty feet from the airplane, well secluded, but was unable to see it unless I raised myself above the two-foot-high tundra brush where I could peer over a burm running parallel to the jeep trail.

I heard no response from Richard and was afraid to speak any louder, or anymore, for that matter. Now I faced the dilemma of figuring out where Richard had gone as well as where the shooters were likely to pop up next. I decided to stay put. I figured that Richard probably had done much the same as I; found some cover and stayed near the airplane, which we needed to defend at all cost.

It was at least two hours when from the jeep trail, less then twenty yards away and from the direction I expected the shooters would come, I heard a twig snap. I waited before making my move to make sure whoever it was would be close enough for me to reach with the shotgun.

Again I heard a footstep; this time, the crunch of gravel under someone's foot. I knew that would not be Richard, for certainly he would not be walking on the jeep trail in plain sight. Someone was approaching the airplane. I wondered if maybe I should toss a grenade. If there were several of them, I could take them all at once. I still was not sure where Richard had ended up and certainly did not want to take a chance on hurting him or damaging the 180. Keeping my head, I decided against the use of bombs.

I, of course, had no idea how many shooters we were dealing with, but it would stand to reason that one or two might take the point position while the remaining shooters played the role of sniper. I decided to wait until they were closer.

BOOOOOM. The blast went off on the far side where I suspected Richard had taken cover. It was clear I was not the only one who had grenades. Leaping to my feet, I saw Deano standing on the trail only twenty-feet from the airplane, looking in the direction of the blast and immediately let him have it in the back with the ten-gage. The right side of his mid-rib section opened up and his body projected forward as if launched from a giant slingshot, slamming face first into the bank on the far side of the ditch.

I immediately turned my attention to the jeep trail and direction of the airstrip. Not a hundred yards away, I saw three more individuals disappearing into the brushy tundra, one to the right on the east side of the trail, and two to the left on the west side. I wondered if they were the only ones or if there were more that I had not yet seen. One thing was for sure, this war had just begun.

We held the high ground now. Diving for cover, afraid for their lives, the drug-runners had given it up. They would soon discover what a huge mistake they had just made. I am sure that none of those goons had ever been to war, so it was not likely they realized the disadvantage they had just put themselves in.

I, on the other hand, had survived two tours of combat in Vietnam as a search-and-shoot squad leader in the infamous "Charlie Company," and knew well that trying to find the enemy is always the hardest. Letting the enemy come to you is the easy part. If they wanted us, they would have to come and get us; we were now in a position where we could both see and hear them when they did. I guess they never had that explained to them by someone shouting into their ears so close the saliva landed on their ear lobes, as my infantry instructor sergeant major could do so proficiently.

"Richard," I called again. This time I spoke in a much louder voice.

"Right here, Dad," he said. A bit surprised, I saw the door of the airplane open as he stepped from the passenger side.

"Did you bring your .300 Winchester Magnum?"

"Yeah, I got it right here." He still concealed himself behind the door.

"Get on your belly under the airplane. Anybody who pokes their head up from that tundra, take it off, I'm going to try to flush them out of there."

With Richard looking out for my backside, I left the place of concealment that I had returned to after dropping Deano and quickly made my way over to the east side of the jeep trail where I believed I only had one of the shooters to deal with.

Working my way northward in the direction of the airstrip, I positioned myself into an indentation in the ground that would give me adequate cover, but also left me—albeit limited—some visibility to the north and east of my position. The problem was, for me to see over the trail to the west side, I would have to reveal enough of myself that a sniper from that side could easily dispatch me if he had a rifle and scope. I had to assume that these people were capable of anything and that although, to this point, I had no evidence that they in fact had a rifle, I must assume that they did or I might wind up in the land of the departed.

CRAAAACK! The deafening sound of Richard's .300 Win Mag reverberated repeatedly up and down the canyon. I had no doubt that there were only two left.

It was a waiting game, and neither Richard nor I could afford to be in a hurry. One mistake would get you dead, and obviously we knew that better then they did, so I just kept my head down and listened.

At least another hour passed, and then I heard it: an airplane, coming in our direction from the south. I was sure it must be Rusty. Closer and closer it came. Then I realized by the sound that it was not the Helio. I searched the database of my experience for another plan. My heart raced faster as my apprehensions grew over the probability that help was arriving for the other side. Oh, well, maybe when it lands we can take a few more of Alaska's drug dealers along with us.

Definitely intending on landing at this deserted but increasingly overpopulated airstrip was a Pilatus Porter, a French-made bush plane that obviously had undergone a turbo conversion, which I presumed was the plane used in transporting the drugs, which was likely returning for another load of methamphetamine.

I decided it was time to make something happen. Lying under the Skywagon, well concealed with the scoped rifle, was Richard, who I trusted would cover me. As the airplane passed overhead, I scrambled from my foxhole to the jeep trail, sprinted as fast as I could toward the airstrip. I was amazed at how far I got before the shooting started. The remaining goon from the west side jumped up and fired a round from what I recognized as a .45 semi auto that went zinging past my head, coming within an inch of carving another trough in my scalp. Swinging the ten-gage in his direction, I touched the trigger in the same moment that I heard the report of Richard's .300 once again echoing through the canyon, which, to my relief, terminated the immediate threat, greatly reducing my level of anxiety.

With only one more shooter remaining that I knew of, and, of course, whatever surprises the Porter had brought to the party, I continued my mad dash to the north, hoping Richard might get a shot at the remaining drug dealer still on the east side of the jeep trail.

I was almost to the end of the threshold of the south end of the runway. The Pilatus Porter had landed and parked at the north end, the feathered prop spinning freely and the whine of the turbo winding down, when I saw movement on my right. Immediately I stopped, bringing the ten-gage to my shoulder and aimed at the moving brush. It was Beltray Gibbons, emerging from the tundra, both arms extended to the sky and screaming, "Don't shoot! Don't shoot!"

I yelled for Richard that he could come out. Approaching Beltray, I turned him toward the runway, and holding the shotgun at the base of his skull, we started a slow walk toward the Porter. I watched intently as three men exited the airplane. They were Rusty and Kevin with the pilot close behind, a man I had never before seen. I was baffled, but very relieved.

"Good timing, son. For a minute, I thought we were outnumbered. What's with the Porter, and who is your pilot?"

"This is Jerry Hansen. He owns a shop in Nome. We developed a magneto problem. We didn't see Deano or his 206 anywhere and Jerry hadn't seen them come in, so he volunteered to help us out."

"Well thank you, Mr. Hansen, we appreciate that. Deano shot us down and for that he is now taking a long nap along with two more of his buddies, and this little guy I got here is going to tell us where his 206 is. Isn't that right, little guy?" I pressed the barrel of the ten-gage a little harder against the back of Beltray's neck. He didn't answer. I looked at Rusty again. "He'll talk later. I don't think he is done wetting his pants yet." I turned to Jerry Hansen. "Well, Mr. Hansen—"

"You can call me Jerry."

"Well, Jerry, I guess if you had known you were flying into a war zone, you might have had second thoughts."

"War zones are actually not new to me. Besides, it looks like the war is over, and you won."

"I would like to believe that, but I'm afraid this was just the first battle. The war just got started."

We took Beltray with us to have a look around. I could smell a horrible odor in the air. Kevin said it was the meth and that was the reason they cook it in remote areas because the horrible smell tends to give away its location.

Turning to Beltray, I asked, "Where's the Stationair?" He just shrugged his shoulders again without answering.

"Do you know who we are?" I asked.

"You're the guys who built that learning center," he said in a disgruntled tone.

"We're also the guys who saved your butt when you bailed out of that Cardinal back at Alfred Creek six years ago, do your remember that?"

Beltray looked at me. His face, though horribly scarred from body surfing on a gravel runway at seventy miles an hour, showed genuine surprise. "You were there?" he asked, perplexed.

I had let loose my hold on Beltray, lowered the shotgun, and turned him around where he was facing me.

"Yeah, we were there, we got the medivac helicopter in there in time to save your scrawny little carcass. I even looked in on you when you were in the hospital, but now I want something in return." I pulled him closer to me, this time placing the ten-gage under his chin and against his throat.

"And if you don't tell me what I want to know, I'm going to toss what's left of you over there on top of your friend Deano."

"The Stationair is under a canopy on the other side of that hill," Beltray blurted.

"Where's the meth lab, and how many people are in there right now?" Kevin interjected.

"No one is there," he eagerly answered back. "We had just got here when these guys showed up." He gestured toward Richard and me.

"Who killed Bill?" I demanded as I shoved the barrel of the ten-gage tighter against Gibbons throat.

Beltray started shaking and stammering, but did not answer. Finally, more terrified of us than the people he had been working for; he directed our attention toward the location of an old dilapidated shack.

Gibbons opened two cellar doors. We made our way down a ladder to an underground level and another set of recently installed steel doors secured with a chain and padlock. Beltray retrieved a key from under a rock and from there, we entered the source of the gut-gagging smell.

Rusty went to the Porter and returned with his backpack. Strategically placing plastic explosives throughout the underground drug lab, he set and activated a small transmitter that he placed in his shirt pocket. He then retrieved the Stationair from under a camouflaged canopy, relocating it to the runway.

Jerry Hansen, the pilot of the Porter, was also a veteran of foreign wars. An A&P mechanic with a full-service shop on the airfield at Nome, Alaska, Jerry was the bush pilots' mobile mechanic for the North Slope, and his Pilatus Porter was literally a flying service truck.

The bullet that penetrated the oil sump of the Skywagon appeared to be the size of a nine millimeter. We were able to patch it sufficiently enough to hold oil, enabling me to fly to Nome where Jerry could make more thorough and permanent repairs.

Rusty waited, making sure we were safely in the air, where we circled awaiting the show.

Climbing into the driver seat of the big Cessna with Richard in the front and Kevin guarding the prisoner in the back, they proceeded to borrow Deano's Stationair indefinitely and with no apparent objection from Deano.

With plans to interrogate more information from the ungrateful Beltray Gibbons, who, like a cat with nine lives, had once again dodged his destiny, Rusty fired the big Cessna and joined us in the sky above the underground meth lab.

Shortly after departure and a climb to a safe altitude, Rusty took the little transmitter from his shirt pocket and pressed the red button. We all watched Deano's meth lab evaporate into a landfill. The explosion lifted the dirt rooftop of the lab forty feet above the surrounding terrain, leaving a huge cloud of dust, and then settled into a sunken indentation in the ground that resembled a construction site for an Olympic-sized, backyard swimming pool.

"I bet that will get their attention. They wanted a war, they got a war," I said.

I have heard it said that "ignorance is bliss." I didn't realize at that time just how ignorant I was. I had no idea who I was actually at war with, how long the war would go on, or that someday it would actually come right to my front door and take my darling Kati.

CHAPTER 16

A few days later, Rusty and I flew back to Nome to bring home the Helio Courier. It gave us a chance to discuss the events that had taken place at the deserted mine where we had destroyed the meth lab. Though it felt as if we had accomplished something significant in our personal war on drugs that we had taken upon ourselves, all we had actually done was swat a couple of flies in a barnyard.

We imagined that sooner or later someone would discover the bodies of Deano and his deceased friends and be looking for whoever was responsible. If law enforcement found them, they would just think it was a turf war, no harm, no foul. However, when the ringleaders learned of it, they would know that someone other than law enforcement had a personal vendetta against them. After the highly publicized murder of Bill Shearer and my personal involvement with him, they would not need a rocket scientist to arrive at the conclusion that I was their huckleberry. We well knew what that meant. To protect our own, we would have to find the top of the organization and bring it down fast.

In the past few days since returning home, both Kevin and Rusty had spent some quality time with Beltray Gibbons and learned several things that would help our investigation. For instance, with the exception of Deano, neither Gibbons nor the other goons who were involved in shooting at Richard and I knew who brought the chemicals in or took the finished product back out. They would just get a phone call, informing

126

them to go cook-off the stuff and package it, and when finished, they would leave.

According to Gibbons, Deano's connections went considerably higher, but how high he either didn't know or was so far reluctant to say. I was then inclined to think that maybe Deano's old man, Gino, was at the top of this ladder, and now that he was in prison, the handling of the business had been passed to the son who received his orders directly from his old man. That being the case, and with Deano now dead, we could expect some serious fallout coming all the way from Chicago—well, actually, Leavenworth.

In addition, Gibbons had revealed that the phone call usually came from Deano, and the reason he was at the old mine that day was to drop off Beltray and the other two characters, who were brought along to help with the cooking and packaging. He also informed us that Deano had spotted us at McGrath and was laying in wait at the old mining airstrip, expecting that we would show up sooner or later. He was also the only one who carried a nine millimeter with a fifteen-round clip, and the only one who had fired at Richard and me when we were airborne. The two goons who Richard dispatched after we were on the ground had only gotten off one shot between them—at me—which was enough to justify there untimely end, mostly because they were so stupid. Drugs do that to a fellow.

It was past midday by the time I dropped Rusty off at Nome. I had planned to head straight to Bettles to the learning center, but on the way, decided to divert and swing by the old mine to see if there was any evidence of activity since the gunfight four days earlier. It was a clear day, so climbing to six thousand feet where it would be unlikely anyone on the ground would pay much attention to me, I passed well above the airstrip.

There was no indication that anyone was there or that anyone had been there since we left. I decided to have a closer look to see if the bodies were where we had left them.

The place looked just like we left it. The mound of ground where the underground meth lab had been was now an equally large depression in the ground with no indication of what it once had been. I let the Skywagon come down and set up once again for a low and slow flyby.

By the time that four-hundred grain slug had finished with Deano, what was left of his body had come to rest facedown on the east side of the jeep trail and about three hundred yards south of the south end of the airstrip. This was adjacent to the spot the Skywagon had ended up after Deano had shot Richard and I out of the sky.

From fifty feet above the ground and on the west side of the jeep trail flying southbound, I was in position to see even the blades of grass growing on the trail. Deano's remains were no longer there.

I made another pass, this time northbound and on the east side, looking for the other two, who, with a little help from Richard's crosshairs, had met their Maker on the west side of the jeep trail. They, too, were missing.

Who else could have known about the gunfight other then Jerry Hansen? Surely he wasn't involved in the drug organization. The only other person would be Beltray Gibbons, and he was a securely guarded guest at my place with no access to a phone or other people. I was beginning to wonder if our new friend Jerry might not be a friend at all.

I decided to turn around, go back to Nome, and have a face-to-face with Jerry Hansen.

Rusty was already gone, but I had been able to get him on the phone and fill him in on the latest development. He told me to call him if I had any problems, and he would turn around and come back. I told him, "Don't worry about me. Just wring some more information out of Beltray. We're running out of time." We needed to know who removed those bodies and, above all, who murdered Bill Shearer.

I taxied over to Jerry's shop and shut down the big Continental. Jerry was in his office doing paperwork as I entered through the shop door.

"Good afternoon, Jerry," I said.

"Hey, there, Lou. Did you find more holes in the 180?"

"Oh, heck no, nothing like that." I looked around to be sure no one could hear what else I had to say. "Listen, I just did a flyby over the old deserted mine that we were at the other day, and there were three missing packages that we had left behind. Do you have any idea what could have become of them?" I paid close attention to every little reaction in his face and eyes. Seeing absolutely nothing suspicious, I continued. "That little guy we took with us has been completely in-comunicado, so we know he could not have tipped anyone, which has us really wondering who else we could be dealing with here."

"Well, Lou, I've seen that little guy in here before, sometimes with that dude you wasted, and sometimes with another great big dude they call Judo. Actually, they just call him that. His real name is Terry Markin, and he flies a Cessna 208 Caravan. I'm sure you know what they look like."

"Yes, I do. The learning center owns several of them, and I know exactly who you are talking about," I said. "Well, that sounds like just who I am looking for: a big guy with a big airplane. What could be more perfect for getting rid of three stiffs? Just one more thing, Jerry, and I'll get out of your way. What color is that 208, or do you happen to remember the tail number?"

"Just a minute," Jerry said as he opened his desk drawer. He fumbled though pens, paperclips, and other miscellaneous items before finally locating a picture, which he handed to me. "He brought that 208 in here with a damaged prop about a year ago, and I installed a new one for him."

As I turned to leave Jerry's office, I pointed at him and said, "I appreciate your being on my team, buddy. Thanks for your help."

The 208 Jerry was referring to was in fact familiar to me, as I had seen it on several occasions but had no idea who the driver was until now. Beige with a light, powder blue sea-wave paint scheme, Judo's 208, when new, was a real sharp-looking airplane. However, every time I had seen it, which was usually at the Gulkana airport, it looked uncared for and unmaintained, probably because he was in and out of the rougher bush-type strips so much. It probably stinks like a meth lab, too. Definitely fast; in fact, almost twice as fast as my 180. The 208 is a real workhorse, capable of flying away with up to 2,700 pounds of payload.

I could see that for me to keep up with Mr. Terry Markin or 'Judo,' which evidently he prefers, I would definitely need something faster than his 208. I headed for the Lake Hood hard surface to pay Ray Sumner a visit.

Ray knew of a Pilatus Porter for sale in Fairbanks that had the turbo conversion kit already installed on it. The Porter, about the only single-engine airplane available that would be faster than the Caravan and still capable of hauling a sizable payload, would prove useful to us in other lines of work besides chasing drug-runners. Ray and I took off for Fairbanks to have a look.

An oil-drilling corporation, whose superintendents traveled to and from a variety of projects on the North Slope, owned the Porter. Evidently, they had recently purchased a new Caravan to replace it because the Caravan was significantly quieter and more comfortable, conducive to high-profile big shots.

I made the deal directly with the drilling outfit, purchasing the Porter as Alfred Creek Mining Enterprises and giving Ray his broker's fee in cash. With the paperwork and the buyer's annual completed, Ray flew the Porter to my place where we left the 180, and I shuttled Ray back to Lake Hood in the Porter.

While at Lake Hood, I called Phillip Later, the flight instructor who had checked me out in the Skywagon almost eight years before. We went back to Portage Pass where Philip likes to make the training real, putting me through the paces in and out of Whittier's field.

I had completely forgotten about Phillip Later. He was an excellent flight instructor, and we needed his kind of experience and dedication to superior teaching at our flight school in Bettles. Therefore, I told him if he ever wanted to join our staff at the learning center to give me a call. Of course, I waited to extend that offer until after he had signed my logbook, approving my checkout in the turbo-prop Pilatus Porter

The Porter had been painted orange probably to satisfy safety regulations on the North Slope. It was a horrible color for an airplane, especially one that was about to be used to discreetly tail a gangster. But there was no time to give the Porter a new paint job. Besides, when this deal was over, orange would probably be a wise color choice for mining work anyway. We decided to leave it the way it was. Maybe it would work to our advantage. Maybe Judo would see it and, by virtue of its color, never think to suspect it as anything more than one of the North Slope project planes, which he had probably seen many times.

Landing at our home airstrip, I parked the Porter outside of the new hangar. Four years before, we had installed an underground office and vault, where everyone in the country assumed we had stashed the seven billion in gold. Everyone accept Beltray Gibbons, of course, for that vault had been his home for the last five days.

Taking turns babysitting Gibbons until I returned from my fact-finding mission, Rusty and Kevin continued to question Beltray. Neither of them condoned the use of torture or any other methods of intimidation inherent in most interrogation technique. Neither did they use the silly good cop/bad cop methods that are archaic and completely ineffective anyway.

The DEA had estimated that the Cardinal that crashed and burned at Alfred Creek was loaded with over three hundred pounds of meth. Although Beltray Gibbons was only a small potato in the organization, he was also the only one who survived, and therefore, the only one charged. The charges were drug possession and drug transport with the intention of distribution, for which he received a five-year sentence at the prison in Fairbanks. Released, a little more than a year before around the time Bill was murdered, he returned to the only thing he knew how to do—make and package drugs.

I wanted to talk to Gibbons, but first I needed to learn what information Rusty and Kevin had managed to get from him.

When Beltray discovered that we were the ones who had saved his bacon at Alfred Creek, he began to see us more as friends than enemies. The more he cooperated with Rusty and Kevin, the kinder they were to him. Although his living quarters were not ideal, they were clean and comfortable. Beltray's trust in Rusty and Kevin had grown, and their humanitarian treatment of him had increased his willingness to chat. He was still totally terrified of me, however.

While Richard watched Gibbons, Rusty, Kevin, and I went to the house where I could do some freshening up.

Kati had made a huge kettle of pot roast stew, and while we indulged ourselves with her wonderful cooking, she prepared a plate for Richard and Beltray, including a generous portion of her blueberry cobbler for each of them. I took the food, and we returned to the hangar.

Richard and Beltray were in the middle of a game of chess, a losing cause when you are playing with Richard.

"Beltray," I said, "I brought you some dinner. Do you want it now, or do you want to finish that game while it gets cold?"

"Oh, hey, thanks. I'll eat it now." Richard moved the chessboard from the table as I set their food in front of them.

Turning to Rusty and Kevin, I proceeded to bring them up to date on the purchase of the Porter and my intention of tailing Judo. I had actually already done all that up at the cabin when we had dinner, but we decided to do it again in front of Beltray and talk to him as though he were one of us. I continued to talk as Beltray finished his meal, scraping every speck of purple from the bowl that had recently contained the cobbler.

I still suspected Beltray knew more than he had told us so far and was hoping the pot roast and cobbler would bring the rest out of him. He had told Kevin that Deano would meet with a man in a fancy suit over at McGrath a couple of times a year, but Beltray did not know who he was, and it was always Deano giving the man a package and never the other way around.

"Beltray," I said. "Are you ready to talk to me?"

"I guess so. I've already told these guys everything I know," Beltray said nervously.

"Kevin tells me you saw Deano give some man a package back at McGrath. Is that right?"

"That's right. I was with him several times when he met with him."

"Do you know what was in the package?"

"Money, whadaya think? It's always about money."

"Did you see the money getting packaged up?"

"I was the one that wrapped it up for Deano. He had me do everything."

"How much cash was in each package?"

"Ten grand in hundred dollar bills."

"What else did he have you do, Beltray? Did he have you kill Bill Shearer too?" I asked this time with an attitude.

"I didn't do that. I ... I ... could never do anything like that," he stammered.

"Well, then, did Deano do it?" I continued pressing.

"I don't know, man. You have to believe me. I really don't know." Beltray was quivering and wanted to go to the bathroom. When he returned, I continued.

"Beltray, I thought you got five years for that drug rap. Did you get out a year early or something?"

"Yes, sir. I made parole after four."

"That tells me that you have it in you to behave yourself, so I want you to understand something. I am not going to hurt you. Even if we find out you are lying to us, we will just turn you over to the cops. Of course, you will wind up back in the joint where you just spent the last four years since that plane crash. Then, I will make sure everyone understands that you willingly cooperated with the law, you can put the rest of your life on fast forward from there, and in about ten years, you can tell me the rest of the story, if you are still alive. On the other hand, I want to offer you a once-in-a-lifetime opportunity. Would you like to hear it?" I was hoping he would say yes, and not sure how I would proceed if he said no.

"What is it?"

"First of all, I want to hear everything you know about that drug organization and everybody in it. I want names, places, the whole deal, all the way to the top. I want to know how the organization operates and who the top people are. Do not leave anything out, and most of all, I want to know who killed Bill. In exchange, you get our protection and a new life. I will get you enrolled in the William Shearer Center of Learning, where you will live in a dormitory while you complete an education in any field or endeavor you choose. Everything—education, room and board, flight training, anything you want—completely prepaid. I will even get your criminal record completely expunged so you can get a job or run a business. You need to think long and hard about this because this is the only moment you will ever get to take your life in another direction. I'll be back in an hour to hear your decision."

I walked away from Beltray Gibbons feeling as if I might just as well have offered a deal to the devil. One could only hope that it did not land on deaf ears.

I had no idea at the time that in less than four years, my very life would depend on the decision Beltray would make when I returned.

CHAPTER 17

Beltray Gibbons was a career criminal who still had the biggest percentage of his career still ahead of him. At least until he met me. Now, he was either going to change careers or die in prison. Either way, his present lively hood as he had known it was over.

I did not know where he had come from or how he happened to get involved in the world of drugs and crime. However, I did know that every present moment is the result of the string of decisions and choices that have gone before it, whether his or someone else's. It didn't matter; he was responsible, even if only by agreement.

Gibbons faced another moment of decision. This time it was the most important one of his miserable life. Yet I had no doubt that he would lie, and as soon as we released him to the school, he would bail out and eventually we would see him again in handcuffs or dead. The epitaph for that stone had already been written. I was hoping he realized there were not many of his nine lives remaining.

I returned in exactly an hour, just as I said I would. Beltray took the offer and said that he wanted to go to school. In fact, he almost made it believable. That wasn't all. He went on to say a lot more, including who killed Bill.

The drug organization stretched all the way to Leavenworth, where Gino sat with an extended stay that would keep him confined until he is about 130 years old. His drug business, confined to the lower forty-eight states for many years, had moved to Alaska only fifteen years before I did. The money he used to purchase our gold was cash he had received in exchange for drugs from the people of Alaska and money he needed to launder. The gold gave him a perfect Laundromat.

He swore he would see me dead for killing his son. The same son who had tried to murder my son-in-law by throwing a hand grenade at him, and who only a short time before had shot the airplane down that Richard and I were flying, attempting to murder both of us.

Carl Brightwater lost his job as attorney general for receiving cash donations from known organized crime members and providing protection from investigation. Carl and Gino became roomies.

Judo did not fare so well.

Rusty and I had been searching for him for about a month. According to Beltray, he would oftentimes make supply pick-ups at a remote mountain airstrip close to the US/Yukon border called, Border Town Aero. Lying next to the Taylor Highway, only a few yards away from the road and a hundred miles from anything else, it provided a perfect drop-off and/or pick-up location.

Rusty and I had been keeping a close eye on the Gulkana airport, and on one particular lucky day, we had been sitting on the tarmac in the bright orange Porter, watching Mr. Markin's Caravan for over six hours. We both perked up when a very familiar-looking Crown Victoria turned into the entrance of the airport and drove directly to where the Caravan sat parked. The man called Judo unlocked the door of the Cessna 208 and slid open the baggage-side door. From the trunk of his car, he took two aluminum suitcases exactly like the ones that our seven million bucks had come in the last time we did business with Gino Pastelli.

Returning to the trunk of his car, Judo retrieved one more item. Though wrapped in a blanket, there was no doubt it was a rifle scabbard, and it was not empty.

"What do you want to bet that's the rifle that killed Bill?" I said to Rusty.

"You'll have to get someone dumber than me to take that bet."

"I'm going to wait till he fires up and gets in the air before I spool up, otherwise we might spook him."

"Good idea."

The second he pushed the power forward, I had the Porter spooling up, and in short order, we too were in the air. I guess you could say I mashed on it. In only ten minutes, we had the 208 back in sight.

We tailed him at a distance until we were sure that his destination was in fact Border Town Aero. Then we diverted to give him time to get on the ground and hopefully shutdown.

We also were not sure if he might be meeting someone of if he was planning on dropping off something or picking up something. I did a couple of 360deg. turns, and my patience ran out.

I did not bother with flying a conventional pattern at the short mountain airstrip at Border Town Aero. Judo was already on the ground and had the 208 sitting in a takeoff direction facing us at the far end of the strip when I emerged suddenly from a long canyon that had concealed our approach and executed a hard right turn to a very short final approach. Just as I turned the corner, we saw a minivan pulling away from the side of the road and from where Judo was carrying a package toward the Caravan. Rusty was already in the back, ready to open the cargo door.

"Rusty, he's on the other side of the Caravan," I yelled.

Hitting the deck just under rotation speed, I let the Porter travel freely past the midway point before reversing the prop and stopping short of hitting the Caravan. With full right rudder, I ground looped the tail wheel clockwise as Rusty swung open the huge cargo door on the left side of the Porter and leapt to the ground. In a dead run toward the front of the 208, Rusty kept the Caravan between him and Judo.

At the time the Porter touched down, Judo looked confused as if he did not know who it was who had just landed or what to do. (I think the orange paint worked in our favor.) The Porter had actually come to a stop by the time he turned to run. Rusty paused in front of the big propeller and yelled for him to stop, at which time Judo spun around, wildly firing off four rounds from a nine millimeter that very nearly spilled some of Rusty's blood. Rusty fired once with his .45 S&W, and Judo's body went limp in mid-stride, planting his face into the turf runway without so much as a grunt or a groan. The 230 grain jacketed hollow point entered the base of his skull at the top of his spine, and Pastor Bill Shearer's murderer was dead before he hit the ground. The war was over. Or so we thought.

We called the Alaska State Troopers, who in turn contacted the DEA, and waited for their arrival.

The ballistics on the scoped rifle found in the back of the Caravan matched the bullet taken from Pastor Bill's body. Along with the sworn testimony supplied by Beltray Gibbons that he had seen Deano give that rifle to Judo the day before Bill was killed, the jury was satisfied that the murder of William Shearer had been solved. Over the course of the next year, the DEA raided and destroyed three more drug labs along the coastal area of Alaska. Within a year, at least 150 additional drug-runners and distributors received sentences along with free room and board at the prison in Fairbanks. Did that end the drug activity in Alaska? No. But it sure reduced it and saved a great many lives and families.

At the realization that I had contributed to the financial aid of a drug dealer by helping him launder his ill-gotten money, I was even more determined to see the people of Alaska benefit from the resources we had been so fortunate to find.

The Eva Creek Mine had sat dormant for the last twenty-two years, and with Alfred Creek apparently played out, Mitchell, Rusty, and Richard moved the operation to Eva Creek. We had reopened the claim as a business, this time under the name of Alfred Creek Mining Enterprises, Inc. My three sons were still quite young and had plenty of energy and vision. I, on the other hand, was getting lazier, at least when it came to mining. After all, I was quite well-to-do.

It seemed that I had turned out to be quite the survivor as well. First, two tours of duty in Vietnam and then twenty-seven years as a commercial truck driver, escaping more than a few situations that could have easily taken my life, along with two major gun fights since moving to Alaska. Sometimes I wondered how much longer my luck would hold out. I do not really believe in the nine lives thing or luck, for that matter, so my reflections soon took another direction. Both Kati and I felt that rather than worry about finding my true calling at this stage of my life, I should just let it come to me.

I called Leonard Gerard, the architect and superintendant of the construction of the learning center.

"Good morning, Gerard's Architectural. This is Hilda. May I help you?"

"Hi, Hilda. This is Lou Worley. Is Gerard in?"

"Yes, Mr. Worley, he is. Just a moment, please."

"Lou!" Gerard answered. "How the heck are you? I have needed to talk to you, but wanted to wait until the trial was over. What can I do for you?"

"Hello Leonard. Well, there has been a lot going on, that's for sure. Priscilla says the learning center is starting to generate some revenue from the aviation and auto mechanics shops, and Genneta Williams informs me that the flight school is also turning a profit now from its charter flights."

"Good, Lou, that's good to hear. You ready to begin another project anytime soon?" Gerard asked.

"Yes, I am. I found a site down by King Salmon, a place called Naknek. If you could give Priscilla a call and get together with her and Gerald Connor, I can get one of the Caravans to come down from the school and take us all down there where we can look at a piece of land I think would work for another center. Can you call me with a date? I will make arrangements for one of the Caravans as soon as I hear from you."

"I'll get right on it, Lou, and get back with you."

"Thanks, Leonard. See-ya."

Gerald Connor was one of three attorneys retained by the foundation to handle the legal matters and finances of the school. They were all long-standing members of the board of trustees for the Shearer/Worley Foundation, the nonprofit organization responsible for the distribution of funds that provided for the budget of the projects.

Under the supervision of both Kati and Sharon—chairperson and vice-chairperson, respectively of the Foundation—Gerald Connor and two of his associates, Beverley Howard and Benjamin Goldberg, managed the money set aside for the projects. I compensated Mr. Connor and his group very well for their services and made one thing perfectly clear to them from the beginning: They had more to lose from stealing from me than they had to gain and more to gain from taking care of me than they ever had to lose. With one project successfully completed, my confidence in Gerard's choice for attorneys had increased significantly.

The William Shearer Center of Learning had become a recognized education center throughout Alaska. Many of those who originally enrolled in the school had successfully finished their training and were entering the workforce. Men and women, young and old, were returning to their villages and starting successful businesses that were contributing to the local economies. I had provided the Shearer/Worley Foundation with an expense account of two billion dollars, financing the projects, and all the costs of the students' education. Even start-up money for small businesses was available from that fund.

Unemployment had decreased throughout the state as the learning center continued to fill positions from teachers and educators, to mechanics, doctors and nurses including complete hospital and clinical staffing, as well as flight instructors, even security personnel.

It was a thrill for me personally, as I watched the stream of uneducated and dysfunctional people that passed through the learning center emerge as educated, functional, and contributing members of society. I only wished that Bill could have seen what his dream for the people of Alaska was accomplishing. Knowing Bill as I did, I knew that he would not take much time to reflect on things in the past with so much work yet to do.

The next day, Gerard called and gave me a date for our site-finding expedition to Naknek. I notified everyone who had indicated they wanted to come along. We all agreed that the Caravan would pick us up at Bold's.

Leonard Gerard the project architect, Gerald Connor and one of his associates, Ben Goldberg, arrived together. Gilbert Riley from the Office of Rural Development, Priscilla Vasquez the superintendent of public instruction, Sharon Shearer, Kati, and I were already waiting.

I did not experience flying as a passenger very often and was a bit nervous about the idea until I realized who our pilot would be. Within ten minutes and right on time, one of the school's Cessna 208 Caravans roared above our heads, crossing midfield for a right traffic landing at our home field. It was a beautiful sight. Genneta Williams had sent us a charter airplane, and as our pilot, she had loaned us her husband, Jeffery. All my apprehensions dissipated while I bragged to everybody about Jeffery's many years of experience as a crop duster.

The flight to Naknek, a distance of 324 miles in the Caravan, was only about an hour and forty minutes. I was a very well-behaved passenger for all of about eleven minutes when Kati let go of my hand and pushed me toward the copilot's seat, where I immediately began my checkout in the 208 Caravan.

On the ground at Naknek, the owners of the property that I had inquired about almost three months prior to our arrival picked us up in an extended van. This time, we would have to pay the going price for the land, as there were no squatters' rights available as there had been in Bettles.

The dickering went two ways. We were the people who had found billions of bucks' worth of gold and could afford any price. That was their position. Then again, we were the people who were going to provide an education center for their community, complete with paid room and board and free education, which, of course, would benefit their economy. That was our position.

The landowners gave us a price for the seven hundred acres. Gerald Connor offered twenty-five percent less, and they accepted. Kati and I went for a walk around the property while the attorneys did the paperwork.

"Lou, baby, how many of these schools are you going to build?" Kati asked as we walked.

"Well, sweetie, King Salmon has a small hospital and Naknek is only three hundred miles from Anchorage where there are two more big hospitals. We could get by with just a good-sized clinic and trauma room at the Naknek center, which would save some money. As for more schools, I think we need another major-sized learning center at Sitka to address the educational needs of the many fishing communities on the Aleutian Chain and along the inland passage. Then I think it would be a matter of wait and see. Well have to look for any smaller communities that are still too far away to benefit and build smaller schools closer to them." We turned around to go back to the van.

Throughout the summer, the Naknek project progressed rapidly. Kati and I had flown the Skywagon down to spend some time in the fishing village, getting to know the local people. After a day of visiting the town and checking the progress of the construction on the learning center, we headed for home.

Ordinarily, I would fly the coastline to stay out of the higher terrain on the north side of Mount Redoubt, but it had been a beautiful day, and a trip through the mountains seemed like a wonderful idea. I knew Kati would enjoy the beautiful scenery, and we expected to see an abundance of wildlife. With our fingers crossed that Mr. Redoubt would blow some other day, we settled in for the long ride home.

Approaching Lake Clark, I descended to two thousand feet above the lake as we proceeded eastbound through the Lake Clark Preserve toward Clark Pass.

Lake Clark is a fifty-mile-long, slender lake not more than a half-mile wide. The boundary to the national park begins about two-thirds of the way up the lake. A thirty-five-mile-wide preserve area had been included to the lower edges of the national park boundary as a wildlife protection act. This preserve provided a wintering zone for the wildlife seeking the lower elevations during the severe winter weather. That zone extended from the national park boundary all the way to the west end of the lake.

As we approached the park boundary, I began our turn to the north following the preserve/park boundary line along the western foothills of the Neacola Mountains in the Alaska Range. Passing Twin Lakes and with Telaquana Lake coming into view, I noticed movement low over the surface of Telaquana Lake.

"Kati," I said pointing at the lake. "Do you see that? It looks like an airplane coming up off the water."

"I don't see anything," she responded at first, then, "Oh! Yes, I do. It's camouflaged."

"I see that, it looks like a Super Cub. Let's have a look." I reduced manifold pressure and began a descent, keeping the Super Cub directly in front so that they would not see us. Dropping to just above treetop level, we got a close look at the shore of the lake where the Cub had departed from. There in the trees were three men and the remains of three illegally poached bull moose. Obviously, the other portions of the animals were on board the Super Cub.

I wanted to circle around and make another pass to get a picture of the poachers and their trophies, but was afraid that they might start shooting at us. With Kati on board, I could not take the chance of her getting hurt, so we stayed with the Cub and followed it.

It was not long before it occurred to me that the Super Cub driver must have received a call from his friends on the ground, informing him that I was on his tail because he began a series of diversionary maneuvers, clearly designed to lose me. Too bad for him, it didn't work. I had way more fuel than he had moose meat and every bit as much daylight. By the time he figured out he wasn't going to shake me, we had explored half the river beds in the Alaska Range and ran a slalom through Merrill Pass to the east side of the range. Kati was as green as grass and wanted out. We took a picture of the tail end of the airplane and headed for our home turf.

I called Cal Trent as soon as I was back into cell phone country and told him what we had observed. When we arrived home, I sent him a picture via e-mail of the Cub we had chased. When he saw the picture, he called me back.

"Yes, sir, Officer Trent. How are you today?" I said, answering my cell phone.

"Lou Worley, when are you going to start calling me Cal, or have you forgotten you're one of us now?"

"Okay, Cal. I guess I thought that badge you gave me was just a gesture. Are you saying that I am really a cop?" I tried to make it sound like I was kidding, but at the same time, I was curious about what official or unofficial authority that badge actually held.

"You're a cop as long as a cop is with you," Cal said, "and if there is ever any question, you just say I'm with you and then call me as soon as you can. I got the picture you sent. I recognize that Cub. It belongs to a fellow named Dale Stanley. Too bad Kati was with you; it would have been nice to catch him with the meat."

"Well, Cal, he only got part of it out. There were at least three animals on the ground, so he would be looking at three or four more trips in there to get it all out along with his clients. If you are ready to go, I am," I said.

"Do you have your amphibian floats on yet?" Cal asked.

"No, not yet."

"Okay. I will grab the Bell Ranger. It's got the pontoons. I'll pick you up at your place in an hour."

"See you then." I hung up.

CHAPTER 18

I grabbed a quick shower and the sack lunch Kati made for me and headed for the Skywagon to get my backpack and shotgun. With the .45 Glock belted to my side, I was closing the door on the 180 as Cal sat the Bell Ranger on the pad, blowing dirt all over my still wet hair.

Cal handed me a blue State Police flight jacket and a helmet. On the way, I pointed out to him from the sectional map where we had seen the poachers and the direction the Cub had gone after we emerged from Merrill Pass.

It was getting late, almost ten o'clock at night, and about as dark as it was going to get for that time of year, but still plenty dark enough that flying through Merrill Pass would not be a very good idea, at least in my mind. Of course, I am not a helicopter pilot. Actually, I was a bit surprised at how much visibility remained as we negotiated the tight S-turn through the low and then the high stages of the pass.

On the western side of the Range, Cal retraced the route Kati and I had taken just a few hours before. Coming up on Telaquana Lake, Cal turned off all his lights and climbed to nine thousand feet to look for campfires or lights that might give away the poachers' position.

Seeing nothing, he flew north and then west as he descended to approach their last known position from treetop level. Less than a quarter-mile from the western shoreline and eastbound toward the lake, a dim-lighted lantern in a tent caught my eye. I called out to Cal as I pointed to the ground. Cal turned on the landing lights and banked the Ranger hard around to the right, returning to the spot at which I had pointed. The landing lights lit up their camp.

Cal held the Ranger in a hover slightly more than fifteen feet above the trees and a bit to one side as he pulled a bullhorn from behind the seat. "Hello in the camp," Cal yelled. "This is the Alaska State Department of Game Management. Step out in the open with your hands above your heads."

One by one, the three men sheepishly emerged from their three tents, holding their hands toward the sky.

The area was not conducive to landing a helicopter due to the scrub brush and the short but thick timber. The only option for landing was the lake, which would not be a problem as the Ranger was equipped with pontoons. However, it was also a good fifty yards away.

"I want everyone to move over to the lake shore and stay together where I can follow you. Is that clear?" Cal ordered. I could see the three men nodding their heads as they turned toward the lakeshore. As the men made their way toward where Kati and I had seen them earlier in the day, Cal slowly followed, holding the Ranger in a hover while keeping the lights on the poachers.

As the men reached the waters edge, we could see the meat from the three poached animals hanging from four different meat poles. Cal let the Ranger descend to within ten feet of the tops of the short trees. Turning to me, he said, "Lou, slide that side door open in the back and roll out that rope ladder. I need you on the ground, and take your backpack. You will need your flashlight to watch them while I land this thing on the lake." Neither Cal nor I heard or noticed the camouflaged Super Cub that had just landed on the lake less than two hundred yards away with its lights out.

Opening the sliding door of the Bell Ranger, I rolled out the coiled-up ladder rope. With my daypack strapped to my back, I started to step out onto the dangling ladder when I remembered the ten-gage. Reaching across the cargo area, I retrieved it and hung the shoulder strap around my neck. I then began my swaying descent down the ladder to the ground.

With me safely on the ground, Cal maneuvered the helicopter out over the lake with the ladder still dangling and set the Ranger down on the water within fifty feet of the shore. Cal then disengaged the rotors as the Bell Ranger sat at an idle. Stepping out of the sliding door, he began to unlash a canoe that he kept strapped to the pontoons.

I watched the three poachers who were now standing on the shoreline and in the half-light of the night sky while I remained concealed inside the darkened timberline less then fifteen feet behind them. With the turbo from the helicopter engine winding down and now whining at an idle at least fifty feet away, I could, for the first time, sense the quiet of the Lake Clark Preserve.

Suddenly, Cal froze in a kneeling position with the canoe only half unlashed. Looking in the direction of the southern shoreline, he looked startled. At precisely the same moment, I heard both a click and saw Officer Trent somersault backward into the water and out of sight.

I recognized the click instantly as the sound of a rifle safety being returned to a "fire when ready" position. Unless a person had some supernatural ears, it would be unlikely one could hear that sound from more than about ten or twelve feet away. So although I still knew nothing of the presence of the Super Cub, I did now know that we had company.

I felt I was reasonably secluded where I was, but knew that the three poachers, who were actually just the clients of the real poacher, knew where I was. I looked for any indication that they might be aware of anyone else's presence or had heard the sound of the safety mechanism that I had heard. It did not appear that they had.

From where I stood, I could see the still idling helicopter but had no idea where Cal had disappeared to. I assumed that he was still in the water. I didn't know how, but I was sure he was aware of the additional threat.

Then, off to my right, where I had heard the sound of the safety, I heard a twig snap. Moving slightly to the right, I was able to see around a large tree that had been not only concealing me but also the area from where both sounds had originated. Taking one and a half steps backward and leaning to my right, I could see the silhouette of a man with a rifle aimed in the direction of the helicopter.

On the chance that he had come alone, I decided to give away my position. I brought the ten-gage to my shoulder and slid the safety to "fire when ready," which made an identical sound to the one I had just heard, and one which I was sure my new friend would recognize.

"Did you come alone?" I spoke softly, just above a whisper. The man with the rifle had been caught by surprise and was not sure who I was or how I got there. "Point that rifle to the sky, set the safety back on, and toss it into the water," I instructed.

"Who are you?" he demanded.

"That doesn't matter," I said. "Do as I tell you. I asked you a question. Are you alone?" I spoke still barely above a whisper. "And don't lie to me because if this goes sideways, you'll be the first one I shoot."

"Yeah, yeah. I'm alone," he said as he tossed the rifle into the lake.

"Cal!" I yelled. "Can you hear me?"

"I'm right here." Cal stepped out of the darkness and from the far side of my prisoner.

"I found this gentleman pointing a loaded rifle at the helicopter and heard him switch the safety off. It looked to me like he was waiting for you to resurface. I think he might have had murder on his mind. What do you think?"

"I think you might be right, Lou," Cal said as he placed Mr. Dale Stanley in handcuffs and under arrest.

"So, Cal, did you see him? Is that why you dove in the water?"

"No, I never did see him. I saw that camouflaged Super Cub tied up about two hundred yards down the shoreline and concluded that we had company, then I made my way through the water to the far side of the Cub and back up the shoreline to approach him from behind. I had just figured out where he was when I heard the safety click off on your ten-gage. I spent the rest of the time just watching you at work, Lou. It was a thing of beauty."

"He must have come in with his lights out while I was going down the ladder."

"You gentleman get that meat down from those meat poles," Cal instructed Stanley's three poaching clients. "Lou, can you take my prisoner back in that Super Cub of his? I am going to have a full load with all that moose meat. I'm just going to write these gentlemen a citation and come back for them tomorrow. In the meantime, I don't think they will be going very far."

"I can do that," I said.

Cal served Dale Stanley's clients with their citations and waded back to the still idling Bell Ranger, finished unlashing the canoe, and returned to shore. With Mr. Stanley cuffed and secured and the clients' weapons confiscated, I set about helping Cal load close to one thousand pounds of moose meat from the two remaining poached animals. Mr. Dale Stanley had obviously taken a whole moose out in the Super Cub earlier in the day when Kati and I had happened upon him. There was still about three hundred pounds left, which we loaded in the Cub, leaving just enough for the three men to have for food until Cal returned the next day to remove them from the preserve.

Cal closed the sliding door on the Bell Ranger, and the turbo began spooling up. As the helicopter struggled its way into the air, I turned my attention to the task of securing my load and prisoner.

Dale Stanley was tall, lean, ugly, and as mean as a junkyard dog. I could tell by his eyes and demeanor that he would not hesitate to kill me if I gave him any chance or opportunity to do so. It was also apparent that he had received some tactical training from somewhere. I assumed that he had been in the military, possibly the Army Rangers or maybe the Green Berets. Either way, I knew this fellow was sure he would be able to escape from my custody before we reached the Wasilla airport and was not above attempting to cause the airplane to crash, gambling that he could possibly survive it and giving him the chance he was looking for.

The Super Cub is a two-place tandem airplane with duel joystick controls that can literally haul anything you can close the doors on. With the remaining moose meat in the baggage area, I placed Stanley in the front with his hands cuffed behind the seat and his legs duct-taped together and secured to the front of the seat so he could not reach the rudders. I then tied a loop in a three-foot-length of rope and placed the loop over Stanley's head and against his throat, letting the remaining twenty inches or so of the rope hang down his back where I could reach it if I needed to persuade him to behave himself while we were in the air.

Stanley got the picture and was as good as a choirboy all the way home. I called Cal, and he met me at the Wasilla airport with another state trooper, who took over custody of Mr. Dale Stanley.

"Lou," Cal said turning toward me. "Thank you so much for your help. Just take that Cub to your place, and put that meat in your freezer. I have all I need for evidence and am out of room for keeping any more. To keep it from going to waste, you and Kati take it."

"Well, thanks, Cal. We can sure make good use of it. Thanks again," I said as I returned to the Super Cub.

"Oh, by the way. Why don't you grab some sleep and call me when you get up? If you want, you can go with me to get the other three."

"No problem, Cal. I'll give you a call. See ya later." I fired up the Cub.

Kati had locked herself in the house and closed all the blinds. When I drove up to the cabin, for a minute, I thought she might be gone. When she heard the Land Cruiser, she timidly opened the sliding door to the deck and peered out. "I saw that camouflaged airplane and was afraid it was that poacher guy," she said as she wrapped her arms around my neck.

"I'm sorry. I should have called you and let you know I would be flying a strange airplane. I have about three hundred pounds of moose meat in that Super Cub that Cal gave us for our freezer. If I put it in the back of the car, can you take it to the butcher and have it cut and wrapped, while I try to get some sleep?" I asked, using my most pathetic tone. "I'll be going with Cal again as soon as I wake up."

"Sure, baby, you know I will." She is always so willing to help.

Showered and shaved and with a whole four hours of sleep, I called Officer Cal Trent.

"Lou Worley, I can't begin to tell you what a huge help you were last night. Have you had anything to eat? If you haven't, I want to buy you lunch." Cal sounded excited.

"I just finished eating, Cal. Kati made plenty of pot roast. Come on over and have some."

"I'll be there in five minutes," Cal said.

I no sooner hung up when I heard the Ranger coming over the hill.

That was the first time Cal Trent had ever been in our home. Kati filled his belly to the brim with pot roast and biscuits while he proceeded to tell us his life story. Finally, two hours later, Cal and I strapped ourselves into the Ranger and lifting off, headed back to the preserve.

As we approached Telaquana Lake at two thousand feet above ground level, Trent circled the area where the three poachers had been camped and where we had left them barely twelve hours before. They were gone, and there was no sign of them.

Cal landed close enough so that we could wade ashore to investigate the campsite. Attached to a tree were all three of the citations Cal had written with two words inscribed on each one suggesting that Cal do something insanely perverted to himself. I could tell it made him mad.

CHAPTER 19

The game warden stared long and hard at the disturbing notation written on the three citations he had issued to the clients of poacher Dale Stanley only the day before.

"Cal, do you think someone picked them up?" I asked.

"I'm sure they did," Cal muttered, still staring at the citations. "The thing that gets me is, before they did this, they weren't in that much trouble. All they had to do was pay the fine. It wasn't like they were going to jail or anything, and it wasn't like they couldn't afford it. If you stop to think how much an out-of-state moose hunt costs these days, anyone who could afford that could certainly afford to pay this citation. Even if they refused to pay the fine and returned to Washington, all that would have happened is the court would have issued a bench warrant. Now, they have spit in the face of the people of Alaska, that's what infuriates me. When I catch them, I will see to it they pay the price." Calvin folded the citations and put them in his pocket.

"Let's get in the air and have a look. There is always that possibility they might have tried to walk out, though I doubt it." Cal headed toward the Bell Ranger still idling next to the shoreline. "By the way, Lou. Did you say those guys called Stanley and told him you were on their tail?"

Trent was referring to the day Kati and I had first spotted Stanley and his clients and we had followed him as far as Wasilla.

"I'm not positive, but he had no way of knowing we were behind him unless someone tipped him off," I said. "All I know is, suddenly he began flying erratically in an effort to lose me."

"That means he had a phone, and before he landed on the lake that night we picked him up, he took time to call someone to come and get his hunters. He must have figured I would just write them a citation."

Trent and I climbed back into the Ranger, and Cal soon had the helicopter above the trees. We circled the area of the poachers' camp. The extra moose meat we had left for them was also gone as was any trace that there had ever been a poaching violation. It was evident that someone with experience had helped with the cleanup.

Two hours later, with no sign of the three men, Trent turned the Bell Ranger toward Wasilla.

"So what will you do next?" I asked.

"Well, the problem is more with the budget than it is the game management end of things. The wildlife issue isn't seen as the most urgent usage of funds. For example, I have to write a report for every trip I make in this helicopter, which I use for both wildlife management enforcement and law enforcement purposes unrelated to game management. Therefore, I have two different sets of paperwork and must keep a log of everything I do with the aircraft.

My time is divided between everything from providing air support for the highway patrol to tracking down poachers and checking the hundreds of hunters and fisherman that are legally hunting and fishing. Along with showing up in court for every citation that gets disputed, I can get spread awful thin sometimes. I will go after these people, but it might take a while, and there are only five game wardens in the whole state. The outfitters who are selling these hunts to their unsuspecting clients and who then take them into the preserves and national park areas to find them a trophy are the ones I want. With no more resources than we have, it can sometimes take awhile for us to catch up to them, during which time they can kill a lot of animals and make a lot of money doing it."

Trent fell silent. I could tell he felt as if his hands were tied, and it seemed like the bad guys were always winning. I decided I wanted to help and I had an idea, but first I would need to consult with Rusty.

As Cal was dropping me off at my place, Kati called my cell phone and insisted he stay for a supper of moose roast, compliments of the poachers. We talked well into the evening.

"Cal, I have an idea," I said. "I need to talk to Rusty, but I would like to run something by you to see what you think. Every year at Puyallup, Washington, they have the hunters and sportsmen exhibition and trade show. I have been to it many times. Many of Alaska's guides and outfitters go there to sell their big game hunts.

"I could hire people to pose as businessmen purchasing those hunting trips. Of course, they would be trips of our choosing and with an outfitter of our choosing. They would take notes, pictures, and names, while documenting the exact locations where they took game along with any other information necessary for convictions. In four or five years, we could have every illegal outfitter and guide out of business."

"Lou, are you talking about using your own money to do that?" Trent asked.

"Absolutely. That gold we discovered is just as much an Alaskan resource as the wildlife, so I feel I have a responsibility, even an obligation, to reinvest it back into preserving any other Alaska resource that may be threatened. As far as the company Bell Ranger that you drive, I can buy us another helicopter that we can use that doesn't include a bunch of paperwork."

Trent was silent for a moment, not sure he had really heard what he had just heard. "It would have to be authorized by Bradley," Trent finally said thoughtfully. "Any kind of privately funded undercover operation that didn't have the sanction of the superintendant's office would run into shaky ground when it got into court. Maybe a special unit could be formed under the umbrella of game management that would have all the authority of the department."

The next day, I placed a call to the office of Arnold Bradley, the Superintendant of Public Safety. His secretary patched me through.

"Mr. Bradley, I would like to meet with you and bring Officer Calvin Trent along. Can you fit us into your appointment book somewhere?"

"Mr. Worley, I can throw this appointment book out and start a new one just for you," he said, jokingly. "When would you like to come in?"

"Well, I wouldn't want you to do that, but if you can meet us at the diner in thirty minutes I will buy you a slice of that homemade cherry pie."

"You got a deal, Lou. See you there."

Cal and I waited for Bradley to arrive before entering the diner, at which time the three of us asked for a table in a back room that was usually unoccupied except during peak business hours.

Trent spoke first. "Arnold, I am filling out the report on a poaching operation and an arrest that Lou helped me with the other night. I was telling Lou how out of control the poaching problem has become and how limited the budget is for effectively doing much about it." Trent paused as the waitress took our order.

"Yes, I heard about that, Cal. That was Dale Stanley again, wasn't it?"

"Yes, sir, it was. He was in the Lake Clark Preserve with his out-of-state clients who had three illegal moose on the ground, ready for transport. I cited the three of them and ordered them to stay put while Lou and I apprehended Stanley who tried to bushwhack me, obviously intending to kill an officer of the law. Lou made the apprehension, and we brought him and the poached moose meat out with us. When we went back, the three violators were gone, and we found their citations nailed to a tree in plain sight with this note scribbled on them."

Trent pulled from his pocket the crumpled citations and handed them to the Superintendant.

"I see," Bradley said as he studied the scribbled notations.

"They are laughing in our face, Arnold, and in the face of the people of Alaska. Lou has a suggestion that I told him he would need to share with you in person."

Trent relaxed in his seat and began to sip his coffee. I was sitting directly across from Arnold who immediately turned his gaze toward me as if expecting a long, drawn-out, less-than-profound dissertation on how to catch poachers, which was exactly what he got.

"Mr. Bradley, what would you be able to do about the poaching problem in Alaska if you had an unlimited budget to work with?"

Arnold appeared caught off guard. "Well, probably beef up our whole game management resources. More officers in the field, more equipment to work with, better pay and benefits. Basically everything we are doing now, we would be able to do more of."

"I'm sure Cal and the other field officers would appreciate that, but if you don't mind my asking, how would that put a stop to the illegal poaching of Alaskan wildlife by maverick outfitters selling illegal out-of-state hunts?" I paused for a moment, not sure how Arnold would take that.

"Actually, the extra money would probably get swallowed up in the bureaucracy, overloading me with more paperwork and very little to show for it in terms of out-of-business poachers," Bradley said. "So, Lou, why don't you tell me what it is you are proposing?"

"I am prepared to finance the expense of a special undercover unit of private investigators posing as hunting clientele. The unit would purchase special hunts at the sportsmen shows and exhibitions that take place out of state where the illegal outfitters advertise their hunting packages.

"During their hunting trip, they would take pictures, names, record events and conversations, use tape recorders, and document any illegal violations that take place. Documentation that, in the event their actions are illegal, could convict them, or vindicate them, if in fact they are conducting a legal operation. But it would necessarily need to be sanctioned by the Office of Game Management." I paused, waiting for some indication from Bradley that my idea may be feasible.

Arnold looked at Trent.

"Cal, have you spoken to the governor about this?"

"No, sir. You know I would never go over your head. But if you want me to, I will."

"I'll let you know, but right now, I want to hear more from, Lou. What about back up? We cannot provide as much air support as the kind of operation you are proposing would need, and I do not want civilians stranded without support. When it's time for them to get out of there, we would have to move fast or they could be in danger."

"I will provide whatever is needed. I can make one phone call and two Bell Rangers would show up at my place within twenty-four hours. However, just so you know, the people who would be involved in this would be professionals, ex-military Seals and Green Berets trained in ways you do not even want to know about. They will not need a lot of back up.

It would be just a matter of picking up the already apprehended subjects along with the necessary documentation collected for their convictions."

"You make it sound easy," Bradley mused.

"With the right people and without the political and bureaucratic handcuffs, there is no reason why it couldn't be just that, Mr. Superintendant."

Bradley thought carefully for several minutes while we turned our attention to the cherry pie alamode that had arrived at our table.

"Cal, I can't authorize a covert operation such as this on my own without a nod from the governor, and I'm sure she will want to talk to the attorney general before she gives the go-ahead. Therefore, I suggest that you and Lou talk to her and then get back with me. One more thing, the privately organized taskforce would need to work under a subcontract with the state, operating in total secrecy. If the governor gives us the nod, I then want you and Lou to be in charge of it, and I will hold the both of you responsible for its outcome. Is that understood?" Cal and I agreed.

Rusty, Mitchell, and Richard had purchased the rights to an active claim at the Eva Creek mine located 185 miles north of Wasilla and only twenty miles north of the McKinley Park entrance. It was a placer mine, and the boys had been working the claim the last two years with a mining subcontractor from Fairbanks who had brought in drilling equipment and a crew of three men.

They were finding gold, but it came in little pockets and sliver veins that involved drilling, blasting, tunneling, and chemical processing to retrieve. The profits were slim in comparison to Alfred Creek, but the boys still had the gleam in their eyes, so they felt it was worth the work. Rusty was providing all of the air support to the mine with the Pilatus Porter, and Mitchell and Richard were supervising the operation.

I called Rusty, and over the next hour, I filled him in on the events of the last week involving the poachers and the conversation Officer Trent and I had with the superintendent. Rusty said he would call Kevin and Brenda and let me know when they could meet with us.

It was two more weeks before the Gaithers arrived from Spanaway. Brenda had spent some time locating the three clients of Dale Stanley who had skipped out on paying the citations. They were all three used-car salesman from the Vancouver area of Washington State.

We all met at the office in the hangar along with Calvin Trent and spent the better part of three hours discussing the planning and execution of a feasible covert operation. Kevin and Brenda had a long list of people who would be perfect for the job, some of which had worked as undercover clientele in Africa, busting both diamond and ivory smugglers. I said to Kevin,

"Kevin, as soon as we get the go ahead from the Governor I want those car salesmen in Vancouver to miraculously show up in Alaska where Cal will be able to personally serve them with a warrant. Also be sure the people that are working for you understand that those guys are not to know how they even got here. Do you get my point?"

"I understand." Kevin answered. "Believe me they will go to sleep in Vancouver and wake up in Alaska and never have a clue how it happened."

At that point, it was only a matter of getting the okay from Mrs. Trent, who un-fortunately was tied up with some political matters in Washington DC. We would have to wait for her return.

CHAPTER 20

C alvin Trent parked his game warden Ford Expedition in front of my office at precisely 3:00 a.m. It was a beautiful Monday morning with clear skies all the way to California, and we had a 10:00 a.m. appointment with the governor and attorney general five hours away in Juneau.

We rolled the 180, mounted on amphibious floats, out of the heated hangar, loaded our bags, and with Kati in the backseat, woke up the chickens as we pointed the spinner south to Juneau Harbor. It would be an overnight excursion due to the fact that Cal hadn't seen his wife in awhile.

The governor had insisted that we bring Kati and join them for dinner later in the evening. Kati was giddy with anticipation. When she gets like that, she has a habit of rubbing the palms of her hands together very fast as if she were trying to warm them. I always look around to see if anyone is watching whenever she does this.

It was a beautiful ride. I leveled off at 9,500 feet msl. The air was as smooth as a magic carpet, and with not a cloud in the sky, it was the truest blue I had ever seen; the vistas were breathtaking. Mesmerized by the incredible scenery, we said very little.

I reflected on the aviation pioneers who had paved the original airways to Alaska back in the early 1920s and 1930s, wondering at the courage and grit that inspired them to explore Alaska's hostile environments. I respected and even honored them, and with my right hand—oblivious to the presence of both Kati and Cal—saluted their memory. Cal's voice interrupted my meditations.

"What was that for, Lou?"

Somewhat embarrassed, I instantly snapped out of my hallmark moment. Kati was rubbing her hands and giggling again.

"I don't know, just thinking," I said. I knew that Cal understood.

After about four and a half hours suspended in tranquility, it suddenly occurred to me that Juneau was straight ahead and only twenty more miles. It would be my first time landing at the Seaplane base next to Juneau International."

Because there was no wind, I was expecting glassy water conditions, so I was pleasantly surprised to find just enough current to provide adequate depth perception all the way to touchdown. As the floats settled onto the water and the airplane temporarily became a boat, I reduced power, dropped the mechanical water rudders, and idled toward the pier. With just enough momentum to maintain effective water rudder control, I cut the engine, maneuvering the floatplane at a slow glide alongside and against the dock. Cal climbed out and, stepping onto the pontoons, secured the floats to the tie-downs.

Cal, who made regular trips to Juneau for family business, headed straight for a nearby parking lot where he kept a little Toyota Camry. It was only eight-thirty in the morning, so we drove to a nearby restaurant for a quick breakfast.

Promptly seated and served at the Capital Street Café, it was evident that Cal Trent was a familiar face to the patrons and servers.

"Have you met the new attorney general?" Cal asked me.

"No, I haven't. All I know is his name is Terrill Bishop, and I understand that he is definitely a step-up from the last one we had."

"His wife has a second cousin who is the mother of someone you know."

"Really!" I said. "Who would that be?"

Cal looked at Kati with a slight grin on his face, hesitating for effect before answering. "Beltray Gibbons."

Kati's mouth fell open as she gasped for air. Before she could start rubbing her hands, I pinned them to her lap.

"You have to be kidding me! Is that for real?" I asked in amazement.

"It's for real. Bishop's wife's name is Pamela, and she has a second cousin named Loraine, who gave birth to Beltray when she was seventeen years old and gave him up for adoption. Beltray doesn't know about it. His biological mother never knew who adopted her son or what become of him. His adopted parents let him run wild, and he grew up more in than out of the reformatory. The attorney general and his wife Pamela, as well as the governor, are aware of what you did for Beltray, putting him in that school and getting him off drugs."

"Does that mean we are going to get their support for this covert operation?"

"I think that is a foregone conclusion, this little get-together is just a formality."

We ordered our breakfast and talked about the day when we could just relax and go fishing like normal rich people do. Cal looked at his watch and motioned for the waitress to bring the bill.

The state capitol building was only a short distance from the café. Traveling back on Marine Way, we turned north on Main. Just past Fourth Street, we entered an iron-gated entrance where the guard, who obviously knew Cal, waved us through to the reserved parking.

It was 9:55 when we were ushered into a private study adjacent to the governor's office. Five minutes later, the door to her office opened, and Governor Nanci Trent entered the room, accompanied by Attorney General Terrill Bishop and his wife, Pamela.

The governor first approached her husband with a warm greeting and embrace, and then greeted Kati and me with the same except I didn't get the embrace. Terrill and Pamela Bishop introduced themselves as the governor invited us into her office. Pamela and Kati remained in the study.

"Mr. Worley." The governor began. "My husband has briefed me on your suggestions for conducting a counterattack on the out-of-control poaching trade that is running rampant throughout Alaska, and I want you to know that I am all for giving you anything you want to get this done. However, I want Mr. Bishop to work directly with you in this operation to make sure it is legal and constitutional. I do not want it coming back and biting me in the hind end. Is that understood?"

I looked at Cal at the same time he looked at me, unable to conceal the grin that had taken over his face.

"Yes ma'am," I said.

"Well gentleman, I have business with those two ladies who are waiting for me in the other room, so I will leave the three of you to work out the logistics and details to all of this among yourselves." Turning to Terrill, she added, "Mr. Bishop, when you are satisfied with their plan, I want you to give Lou and his people your full support and the authority of the state's law enforcement powers. This is to be top secret. I want a sealed, documented file of the operation on my desk as soon as you can get it there. No one in this office is to know about this except the four of us and Mr. Bradley the Superintendant." As she walked toward the door, she paused.

"You may use my office for the rest of the day. I am going shopping with some lady friends. Oh, Cal, the dinner at the Governor's Mansion is at 8:00pm. We will have your tuxedoes ready by 6pm. Don't be late." The governor closed the door as she left. I looked in bewilderment at Cal.

"What are the tuxedoes for?"

"Oh, didn't I tell you? We have all been invited to a formal banquet tonight at the mansion."

For the next four hours, the attorney general discussed with Cal and me the existing game laws and the loopholes that many lawyers were using to successfully plead the cases of their out-of-state clients. By the time the majority of the cases reached the overcrowded court systems, they were either plead-out with a reduced fines or completely thrown out for lack of evidence.

Terrill made it clear that certain specific evidence would be required in order to prove a case that, by the time it came to court, may be two or three years old. We would need undeniable proof, such as video of the kill; proof of the illegal location; proof of the month, day, and year of the hunt; receipts connecting the hunter to the outfitter, etc. With those types of things for solid evidence, the hunters and the outfitters would find it difficult to retain a lawyer who could do much more than take their money.

The covert task force would operate as a subcontracting undercover unit on special assignment by the attorney general's office. Though separate from the existing game management division, it would work in cooperation and under the direct supervision of the head game warden Calvin Trent, who in turn would answer only to Superintendant Arnold Bradley. The authorization was for one year and would come up for re-evaluation annually in December. We knew we would need to work fast.

With that business completed, we went in search of the wives. We still had a few hours left before the banquet. Cal called his wife and dropped me off where the ladies had stopped for lunch. Mr. and Mrs. Cal Trent then disappeared for a while.

Three hours later Cal called me and said he would pick us up at the same place he had dropped me. A half-hour later, we were in the Governor's Mansion a few blocks away between the two streets named Calhoun and Indian. Kati and I followed one of the mansion's aids, who escorted us to a guest room where we found her evening gown and my tuxedo lain out on the bed.

With a seating capacity of one thousand, the banquet hall was vary large, at least the same size of the assembly hall at the Bettles Learning Center. Decorated with a huge display of flags, flowers, ribbons, and bows, it reminded me of the Republican National Convention I had seen televised prior to the last presidential election.

Kati and I followed Cal as we were ushered to a large table set with twenty-five place settings that was located next to an elevated speaker's platform and situated in such a way that the seated dinner guests could see both the podium and banquet hall.

Folded name cards placed in the center of each plate established the pre-determined seating arrangements. Obviously, six of those seats were reserved for the governor and her husband, the attorney general and his wife, and, of course, Kati and me. I assumed the additional place settings were simply for effect since there were no name cards with the exception of two settings bearing the names of Arnold and Megan Bradley, who had not yet arrived.

I smiled at my wife, who was rubbing her hands again from her giddy anticipations. At least she was doing it under the table, somewhat concealing her uncontrollable urge. She is so funny and so genuine. I leaned over and whispered in her ear, "I love you, sugar." Immediately, the hands came up and around my neck. At least the rubbing stopped for a minute.

"I love you too, baby. I'm so proud of you." The hand rubbing started again.

"Cal," I said. "This seems a little much for dinner out. Wouldn't it have been cheaper to go to the Capital Café, just the six of us?"

"We just happened to show up at the same time a special guest flew in that the governor is throwing a big party for," Cal said. "Plus, it's a last hurrah for Nanci, who will be leaving office next month. There are dignitaries here from at least thirty other states, including Washington DC. I also understand that one of the former presidents along with a country music artist will be here."

"Wow, did you hear that, sugar? Which president?"

Cal had turned to talk to one of the other guests. Kati was rubbing the palms of her hands fast enough to start a campfire in a downpour.

Suddenly, I heard movement behind me, but before I could get turned around, two arms were wrapped around my neck and someone—who I instantly recognized as my daughter Keera—was kissing my cheek. As I stood up and looked behind me, I realized our whole family had arrived: Rusty and Keera, with the twins, Manson and Michelle; Mitchell, Kelly, and their three children, Walker, Rhiannon, and Tristan; and trailing close behind were Richard and Kathy with Randy and, of course, little Elaine. It seems Kati had been responsible for the missing name cards because she wanted to surprise me.

I was so busy greeting, hugging, and kissing my daughters and grandchildren, that I was completely unaware of the applause my family's arrival had generated. Gradually, the rest of the guests, including Arnold and Mrs. Bradley, arrived along with Terrill Bishop and his wife.

Excusing himself from the table, the Attorney General stepped to the podium, gaining a brief applause. Pausing until the applause subsided, he began speaking. "Ladies and gentleman, dignitaries and special guests, we welcome you to Juneau, Alaska."

The audience once again responded with a round of applause.

"Allow me to introduce to you tonight, and please give a warm welcome to a very special guest ..."(more applause) " ... from the *other great state* of *Texas* ... (more applause, whistling, hooting, yelling) " ... the former president of the United States of America ..." (screaming, whistling, applause, hollering) " ... Mr. ..." The roaring was so loud I couldn't make out which ex-president he said it was.

I leaned over against Kati's ear.

"Who did he say it was?"

"Sssshhhh. Listen."

"Oh, there they are. I see who it is now."

As the former president and his wife stood waving and greeting the assembly, I thought the applause and screaming would never end. Kati and Keera were both covering their ears.

The attorney general continued. "We have another special guest tonight who has generously consented to sing the National Anthem. Please give another warm welcome to country music artist and performer Mr. ..." Again, the noise level reached eardrum-damaging proportions, and again, I missed who he said it was. Then he made his way to the podium, and I recognized him.

With the applause for George's countrified rendition of the National Anthem subsided, Terrill Bishop returned to the microphone. "Ladies and gentlemen," he began. "Let me now introduce the lady who has put Alaska on the map in a whole new way and who singlehandedly has changed the world's understanding of Alaskans and Alaskan life. Please welcome the governor of Alaska, Nanci Trent!" Everyone in the place rose, and the roar of applause was once again deafening as the governor emerged from behind a curtain and stepped to the podium. Patiently, she waited for the noise to diminish so that she could speak. Each time she was about to begin, the applause would once again increase. Finally, the assembly of over nine hundred resigned themselves to quiet.

"Ladies and gentlemen, constituents, dignitaries, honored guests, and citizens of this great state, welcome to Juneau, Alaska. We are here tonight to pay tribute to a special friend of Alaska. This banquet is in honor of that special guest.

"Before we introduce this individual, however, I would like to take this opportunity to thank the people of Alaska for your support and for the opportunity and privilege of serving as the governor of this great state during this last term. As you know, I will be leaving office in a month. I have accepted ..."

I leaned over to nudge Kati.

"Is she talking about G. W.?" Kati just squeezed my hand, which I think meant "be quiet."

The governor continued, addressing economic goals for Alaska in terms of trade and industry, and the responsibility of government to expend whatever means necessary to protect Alaska's natural resources for future generations.

"Now I would like to introduce a very special and honored guest along with his family. Please give a warm welcome to Mr. Louis Lowell Worley. Mr. Worley, would you please join me at the podium?"

I was stunned. I wanted to say no, but did not dare. The place was roaring with applause, and I could barely find my way around the table. Keera—always looking out for her daddy—got me headed in the right direction. My legs felt like they were full of lead and it seemed as if I was walking in slow motion as I made my way to the steps leading to the podium where the governor of Alaska stood applauding vigorously as I approached her. First, she greeted me with a firm handshake and then a courtesy hug. Then turning toward my family, she motioned with her arms for them to stand.

"Ladies and gentlemen, please also welcome the Worley family." The applause continued, and the stage-lights from the balcony lit us all up like a Christmas tree as the governor introduced each member of my family, beginning with Kati all the way to my youngest grandchild, Laney.

The applause gradually diminished until it was again quiet, and the governor was able to continue.

"Ten years ago this coming spring, a truck driver on vacation from Washington State, flew his private plane to Alaska in search of adventure. Not only did he find an adventure, he fortuitously discovered a fortune in gold.

"Most men, I would venture to guess, would have taken their newfound wealth and returned to where they came from. But not Lou Worley, he instead, relocated his entire family to Alaska and has reinvested over two billion dollars back into the people of this great state.

"I doubt there is anyone here who has not heard of the William Shearer Center of Learning in Bettles, Alaska, that the Shearer/Worley Foundation has funded. Let me tell you that from that learning center there emerges a constant stream of educated, trained, and contributing members to Alaska's communities and economies. There is, as I speak, two more of the learning centers under construction in Naknek and Sitka scheduled for completion within the next two years.

"Lou Worley has been responsible for the restoration of hundreds of dysfunctional communities throughout Alaska's interior and beyond, bringing the drug organizations operating in Alaska practically to extinction by eliminating the customer base for their product.

"Tonight, we are here to honor this man and his family. These are the people and others like them who guarantee the future of Alaska and its communities. This is the standard of character needed in our leaders, who serve as role models to our children."

The governor stepped away from the podium, turning toward me as she initiated another spectacular round of applause.

I was soaked with perspiration. My knees were shaking, and I would have run had I not been so paralyzed that I was unable to move.

Stepping back to the microphone, the governor continued, "There is a medal that Alaska has reserved in honor of citizens who have exemplified the highest standard of selflessness and contribution to the people of Alaska. We call it The Alaska Citizen Medal of Honor."

Opening a silver box with the Governor of Alaska state seal stamped on its lid, she removed a gold medal bearing the same emblem attached to a braided, gold-silver-and-purple cord and placed it around my neck.

"People of Alaska and of America, the greatest need of our societies, is for role models. Our young people need role models for character and integrity, role models for citizenry and patriotism, but most especially, role models for functional family life. Ladies and gentleman and all of America, please allow me to present *your* role model Mr. Louis Lowell Worley!

"Thank you, Mr. Worley. Alaska thanks you, and America thanks you."

The whole thing in Juneau finally ended with several television interviews from local and national news agencies that no matter how hard I tried, I was unable to avoid.

Shortly after returning home, Cal and I attended a meeting in the new hangar with Rusty, Kevin, and Brenda Gaither. It was the last week of February, and the sportsman show in Puyallup, Washington, had already been held the third week in January.

Cal laid out the rules and guidelines set forth by the attorney general for the undercover operation we were planning. He also handed Kevin a list of the legitimate outfitters that had operated in Alaska for many years and whose outfitting services were economically impacted by the illegal hunters. On the list were the suspected illegal operators he wanted to begin investigating immediately. At the top was the outfit Dale Stanley had run and was still in operation, even while he was out on bond awaiting trial.

Kevin handed Cal a list of thirty-six people available for the operations, complete with their pictures, background checks, qualifications and verifiable covert work history. Of those, twenty were immediately available and under retainer; sixteen had already been enlisted in anticipation of the approval of our proposed operation. Cal and I had given Rusty and Kevin the go-ahead, and eight of the big-game outfitters on our list of suspect operations had already sold big-game hunts to sixteen of our undercover operatives working together in pairs.

Once we had brought an outfitter up on charges, none of the agents involved in that bust would be useful as undercover agents again due to the risk of detection. Therefore, a long list of potential ex-military operatives would be necessary for future cases. I really would have loved to be more involved in it all, but, of course, that was out of the question due to my now very high visibility.

Coincidently, Dale Stanley's three car salesmen clients from Vancouver Washington were discovered sitting on the steps of the Office of Public Safety building in Wasilla with their copy of the citations Cal had written them stuffed in their shirt pockets. Imagine that!

CHAPTER 21

J ust over two years had passed since the banquet at the Governor's
Mansion. Nanci Trent's political career was on hold as she pursued
more personal celebrity status.

The undercover covert operations we had conducted using Kevin's
operatives had succeeded in busting twenty-three illegal hunting guide
operations, mostly involving international clients.

Dale Stanley lost his bid for freedom and was doing ten-to-twenty at
the penitentiary in Fairbanks for attempted murder of an officer of the law
while in the performance of his duty. Three vary reliable witness's from
Washington were among those who testified against him.

The doors to the learning centers at Naknek and Sitka had opened,
and the classes and dormitories were already bulging with students of all
ages. Genneta Williams turned the flight program at Bettles over to her
husband, Jeffery, while she supervised the construction of the runway and
establishment of another flight school and air taxi service at both Sitka
and Naknek.

The center at Sitka was now the largest of the three centers. Spread out
over 150 acres on a three-hundred-acre parcel of land, the school included
a hospital complete with a surgery department and trauma center, drug
rehabilitation and psych wards, as well as an air ambulance operation
hosting three Sikorski 76A, medivac helicopters.

Although Gerard had appointed and supervised the superintendents
responsible for the construction, Keera had overseen the establishment of

the medical facilities and medivac operations at the two new centers. An additional fifteen fixed-wing airplanes of various makes and models made up the flight school fleet as well as four Cessna 208 Caravans the school used for air taxi operations and student transportation.

It had been eleven years since I had arrived in Alaska in my little straight tail 172. It was mind-boggling how much had happened since then. With the family spread out among the three learning centers and the Eva Creek mine, Kati and I spent way too many weekends at home alone wishing they were with us.

Our youngest grandchild, Elaine, almost nine, had grown up with Calvin and Nanci Trent's son Anthony, who just turned eleven, and we all anticipated that the Trent family and the Worley clan eventually might become related.

Kati and Keera were in Paducah, Kentucky, visiting her mother, whose husband—Kati's stepfather—had passed away the month before. My mother-in-law, still mentally sharp as a tack and eighty-five years young, was now ready to come to live with her daughter. Mom would fly back with Kati and Keera commercially.

While finalizing her mother's financial matters and arranging for her belongings to be shipped to Alaska, Kati was busy showing Keera where she was born and had spent her childhood. I did not expect them to be home for at least another week to ten days.

Spring had arrived. I had been planning an adventure for several years that I was sure Kati would not approve of, so, with her and Keera in Kentucky, I felt it would be the perfect time to go for it.

A package had arrived in the mail over three years before from Genneta Williams, about the time of the Dale Stanley incident. Included was a letter from Genneta along with a large manila envelope bulging with old pictures, maps, and newspaper articles.

"Mr. Worley," the letter began, "my father wanted you to have this. He never got around to finding the downed aircraft, but said if anyone could, it would be you."

Forty-three years prior to the year I landed my little Cessna on the gumbo-covered airstrip at Alfred Creek and during Arthur Bold's long flying career in Alaska, the local news media reported that a Russian pilot, thought to have smuggled diamonds into the US, had apparently gone down somewhere north of Nome. The date was given as October 1953.

Canada had held the distinction of being the third largest producer of diamonds for at least a dozen years, the majority of which were coming out of the northwest territories and the Yukon. Much of Canada's diamond revenue was being lost in the smuggling operations that were bringing the precious stones into the US and selling them through black market sources significantly affecting the market price of the homegrown diamonds. In those days, there was little man-power and even less technology for pursuing or apprehending smugglers.

Canada was not the only source of uncut diamonds for the smuggling operations. Siberia was a less traveled but nonetheless frequently used route from the far east to the US underground market. The popular conjecture was that the Russian had crossed the icy waters of the Bering Sea with a fortune in diamonds—and who knows what else—bound for some remote rendezvous in the territory of Alaska.

I had spent a hundred hours pouring over the information that Arthur Bold had provided. He had obviously been quite fascinated with the story, for he had preserved every newspaper article including any maps that pertained to the mysterious sighting of the presumed downed aircraft.

No one would have even known there was such an airplane, or if it was loaded with diamonds or chicken feed for that matter, except for an old timer and his dogs that were out for a walk one evening near the little town of Port Clarence on the west coast of Alaska, fifty miles northwest of Nome.

The Russian-designed Antonov came out of the north-northwest, flying low under a solid overcast in less than two-miles of visibility due to fog and light snow and fifty feet above the old-timers head. Over the little village of Singigyak, the huge floatplane turned due east toward the Feather River airstrip, which, at that time of the year, would most likely be covered with a layer of ice and snow. After circling the field at Feather River several times—possibly calculating if there was enough room to land and take-off—the AN-2 turned east up the Glacial Lake drainage toward Salmon Lake.

The old man notified the coast guard the next morning, but no one ever saw the aircraft again. Some say it flew all the way to the Yukon without landing in Alaska at all. Others speculated that it crashed in the Kiglua mountains from fuel exhaustion. Arthur Bold was sure that he knew exactly where.

There was a note from Arthur attached to one of the maps:

To Lou Worley:

I always said if I ever got the time I would go look for the Russian smuggler. I never did, but I sure hope you will. I want you to have everything I compiled over the years. All the information you need is in this envelope. Take my word for it, that old Russian airplane is right where I believe he is.

I don't know exactly where the Russian plane took off from, but if he was indeed a smuggler, he probably had a load of diamonds coming from India or Russia, in which case he had flown all the way across Siberia to the Alaska territory on his way to either a fuel cache or a rendezvous. One thing is sure: He would have had some fuel quantity issues by the time he reached the northwest coastline. It is my guess that, due to the weather conditions at the time, he had burned too much fuel trying to figure out where he was in relation to where he wanted to go. I do not think he got very far after the old man last saw him. If I were you, I would start where I have made an X on the map about twenty-five miles due east of Singigyak. You may find him at the bottom of Glacial Lake, and I will tell you why I think that.

Judging from the description of the airplane provided by the eyewitness, the Russian was flying a 1947 Antonov AN-2, a Russian-designed and Polish-built bi-wing with an eight-hundred nm (nautical miles) fuel range under ideal conditions. The weather that night was anything but ideal, and the pilot may have already been running on fumes as he crossed the Bering Strait and the coastline at Port Clarence.

It occurred to me that he may have had extra fuel on board in the form of four or five fifty-gallon drums, giving him an extra two hundred or more gallons; enough to get him to his next rendezvous, if he could find a frozen lake where he could land the big floatplane and refuel.

I believe that is why he paused to circle the airstrip at Feather River.

At that time of year, it would have been unlikely that the pilot would find a lake frozen with a sufficient amount of ice to support the weight of the AN-2, even if it were loaded lightly. However, most of the lakes would have had more than enough ice to support several inches of snow, which could deceive a tired pilot in poor visibility conditions. He would have been looking for a lake remote enough that he could refuel and wait out the deteriorated weather without detection. Glacial Lake would have met every criterion, and with the freshly fallen snow on the thin layer of ice in reduced visibility and out of fuel, attempting a landing on Glacial Lake was probably the only option he had left. As the big floatplane transitioned its weight onto the thin layer of ice, it broke through and flipped the airplane upside down, which immediately sunk to the bottom of the lake. I am sure that by the time anyone investigated that area for the wreckage of a downed aircraft, the lake had again frozen over, leaving no trace of what had happened. I know it is speculation, but I'm sure you can see why I believe that Glacial Lake is precisely where he ended up.

For the last three years, I had pondered Arthur's speculations, and the more I did, the more they metamorphosed into solid evidence. I was ready for another great adventure and diamonds were as good as gold, as far as I was concerned.

The 180 Skywagon was in the hangar having the main gear and skis replaced with the amphibious floats. I loaded my scuba gear and eight-man emergency life raft along with a substantial amount of camping supplies and food for at least two months.

It was a gray day, with ceilings of two thousand feet overcast, when I lifted into the air from our home airport. Sliding through Shellbarger Pass, I emerged from the west side of the Alaska Range and pointed the nose toward McGrath, my first fuel stop. Another three hours, and I was having a late lunch and visiting with Jerry Hansen in Nome while the Skywagon, once again was refueled.

Glacial Lake was only twenty-six miles north of Nome as the crow flies. The coastal weather always stacks up against the Kiglua Mountain Range where the three-mile-long lake lies in a north to south position perpendicular to and on the south slope of the east-west range of mountains. Two, three-thousand-foot-high ridges guard the east and west shorelines of the lake that also provide a venturi for high winds in unstable conditions.

On the day I flew into Glacial Lake, however, it was dead calm. Conditions were ceilings of seven hundred feet and ten miles visibility until the far north end of the lake where the cloud layer that stacked directly against the towering cliffs made a go-around impossible. A cloudless day would have allowed me to do an over-flight of the lake from a much higher altitude, enabling me to see into the depth of the water. However, due to the lower cloud levels, I dragged the lake from only one hundred feet above the surface.

The lake was narrow, but I still had a half-mile of turning radius as I slowed the floatplane to maneuvering speed, checking for logs or other obstructions that could eat my floats. The water was dead calm and eerily dark, suggesting that it was deep or at least green with lake-weed on the bottom.

The first one-quarter of the lake on the south end was semi-separated from the north end by an outcrop of land extending westward from the east shoreline one hundred yards wide that reached nearly halfway across the lake. Sparsely timbered with short scrub and a sandy beach on the north side, it appeared to be suitable for camping and beaching the floatplane. I decided I would set the Skywagon on the water just north of that outcrop, do an about face, and taxi back to the sandy shore.

Completing my third turn over the landing zone, I was satisfied I had sufficiently memorized the surroundings and was ready to fly the approach. Descending through two hundred feet with flaps at thirty degrees, I set up the glassy-water landing attitude.

The problem with landing on glassy water is it confuses your depth perception, without which you may arrive at the water before you expect or after. Either case could mean catastrophe. With pitch attitude and power preset for a one-hundred-foot-per-minute descent rate, I let the airplane settle itself onto the glassy surface.

As the airplane touched the water, I reduced power gradually, letting the floats transition off the step and settle into the water. WHAM! The 180 violently lurched toward the right. I saw what appeared to be a large portion of the right pontoon come out of the water and tear into the underside of the right wing while at the same time the left float collapsed from the sheer force of the side load. The airplane was in a forty-five-degree angle to the right, but still moving straight ahead and the left float, unable to sustain the side load, collapsed. The left wing dipped straight into the water and buckled like a straw.

As suddenly as it happened, it was over. I had been violently yanked from one direction to another so fast that it was all still a blur. Then I realized that the airplane was sinking rapidly, and I needed to get out. Clawing at my seat belt, I set myself free and opened the pilot-side door.

The eight-man emergency life raft, strategically located directly behind the pilot seat, was the first item I tossed from the sinking craft that was rapidly filling with water. Yanking the self-inflation cord, the rubber raft exploded into the most beautiful boat on the planet.

I stayed in the icy glacier water as long as the cabin of the plane was still accessible, retrieving one emergency pack, the scuba gear, and my trusty ten-gage. All of the two-month supply of additional provisions—food, stove and stove fuel, water, extra clothing, tent, and a hundred other miscellaneous items that I had esteemed as useful and necessary for my wonderful adventure—were now on the way to the bottom of the lake. Shivering uncontrollably, I climbed into the raft and watched the tail of my beloved 180 disappear into the dark water.

CHAPTER 22

I guessed the air temperature at around forty-six degrees Fahrenheit. Having just emerged from the glacial water, whose temperature I also estimated at something significantly lower than the air temperature, my body was shuddering violently in an attempt to stave off the effects of hypothermia. I fished through my survival pack for the miniature pit shovel, mumbling something about paying five thousand dollars for a life raft that had not even come with an oar.

Stripping off my wet clothing, I paddled toward the spit of land I had seen from the air as furiously as possible in an effort to increase my body heat. Upon reaching the north shoreline of the spit, I then retrieved my wetsuit from the scuba pack. It was a bit of a chore getting it on, but finally accomplished, I began to feel warmth gradually returning to my body.

The life raft was equipped with a built-in rain hood and fly, a mosquito netting-type of material. From my emergency pack, I took a portable propane heater and, lighting it, returned to the semi-enclosed raft. As I waited for the warmth of the heater and the wetsuit to return my core temperature to normal, I plaintively considered my options.

I had the scuba gear and with it an underwater light, but the portable camp generator with the extra five gallons of gas had gone down with the ship. The underwater lamp was only good for two hours and then would need recharging. I had the ten-gage shotgun, but my Desert Eagle was also underwater. All of a sudden, whatever was in the Russian airplane—if it even existed—was worthless, and all that was in my airplane was far more valuable than any diamonds.

On the bright side, providing that the lake was not too deep, I would be able to make several trips down to the 180 before my light battery and oxygen level were all gone. The .44 magnum, portable generator, and additional gas and spare oxygen tanks were the priority. Feeling sufficiently warmed, I turned off the little heater and set about to gather wood for a fire.

It was indeed a beautiful location. Unlike Alfred Creek where the pounding of the water eventually numbed your ears into not even hearing it anymore, this place was so quiet I could hear my own heart beat.

Still early in the evening, I loaded my gear into the raft and made my way toward the spot where the airplane had sunk. Then I remembered. I had hit something. I almost forgot about that. Something just under the water, maybe a foot or less, had opened my right float like a sardine can. Looking back over my shoulder, I tried to remember the exact approach path I had taken as I set up for the glassy-water landing—which, by the way, had been perfectly executed up to the point of impact with the underwater float opener.

Gradually, I worked my way northward correcting and re-correcting my path, searching and fishing with the pit shovel for whatever it was I had encountered. Suddenly, I felt it. Hooking the corner of my shovel onto the edge of a large piece of sharp granite, submerged less than five inches under the surface of the water, I pulled the rubber raft alongside to gaze at the steeple-shaped pinnacle of a granite spire, protruding straight up from the bottom of the lake like a giant stalagmite.

I cut a three-foot-length of rope from the sixty-foot coil I had brought with me in the emergency pack and tied it to the granite vertex. Removing one of the eight built-in life jackets from the raft, I then secured a floating buoy, visible from the air.

From there, I proceeded toward the place I had last seen my Skywagon. I had to use my imagination to select the spot. There were so many things I was wishing I had paid attention to— for instance, some object on shore abeam the spot where it had sunk. Suddenly, I saw a water bubble emerge to the surface and realized that would be trapped air from the baggage compartment, marking the spot for me. Immediately, I made a mental note of the details of the shoreline abeam that spot.

Tying the end of the long rope to the bottom rung of the manufacturer-provided stepladder attached to the side of the raft, I tossed the remaining rope into the lake. It was now time to dive. I had no idea how deep the water was at this midpoint of the lake, but was hoping it wouldn't be more than forty or fifty feet. I only hoped my rope would be long enough to tie to the top of the sunken aircraft and still reach the surface.

I strapped on my tanks, belted on my waist weights, and with the underwater light attached to my chest, rolled backward off the raft, taking the rope with me. Slowly, I let the two weights take me down. Past ten feet it became so black; I could not see my hand in front of my face.

I had descended at least thirty feet by the time I switched on the light to have a look. There was nothing there but more blackness. I was wondering if the air bubble had come from the 180 or something else. I turned the light out and descended further. At a depth of forty-five feet, I again, switched on the light and, to my surprise, was staring directly at the corroded remains of an Antonov AN-2. I felt both excitement and disappointment at the same time. Turning toward the north end of the ancient Russian floatplane, resting tail down on the crumpled remains of its badly corroded pontoons, I detected a shadow close by. Moving closer, I could see the maroon-and-black color scheme of the 180's vertical stabilizer.

The Skywagon was lying on its left side in a nose-down, tail-up attitude with the right wing extended upward at a forty-five-degree angle toward the east. I slid over to where the wing strut fastened to the bottom of the right wing and tied off the rope. Following the strut down toward the fuselage, I made my way into the cabin of the airplane through the passenger-side door opening. The windshield had popped out, and the-three-bladed McCauley propeller was twisted and curled on the ends like a pretzel. Evidently, it had made contact with a section of the right float assembly before the engine expired. The passenger-side door was missing. I wasn't sure why, maybe the door had popped open just before the pontoon hit it ripping it off, but to me it meant that retrieving my gear would be easier than I thought.

The first item of business was the Desert Eagle. With that strapped to my waist, I went to work retrieving the rest of my property. One by one, I brought up the spare oxygen tanks. Five more trips down to the airplane provided me with, the small gas generator and gas can, my tent, camp stove and fuel, as well as extra food and clothing.

My first day of diving had been successful, and finding the Antonov had revived in me the enthusiasm for continuing my quest for the diamonds. After all, just because I got off on the wrong foot didn't mean the whole trip had to go down the river (I mean lake). On my last dive with my arms bulging with stuff, I reached for the rope to haul myself to the surface one last time. Suddenly, all went dark in front of my light. It took a moment for my eyes to adjust to the strange shadow passing not more than two foot in front of my face. Then I saw a huge dorsal fin attached to a wall of scale-less fish skin at least two and a half foot high. Another five seconds went by until I saw the very large tailfin of a great fish pass by my face, disappearing into the blackness of the water. Whatever it was, it was close to thirty-feet long and easily three feet or more at its deepest point.

My first urge was to get up that rope as fast as I could. But I knew if I did that, I would take a chance on suffering the bends, which could kill me faster than the monster fish I would be running from. Slowly, I ascended, stopping every ten feet to let the oxygen in my lungs readjust to the changing pressure of the water as I had done in my previous descents. Finally, with all of my booty loaded in the raft, I tied another of the life jackets to the upper end of the rope that I had left tied to the wing strut of the airplane below, marking with a buoy the spot of the sunken 180.

My pile of provisions had grown a little, and I set about to organize my camp, cook a meal, and recharge the battery of the underwater light.

My take on the big fish, which was purely speculation, was that it was likely a sturgeon. However, the largest sturgeon on record on the North American continent, taken out of the Frasier River in British Columbia, was only eleven feet long, weighing in at one thousand pounds. They figured that fish was at least 120 years old. I didn't see all of this fish, but I guessed it for a good thirty feet and six thousand pounds. The only sturgeon I know of that size would be the European beluga, found primarily (but not exclusively) in the Caspian and Black Seas. However, those are landlocked seas and other than the Mediterranean the Beluga Sturgeon has never been known to travel away from that region. If that were indeed what this fish was, I was seriously baffled as to how it managed to wind up in Glacial Lake. I wondered how much of a threat the big fish represented to my underwater activities. I suspected that it was more curious than anything else. Most sturgeons are a harmless bottom-feeder. However, considered a predator—at least of other fish—this particular pre-historic monster could possibly be capable of much more. I was hoping he would not mistake me for an overgrown salamander.

I spent the rest of the day batting mosquitoes and packing firewood. I had spread my clothes out to dry in the breeze coming off the slopes of the Kiglua Mountains. As I retired for the evening beside the hospitable campfire, my thoughts turned to Kati and my family.

I wasn't too concerned about being stranded without an airplane. I had emergency locator beacons in my survival gear that I could activate whenever I wanted a ride home. I really wasn't ready for extra company. I was anxious to have a look in that AN-2 to see what the Russian had brought with him from the far east, or was it west?

I hated to break the almost sacred silence, but I needed to make sure the Desert Eagle was functioning properly, and my powder was still dry. As the last of the .44 magnum shots reverberated into the evening, and silence returned to the valley, I pulled my ten-gage to within reach on my left side, and with the big handgun on the right side, lapsed into another familiar, nine-hour, fatigue-induced coma.

When I awoke, I thought at first I had gone to heaven judging from the stillness, the beauty, and the chirping birds—but then I heard the dreaded buzz of the mosquitoes, reminding me I was still on mother earth and that my situation remained unchanged. However, it was my certain belief that the only difference between where I had awakened and heaven were those annoying mosquitoes. I would soon learn, however, that the mosquitoes would prove to be the least of my concerns.

I took my sweet time savoring every moment as I built a fire and prepared a breakfast that would have made my Kati proud. Knowing I would need to wait at least a full day before diving again, I set out for a hike.

The immediate leg of the L-shaped valley lay south to north from its mouth at the south end of the lake—forming the bottom of the L—the main leg of the L lay east and west and extended some forty miles to its crest. A saddle-shaped pass, rising to an elevation of four-thousand-feet, made up the northeast extremity of the Kiglua Mountains.

I worked my way along the increasingly steep hillside coming off the small mountain on the east side of the lake until I reached the far north end and more traversable terrain. A mile past where Glacial Creek spilled into Glacial Lake, the valley made a ninety-degree turn toward the east and widened out into a huge basin of meadows and timber stands over thirty miles in length where dozens of isolated herds of forty or more elk per herd fed and napped in the huge, sleepy valley. I watched the animals as they went about their interpersonal relationships with one another and wondered at their ability to survive in such a harsh country.

Later in the afternoon, as I made my way back toward camp, I noticed three elk feeding at the inlet to the lake. Standing in the marsh grass and knee-deep in the water, the two cows and the year-old calf seemed like a picture perfect Kodak moment.

Suddenly, in one second, the water turned to a boil, and a huge monster fish twisted out of the water like a giant corkscrew. With its tail, it slapped the small elk sideways into the deeper water of the lake, disappearing as suddenly as it had appeared. In a matter of moments, with the exception of the ripple effects finding their way toward both shores, the water was as still as it had been before the attack. The two cow elk scampered up the creek, pausing briefly to look back, baffled at the disappearance of the yearling.

I had wondered what a fish that size could find to eat in a lake only three miles long and a half mile wide that would sustain its appetite for at least 200 years or more. For the first time, I had reservations about diving into a world that obviously belonged to a sea monster. Completely astonished at what I had just witnessed, I continued to my camp to reconsider my intentions.

I was beginning to think I would be smart to give up this crazy notion of finding those diamonds. On the other hand, I am a pragmatic sort of individual. As I considered the circumstances, it occurred to me that the fish had probably happened quite accidentally onto elk as a food source. Maybe one drowned in the lake and the great fish fed on its remains, developing a taste for the elk meat. Who knows?

The next day dawned more beautiful than the first, but I could tell from the horsetail-like, high-altitude, cloud formations that the weather would soon deteriorate. I loaded my gear into the raft, pushed off, and began rowing my way toward the buoy.

CHAPTER 23

The five oxygen tanks I had brought with me limited my time underwater to one hour each. I had already depleted one and a half of them retrieving my supplies from the 180. However, I felt that the three and half hours of underwater time still available should be adequate, if only my luck would take a turn for the better.

The aggressive actions of the great fish had not only surprised me but also alarmed me a bit. I knew the monster fish had to be close to a couple of hundred years old, and confined to a lake only three miles long and a half-mile wide, the normal feeding characteristics of the beluga would have—for purposes of survival—obviously gone through some considerable adaptations.

Just the same, it is not as if it were a shark or a barracuda. Its mouth is very small and designed for bottom suction-type feeding. Its teeth are tiny, and though it also feeds on other fish, the only kinds it can eat are the ones that would fit into its small mouth. It would probably let the elk decompose for a while until it could more easily feed on its decomposing flesh. I also realized that if indeed that were the case, it meant the fish had achieved a very high level of cognitive thinking. That was in itself a bit disconcerting.

Nonetheless, I told myself only what I wanted to hear. It was the second day of my excursion in the great valley, and if I was going to go forward with my endeavor, I had to alleviate my apprehensions somehow, and get started. Therefore, I continued my reassuring reasoning, with the conclusion that the fish would likely not see me as anything more than a curiosity.

I tied the raft to the buoy that marked the location of the Skywagon. With my underwater light mounted to my chest, I began my descent to the Antonov.

I wondered if the AN-2 had snagged the same granite spire that had destroyed the right float on the 180. It certainly seemed logical, as the 180 wound up practically on top of the Antonov at the bottom of the lake. I had assumed that the lake was partially frozen and the Russian floatplane had broken through the ice, but maybe it wasn't frozen, maybe the lake had little or no ice on it at all the night the Russian smuggler tried to land; which raised the question of what then, made the airplane sink.

Upon reaching the end of the rope still tied to the right strut of the 180, I turned on the underwater lamp and made my way to the ancient wreckage. The floats were so badly corroded they had succumbed to the weight of the huge Antonov and lay crushed on the bottom of the fuselage practically covered over by silt and freshwater lake-weed. There was no way of determining what might have sunk the airplane.

Carefully, I worked my way into the jagged opening that had once been a cargo door. The crushed floats had actually done me a favor as they had kept the fuselage from filling up with the silt that surely would have buried the floor and most of the interior of the hull.

I searched through the tall lake-weed, inspecting every square-inch of the deteriorated floor. Back and forth, up and down, I searched. There were no diamonds.

When the gauge on my tank read ten percent, I began making my way slowly to the surface. I was beginning to wonder what I was doing this for. Had I wanted another adventure in my life so desperately that I ignored all logic and not only sacrificed my all-time favorite airplane, but also placed my life in danger, just to chase a myth?

On the other hand, maybe I was looking in the wrong place. Maybe the diamonds were stored in some kind of a false bottom specially fabricated within the aircraft. With my expectations revived, I changed tanks and began rowing once more toward the buoy.

Suddenly, the buoy took off. At first, it was as if someone was jerking on it, and then it began to move steadily northward at a faster and faster pace. Occasionally, it would briefly stop, and then, off it would go again. The sea monster was stealing my airplane.

My heart was pounding in my chest. It occurred to me that I had indeed found the excitement I was seeking, but was rapidly turning into more than I had bargained for. I definitely had underestimated the impact this huge fish was going to have on my expedition.

I watched the buoy make its way northward for a good three hundred yards before it disappeared into the water. It was obvious that the airplane had found the deeper end of the pool. However, I no longer had a buoy for the Antonov and had lost sixty feet of valuable rope. I turned around and headed back to the spit to review my options.

The fish had become more than just a distraction. I was still wondering, however, if it was just playing or actually warning me in some way. Was it vying for attention, or out to kill me? One thing was certain: My job just got more difficult.

I only had five feet of rope left. There was now nothing to tie the raft to while I was on the bottom and no rope with which to descend and ascend. It was not only getting more difficult, it was bordering on unsafe. Just the same, I decided to try one more time.

I found a large rock, weighing about forty pounds, and placed it in my daypack. This was about the closest I could get to an improvised anchor. I rowed out to a point adjacent to the landmarks I had located on the parallel shorelines and about two hundred yards from the eastern shore. I was sure this was pretty close to the spot. If I was a little north, I could always pick up the trail the Skywagon left in the lake-weed and backtrack to the Antonov. Tying one end of the rope to the daypack and the other to the raft, I lowered the short anchor over the side. Carefully, so as not to disturb the water too much, I slowly descended.

For the first time, I felt not just vulnerable but practically defenseless. Armed only with the Desert Eagle, which I wasn't sure would be that effective underwater, I began my last descent. I just wanted to find the diamonds and go about the business of getting away from Glacial Lake and back home. I had thought about activating one of the two emergency locator beacons that I still had in my survival pack, but I still was not quite ready for the company that would surely show up. I was less than thirty miles from Nome and airplanes flying directly over the lake were a common thing. I knew I only had one more shot at finding the diamonds.

Gradually, I descended to the bottom, timing my descent. The dark water created a feeling of vertigo, and I had to use my underwater altimeter to determine if I was indeed descending and how fast.

I turned on the light and adjusted its beam toward the bottom. There was the path the 180 had made on its way north. I felt a chill go up my spine at the realization of the power it took to swim off with that airplane. I backtracked my way to the Antonov. I had already searched the back half of the fuselage and was satisfied there was nothing more to look at on that end, so I focused my attention on the cockpit and the first baggage area directly behind.

Laced with cracks and peppered with holes, I carefully examined the floor. Then I saw it: a gap in the floor where there should have been no more than a foot of space separating the concave belly of the fuselage from the deck of the floor. It was at least two-feet down to a flat bottom. As I reexamined the floor deck, I noticed that it appeared raised somewhat from the deck directly behind. I used a two-foot pipe that lay among the wreckage to rip an opening large enough to get my head into and tried to look inside. It was pure darkness and too small to get the light into along with my head. Reaching my arm into the specially improvised compartment, I felt around until my hand found a large box that I estimated to be about twelve-inches high, eighteen inches long and one foot wide. I scratched and clawed the box closer where I could get a better look. It appeared to be a wooden chest made of teak or maybe gopher wood; perfectly preserved.

With the old pipe that kept bending and crumbling, I gouged and ripped at the hole until I was finally able to get the wooden chest out of the compartment. Its lid was shaped like a hope chest and at one time there were handles on each end probably made of leather that long ago rotted away. With the chest cradled in my arms, I slowly made my way up toward the surface.

Emerging only ten feet from the raft, I rolled the chest over the edge of the rubber boat, letting it fall to the bottom, and then removed the tank from off my back. As I was boosting it over the edge of the raft, something bumped the small of my back. I instantly new what it was. Frantically, I attempted to climb into the raft, but it was too late. The great fish, with his nose buried in the small of my back, shoved me forward a good fifty yards and then briefly let me go. Suddenly, with his tail fin planted firmly under my posterior, the monster fish launched me straight into the sky. The next thing I saw was a view I normally only see from the window of an airplane. The massive tail of the great fish had propelled me through the air in an arc like that of a rainbow. Cresting at a height of at least a hundred feet above the surface of the lake and a distance of over a hundred yards onto the shore where I landed in a mangled heap on the sharp, jagged rocks that formed the foundation of the mountain guarding the east side of Glacial Lake. At the far end of the rainbow, where there should have been a pot of gold, everything went black.

When I awoke, I initially had no recollection of what had happened. I lay where I had landed some twelve hours earlier, a good twenty feet up-slope from the shoreline. The darkness of night had settled upon the valley along with dark and angry clouds. It began to rain.

I struggled to understand why I was laying in the middle of nowhere staring at an unfriendly sky. I figured I must be dreaming. In an attempt to sit up, I realized it was no dream, and I had definitely not died and gone to heaven. Pain shot through my midsection like a dagger. Then it started coming back to me. That fish! Again, I tried to move, and once again, I almost blacked out from the pain. I tried to move just my right arm but couldn't feel it, so I tried the left one. It was practically dead from lack of circulation but seemed to be the only part of me that still worked. Gingerly, I checked the parts of my body I could reach, beginning with my right arm. It appeared to be broken in several places.

I tried to raise my head, but could not do that either. Placing my left hand behind my neck, I was able to lift my head enough to see the mangled pile of flesh and bone that had once been my body. It did not look good. From my limited perspective, it appeared I had broken more than just a few bones, which included hips, various ribs, legs, my right arm, and who knows what else.

My twisted remains lay in a pile of boulders a good conditioned hiker would need to use caution traversing through and was a good six hundred yards from my camp. At least a hundred yards of huge rocks and boulders, a shale slope that angled steeply down directly into the lake, and three hundred yards of tundra brush lay between me and the spit where my camp was located, and yet another hundred yards out onto the spit itself.

I reached my left arm as far around to my right side as I could to see if the Desert Eagle had come along for the ride. It was there, but it had ended up under my butt where I was unable to reach it. Somehow, I would have to work it from under my rear end and manipulate it around to my left side.

It took two exhausting hours of pain and suffering to finally position the .44 magnum where I could get to it in case I needed to defend myself against wild animals. I had hoped I could move enough to drag myself a little at a time toward my camp, or at least into a place where maybe someone flying by might be able to see me.

It wouldn't take a rocket scientist to figure out that I was in serious trouble. I could not tell if there were any compound fractures or not, but I knew if there were, gangrene would become a life-threatening issue in only a short time, which would surely attract bears or wolves, or both. Too bad I had not activated the ELT (emergency locator beacon). Those diamonds were not doing me much good floating around in that raft, and I was suddenly feeling somewhat stupid for even going after them in the first place. On the other hand, who would have thought that a giant sea monster was protecting them and would insist on being so downright un-neighborly?

When I again awoke, it was raining harder and the wind was whistling through the natural venturi the mountains created, increasing its velocity by at least four times. I was freezing cold but noticed that when I tried to move there was less pain. I figured it was due to the cold so I may as well take advantage of it.

Painfully, I lay my right arm across my chest to keep it from dragging in the rocks. Working myself up onto my left elbow, I could tell from the excruciating pain that there were several broken ribs. Inch by inch, I managed to move a couple of feet. It was not much, but it straightened my legs out a bit and gave me a flat spot on a rock I could lean back against, enabling me to better see my surroundings. It was all I could do for the time being. The pain had awakened. I don't know if I passed out or simply fell asleep, but the next time I awoke, it was morning.

I had made it through the night, but that only meant I had about eighteen less hours of survival strength left. I had no hope of being found, seen, rescued, or, for that matter, surviving, this ordeal. It appeared from every human perspective that it was just a matter of time until I would be fish food. I almost laughed at the thought of that monster fish corkscrewing his thirty-foot body out of the lake to swat my decomposing remains back into the water where he could eat me. I knew that nature's way would prevail, and the wolves would get me first.

My thoughts took another turn. I remembered my friend Pastor Bill Shearer and what he had once said to me. "Lou," he said, pulling at his scraggy beard. "God is not off somewhere fishing. He doesn't have something more important to do than to care for you. Someday, you will find yourself in a place where you are helpless. I want you to remember, *that* is where the good Lord put you, and *that,* is where He wants you to look to Him for your help. You will find it hard to let Him, or even to ask Him. But you must do it anyway. He has a work for you to do for Him that you know nothing about. Wherever you go and whatever difficulty you are in, He has engineered the circumstances for your good and your salvation."

I knew I had put off taking spiritual matters as seriously as I should have. It was always Kati who did the praying, said the blessing over the meals, and insisted on going to church on Easter weekend. I was always too busy working and doing stuff—like looking for gold or diamonds. My life was too occupied for religious matters.

Kati and I had been together forty-three years by the time I took off on my diamond expedition. Our life had been prosperous, happy, functional, and blessed with three of the most wonderful daughters a man could ever hope to have. My family was the most important part of my life, and the thought of dying alone and their not knowing what had become of me was more than I could tolerate. With tears streaming down my face, I prayed, "Lord in heaven. I understand that you sent your Son Jesus Christ to save the lost. *I am lost.* I guess I always have been, but you had to bring me to this for me to realize it, At any rate, I need help. I need the God of Bill Shearer to come and get me before my family loses me forever."

It felt like I had taken a huge hit of morphine or something. The pain subsided, and a blanket of euphoria and well-being pervaded my whole body and mind. Again, I fell asleep.

I heard the airplane, coming from a mile away as I awakened another six hours later to broken skies and warm sun in my face. I wanted to wave something. It seemed obvious that the airplane was coming my way, but was it going to fly by. Or would the pilot see my camp? Maybe he would see the raft and land out of curiosity, at which time I could fire a round from the Desert Eagle to gain his attention. Hope sprang up, but all I could do was wait.

The Cessna 208 Caravan circled the lake and flew north bound directly over the big hill to the east of the lake, and as it made a left 180-degree turn, I could make out the insignia of the Bettles Learning Center on the empennage. It was descending, apparently planning an approach from the north. I watched the big Caravan settle into the water, almost expecting one of the floats to come flying off. Thankfully, history did not repeat itself a second time.

The pilot taxied to the raft where he feathered the prop while investigating it. From where I lay in the rocks facing to the north, I could not see that part of the lake, but listened for the sound of the pilots foot steps on the pontoons. When I was sure the pilot was outside the airplane, I fired a round from the handgun and tried to holler. I could barely speak, but it was enough.

The pilot hollered back. "Hello, there in the rocks! Do you need help?"

"Yes," I feebly responded hoping he could hear me.

"Hang on, buddy. I'll be there in a minute."

There was something familiar about his voice, but I could not place it. I considered for a minute thinking it might be Jeffery, but when I heard him speak, I was sure it was not him. Who then could it be?

The pilot immediately left the raft and continued his taxi to the north shore of the spit, where he quickly tied the floatplane and ran toward where I was lying. I could hear him getting closer, and as he approached the rocks, I again called out in not much more than a whisper. "I'm over here."

Stepping around the boulder I was resting against, the pilot was suddenly looking down at me, and I up at him. I was so shocked that I could barely speak.

"Lou Worley," he said.

I could hardly believe my eyes. Ironically, I was staring into the still horribly scarred face of Beltray Gibbons.

CHAPTER 24

I was stunned to see Beltray and even more amazed that he was piloting one of the school's Caravans. I lay still cradled in a cleft of the rocks, listening as Beltray scurried back to my camp for food, water, and a blanket. Since I had to wait four hours after eating to start diving, it had been over thirty hours since I had eaten anything or taken any liquid.

Not only had Beltray impressed me by actually making something of himself and obviously turning his life around, I could tell that his whole demeanor had changed as well. Gone was his belligerent attitude and deceptive spirit. Before he went for the water, he even covered me with his coat and reassured me that I would be okay.

"You just rest, Mr. Worley," he said. "I'll get you a blanket, some food and water, and be right back."

"Thanks, buddy," I said, hardly able to talk above a whisper due to the broken ribs. I wanted to ask him a million questions, but knew it would have to wait until later.

I heard him returning to me, scrambling through the rocks as though every second I remained cold and hungry mattered to him. I thought back at the last time we had seen each other.

At least four years before, Rusty, Kevin, and I had locked him in that walk-in safe I had built into the floor of the big hangar. It was there I had given him the ultimatum. "Go to school and turn your life around, or go back to prison." I gave him an hour to make up his mind, more to ease my own conscience than anything, I certainly never expected him to accept the offer, and even when he did, I didn't expect him to follow through with it. I was sure he would go to the school just to play the game that he thought would get me off his back and keep him out of prison.

The Foundation funds had provided for his room, board, and education, so the sky was the limit as far as what he could do. When Genneta Williams informed me that he wanted to take flying lessons, I managed to pull some strings to get his criminal record expunged so that he could get a pilots license. Until this moment, I never knew if he had completed the training or not.

Beltray quickly returned, covering me with a blanket and putting a pillow behind my head that he had retrieved from my tent. As he placed a handful of energy bars and a canteen of water beside me, he said, "Mr. Worley, I'm not going to be able to get you into the Caravan, so I will need to takeoff and get up to around ten thousand feet or so to contact Search and Rescue. Then I'll come right back and stay with you till they get here. Will you be all right for a few minutes while I do that?"

"I'll be just fine, Beltray. Thank-you I appreciate it. Watch out for that yellow buoy you see out there. It is marking the spot of a hunk of rock that will sink your plane, take my word for it."

Beltray paused a moment, looking at me, and then almost affectionately squeezed my forearm before returning to the big floatplane.

It seemed like it took awhile, but eventually I heard the turbo spooling up on the Cessna 208. Once he began the water taxi, Beltray wasted no time getting the Caravan into the air and up to altitude. In a short time, he was back. This time, he taxied the floatplane right up to the shoreline, just below where I lay helplessly in the rocks.

"Search and Rescue is on the way, Mr. Worley. I explained the situation to them, and they are going to lower a basket from the helicopter and, from a hover, transfer you over to where we can slide you in through the baggage door into the Caravan. One of the EMT's (emergency medical technicians) will ride with us while I take you to the trauma unit at the Bettles Learning Center hospital."

"Beltray, I have to tell you. I'm more than a little impressed with what you have made of yourself. You've come far, young man."

"Thank you, Mr. Worley. However, you don't owe me any thanks. I have *you* to thank. You gave me a chance, and God gave me a new heart."

"God gave you a … *what?*" I asked, a little bewildered.

"A new heart," Beltray repeated. "I had just started my second year at the school when I met one of the theology students who had been converted to the Christian faith through the ministry of Bill Shearer. His name is Gray Gillis; we call him Pastor Gee-Gee. He was studying to become a minister. He has since finished school and currently is pastoring several churches, carrying on Pastor Bill's ministry work in the villages. We became friends, and over the next year, I, too, became a born-again Christian and have chosen theology as my major. I will finish my bachelor's degree next year and also intend to carry on the ministry of Pastor Bill."

I stared at Beltray, amazed at what had taken place in him. I could hardly believe it was the same person. "Beltray, last night I thought I was a goner. I really did. I was so sure my time had come, I actually prayed to God. It felt like I got warm all over, and I wasn't afraid anymore. When I woke up, you were landing on the water. How did you know I was here?"

Beltray was about to speak when the sound of the Search and Rescue chopper could be heard closing in. Moments later, it was directly over our heads.

An EMT team of two repelled from the helicopter, escorting a basket.

"Sir, can you understand me?" one of the medics asked.

"Yes, I can, but I'm kind of busted up and might not stay with you long once you start moving me," I said.

"Don't worry, I'll give you something for the pain as soon as I get an IV started." In only moments, the very proficient medic had me hooked up to an IV of saline solution, through which he administered a dose of morphine that in no time at all rendered me completely painless and totally incapable of any sensible level of conversation.

Very soon, they had me secured in the Caravan. I could hear the turbo spool up and feel the thrust of the twelve hundred horsepower engine lift us effortlessly into the sky and finally away from the fish that had literally spanked me nearly to death. Then it hit me: the diamonds, my camp, the raft, my shotgun! I glanced at the cockpit where Beltray masterfully manipulated the controls of the big Caravan. Seated in the pilot seat, wearing an old tattered military surplus flight jacket that was about a size and a half too large for him, he appeared completely confident in his demeanor. Then I glanced back at the rear of the baggage compartment. There was the deflated raft, all my camping equipment, and, in the far corner, almost completely concealed, the teakwood chest, still unopened. I laid my head back, wondering how Beltray knew where I was and what might have been had I not said that prayer.

There were a great many people scurrying around, but everything was such a blur that I thought it must be a dream and didn't really try to make much sense of it. The morphine had instantly replaced my nightmare with euphoria, and I thought if going to heaven felt anything like that, I knew I wanted to go no matter what it involved. No wonder people get addicted to drugs! I guess some people's lives get so screwed up the only way they can escape it is stay on the stuff, which makes no sense because it just screws up their life even more.

When I awakened, I was in a room and everyone was wearing masks. There were hands on me that gave me a sense of reassurance until someone placed a mask over my nose and mouth. The next thing I knew, I was waking up from another deep sleep.

Gradually, I regained consciousness, realizing I must be in a recovery room, which could only mean that I had just come from surgery. Before Beltray arrived, I knew that I was in rough shape. I had surmised that my right leg was broken in a couple of places, judging from how twisted it was when I was lying in the rocks. I also concluded that my right arm was broken in several places, but still was not sure what all they had done to me in surgery. Again, I fell asleep.

Once more, I awakened. This time, I was no longer alone. Kati was there and so was Keera. I felt an enormous relief, and then grief. I began to sob. "Kati," I said. "The 180 is gone."

"Its okay, Lou. Don't worry about that right now. You are just coming off of the morphine and experiencing some dysphoria. Keera is here and all the kids are in the waiting room. They can hardly wait to see you. I love you, baby. You just rest now."

Keera was holding my hand on the other side of the bed, desperately trying to hold back the tears.

"It is all going to be okay, daddy, I was so afraid we had lost you. I love you so much." Keera buried her face on my chest and, unable to hold back any longer, burst into uncontrollable sobbing.

"That's okay, sweetie. You just got dysphoria. Everything is going to be okay," I said, recovering somewhat from my own dysphoria.

I looked back at Kati. With tears steaming down her face, she pointed at me and said, "Lou Worley you barely survived a terrible accident and here you are trying to be funny. I don't feel one bit sorry for you."

A few hours later, after I had taken another nap, the surgeon who had performed his cutlery on me appeared at my bedside with chart in hand. "Mr. Worley, my name is Dr. Becker. I'm an orthopedic surgeon. I had to do a considerable amount of repair work on you today. Can you remember what happened to you?"

"Glad to meet you Doctor, yes, I remember, but I'd rather not go into the details right now. Just suffice it to say that I had a hard landing on a pile of rocks."

"Well, Mr. Worley, you are quite a famous man around here, and we all are committed to your recovery. But if you want to keep that part a secret, you go ahead. However, I need to talk to you about your condition, if you are up to it."

"Go ahead, doc. I'm listening."

"Your right leg was broken in two places. To set it, we had to realign it by inserting a tibial rod. Your right arm also had two displaced fractures that we set with plates and screws. However, you still have a fractured right hip that we were not able to do anything with at this time, In fact, it is so badly shattered that we were unable to pin it back together. You will need a hip replacement.

"We are sending your medical transcripts and X-rays to a hip specialist in Seattle for her evaluation. If she is willing to do the surgery, we will medivac you to Seattle. Last, and the least, of your problems are the six broken ribs that are going to cause you more discomfort than anything else. There is really nothing we can do about them. They are not displaced or anything, but they will be uncomfortable for awhile. I have a prescription for you that should help you manage your pain. After you have had a chance to rest up, and we see what the specialist has to say about the hip, we will proceed from there. Right now, just get lots of rest. Other than that, it certainly looks like you are in good hands. I'll be back a little later to check on you."

"Good grief, doc, is that all?" I asked incredulously. Dr. Becker glanced back and grinned as he walked away.

The next day, they sent me to X-ray where the technician insisted on turning and positioning me in the most painful postures imaginable in an effort to get pictures of the shattered hip from every angle requested by the specialist. Shortly after I returned to my room, the doc showed up.

"Mr. Worley, are you awake?"

"I am now. Why? Am I going to Seattle?" I asked, already sure of the answer.

"Yes, sir, you sure are, the Foundation has chartered a private jet that will be here inside of an hour. You will have two private nurses traveling with you, and you can take up to four additional family members. Your family will be staying at a hotel within a couple of blocks of the hospital, which will also provide their transportation and meals at the cafeteria. You will be admitted to N.W. Hospital in Seattle. Your surgeon's name is Dr. Gharib; she is the most highly recommended practitioner in the field of hip surgery. I wish you all the best and pray for your speedy recovery." With that, Dr. Becker left as quickly as he had arrived.

I turned to Kati. "Who all is going with us?"

"I'm not sure. Let me go ask," she said. In a few minutes, Kati returned with Keera, Rusty, and Kelly.

Two hours later, the hospital personnel along with my two private nurses carefully loaded my gurney into the Cessna Sovereign Citation. The Sovereign can carry nine passengers and has a range of over 2,800 miles. In less then four hours, we were on final approach to Boeing Field in Seattle, Washington.

In another hour, I was resting in a room, awaiting the arrival of the surgeon.

A short time later, a slender, middle-aged, Pakistani lady Doctor, dressed in a blue surgery gown and cap with a matching mask dangling loosely around her neck, stepped into my room.

"Mr. Worley?"

"Yes."

"My name is Dr. Gharib, and I will be your surgeon. Are you the infamous Lou Worley I have heard so much about?" she asked in her eastern accent.

"I think you have me confused with the other Lou Worley," I answered.

"Mr. Worley, we have you on the fast track to get this surgery done as quickly as possible for several reasons. First, with your other fractures, we need to get you up and moving as soon as we can to avoid the potential of what we call a pulmonary embolism. That is, a blood clot that can make its way to your lungs and often leads to pneumonia, which in your case could be fatal due to the severity of your rib injuries. The plan is to do this surgery first thing in the morning and have you on your feet by the afternoon of the next day. How are you feeling after your flight?"

"I'm good. Why can't we do it today?" I asked, just out of curiosity.

"Because I am booked in another case the rest of the afternoon, and you need to rest up while we monitor your vital signs for at least twelve hours. The nurses will be in and out checking on you, and your anesthesiologist will come by some time this afternoon to see you and have you sign a consent form." Dr. Gharib then excused herself and retreated from the room.

Kati reached over and took my hand. I really was glad she was with me. After the surgeon left, I told her the whole story of my ordeal with the fish, diving and finding the wooden chest, and even the prayer I had prayed when I thought I would not survive. She laid her head on my shoulder and wept.

"I have been praying for years that the Lord would bring you to the foot of the cross," she said between her sobbing gasps for air. "I never had any idea it would take all of that to get you there. It reminds me of the story of Jonah and the whale. I am here for you, baby. I will never leave your side."

"Who was Jonah?" I asked.

Kati brought me a Bible and another book written by an oriental minister who spent the last twenty years of his life in a Chinese prison because he believed in Jesus Christ. I wondered why he hadn't prayed and asked God to get him out of there. Prayer certainly had worked quite well for me.

For the rest of the day Kati read to me from first the bible and then a book called the 'Normal Christian Life.' By Watchman Nee. It must have brought me a lot of peace and comfort because I kept falling asleep. From that day to this I am never without those two books.

Dr. Gharib performed the hip surgery the following morning. I spent the next few months in physical therapy teaching my titanium hip to walk. During that time, I studied and read from those two books. Little by little, God's plan of salvation for fallen man began to unfold in my mind. I started to get a glimpse of the force that drove William Shearer who committed over thirty-five years along with the sacrifice of his very life for the work of sharing the gospel of Jesus Christ.

I had spent my life totally self-reliant. I had respect for religion, but felt no need for it in my own life. I had never been in a situation before that I couldn't fight or shoot my way out of. I always felt that the higher powers were going to be on my side because I was a defender of the right. I felt bad about being in situations that required the taking of human life, but never felt any guilt over it because those people were the enemies of human decency and right principles. They chose a way that put them at risk; it was their choice.

I wished that Bill Shearer was still around to talk to about it all, but he wasn't. So I decided I would to talk to Beltray again.

Beltray had come to see me while I was in the hospital in Bettles, but our visit was short. Since I had returned home, I hadn't seen him at all. I placed a call to Genneta Williams.

"Bettles Flight Center. This is Genneta. May I help you?"

"Genneta, this is Lou Worley. How are you?"

"I'm fine, Mr. Worley. How are you? Are you up and around yet?"

"I'm doing well, actually better than ever. Does Beltray have any free time these days?"

"Beltray shuttles students and faculty to and from places they need to go when he is not in class or study room himself, so this time of year he is pretty busy. Why? Do you need him for something?"

"Just tell him I called and if he has any spare time, I'd like to talk to him."

"I will do that," Genneta said. "You take care of yourself, Mr. Worley."

As I hung up the phone, I suddenly realized there was something else I needed to ask Beltray. He still had all my gear and the teak chest. Once again, my curiosity for whatever was inside that box returned.

CHAPTER 25

I t was nearing October, and the hint of winter was in the air. The days were getting shorter, the cold fronts were becoming more frequent, and I was going through some serious withdrawals without my beloved Cessna 180 Skywagon.

I was remembering when Kathy was little. She had a kitten that died, and no matter what we said, she would not hear of having another one anytime soon. I can remember shaking my head over it at the time, but I was able to relate to it a little better now. All I would have to do is give Ray Sumner a call, and he would have me in another sweetheart of an airplane in no time, but it wouldn't be the 180. So there I sat, feeling sorry for myself.

The ringing phone interrupted my pity-party. I didn't recognize the number. "Hello, this is Lou Worley."

"Mr. Worley, this is Beltray. Genneta said you called."

"Beltray Gibbons! Yes, I want to talk to you. Can we get together? I know you're busy, but I was wondering if maybe I could go with you on a few of your runs, and we could spend some time talking. I also need to get my gear that you salvaged for me from Glacial Lake."

"That would be great, sir. Do you want me to come down and pick you up, or can you come up here?"

"When do you do most of your shuttling?" I asked.

"On the weekends mostly. I have to get the adult students home for the weekends and then back again by Sunday evening for their classes during the week. Most of the younger people just stay here the whole semester."

"Okay, Beltray. Will Friday work better for you?"

"That will be perfect, Mr. Worley."

"Okay. I will grab one of the Helio Couriers and meet you at the flight school Friday morning."

"Sounds like a plan, Mr. Worley. I'll be looking forward to it. By the way, I put all your gear in a storage room at the flight center. I meant to tell you, but never got the chance. I'm sure its still there, but I'll check to make sure."

"Great. I'll see you then." Suddenly it struck me that Beltray had not even asked about the teakwood chest or inquired about where it had come from, or even what I was doing at the lake. It just seemed so out of character for him. He was such a little thief, scoundrel, and liar. I couldn't get over the difference. The old Beltray would have opened that chest by now and disappeared without a trace along with whatever was inside.

Carefully, I climbed into the pilot seat of the Helio Courier parked closest to where I parked the new Land Cruiser. Rusty had built a row of open hangars along the south side of the runway to house the two Couriers and a whole array of construction equipment—dozers, loaders, track-hoes even drill rigs—occupied the rest of the enclosure.

I hadn't flown an airplane since the day the Skywagon sunk to the bottom of Glacial Lake four months before. I still wasn't my old self, but the doctor told me to push through as much of the pain as I can; "the more you do, the more you will be able to do," he said. My leg and arm were both healing fine, but the broken ribs were still sore, and the hip was stiff every morning.

I fired up the Courier. As soon as the run-up was completed, I stabbed the power forward, hauling the freighter off the ground in less than forty feet. I grinned to myself as I pointed the nose north toward Denali Pass. Did I mention that it was empty?

It felt great to get back into the air. I had flown this route a hundred times and yet this day was like the first time I had ever seen it. Normally, I would have taken in the beauty of the land and the privilege of seeing it from the air without a single thought of the One who had created it all, but not any more. Something had happened in me that I was unable to explain.

Everything I looked at and everything I experienced was like a special gift from God himself, just to me. I breathed a prayer of thanksgiving.

It was mid-morning on Thursday, and I had the whole day to get to Bettles. I usually stay in one of the guest rooms at the flight center unless they are all occupied, in which case I just crash (I mean, sleep) in the pilots lounge. But this late in the year, it was a sure bet there would be at least one guest room available.

When I arrived, Genneta saw to it that I had a car to use and gave me the key to one of the rooms. It was late in the evening by the time I had settled into my small apartment. The next morning, I returned to Genneta's office and inquired where I could find the storage room where Beltray had stowed my gear. Genneta took me around back of the flight school classrooms to the far end of a row of small apartments reserved for the out-of-town student pilots who were unaffiliated with the learning center except for their flight-training curriculum.

There were several quite well-constructed wood and metal portable storage sheds—seven-feet high, eight and a half feet wide, and fourteen-feet deep—that sat on pier blocks with a white metal roll-up door on the front.

Genneta unlocked the padlock and stepped away as I slid the sliding bolt and raised the door. There, stacked neatly in the far corner, was all my gear with the teakwood chest sitting on the floor beside the neatly stacked pile.

"Thank you, Genneta, I will get the car and put all of this stuff in the airplane."

"I can get someone to do that for you, Mr. Worley."

"No, that's okay. I'll do it. Thanks anyway."

I closed the door of the shed and returned to get the car. As I began loading my gear into the trunk, I noticed that in the back of my mind I was half-expecting to find something missing. After it was all loaded, I felt guilty for having doubted Beltray's new character, or new heart, as he chose to describe it. A quick inventory verified that it was all present and accounted for: the ten-gage shotgun (which Beltray had unloaded), the Desert Eagle (also unloaded and safely secured), all the camping gear, oxygen tanks, and, of course, the teakwood chest; everything except the wet suit that the trauma unit personnel had cut off my body moments after my arrival.

With my gear finally stowed in the Helio Courier and the teakwood chest beside me on the front seat, I parked the car in front of the guest room. Finally, I was about to discover what secrets lay hidden under the lid of the wooden treasure chest that had cost me my beloved airplane and practically cost me my life.

I sat in my room, staring at the small teak box barely larger than a baby bassinet. It almost seemed like a crime to open it. It was not about diamonds anymore. Somehow, it had become a discovery of who that man was who risked, and apparently sacrificed his life bringing that chest into the country.

What could be locked under that lid that was so valuable to him that he would risk flying over two thousand miles through barren terrain and unpredictable, even severe, winter weather to enter the territory of Alaska through such a remote and irregular route. Suddenly it occurred to me. Isn't that exactly what I had done?

I fiddled with the hasp that fastened the lid shut. There must have been a key somewhere, but even if I had it, the key hole was so corroded it wouldn't work anyway. I really did not want to break into it. It would be such a waste of a beautifully handcrafted piece of craftsmanship. I headed to town to get a drill to drill out the corners of the hasp.

Returning from town, I again set about to open the chest. Carefully, I drilled each corner. One by one, using graduating sizes of drill bits, I bore a hole through the lock itself until it finally released its hold on the lid. With the application of a small amount of penetrating oil applied to the hinges, they gradually gave way. Carefully, I opened the lid.

The chest was completely full of silt and mud. I took the waste can from beside the guest room bed and began to scoop the silt from the inside of the box, examining each handful carefully for the possibility that diamonds might be in the mix.

After removing only a few handfuls of mud, I soon encountered stones. Taking one of them to the sink, I rinsed it off, instantly realizing that I was holding in my hand a raw, uncut diamond. Even in its natural condition, it was the most beautiful thing I had ever seen.

Obviously, I had approached this little endeavor somewhat unprepared. I locked the door to my room and went in search of a large stainless-steel pan or tub of some sort.

Genneta directed me to a broom closet where I found a mop bucket on wheels. Soon I was back in my room, dumping the entire contents of the chest into the mop bucket. to my astonishment, the silt was only a few inches thick, beneath which were enough diamonds of various shapes, sizes, and colorations to fill a five-gallon bucket to a little over half full. Under the diamonds was a quart jar sealed in wax, containing an assortment of documents, maps, and old, black-and-white photographs.

Carefully, I washed the diamonds, thoroughly cleaned the box, and returned the diamonds to the chest. In the trunk of the car, I found a rubber bungee that I used to secure the lid and locked the chest in the trunk.

Back in my room, I removed the wax from the jar and carefully investigated the documents. Would they tell me the rest of the story? It was soon obvious that there was more to the smuggler than I had ever imagined.

The first picture was of a young, beautiful Chinese girl maybe twenty years old or so, dressed in a nurses uniform and standing in the midst of a group of what must have been fifty or more young Chinese children that appeared to be all the same age. My guess was around seven years old, some boys, some girls. They were smiling. However some appeared to be either all or part Japanese.

The next picture was of two men standing under the huge cowling of an Antonov AN-2. Both men appeared to be American. One of them, the tallest and youngest of the two, was wearing a sealskin, fur-lined, full-body flight suit with matching headgear consistent with cold weather operations. The other man, much older, but not much shorter, appeared to be a mechanic. Written on the back of the picture was, "Jay and Elmo, Manchuria 1949."

There was a passport in the jar with a picture matching that of the younger man bearing the name, "Jay Baldwin." I assumed he was the pilot of the AN-2. Another picture showed Mr. Bold standing beside what appeared to be the same DC-3 parked on a familiar dirt strip. I flipped the picture over; the writing on the back read: "Brother Jay Bold and his D3, visiting: 1946." Obviously, whatever he was into, it could very well have involved Arthur, a younger brother, and my home airstrip in Wasilla.

The knock at the door suddenly reminded me that I was expecting Beltray. I wondered what had taken him so long.

"Good morning, Beltray," I said as I swung open the door of my room.

"Good morning, Mr. Worley. Sorry I'm late. I was involved in a Bible study with one of my passengers at Chandarlar Lake and lost track of time."

"That's okay, Beltray. Come on in and have a seat."

Beltray removed his hat and coat and settled into a recliner next to the window while I gathered up the papers and pictures I had been looking at. I then took a seat on a short couch located in the opposite corner of the room.

"What did you want to talk about, Mr. Worley?" Beltray asked.

"Well, first off, I would like to know if you answer to any other name than Beltray?"

"When I was in prison, they called me B'tray, but I didn't much like it. If you want, you can call me Tray or Gibbs."

"Perfect," I said. "I'll call you Gibbs. I have a hundred questions. First of all, I am dying to know how you happened to show up at Glacial Lake when you did, just in the knick of time?"

"I was on my way to Nome, and on that run, I often fly low through the valley and over Glacial Lake to see the elk. That's when I saw the yellow raft. As I flew over the Lake, I spotted your camp and decided to land to see if there might be a camper in trouble. I was a little suspicious that there wasn't an airplane tied up somewhere and figured that was way too much gear for someone to pack in on their back. Also, it was the first time I had ever seen anyone camping on that lake. Most people are afraid to go there. Some say there is a monster in that lake."

"Imagine that!" I exclaimed. "So, tell me. What turned your life around? You are not the same man I busted for drug-running back there at the old mine and detained in my vault four years ago."

"I told you about Pastor Gee Gee, the one who led me to the Lord in the first place. I was floundering around, not sure what I wanted to do with the opportunity you had given me. I really didn't want to be in the school, but I knew that if I left, it would result in the end of me. So, I reluctantly stuck it out. Then one day, I overheard Gee-Gee sharing his faith with one of the fellows in the aviation program and something he said really spoke to me. He said to him, 'God made you, and He has never made a mistake.'

"I couldn't get those words out of my mind. I had always been convinced that I *was* a mistake. I knew I had been adopted out, I had no idea who my real parents were, and the people who adopted me certainly did not care anything about me. So when I found Pastor Gee Gee alone, I approached him, and he prayed with me and led me to an understanding of my purpose for being alive and to an understanding and acceptance of the gospel of Jesus Christ. My life immediately took on new purpose, and I fell in love with Jesus, my Savior. Where I go in the future will all be according to His divine will and purpose for my life."

I was fascinated by Gibbs's testimony and was emotionally touched by the evidence of God's love and grace that had saved this lost and abandoned soul from the gutter he had been born into, raised in, and lived in his whole life. Now he sat before me, horribly scarred on the outside, but completely renewed on the inside. Although real, it was as impossible to believe as the fish story that brought me to the place where I found myself completely helpless and in need of divine intervention.

For the first time, I felt that Beltray Gibbons and I, who until now had barely known each other and who certainly came from two completely different cultures with vastly different ideals, suddenly shared a common bond that in the Christian world describes as "brothers in Christ."

Gibbs rose from the recliner and handed me a tissue from the nightstand. "I can tell the Lord has had His way with you as He has with me, Mr. Worley. You never got to tell me how you managed to wind up in those rocks all busted up like you were."

Gibbs pulled up a chair from the desk and sat closer as if afraid he might miss some detail of how the gospel had reached the self-sufficient heart of Lou Worley. I proceeded to tell him of my quest for the lost diamonds and my fight with the fish. Gibbs proceeded to tell me of a story in the Bible of a man named Jonah and a similar experience he had with a fish that had a significantly larger mouth.

"Gibbs, what would you do if you were able to locate your biological mother?"

Gibbs drew a long breath and slowly let it escape as if waiting for divine instruction on how to answer the question. "I would go to her and tell her what has become of her son."

"Would you like me to go with you?"

Gibbs could not hold back the tide of emotion any longer. This time it was I who handed him the box of tissues. "Her name is Loraine, and I know how to find her. When you are ready, just let me know."

CHAPTER 26

Gibbs and I spent the rest of the afternoon discussing questions I had concerning my new spiritual experience. Unlike Beltray, who had gone through a dramatic change of lifestyle and character—even personality. I, as far as I could tell, hadn't changed much at all. The most noticeable change in me that I could actually put my finger on was my awareness of a new spirit and power at work inside of me that I was learning to submit to. I didn't need to quit drinking because I didn't drink. I didn't need to overcome or have miraculously removed any other of the vile habits or downfalls that are common to the fallen sinful nature. I was fortunate in that I never got involved in any of those habits in the first place. What I did have, which may even be worse than all of the above, was a sense of pride and self-approval that comes from receiving so much commendation and praise from family, friends, community, and peers. I knew that to be humble is the better part of valor, but inside I knew I had a swollen ego. It was more than just the principle of right versus wrong that drove me to risk life and limb for the cause of justice.

I had already read Watchman's book several times; the last two chapters dealing with the soul life were of special interest. Slowly but gradually it was becoming clear to me that whatever I set out to do, I must never do until first giving the thing to God to bless and sanctify and to return to me with the stamp of divine approval. Only then can it be truly successful and bring glory to God

Gibbs returned to shuttling students, and I prepared to fly home the next day. However, I needed to pay Genneta a visit first. I approached her office door with the teak chest under my arm and patiently waited for her to finish her phone conversation. She then motioned me to enter and have a seat.

"Genneta," I said. "I have something that I believe belongs to you more than it does to me."

Puzzled, she glanced at the teakwood chest as I placed it on her desk. "That doesn't look like anything that belongs to me. In fact, I have never even seen it before. But it *is* beautiful."

"Remember the manila envelope you sent to me from your father?"

"Yes, something about a Russian airplane that went down somewhere, supposedly smuggling diamonds."

"That's right. I found the airplane, and this chest was hidden in a secret compartment that I would never had found if it hadn't have been rotted out. I think you should have a look inside. There are some documents and pictures that you might be interested in." I opened the lid.

Genneta Williams inhaled so deeply I thought she would explode. "Oh, my God! Are those diamonds?"

"Yes, ma'am, they surely are. And I believe they are yours."

"I want you to be right, but why are they mine?"

"Have a look at the pictures and documents and see what you can find out about those people. I think they may be some members of your extended family. Oh, and don't make this public. It would not be in anyone's best interest for the news media to know anything about it. Just take them home, and if you want to sell any of them, let me know. I will buy some or all of them from you for fair market value. Or, if you want, just keep them."

"Mr. Worley, I don't know what to say! Thank you very much!" Genneta scrambled from behind her desk and gave me a bear hug. That was good enough for me. It also served to remind me that my ribs had not completely healed.

The next morning, I gingerly loaded my gear in the Helio Courier, tossed the car keys on the front seat, and pointed the spinner south.

During my four months of rehab, Calvin Trent had stopped in to see me at least once a week. I had refrained from mentioning anything about the great fish or the diamonds. I didn't want him to think I had been hit on the head too hard. I just told him I went camping, sunk my airplane, and managed to make it to shore where Gibbs found me and, with the help of S&R, managed to get me out of there.

Since then, I had entertained the idea of not only retrieving the airplane, but also somehow, removing that monster fish from his tiny little world and set him free, hopefully to find his way to some place where he could feed on something besides elk meat. I decided to call Cal and tell him the whole story.

It was late in the evening when Cal returned my call. He had been on a game-management-unit patrol. I told him I had a long story and he said he would stop by.

Kati was fixing supper for three, expecting that Cal would join us. Soon we heard the Bell Ranger coming in from the northwest. I climbed into the Land Cruiser and met him as he settled the State Police helicopter onto the pad.

"What's up?" Cal asked as he climbed into the Land Cruiser.

"Kati's got supper on the table. Let's eat then talk," I said as I turned the truck toward the cabin.

Since our episode with the poachers Cal had shared many a meal with Kati and me in our home, and my wife always loved to watch him devour her cooking as though it were the first home-cooked meal he had ever eaten. It was obvious that his wife was not the cooking type. Finally, we settled onto the couches in the family room where I started at the beginning with the manila envelope I had received from Genneta Williams. When I got to the part about the big fish, I watched for any response from Cal that indicated he might be thinking I had lost my biscuit. Instead, he stroked his chin and stared intently at the coffee table, glancing only occasionally at me until I had completed the story with my hard landing on the rocks.

"I have heard stories about that monster fish off and on for the last thirty years," Cal said. "About twenty-five years ago, a fisherman disappeared up there, and all anyone ever found was his deserted camp. It was presumed by all who believed in the monster that the *fish* caught the *fisherman*. This is the first real evidence to me that the creature actually exists."

"Well, there is no question he exists. I even watched him steal my airplane. The thing is gigantic. My guess is he is thirty feet long and a good six thousand pounds. I actually watched him slap a yearling elk from the waters edge into the deep water and take it down. I'm sure he lets them rot until he can feed on the decayed flesh. I am guessing, he must be close to two hundred years old."

"I believe you, Lou. You are probably the only one who could convince me, but I do believe you."

"So how do we get it out of there?" I asked as I watched the astonished look on Cal's face.

"What do you mean get it out of there? Where do you plan on putting it?"

"Maybe we could get together with some marine biologists and figure out some way to get it into the sea. I'm sure he would appreciate the wide-open space. Besides, I want to retrieve my 180 from the bottom of that lake and have it restored."

Calvin had been sipping hot chocolate. Apparently, some of it went down the wrong pipe because suddenly he started choking. "That sounds kind of expensive. Why don't you just buy another 180?" Cal knew as soon as he uttered those words that it was a preposterous idea to let that fish keep my airplane. "I do happen to know some people at the marine biology institute. I'll see what they have to say, and I'm sure they will want to hear your story. Are you willing to tell it all over again?"

"That's no problem. Tell them I have an idea how we can isolate the fish to one end of the lake while we bring up the 180."

After Cal left, I began to second-guess myself, something I hardly ever do. Usually when I set my mind to something, I never look back. Sometimes even to my own detriment. By the time I actually start an endeavor, I have already considered just about every eventuality and determined that the end justifies the means. Now I found myself wondering if I was doing the right thing, or was I still driven by my ego? I decided to give the whole idea over to God and see if He would give it back to me blessed and sanctified like Watchman said He would.

"God in heaven, I pray to you on the ground of redemption and by the blood of the Lamb who is your beloved Son, Jesus Christ our Lord and Savior. I have the ambition to go forward with this project. I don't want it to be about my ego. If that's all it is, I am willing to walk away from it. However, if you can cause this endeavor to ultimately bring glory and praise to your name, give it back to me with your divine stamp of approval. Amen."

I searched through my file for the business card Mr. Terrill Bishop, the attorney general, had given me with his private phone number written on the back. I wanted to get some updated information as to where I could find Beltray's biological mother.

"This is Terrill Bishop. Leave your name and number."

"Mr. Bishop, this is Lou Worley. Could you help me locate Beltray Gibbons mother, Loraine? Please give me a call. Thanks."

Within thirty seconds after hanging up, my phone rang. It was the AG.

"Mr. Bishop, thanks for getting back to me so quickly."

"Glad to do it, Lou. So, you want to find Loraine. What brought this on all of a sudden?"

"Well, Terrill, I am happy to report that Beltray Gibbons has turned over a new leaf and is actually studying to become a minister. I don't know if you were aware of my accident, but, ironically, it was Gibbons who saved my life."

"Yes, I heard about that, but never got the details. How did you manage to sink your airplane?"

"It was a submerged protrusion of granite that snagged my right float and opened it like a sardine can."

"So why are you looking for Loraine? Does Beltray want to see her, or are you just curious?"

"The irony is, four years ago, I almost took Gibbons head off with my shotgun but instead gave him a chance to turn his life around. It is clear to me that he has done just that. Now in the last four months, he has not only saved my physical life but also led me to an acceptance and faith in the gospel of Jesus Christ. I want to help him discover his roots and possibly salvage some of his past, Lord willing."

There was a long pause as I waited for Mr. Bishop's reply. I was about to hang up, thinking I had lost our connection.

"That is some testimony, Lou. I am going to give you my wife's phone number. She will be able to help you with this. You need to realize that according to the laws of adoption no information can legally be given out as to her whereabouts without her consent."

"I understand that, Terrill. When would be the best time to call Pam?"

"You can call her anytime. It may go to voice mail. Just leave your name and number. She will get back with you. Good luck."

"Thanks, Terrill." I hung up.

I really had not planned sharing all that with the attorney general; it just sort of spilled out of me. It sure must have sounded strange coming from me. The thing of it is, I would not even be alive right now if it was not for Bill Shearer telling me to pray when I found myself in that fix, or for God who heard that prayer and sent Beltray, who I almost killed. The cycle of circumstances still amaze me.

I had just finished a sandwich and cup of coffee when my cell phone started ringing again.

"This is Lou Worley."

"Mr. Worley, this is Pam Bishop. My husband just called and told me about your conversation concerning Beltray Gibbons. I think it is so wonderful that you want to do that for him. I did not know that Beltray had found the Lord and desires to find his mother. I know right where she is and am on my way to see her now. I will call you as soon as I find out if she is okay with this. I am so excited! Thank you, Mr. Worley. Bye."

I just sat there looking at the phone with a blank stare. So, this is how God works. I think I am getting the hang of it.

I still had Gibbs's number in my cell phone, so I scrolled him up and mashed on the green button.

"Hello, Mr. Worley."

"Beltray, I need to know when you could come down here and go with me to meet your mother."

"I can come anytime. Does she want to meet me?" I detected a quiver in his voice.

"I just got off the phone with your mother's cousin, well actually, second cousin and she is on her way to ask her as we speak. She will be calling me back any minute to let me know. As soon as I hear from her, I will get back with you. The message I am getting from the Lord on this is that you need to prepare yourself to meet your biological mother. I'll call you later."

Within an hour, my phone was ringing again. It was Pam.

"Mr. Worley, I have someone here who would like to talk to you."

"Hello, Mr. Worley?" I knew instantly that the quivering voice was Beltray's mother. There was something about the tone of her voice.

Whatever you call it, there was no mistake that this person and Beltray Gibbons had the same *voice* genes.

"Hello to you too. Is this Loraine?" I asked.

"Yes."

"Are you the mother of Beltray Gibbons?"

"I think so, accept until recently I never knew his name. Do you know my son?" Her voice broke, and I had to wait for a minute before I could answer. Finally, she recovered enough for me to continue.

"Yes, I do, Loraine. You can be very proud of your son. He saved my life."

"When can I see him?" she asked, the emotion clearly apparent in her broken voice.

"Beltray is living in Bettles and is one of the school's pilots. He flies a Cessna Caravan and can be down here tomorrow. I am guessing that you live in Juneau, is that right?"

"Yes. I live on the west side, across the channel."

"That's fine. I will call him and get him started this way. If you don't mind, my wife and I would like to come along, if that is all right."

"Yes, of course. Thank you, Mr. Worley. Thank you, thank you."

I was not sure I would be able to witness this reunion without turning into a blubbering mess, but I certainly wasn't going to let that stop me from being there when Beltray got to meet his mother for the first time in his life. I scrolled up his name again and placed the call I knew he was now waiting for.

"Beltray, this is Lou. I just spoke with your mother. She is excited and anxious to meet you. Get an overnight bag together, and I will have the Foundation jet pick you up at Bettles. I will meet the jet in Anchorage, and Kati and I will go down with you. I will give the pilot your number, and he can call you with his arrival time at Bettles. See you in a few hours."

I had no doubt Beltray would call me when he got the message even though there was no need. I called the Foundation and asked to speak with the president.

"Hello, this is Kati."

"Hi, pumpkin. Can I get the jet for a couple of days?"

"Hi, baby. Sure. But where are you going?"

"You and I, sweetie. I am sending the Citation to pick up Beltray, and we are going with him to Juneau to meet his biological mother. You wouldn't want to miss that would you?"

"Oh, Lou, absolutely not! I wouldn't miss that for the world! Why don't we go with Eric when he picks up Beltray and make it a direct to Juneau?"

"Perfect, sweetie. Great idea."

I packed a few overnight essentials for both of us and spooled up the Helio Courier. In fifteen minutes, I was on final approach to Merrill Field in Anchorage. I found a tie-down next to the jet ramp and transferred our things into the Cessna Citation II. Eric Campbell, the chief pilot, greeted me. I had only known him a short time, but had every confidence in his ability. Within minutes, Kati joined us.

"Baby, do you know what I am feeling?"

"What is it, Lou?"

"I am feeling like I have been given another son."

Kati looked at me and after a short pause said, "Maybe you should tell that to Beltray."

CHAPTER 27

T he flight from Anchorage to Bettles was barely over an hour. I gave Beltray's number to Eric and requested that he not mention that Kati and I were aboard.

As he walked through the door, we jumped to our feet and hollered, "SURPRISE!"

That was all Kati's idea, of course. With a short fuel stop in Fairbanks, we were landing in Juneau in barely over two and a half hours from Bettles.

"How much longer are you going to be in school?" I asked Beltray.

"I am working on a bachelor's degree in sociology and theology and hope to finish by the end of this next year. After that, I will need to spend at least three years in the field as an associate pastor or missionary. Maybe my mother would let me move her up to Bettles where we could be together and I could look after her," Beltray mused.

"She could be the second fruit of your ministry, since I hold first place in that category," I said.

It was a rainy and cold early November day in Juneau, Alaska, when the Cessna Citation II settled onto the runway. A black Cadillac Escalade sat in front of the General Aviation Fixed Base Operations Office, awaiting our arrival. Pam Bishop met us at the door.

Our pilot remained behind with the Citation while Kati, Gibbs, and I eagerly climbed into the Escalade.

"We are only a half an hour away from Loraine's place," Pam said. "Would you like to get a bite to eat before we go?"

I looked at Kati and Gibbs, who were both shaking their heads no.

"Let's just go. Maybe we can get something later," I said.

In no time, we were headed west on the AK-7 for West Juneau and the residence of Beltray Gibbons's mother. I glanced toward Gibbs and noticed that his hands were shaking. He had his eyes closed most of the time, probably praying.

Pam turned onto Peters Place and into the parking lot of a very well-kept church. We walked around back to the front door of a duplex apartment that apparently was part of the church's facilities.

The chime was still ringing in my ears when the door opened and a petite, dark-haired woman, appearing to be in her middle forties, emerged from the doorway. Her face bore the impression of years of hard living, but still the beauty of her youthful features were detectable. She and Beltray's similar features made it evident that they shared the same DNA.

With her arms extended toward Pam, Loraine greeted her second cousin. As Pam ushered Beltray toward his mother, their eyes met for the first time. Loraine lifted her hands toward her son, and in that instant, the strength in her legs gave way. Beltray gathered his mother into his arms, lifting her to his bosom. There they remained for several minutes, the tears flowing freely. While, not a sound came from either of them. Finally, Beltray carried his mother into her apartment and placed her on the couch.

For the next two hours, Pam, Katie, and I sat in a circle in witness to their moment. The overwhelming, maternal love for her son, dormant in Loraine for over twenty-eight years, could no longer be hidden. She wondered year after year what he looked like. How tall was he? Was he right-handed or left-handed? Now she no longer had to wonder. Carefully, she memorized every feature; the shape of his eyes, and the creases around his mouth from his smile. Oblivious to his scars, Loraine beamed with pride. Every feature she saw in him was a mirror of herself. Beltray saw himself in her as well. The need he felt to connect with his roots had lain buried for too long, like a gut-ache that had lasted a lifetime. Embraced in his mother's arms, he suddenly belonged; he had found his family. Holding her, he felt comforted and at peace for the first time in his life. We all knew that the love we were a witness to was as pure as the divine hand that had reunited them.

"I'm going to go for some takeout," I said, rising to my feet. "How does Chinese sound?"

"Just right," Kati said. "I'll go with you."

"Wait for me. I'm going too," Pam added as she grabbed her coat and purse.

As I headed toward the door, I noticed a framed wedding picture on the wall of an American man and a Chinese woman approximately thirty-years old. I instantly recognized both of them from the pictures that had come with the teakwood chest. I was shocked, to say the least, and almost turned to ask Loraine why she had a picture of a diamond smuggler and Lord knows what else hanging on her wall. The Lord told me to keep my mouth shut.

"I know a great place on the eastside," Pam said. Turning to Loraine and Gibbs, she continued. "We will be right back. You two could use some time alone to get to know each other." With that, we closed the door behind us and climbed into the Escalade.

As we crossed the bridge to east Juneau, I mentioned to Pam Beltray's desire to relocate his mother to Bettles where he could look after her.

"I'm not sure what Loraine will do with that," Pam responded. "She has been staying at that church for almost five years and is very involved with the congregation. The pastor, whose name was Jay Baldwin, passed away about six months ago, and he had only just lost his wife who was Chinese a short six months prior to that. They were both in their late eighties or early nineties no one really knows for sure. The congregation, more than half of which are of mixed race, Chinese and Japanese descent, are looking for a new pastor. The duplex on the other side from Loraine is the parsonage where the pastor and his wife lived."

"Were they the same couple in the picture by the door?" I asked Pam.

"Yes. Isn't it sweet? I understand they met in China when Jay was there as a missionary."

"Is that a fact? Well, I think that would be a good ministry for Beltray." It suddenly occurred to me that there was more to the Russian smuggler than a sunken floatplane and a chest full of uncut diamonds. I was sure the couple on the wall, were the same two people that were in the pictures from the teak chest and Jay Bold, obviously had something to hide or he wouldn't have changed his name to Pastor Jay Baldwin.

It was also clear that Beltray and his mother would never let circumstances ever separate them again. Her need for her son was matched only by Beltray's need for his mother. Nonetheless, their future together necessitated Gibbs returning to Bettles to initiate the transfer of his scholastic program to the Sitka Learning Center. I decided that a call to Priscilla Vasquez, the head of the educational department, might help to expedite the process.

"Education Department," Priscilla answered in her Latin accent, strongly hinting of her Venezuelan heritage.

"Ms. Vasquez, this is Lou Worley. Do you have a minute?"

"Of course, I do. Mr. Worley. What can I do for you?"

"Were you aware that Beltray Gibbons has been reunited with his birth mother?"

"No, I wasn't. I wasn't even aware that he knew who she is."

"Well, with some help, I was able to locate her. She lives in West Juneau and the little church she belongs to just lost their pastor and Beltray may be taking over the responsibilities of their church." I realized that I might have been jumping the gun a little, but if the Christian life is based on the premise of living by faith, what better way to start?

"What about his classes?" Priscilla immediately asked. "Is he planning on completing them?"

"Oh, yes! He wants to know if he can transfer his scholastics to the Sitka Center."

"Absolutely," Priscilla replied, obviously relieved. "I will take care of all that for him. Can he finish this quarter? If he can, the transition will happen much more smoothly. I assured Ms. Vasquez that Beltray would have no problem with finishing the quarter at Bettles.

We took lunch to go and returned to Loraine's. Gibbs and his mother visited and held each other well into the evening.

On the plane ride back I explained to Beltray the situation with the Church and he was so overcome with emotion that I almost wished I hadn't said anything.

"Mr. Worley, I never imagined that life in Christ could be so blessed. The thing that makes me saddest is the wasted years of dysfunction apart from God. I am so blessed and thank-full."

"Believe me Gibbs, I know just how you feel."

"Gibbs," I said. "This Citation is only going as far as Anchorage, so when we land, we can take the Helio to my place, and you can drop us off and either stay the night or go on to Bettles, whichever you want. Then when you have finished your business at the school, just take the Helio to Juneau and use it to go back and forth to Sitka. When the congregation makes their final decision on taking you on as their pastor, the Foundation will see that you get an airplane and a car that you can use."

The tears were streaming down Beltray's face again. It had been a lot to deal with for one day—meeting his mother for the first time in his life, finding a pastorate, and taking on the responsibility of a church while caring for his mother who was still more a stranger than a mother. Now also faced with changing to another school, it was a huge order for someone who just a few years ago was a lost drug addict who could not even tie his own shoes without someone removing his handcuffs. However, it was obvious that for Beltray there would be no turning back. The choice he had made over four years before along with his born-again experience had changed his heart and mind, resulting in a new life that held exciting promise for the future.

Once again, I was without an airplane. Beltray had taken the Helio to Bettles, and I needed transportation.

I wasn't sure if Rusty and Mitchell were using the still orange Pilatus Porter at the Eva Creek mine or not. I scrolled up Rusty's name and mashed on the green button.

"Hey, Dad, how are you?" Rusty answered.

"Doin' just fine, son. How is the hard-rock mining going?"

"All right. Just chasing one small vein of ore after the other. They are laced all through this mountain. If all the gold that is in these rocks were in one place, we would have almost as much as we got out of Alfred Creek, but it is all scattered in little pockets and veins. Maybe one of these days we will find another mother lode. So what can I do for you, Dad?"

"I was wondering if you were using the Porter. I let Beltray use the other Helio."

"Not a problem, Dad. You can use it all you want. I thought you were going to see about retrieving the 180?"

"I am. I just haven't had time until now. Can you pick me up in your Stationair in the morning? I'll ride up to the mine with you and bring it back."

"I'll just bring it down to you tonight, Dad. I have been flying it to work lately. My 206 is at home."

"Great!" I said. "I'll give you a ride to your house when you get here. See you tonight, son."

I had known for a long time that the profits from the Eva Creek mine were scarcely worth the labor and materials. I think the boys continued with it primarily because they wanted something to do. They certainly didn't need the money. On the other hand, it was entirely possible that at any time they could hit a vein of yellow gold that could meet or exceed the Alfred Creek strike. I had left all that hard work to my sons. I no longer had the ambition or intrigue for it.

Thanksgiving, Christmas, and New Years came and went with our whole family together. Beltray and his mother joined us as adopted members of our extended family. We spent all three holidays in the lodge retreat at Loon Lake.

I was trying to make arrangements for the rescue of my 180, but it seemed that it was going a little slow. Calvin Trent had written a letter to the marine biology department at the Alaska State Oceanography Institute in Anchorage. It read:

> Dear Sirs:
> One of our off-duty law enforcement officers encountered a monster fish in Glacial Lake twenty-five miles north of Nome, suffering not only the loss of his personal aircraft, but barely surviving life-threatening injury.
> I am writing this letter as an inquiry of any knowledge you may have concerning this anomaly as well as a suggested method for retrieval of the aforementioned aircraft.
> In consideration for the safety of the obvious natural phenomenon this great fish represents and the safety of all involved in the retrieval process, this inquiry is therefore submitted.

Officer Calvin Trent
Fish and Game Management
Office of Public Safety, Wasilla, Alaska.

Within a month, Trent received the following reply:

Office of Public Safety
Wasilla Alaska
Attn: Calvin Trent
Fish and Game Management

Dear Officer Trent:

The Marine Biology Department has been aware of the beluga sturgeon for the last twenty years. Our studies have revealed a specific pattern of behavior. It is our recommendation that all parties involved meet with representatives of the department for a verbal briefing of the beluga's seasonal activities.

I am sending an application form. Please include along with the completed application a full disclosure of the incident, events, and proposed recovery plans along with a complete, detailed description of the animal's behavior at the time of the encounter.

A review board responsible for granting the applicant a hearing will then consider the application and disclosure. The applicant may expect notification by mail when the hearing date has been set.

Melissa Macomb, PhD
Exec. Professor, Marine Biology Dept.
Anchorage, Alaska

Cal had sent a copy of both letters along with the application to me. I gave Ray Sumner a call.

"Aircraft Sales and Salvage. Ray speaking."

"Ray Sumner, this is Lou Worley. Do you have a minute?"

"Always got a minute for you, Lou. What can I help you with?"

I brought Ray up to speed on the application and hearing process required by the biology department and my need for a written, detailed salvage proposal.

"That's no problem, Lou. I'll get that to you right away."

"Thanks, Ray. As soon as we get a green light from them, we can set a date for moving the equipment in. Will you be able to go with us to the hearing?"

"You bet, I can be there. We have worked with them on salvages before numerous times, so we have a good working relationship."

"Excellent! They said they have been monitoring the behavior of that fish for the last twenty years, so maybe they will be able to advise us as to a time of the year when it would be less likely to adversely effect the operation."

"I sure hope so, Lou. I can't imagine why you even want to go back up there, but if that's what you want, we will sure get it done."

"I know you will, Ray. I'll get back with you when I hear from the biology department. Don't forget to send me that proposal."

The next week, I inserted the last of the required documents, sealed the large manila envelope, and mailed it. Ray's proposal for retrieval of the 180 included a portable dock airlifted in four separate sections by helicopter from which the divers could work. The plan was to attach four rubber bladders to both ends of the airplane and under each wing as close to the empennage as possible. Four huge air compressors would inflate the bladders individually, lifting the airplane to the surface. A Sikorsky (primarily used for logging) would lower a specially designed canvas crib attached to the helicopter cable system. From there they would airlift the 180 to Nome where Jerry Hansen would restore it to its original condition.

Ten days later, Kati handed me the letter from the Institute of Oceanography Biology Department.

It read:

> Dear Mr. Worley:
>
> A hearing date has been set for September 26 of this year at ten o'clock a.m. The biology department is very interested in seeing any documentation you may have

supporting your claim of the beluga attacking an elk. Our biologists have never observed that particular behavior.

In addition, you stated that the fish stole your airplane. We would like to understand more about that.

We are looking forward to meeting with you and your team.

Sincerely,
Melissa Macomb, PhD
Exec. Professor, Marine Biology Dept.
Anchorage, Alaska

It was only June, and our appointment was not until September. I was not happy about the long delay, but I figured that waiting a couple of months would be better than getting into another argument with that dang fish.

I packed some gear, had the floats installed on the Porter, and headed to Loon Lake for some fishing and mild hiking. Kati came with me, and we spent the next three months enjoying another honeymoon.

Finally the day came, Cal had picked me up in the state helicopter, and Ray and another man were waiting for us at Merrill Field.

The oceanography building was located within a mile of Merrill Field next to the Glenn Highway

"Lou Worley and Officer Trent, I would like you to meet Jason Sorenson. He will be in charge of the salvage operation and is the owner-pilot of the Sikorsky that will be used for all the lifting."

Cal and I greeted Mr. Sorenson with a firm handshake and climbed into Ray's Suburban.

From the airport, we turned east on the Glenn Highway for one mile and soon were parking in front of a four-story glass building at least two blocks long with an array of antennas on the roof that must have included every band and wavelength known to man.

We entered the building into a large lobby, the far side of which sat an information desk framed in a half-circle. Two young ladies, sitting at separate stations, looked up as we came through the door. I addressed the nearest one as we approached, making note of the name on her name-tag.

"Good morning, Carman. I am Lou Worley. We have a ten o'clock appointment with the review board."

"The board is expecting you, Mr. Worley. That will be Room 4B. You may take one of the elevators, if you like."

Room 4B was a conference room with a seating capacity of approximately fifty, generously decorated with pictures and charts pertaining to oceanography and biological studies. A long conference table sat at the front of the room where a middle-aged woman, who I assumed was Melissa Macomb, stood conferring with two older gentlemen. All three stopped talking and looked our way as we entered the room.

"Mr. Worley?" she asked, glancing at all four of us, searching for some clue that would distinguish me from my three associates.

"Right here," I said, slightly raising my hand and forefinger. "You must be Ms. Macomb."

"Yes, Mr. Worley," she said, briefly shaking my hand. "Let me introduce you to the head of our oceanography department, Dr. Clyde Belechek and"—gesturing toward the other gentleman—"this is Dr. Arnold Camas, a world-renowned professor of oceanographic aqua thermal research."

I wasn't quite quick enough at introducing Cal, Ray, and Jason, but they managed to get it done on their own. After the brief moment of introduction and small talk subsided, we seated ourselves across the conference table from the members.

"Mr. Worley," Melissa began "we would like to hear, in your own words, the details of the elk attack and just exactly how you say the beluga stole your airplane. If you don't mind, I would like to record it."

For the next twenty minutes, I told the story that by now had become much less surreal.

"So, is it your opinion that the fish intentionally kills the animals as a food source?" Ms. Macomb asked.

"That is what occurred to me," I said. "I know that it is limited as far as what it can eat by virtue of its species, but if it lets the carcass decay underwater for a long enough period of time, I am sure the meat would soften and fall apart so that the beluga could consume it."

"You stated that the fish ran off with the airplane. How do you think it managed that?" Melissa asked.

"I had made several dives down to the 180. The position that it lay in on the lake bottom with the passenger-side door torn off provided an opening large enough for the fish to possibly get its head into. I am speculating, but I suppose it is entirely possible it was powerful enough to just swim off with it."

"Mr. Worley, you stated that the fish actually attacked you, causing you bodily harm. What do you think you did that might have provoked that attack?" Melissa asked. I did not want the conversation to get to close to the real reason I had flown into Glacial Lake so I knew I needed to divert the subject a little.

"I'm not sure that I did anything unless retrieving my belongings from the Skywagon provoked him. I'm wondering that if you all have known about this monster fish for the last twenty years like you say you have, why were there no warnings provided to the public? Officer Trent tells me that a fisherman went missing up there about twenty years ago, and all anybody found was his rubber rowboat."

"We didn't want the public to know about it because it would have interfered with our behavioral studies and maybe created a firestorm of tourist and media sensationalism that we certainly didn't need. Not to mention the threat to public safety," Melissa responded.

"Well, I understand that, and I'm not suggesting that you were not regarding public safety by not providing warnings, but people are going to continue using that lake occasionally, and it is just a matter of time before the word gets out. My question is, how did the thing get into the lake in the first place and how are you planning on removing it? Also, how can we go about the salvage of my aircraft without provoking more interference from that fish?"

Ms. Macomb turned to the head of the oceanographic institute.

"Dr. Belechek, would you share with these gentlemen your conclusions based on the behavioral studies we have gathered?"

"I would be pleased to, Melissa. Thank you. Gentleman, we have monitored as much of the activities of this fish as we were able to, using motion detectors and underwater recording devices powered from portable solar panels. We have been able to detect its presence at only certain times of the year, primarily the months of July and August. Occasionally, we have picked up movement as early as the middle of June, corresponding with the El Nino weather systems. Dr. Camas believes the fish comes and goes with the warmer currents also corresponding with El Nino."

"Excuse me," I interrupted. "Are you telling us that the fish comes and goes from the sea?"

"Yes, we believe it does," Dr. Arnold Camas responded. "It is entirely possible that an underground or underwater cavern exists somewhere near the bottom of the lake and extends all the way to the Bering Sea some twenty-six miles west. This species found usually but not exclusively in the Caspian and Black Seas, is also prevalent in the Mediterranean. We believe it follows warm water currents that migrate from sea to sea all over the world. Normally, the best feeding for the beluga sturgeon would be in warmer waters where it would be more apt to find its natural feed, but very likely travels to various parts of the world in search of new feeding sources."

"Mr. Worley," Melissa interrupted. "From your account of the attack on the elk, we are now speculating the possibility that the beluga might have inadvertently happened on a dead elk in the water long ago and fed on its decaying flesh, acquiring a taste for elk meat as an entirely new food source. We would like to thank you for sharing this information with us. It has contributed to our insight into this ancient wonder."

"This is your permit for the salvage operation." Melissa handed me an envelope. "We have determined that the beluga has left the lake for the year, and you should be able to go ahead without concern. The lake will be freezing over in less than a month, but that should give you enough time. The permit has some stipulations associated with it, so please read them carefully."

We thanked Melissa and her review board members for their time. On the way to the car, I asked Ray and Jason, "When can you guys start moving in?"

"We will get started the first of the week," Jason said.

CHAPTER 28

I felt a small amount of apprehension over returning to Glacial Lake, especially the part where I had to land on the water.

It was October 5. We were already six days late getting started due to a persistent fog that had blanketed the Glacial Lake area for over a week. The floats were still on the Porter from my summer of flying in and out of Loon Lake. It was a clear day, and I circled the lake several times looking for the fish, I mean, logs and granite spires.

I beached on the north side of the spit where I had camped the year before. In the orange floatplane, I had included provisions for two weeks even though I didn't expect the salvage to take much more than three or four days. With the extra space in the Porter, I just made my bed inside the plane.

I had arrived a day early, mostly to reminisce and thank the Lord that this whole deal was working out. Jason would be bringing in the first section of the floating deck sometime in the early morning, and I expected Ray to show up with the crew in his DeHavilland Beaver in time to prepare for Jason's arrival.

I sat staring at the campfire until I could no longer keep my eyes open. The night was beautiful, with the cool nip of fall in the air. I hoped and prayed the fog would not return. With flashlight in hand, I made my way back to the Porter and my floating camp. Snuggled into the sleeping bag on an oversized air mattress, the gentle rocking of the waves against the pontoons soon put me to sleep.

I awoke to the shrill bugle of a bull elk high in a mountain meadow. The rut was on, and the bulls were making their play for breeding rights. The fall colors were about to make their brief but beautiful appearance, painting the land in brilliant displays of red, gold, and purple. It seemed a shame to disturb the quietness of the place with the hammering blades of a Sikorsky helicopter, but at the bottom of that lake was the mangled remains of what had once been a perfectly good airplane, and the time had come to restore it to, not just its original condition, but even better. I thought about the parallels of that to the work of God in the lives of fallen man.

The drone of Ray's Beaver, trudging its way to Glacial Lake, interrupted my thoughts. The day I had been anticipating for more than a year had arrived.

Ray circled the lake, setting up for a glassy water landing from north to south. The orange life preserver I had tied to the granite spire the day before marked the spot of the underwater float opener. The Beaver idled its way to the spit until the pontoons slid to a stop on the sandy shore.

Two divers emerged from the cargo door of Ray's floatplane and began unloading their equipment. Ray climbed down from the cockpit and made his way toward me.

"Lou," he said. "Can you go with the divers in the raft and show them where you think the Skywagon ended up after the fish ran off with it?"

I approached the two men whom I had never met before.

"Good morning, I'm Lou Worley. You boys want me to ride out with you and give you an idea where to find that airplane?" I asked, simultaneously shaking their hands.

"How do?" The larger of the two men answered. "That would be great. By the way, I'm Elroy, and this is Lester." He referred to the shorter man who briefly stopped working to nod and shake my hand.

"We should take a hundred feet of rope and a spare life preserver to use as a buoy for marking the spot where we find the wreckage," I said. "The buoy that I had tied to it might still be attached. I don't know how far it went after the buoy disappeared underwater."

Ray Sumner hollered, pointing toward the south. "I hear Jason."

The three of us looked at each other, knowing that what we were about to do would have to wait until Jason's load was detached.

From Ray Sumner's Beaver the two divers had unloaded a four-man Navy SEAL-type rubber raft with torpedo-shaped pontoons and an huge outboard motor mounted on the rear. As the Sikorsky came over the ridge, I slid into a life preserver and climbed into the boat, making my way to the bow. Lester was directly behind me with a coil of rope. Elroy checked the fuel and fired up the Johnson 550. I pointed to the north end of the lake just as Elroy poured on the coals, almost landing me in his lap. If it were not for Lester, I probably would have sailed right out the rear of the boat.

Jason slowed the helicopter with his cargo dangling a hundred feet below him, giving us time to get into position. He was definitely good at what he did. About a half-mile north of the spit, I held a clenched fist above my head signaling the spot where we should set up the platform, putting us, I hoped, in close proximity to the wreckage.

Lester dialed up Jason on a two-way radio as the Sikorsky settled the first twelve-foot-by-twelve-foot section of the floating platform onto the surface of the lake. Quickly, Elroy maneuvered the Kodiak alongside where Lester mounted the platform and set free the four corner cables attached to the deck. In the center of the platform was an anchor attached to a small winch that Lester quickly released, establishing the platforms position on the water.

As Jason and his helicopter, which looked like a giant C-clamp with a hornet's head and rotors, returned to Nome for the next section of the platform, the two divers began unloading their equipment onto the twelve-foot by twelve-foot dock. Soon they were ready to submerge. Lester had a hundred feet of fluorescent nylon rope fastened to a belt full of carabineers along with a life preserver to use as a buoy. Four two-foot-by-two-foot trap doors surrounded the anchor winch assembly from which the divers could descend straight down the cable, which was marked in one-foot increments. The anchor had come to rest at a depth of seventy-three feet.

I pointed them in the direction I had last seen the buoy and where they would likely pick up the path, which should lead directly to the wreckage. I then returned to the spit to pick up Ray. After a cup of coffee, we returned to the platform to wait for the marker.

Almost an hour had past when to our northwest and a hundred yards away the yellow life preserver broke the surface of the water. I started the Johnson outboard and carefully idled the Kodiak in the direction of the

225

yellow marker, expecting that at least one if not both divers would be following the rope to the surface. At the halfway point, one diver surfaced and within another fifty yards, the second one joined him. I added throttle and moved alongside the buoy, killing the motor.

Ray reached over the side, and in a Navy SEAL-type motion, Elroy was in the Kodiak in the blink of an eye. Moments later, Lester was beside him.

"How does it look?" Ray asked. "Is it still in one piece?"

Elroy pulled off his goggles and mask. "Yeah, it's in one piece. Should be a piece of cake except it has a lot of mud and lake-weed in the floor of the hull and empennage. We will have to clean that all out before it can go for the ride."

"Is it still right side up?" I asked.

"For the most part it is lying on a hill, nose-down, tail-up. We will have to approach it from the downhill side with the bladders," Ray continued.

It had been an hour and a half since Jason had left, and we could hear him in the distance, returning with the second section of platform and one of the air bladders.

I was getting really excited. Though we had just started, it seemed we were only within hours of actually seeing my 180 back on the surface of the water once again. The Sikorsky finally free from its payload and swinging the dangling cable away from our operations area, Jason once again headed south.

Elroy and Lester geared up for their next descent. Jason had brought two of the four bladders necessary to raise the airplane, along with four air compressors. The first item of business was to join the two sections of platform together and bolt them into place, and then raise the anchor and tow it with the Kodiak closer to the buoy marking the location of the 180. That accomplished, the divers dropped each anchor on the two sections and prepared the bladder for submerging.

Elroy and Lester first lowered two cables, the upper end of which fastened to the platform, and descending with the other ends, fastened them to the Skywagon to hold it from sliding further down the underwater hill it was resting on. Then, with fifty pounds of weight attached to the lower end of the first bladder, they took it down to the 180, sliding it through the opening between the strut and cabin of the aircraft. Attempting to do the same thing on the other side proved somewhat more difficult, but their long experience in salvage overcame the problems they encountered due to the collapsed wing.

Jason soon returned with the third and then the fourth sections, and by the end of the day the 24X24 foot square platform was in place. All that remained was the placement of the two remaining bladders. The divers could not dive two days back to back, so the next day Ray Sumner would bring in another team of divers while Elroy and Lester worked on the surface. Each evening, Ray would return the crew to their motel at the airport in Nome. Suddenly alone with my reflections of a year ago at this same lake, I enjoyed the evening by a campfire before retiring to my floatplane apartment.

It seemed like it took hours for me to get to sleep. My mind was working overtime reliving the ordeal I had gone through. I still had pain and discomfort in my hip and walked with a slight limp—the cold weather was returning and the additional aches and pains associated with it—but overall I was actually doing quite well. I thought about a man I read about in the Bible named Jacob who also had to live his life with a lame hip as a reminder of Gods grace and provision regardless of what things seem like at times.

Although relieved by Dr. Camas's report that the sturgeon would likely be gone, I still, for some reason, was not completely convinced. After a couple of hours lying awake fretting about it, I finally remembered that I placed the whole thing before the Lord for Him to bless and bring about, according to His will. Content with that, the fretting ceased, and I fell asleep.

The morning came and with it a three-foot layer of ground fog that laterally obscured the lake. I knew, however, that a good float pilot would still be able to land in-spite of it, and the vertical visibility from Jason's perspective in the helicopter would be virtually unaffected. By the time I had completed preparing breakfast and coffee, Ray and his four passengers were already on final approach with the big Sikorsky; close behind and already thumping its way over the ridge.

Ray and I, along with the two additional divers Leo and Robert, climbed aboard the Kodiak and fired the outboard. The fog had already more than half dissipated as we made our way toward the platform. Jason hovered directly overhead as we disengaged the rubber bladders from the canvas cradle and set the huge chopper on the only available landing pad at the far end of the spit. Leaving Ray on the platform, I made my way to where Jason had landed the Sikorsky and turned the Kodiak over to Elroy and Lester who had been waiting on the shore.

Jason and I chatted over coffee while Leo and Robert went below to set the last two bladders. Elroy and Lester would work the top side. Within three quarters of an hour, Leo appeared at the surface, giving the thumbs up to start the four air compressors. With the air now flowing simultaneously into all four bladders, the two divers traded off going below to check the inflation of the bladders, each staying below about an hour.

After the first hour, Leo again descended to the Skywagon relieving Robert. The only communication between the platform and the divers on the bottom was a rope connected to a bell. one yank on the rope would indicate that all is well, keep pumping. A continual ringing of the bell meant shut down the compressors.

"Jason, how long will it take to fill the bladders?" I asked.

"About six hours."

"Is that going to give you time to get the wreckage back to Nome?" I ask a little tentatively.

"Well, hopefully, we will be able to get it on the surface where we can hook up to it and lift it with the chopper onto the platform. Then tomorrow it will have to be cleaned out and secured to make sure nothing is going to fall off in-flight before we transport."

For the rest of the day, we listened to the drone of the four air compressors. Suddenly the bell started ringing. Jason and I ran for the Kodiak and quickly sped out to the platform where Lester had shut off the pump, waiting for more communication. Robert quickly descended to the bottom to see if Leo needed his assistance.

For twenty minutes, we all watched and waited. Then the bell rang again, this time just once. Lester started the compressors and checked the gauge; the bladders were at sixty percent. Another hour and a half went by when suddenly Leo appeared on the surface.

"It's coming up," he said.

The gauges were at eighty-five percent when the 180 suddenly broke the surface of the lake. Elroy and Lester were already in their wet suits. Though they would not be diving, they still would work in the water to secure the cables.

The whine of the Sikorsky turbo told me that Jason was about to get in the air. Elroy and Lester fired up the Kodiak loaded with cables and slowly motored their way toward the Skywagon. The air bladders on each end and under each wing had lifted the top one-third of the airplane above the surface. Draped in lake-weed with the left wing folded upward at a ninety-degree angle and the floatation carriage ripped and mangled, I wondered if Ray would even be able to restore it, but I knew he had rebuilt worse. Before we decided to go ahead with the salvage, I had described the damage in detail. He just shook his head and said, "No problem."

All four divers were on the wreckage attaching the carrier cables and straps. Jason lifted off the spit in a clockwise loop keeping the one-hundred-foot stinger away from the work area, hovering well above the wreckage. Jason had used his Sikorsky workhorse for everything from logging to hauling pipe for the pipeline from Prudhoe Bay to Valdez; salvage was just another day for his crew and, compared to many, this one was a walk in the park.

Jason descended to where the end of the stinger was only fifty feet above the crew. There he held the hover activating the winch and slowly lowered the stinger. Two, twenty-five-foot ropes hung from the ball and hook that provided a means of controlling the swinging stinger, which, uncontrolled, could easily kill a man. Leo and Robert held the control ropes while Elroy and Lester connected the cables and straps, securing the wreckage to the ball/hook.

With the connection made, Jason slowly began to wind the winch, reeling up the cable until snug. Lester communicated with Jason on the handheld radio as they checked and rechecked every connection. Satisfied that all was secure and the helicopter now supported the weight of the airplane, the four divers simultaneously opened the air valves to empty the bladders. Once deflated, the crew re-boarded the Kodiak and circled the wreckage removing the bladders. Then, satisfied that nothing would slip or give way while in transport to the platform, Lester signaled for Jason to initiate the hoist.

The Skywagon slowly rose from its watery grave and was once again airborne, albeit in pitiful condition. Slowly and carefully, Jason slid the 180 over to the platform where the four divers were waiting, positioned at all four corners. As the weight of the wreckage settled onto the floating platform, Elroy scrambled up on the top of the cabin to unhook the stinger.

What a beautiful sight. There wasn't a lot of room to move around on the twenty-four-foot-by twenty-four-foot platform that now was completely taken up with the salvaged airplane, but at least we were able to examine firsthand the extent of the damage. I could tell that Ray Sumner was anxious to see it restored once again as well. Again, I reflected on the work of the Lord in the saving of a man wrecked by sin.

I was hoping Jason would be able to get it on to Nome and to Jerry Hansen before nightfall. However, it was obvious when I looked inside that the cabin and empennage would need to be cleaned out and a few loose pieces secured.

Before they left, Jason had the crew secure all four corners of the airplane to the platform, tow the platform itself to the shore where the spit joined the mainland, and tie it off to a couple of trees. Then, climbing into the Sikorsky, Jason once again disappeared over the ridge.

With all four divers aboard the DeHavilland Beaver Ray shoved the floatplane away from the spit and fired up the huge radial engine. Within ten minutes I was once again alone at Glacial Lake.

Ray and the four divers returned the next morning with Jason and the Sikorsky in-trail. After several hours of preparation, they lifted my poor old 180 into the air and back over the ridge to Nome and Jerry Hansen's shop, where it would undergo a complete restoration. I had given Jerry the green light. I wanted it done perfect and painted the same color, with no time limitations.

I spent another week at Glacial Lake, fishing, airplane camping, and reflecting on the similarities of what I was doing with my destroyed airplane and what God had done in both mine, and Beltray Gibbons, life. I could only arrive at one conclusion as my reasoning or the reason for God giving his only begotten Son. If God loved the world as much as I loved my one-eighty, it was a no brainer.

I could see that the weather was about to turn so I loaded my camp into the Pilatus Porter and pushed away from the spit. As the airplane drifted clear of the land I fired the turbo, let it wind to full power and twisted in just enough prop pitch to taxi to the north-end of the lake for a southerly departure. Along the way I checked for anything that might be floating on the surface that would once again ruin another good airplane.

I prayed a prayer for traveling mercies as I went through the pre-takeoff check list.

With all the instruments registering in the green, I twisted the propeller to full pitch and the pontoons began their plow through the water. Suddenly my peripheral vision detected movement out of the left window. With all but one-percent of my attention dedicated to the take-off, I had barley a moment to identify what it could be.

Quickly glancing to my left I saw the most un-expected and fascinating scene I could ever imagine. The great monster fish was keeping pace with the aircraft; porpoising out of the water along side the floatplane as it rapidly increased in speed. Faster and faster, the floatplane continued until the smooth surface of the lake gave up its hold on the craft, letting the pontoons rise up onto the step.

I was enraptured with the spectacle. The sturgeon was much longer than I had first thought and much greater in mass. Rising out of the water to an elevation that almost put it in contact with the bottom of the wings it continued its porpoising until the Porter finally lifted off the water and into the air. However, just moments before its rotation their was a brief moment when time slowed down and everything went into slow motion as the prehistoric fish seemed to be close enough for me to reach out of the window and touch, and I swear it looked me square in the eye, and smiled.

I continued my climb to about four-hundred-feet above the water and began a steep turn that would take me around the lake for another flyby. Descending to one-hundred feet above the lake surface, I positioned myself south bound, and a little west of the point that I had departed from just moments before. There in the water was the most awesome thing I had ever seen. There was not one, but two beluga sturgeon, one only slightly smaller than the other, the largest well over forty-feet in length. I dipped my wings to say good luck, and never returned to Glacial Lake. The fishing was not that great anyway--*I wonder why.*

CHAPTER 29

E
ight months had passed since the salvage of the Skywagon from
Glacial Lake. The Juneau Bible Church had requested a new minister
and the Christian Ministerial Society acknowledged by ordaining
Beltray Gibbons and giving him the job. Gibbs had become so involved
in his pastoral work and ministry that he had temporarily postponed his
pursuit of a doctorate.

The Shearer/Worley Foundation responded to the need for a Christian
radio broadcast in the Juneau area and Pastor Gibbons was soon broadcasting
every week from the little church where less than a year earlier he had
found his mother and his calling. In addition, Sharon Shearer donated
the Cessna 185 that Bill Shearer had flown since we first met on the banks
of the Yukon river, where Bill had flipped his Piper Clipper. Now the big
Skywagon would meet the needs of Pastor Gibbons, enabling him to serve
people in the outer peninsulas and up and down the Aleutian chain.

There was still, however, one thing that troubled me, a loose end
dangling in the back of my mind that I needed to tie-up. I was taken aback
when I saw it, but at the time it did not seem appropriate to inquire about
the couple in the picture. Later, when I brought it up to Pamela Bishop
she mentioned that the young man was the pastor of the Juneau Bible
Church and that he and the young girl had met when he was a missionary
in China. It seemed to me that something wasn't adding up—but then
again, maybe it was. I reached for my cell, scrolled up Genneta Williams,
and mashed on the green button.

"Good morning, Mr. Worley. How are you?"

"I am fine, Genneta. Good morning to you also. How are you, and how are Jeffery and the kids?"

"Living the dream, Mr. Worley, thanks to you. What can I do for you?"

"Did you get a chance to look through those pictures yet?"

Genneta paused for a moment as if she were about to start up a long, steep hill and needed to shift gears. "Yes, I have studied them quite a bit since that day, and I have a lot of questions. The problem is, I have no idea who can answer them."

"What kind of questions?"

"Well, for instance, why didn't my father tell me I had an uncle? Was it none of my business, or was he ashamed because his brother was a diamond smuggler? Furthermore, if he knew his own brother was smuggling diamonds and had crashed somewhere, why did he not try to find him instead of waiting all those years and leaving it to you? It makes me wonder if my dad was involved in the whole operation. Maybe that is why my mother left him and took me back to Missouri to avoid any potential ramifications that could come from it. Now I'm not even sure I want that box of diamonds."

I wasn't sure if Genneta should be bitter over the whole deal or happy for the opportunity to learn something involving her family history. I felt obliged to tell her what I knew and what I had deduced from the wedding picture.

"It may not be what you think, Genneta."

"Well, that is the problem, isn't it? I have no idea what to think."

I sensed Genneta's frustration, anger, and even possible betrayal. I was glad, however, that she felt comfortable enough with me to let it out. I was about to speak when she broke in with other questions, throwing them out on the table like pieces of a puzzle that not only didn't fit but had no business being in the box.

"And who is the Chinese nurse, and who were all those kids?" Without realizing it, she had asked her question in two opposing tenses, as if the girl who was much older was somehow a pertinent part of her dilemma, but the children never were.

"Genneta, do you remember when we took Beltray to meet his mother for the first time?"

"Yes," she answered, almost in a whisper.

"His mother, Loraine, is a member of a church in West Juneau, the one that Beltray has become the pastor of. He lives in a duplex next to the parsonage."

Her voice this time was stronger. "Yes, I am aware of that."

"The congregation's pastor passed away only six months before Beltray met his mother, and the pastor's wife had passed away only six months prior to that."

"Yes, I am very glad for Beltray, but what does this have to do with me?"

I paused a moment, not sure exactly if I even knew that answer. I decided to let her arrive at her own conclusion from the same information I had. "She was Chinese and the majority of the church members were of mixed Chinese/Japanese descent." I paused again.

"And?"

"When Kati and I were there, we saw a wedding picture on Loraine's wall of a young man and his bride. They were both about thirty years old. *It was your uncle and the girl in the picture that you have.*"

I could hear Genneta quietly crying. She didn't say anything for several minutes. Finally she spoke. "Mr. Worley, thank you … thank you, but there is still so many unanswered questions." She paused again, regaining her composure.

"Are you saying he was the pastor of that Church?" "It seems that he was, yes." I said.

"What do you think happened? Who were all those children? How did they …?" Again, she wept.

"Genneta, I can find the answers to those questions for you if you truly want them, but there is no telling what else may come to the surface. Maybe wonderful discoveries about your family history and maybe some not so wonderful, you will have to let me know. I can also tell you what *I* think if you like, and you can either let my speculations be your truth, or give me the go-ahead and I will begin an investigation that will reveal the whole unadulterated facts of the story from the beginning."

Again, she waited a long moment before replying, "I would like both, Mr. Worley."

"According to the information that I have—which is purely here-say—your uncle's name was Jay Baldwin. I am not sure if he had a different father than Arthur or if he just changed his name from Jayson Bold for some reason.

My source also suggested that he may have been a missionary in China, where the two of them met."

"A missionary? I find that hard to believe."

"Why?" I asked, surprised.

"I don't know. I guess because I never heard of anyone in our family who was a Christian."

"Well, either way, he was in China for some reason. Maybe he was in the army or something. Maybe that is why he changed his name and Arthur never spoke of him. Maybe your father was trying to protect him from his past. Maybe ..."

"Maybe what? Mr. Worley, please finish your thought."

"Maybe he was in the army when he met the girl and deserted to run off with her. I told you that you might not want to know. What may be theory at this point could very well be fact at another."

"Isn't that the best way to arrive at the facts? Through theories?"

"Sometimes, but the theories at some point must be substantiated."

"That's why I would like to have both. So would you please continue? Where do the children fit into all of this?"

"I'm not sure, but it is possible that she was a teacher as well as a nurse and they were her students, or maybe she worked in an orphanage or something. Anyway, my perception is that Jay was trying to get her and the children out of China and for some reason, had to resort to smuggling diamonds to fund the operation. This could have placed the timeframe around the time of the fall of Shanghai to the Japanese and the 1937 invasion and rape of Nanking where over 300,000 Chinese were massacred in less than a month. During that month over twenty-thousand woman and young girls were raped, most of which were murdered. You cannot help but notice that all of those children in the photograph are apparently the same age. I would venture to say that their birthdays are all within three weeks of one another, which explains why they are mixed race, Chinese/Japanese. Whatever Jay Bold was doing in China, I believe he left off doing it to concentrate on saving those children. During that time he and she, fell in love.

It is possible the mechanic was involved in it all as well; maybe he was the one who owned the Antonov. Who knows? At any rate, that's about all I can come up with that has any feasibility to it. One thing seems clear, though. He hid them all in Juneau, started a church, and apparently changed his name. If I were you, I would let it go at that. In my opinion, the guy was a hero."

"Thank you, Mr. Worley. I think I will. Can I see their wedding picture?"

"I see no reason why not. I will ask Loraine to make you a copy."

"If you are right, and I hope you are, it is an exceptionally beautiful love story." Genneta again began to cry.

After my conversation with Genneta, I placed a call to Kevin Gaither.

Brenda answered, "Gaither residence,"

"Brenda, this is Lou. Is Kevin there?'

"No, he is in Seattle for a few days. Do you want his cell number, or is there something I can help you with?"

"Actually, both. Remind me to get his number before we hang up, but I need someone to do some international investigation for me. I would rather not involve anyone who is a member or in anyway close to my family."

"Sounds serious. Is it your family's welfare you are concerned about, or just the nature of the information that you want to protect?"

"The latter."

"Okay. I will text you Kevin's number, and between the two of us, I am sure that we can find an international detective agency. Actually, I know of several that have a very good history of success. What other countries will be involved, do you know?"

"China for sure, before and during the invasion of China by the Japanese, including, Manchuria, Russia, Siberia, and Alaska. It would involve certain people who may still be alive or at least who are descendants of those people. I would like to tell you more, but not over the phone."

"Very good, Mr. Worley. I will pass this onto Kevin, and it might be a good idea if the three of us got together and discussed this a bit more. I take it you want this to be anonymous, am I right?"

"That's right, Brenda. Call me when Kevin gets back. When we meet, I will brief you both on the rest of the details. In the meantime, I will make copies of some pictures and documents that are available that might help."

"Yes, that would help. I will call you when I hear from Kevin."

The 180 had been sitting in my hangar for a whole week. The completed restoration had left not a trace of the crash or the year it had spent underwater. The new glass panel G-1000 IFR-approved GPS navigation system was the latest technology for light general aviation aircraft, and I still needed many more hours of dual instruction before I would become proficient and completely comfortable with it. So three to four times a week, I would pick up Phillip Later, my favorite instructor, at Lake Hood in Anchorage and spend five to six hours each day practicing instrument approaches and cross-country flying under instrument flight rules.

The Skywagon, along with a retrofitted 475 horse IO-550 Continental engine, had come with a new set of 439-2705 EDO amphibious floats that permitted me to land on water, turf, or hard surface runways as long as the turf was reasonably smooth. Obviously, when the temperatures turned too cold and the snow piled up, I would have to transition back to wheels or skis.

I was impressed with the job Jerry Hansen had done. The 180 flew as true as it ever had. It takes a special talent to rig an airplane; not everyone can do it. Although there are a great many who claim to have the gift for it, only a few actually do. Jerry was more than just good; his ability to set wings and rig them was as much a natural talent as any acquired skill or ability.

It felt good to have my own airplane back again. We were getting well into the summer season, and the weather was exceptional for flying. I wanted to bag a moose for the winter and decided to give Calvin Trent a call to see if he would like to take a few days off to go along. Scrolling up his name on my phone, I mashed on the green button.

"Officer Trent. Please leave a message."

"Cal, this is Lou. I am going up to the lodge moose hunting. Do you want to go? Give me a call when you get a minute or just show up. See ya."

While getting a few things together to take with me to the lodge, I heard a car door slam and looked up to see Kati coming through the door with Keera not far behind.

"Hi, baby," I said to my wife.

"Hi, sweetie. Keera, your daddy is home," she hollered to my daughter who had not yet come through the door.

"I'm going moose hunting tomorrow, Kati. Is there anything you need me to do before I leave?"

"Your not going alone, are you?"

"I'm waiting to hear from Cal. I guess if he can't, I could see if any of the boys want to go."

"Well, I don't want you going by yourself, Lou. You know how I feel about that. You're not as young as you used to be."

"Daddy, where are you planning on going for your moose?"

"Loon Lake."

"Oh, I love it up there. I wish I could go."

"Why can't you?" I asked.

"Business meetings, Daddy. A constant stream of business meetings, interviews, and schedules."

The next morning Kati went to work at the Foundation, and Keera was off to Bettles in her Cessna 206 Stationair. Cal still had not returned my call. The first year I bought the lodge, and the approximately 330,000 acres and the several thousand lakes that speckled it, Cal and I had each taken a moose, which was the first time I ever went hunting with him. That was ten years before and almost six years before the poaching sting operation I had sponsored. Though we had been there numerous times since for other occasions, that was the last time Cal and I had hunted together.

Since I told Kati that I would try to get one of the boys to go with me, I gave Rusty a call. He, Mitchell, and Richard were tied up with work stuff and could not get away, so I left a note on the table, loaded the 180, and left. Along with a month's supply of provisions, I took my .300 Weatherby magnum hunting rifle, ten-gage shotgun, and Desert Eagle.

Illegal activities by a hunting outfitter had resulted in the mandatory auctioning of his hunting lodge and property due to fines levied by the state. In addition to losing his hunting outfitter and guide license, the state had seized the property. I knew it would eventually go to auction. This was early spring of 1998. Over a hundred outfitters and guides had come, hoping they could get lucky, but soon those bidding against me eventually realized I wanted it and had the means to stay till the end, which is what I did.

Located approximately seventy miles west of Wasilla and twenty-five miles northwest, of Beluga Mountain, the hunting lodge sat on the southeast shoreline of Loon Lake. The original hunting cabin, built by a couple of trappers back in the 1940s, sat on the far northwest shore and was primarily used as a hunting blind. The area was a hot spot for trophy moose, and several of the record-sized moose heads hanging in the main lodge had met their demise in the front yard of the old trappers' cabin.

Since it would be at least a day or two before I would actually be hunting, I flew somewhat of a grid within the perimeter of the 512 sections of prime hunting land to locate a nice bull that I would be proud to hang a tag on. I knew I did not expect to be out thrashing the brush that much anyway and would probably take a moose right off the porch of the lodge nearby the shoreline. However, it was fun looking for them and especially fun knowing we had some gigantic trophy bulls on our place. It was early afternoon, so it didn't surprise me that I only saw a few cow moose with their late spring calves. The large bulls are seldom out in the open during the middle of the day. I headed for the lodge.

Soon the lake came into view. Dropping low over the trees, I circled the two-mile-long lake twice, looking for floating objects that could potentially re-sink my recently re-furbished 180. Other than a few logs along the shoreline on the north end, the lake was perfectly clean. On the third pass, I set up for a glassy water landing, carrying power through to the touchdown. It was not until I came off the step that I realized I had been holding my breath throughout the approach, subconsciously expecting the pontoons to come flying off, no doubt.

The floatplane settled into the water. Lowering the rudders, I taxied to the tie-down. The dock extended out two hundred feet from the shore, terminating in a T-shape, capable of accommodating at least four floatplanes and several boats. Maneuvering alongside the closest tie-down to the shore, I closed the throttle on the big Continental and scrambled out of the passenger-side door and onto the pontoon, where I secured the plane to the dock.

The huge log-constructed lodge with the five acres of cleared meadow behind stood 150 yards beyond the shoreline, directly above the dock. It was an awesome scene. Dark green sheet metal roofing covered the weathered and aged twenty-inch fir logs that formed the twelve-by-twelve degree pitch roof, a beautiful contribution to the already aesthetic setting.

One-hundred-and-eighty degrees in the other direction, looking across the lake, the mountains of the Alaska Range loomed high into the western sky, framing a backdrop fit for the most renowned of artists.

The front of the lodge sported a fifteen-foot wide, split-log deck that extended the full length of the structure. Twelve-foot-wide-by-eight-foot-high double-paned glass windows lined the front wall of the lodge overlooking the lake. Inside, a huge stone fireplace took center stage along the front wall of the great room surrounded by three eight-foot-long leather couches and six plush recliners that faced the view across the lake.

Upstairs, there were twelve private bedrooms with accommodations for four people each. The guest rooms were located at the rear of the lodge on the east side of a huge banquet room under a magnificent cathedral, log roof. The dining room table could seat fifty people with a dozen four-place tables lining the front wall and its view of the lake. The kitchen, located directly under the guest rooms, was more than adequate for preparing food for a hundred guests, providing there were enough cooks.

Our family had become quite large, and I knew that in a few years it could very easily double in size. The lodge at Loon Lake had already accommodated us all on many Thanksgiving and Christmas holidays during just as many long winters. We also spent Memorial Day, Fourth of July, and Labor Day weekends at Loon Lake almost every year. The Trent's and many other friends along with their families often joined us.

We had also rented or loaned it out for everything from political banquets to spiritual retreats and, of course, hunting parties. Its location and new owner were no secret as far as the public was concerned, and many moose, bear, and fish taken from our property's lakes and streams adorned the walls of Alaskan homes. I did not mind if the local people hunted on the place as long as they hunted legally and were not outfitters or their clientele. I hate "No Hunting" or "No Trespassing" signs, so I never posted any. As far as I knew, no one had ever misused the privilege. My purpose for buying the place was not only for a family retreat but also, to preserve the land as a resource for Alaskans. It is my opinion that too much land is bought up by the rich and then privatized to keep the public out, until the public have no where else to go. I didn't want to be guilty of the same crime.

I unlocked the equipment shed containing several Yamaha 700 four-wheelers, one of which I hooked to a basket trailer we used for baggage and/or meat, and headed for the dock. Within an hour, the 180 was unloaded, and I was sitting on the front porch with a pot of coffee and sandwiches my sweet Kati had put together with her two precious little hands.

Tethered to the dock with its back to the shore, the Skywagon glistened in the early afternoon sun, the fresh maroon paint reflecting the dancing sparkles of shimmering light from the mirroring water. On the far shore a half-mile from my porch swing, a dozen loons perched on a snag protruding from the bank, wings outstretched to dry. A hundred yards from the loons, a cow moose and her calf stood with their faces submerged, grazing from their underwater pasture. In an hour, the sun would disappear behind the range of foothills fifteen miles to the west, abruptly rising from the plateau of marsh, lakes, and forest that comprised our front yard.

My thoughts turned nostalgic, traveling back to the day I pointed the little Cessna north to Alaska a little over thirteen years before. Never in my wildest dreams did I imagine the direction my life would take once I reached my destination. At the time, I just thought it was another vacation from which I would return, go back to work, living from paycheck to paycheck, scratching out a moderate living for my family. Even before I came to Alaska while on a truck driver's income, I owned an airplane, which to some may have seemed a bit extravagant. However, it was just a lifestyle Kati and I had chosen. We made it affordable by the sacrifice of many other conveniences, such as bigger home, more land, new cars, buying tickets to football games and so-forth, things that many average working families chose to not live without

The wealth we encountered had not changed our family as far as our relationships were concerned. Of course, it did change our lifestyles, but more than anything, it changed the purpose of our lives. The learning centers had become our family's life work. Keera was the director of all three of the centers as well as the medical facilities. Kelly worked directly with Priscilla Vasquez in charge of the educational departments, and Kathy was charge nurse in the surgical department at the Bettles medical facility. Kati, of course, was still the chairperson of the Shearer/Worley Foundation.

With the grandkids either entering or about to finish high school, my summers with them fishing and hunting at our Loon Lake paradise were becoming less frequent. My hope was that some of those grandkids would get married and present me with some great-grandkids that I could teach to fly, hunt and fly-fish while I could still hunt, fly, and fly-fish myself.

The sun had gone down and a roaring fire in the fireplace lit the dining hall with dancing flickers of yellow-orange light, illuminating the moose heads adorned with gigantic antlers that were silhouetted against the shadows of the great room. A chill ran down my back. I squirmed my way farther into the sleeping bag and adjusted the pillow, staring into the hypnotic flames. Shortly, I was fast asleep.

The couches were too soft for me and I like sleeping in the great room in front of the fireplace so I borrowed a mattress from one of the guest rooms that did not look near as comfortable as it actually proved to be and to which the nine hours of undisturbed sleep testified. The fire was still smoldering when I awoke, and I quickly brought it back to life with some help from the kindling box. The morning was so unbelievably beautiful. I sat on the porch swing, mesmerized by the beauty of the place.

The distant sound of an approaching helicopter suddenly shattered my tranquility. "Probably Cal," I muttered to myself as I rose to refill my coffee cup.

I returned to the porch, stepping out to the outer edge above the twenty-foot-wide split-log staircase descending to a path that extended from the bottom step out to a fork in the path. The lower extension led to the dock and the upper one to the helicopter pad. The Bell Ranger appeared low over the trees from the north, the Alaska State Police emblem glistening in the morning sunlight. Cal waved from the window of the copter as he passed over, executing a counterclockwise turn around the lodge, and set the Bell Ranger on the heli-pad at the south end of the lodge. Within a minute, the turbo began to spool down, and Officer Trent climbed down from the driver's seat to make his way toward me. Dressed in camouflage hunting pants and a khaki shirt, he looked like any ordinary hunter.

"Glad you could make it, Cal. How are ya?"

"Great, Lou. I didn't get your message until yesterday afternoon. Have you seen any bulls yet?" Cal extended his hand, greeting me vigorously and spilling half my coffee.

"I saw a dozen or so cows and calves yesterday when I was coming in, but no bulls. I just want to fill the freezers for the winter, so it doesn't really matter. However, if it turns out to be a nice wall mount, so much the better."

"I have been keeping my eye on this place. I know there are several monster bulls that hang out between here and Mount Spur." He waved his arm in the direction of the lodge and the Alaska Range to the west looming high above the landscape.

Loon Lake was located in the southeastern corner of 512 sections of land or 327,680 acres. The western thirty-two-mile boundary lay adjacent to the national forest and protected land of the Alaska Range. I had picked it up for two dollars an acre and what amounted to $200,000 for the lodge at the state held auction. Including the auction fees and taxes, the whole thing set me back a little over $900,000. I thought it was a great deal. Most importantly, it kept the sixteen- by thirty-two-mile chunk of prime hunting land out of the hands of outfitters and potential poachers. It was common knowledge that the property owner was also associated with law enforcement. Some of those who had bid against me had even cried foul because of my affiliation with the game warden and state police, but the attorney general gave the okay for me to bid on the place, and that was good enough for me.

"I have fresh coffee inside," I said, motioning toward the lodge.

"I believe I will, thanks." Cal followed me up the stairs.

Cal travels light. The only thing he brought was a backpack for hunting and a small travel bag of personal effects. We both had rooms in the lodge with more then enough gear that stayed there year around, so there was no need to bring much anyway.

"How long can you stay?" I asked. We had fixed a little breakfast and were sitting on the porch, sipping on another cup of coffee.

"I can only stay away about a week. This three-month moose season will start kicking into high gear in a couple of weeks, and I will need to be out there checking everyone's paperwork."

"So what do we need to do to find a couple of those monsters you were telling me about?" I sat my empty cup on the porch banister.

"Are you up to hiking a little ways?" Cal asked.

"How far is a 'little ways'?

"About ten miles that way." Cal pointed in the direction of Mount Spur. "About five or six miles this side of your property line."

"Can we take the four-wheelers?"

"Yeh, I suppose, but it's a lot of marsh until you get to where the terrain begins to rise. Have you been through there before?"

"Yeh, I've been all over this country with those Yamaha's. I think we can find our way through, but you will have to say when we park and mark them so we don't get to close to where we are going to hunt."

"When do you want to get started?" Cal asked.

"Lets get you put away and load the four-wheelers," I said as I headed for the equipment room.

CHAPTER 30

C al and I fastened our hunting gear on the luggage racks of the Yamaha 700s to which we connected the six-foot-long, two-axle meat wagons capable of carrying large deer or small elk. Between the two of us, we could bring out at least three-fourths of a whole moose in one trip. In the event both of us filled our tags, it may require three or four trips to bring out all the meat plus our camp. I had no doubt that would be the case.

We had extra gas for the four-wheelers and a small chain saw if we needed to cut a path through downed trees. Most of the terrain was marsh interspersed with dry land and patches of stunted scrub trees. With an abundance of all of life's essentials—cover, food, and water—it was the perfect moose habitat. Mounted to the handlebars of the four-wheeler was a scabbard into which I placed my scope-mounted .300 Weatherby magnum. An additional gun scabbard lashed alongside contained the ten-gage shotgun loaded with grizzly bear protection. On my hip, of course, I carried the .44 magnum Desert Eagle.

Cal hunted with an open sight .45/70 Winchester lever action that launched a 300-grain partition gold bullet 1880 fps (feet per second) out of a twenty-two-inch muzzle. It was his moose gun, bear gun, and man gun. Unbelievably, he even used it for grouse. He would aim to the right or left of the bird about five or six inches and a little to the front, and the concussion would kill it without destroying any meat. Like I said, Cal traveled light.

We used one of the four-wheelers to drag my one-eighty up on the dry land by the dock and lashed it down in case a windstorm come up while we were gone. We were finally on our way. It was three o'clock in the afternoon by the time we left. Cal followed me, as I was most familiar with the terrain at least from the perspective of a four-wheeler. I had studied it thoroughly from the air as well as traversed it on a machine many times. I had a good idea where he had seen the big moose, and I too had seen big bulls around that area during the rutting season on occasion. It was that time of the year again, so we were optimistic about our chances of scoring big. I had already made up my mind that I wanted to see Cal get a real trophy bull even if there was only one available. He certainly deserved it, and I planned to do everything I could to see it happen. One week is not a lot of hunting time but it was all that Cal would have before he had to get back to work. I, on the other hand, had the whole season and push come to shove could score a young bull from my front porch.

Cal said he had last seen the critters about five miles in from the western property line and the Alaska Range boundary. The property was sixteen miles wide and thirty-two miles long. The lodge and lake were located a mile and a half from the eastern property line, which meant we needed to work our way through about eight miles of hard-going marsh and stunted growth timber, not to mention dozens of creeks and streams. It stayed light about sixteen hours a day that time of year, so we had plenty of daylight, but it would still take a good eight hours to get to where we needed to leave the noisy machines and where we would make a camp.

We had churned our way through a bog and up on some higher ground when Cal said, "We should make camp here. Tomorrow, we can hunt the rest of the way on foot."

The small chain saw with its twelve-inch bar was perfect for cutting poles for a tent frame. In short order, we had an eight- by ten-foot wall tent erected complete with camp stove and chimney pipe. A lantern provided the little light we needed during the four hours of semi-darkness.

We had begun to see some recent moose tracks in the area, which was the reason that Cal suggested we pitch our base camp. Too much camp noise and smoke from a campfire or stove would only serve to alert the big bulls that there was unwanted company in the area. With a few hours of sleep and food in our bellies, we would hunt a five-mile radius from our camp. We both had GPS hand-helds and cell phones, so we could hunt in different directions, covering twice as much territory while making half as much noise.

"Cal, do you have an idea where those bulls might be holding up?"

"They could be anywhere, but I'm betting they are sticking close to that bog where I saw them a couple of weeks ago. It's not quite two miles from here due west. If you want, you can head straight toward it, and I will move northwest for about a mile and then turn west toward the bog on the north end. If they are still in there, one of us should run into them."

"I better give you a thirty-minute head start so that we arrive more or less at the same time, don't you think?" I suggested.

"That will work," Cal said. "I'll move along a little faster than you, what with your plastic hip and all." I saw the facetious little grin on Cal's face and knew he was trying to be funny, so I chuckled to make him feel good.

"Just for that, I'll shoot the biggest bull and take home the bragging rights."

"That's okay. Just be sure you notch the right date on that tag or you might get a ticket," Cal said, his grin growing wider.

"You probably would too. I wouldn't put it past you. Just remember, I got friends in high places," I said chuckling. I do not think Cal was sure if I was referring to the attorney general or a divine Being, but he left my comment alone as he slung his backpack onto his shoulders. "By the way," Cal added, "don't forget to put your cell phone on vibrate. I will send you a text when I am in position along with my lat and long." I watched him move off into the woods, noting the time and direction he took.

Exactly thirty minutes later, I too donned my daypack filled with water, snacks, three hunting knives, rope and pulleys, hatchet, saw, whetstone, game-bags, and some emergency essentials, and headed into the timber due west. Cal was right; I *was* slower than I used to be. It was harder to get over and under the downfalls than it was before my hip replacement. However, there was no reason to be in a hurry anyway. I was hoping, Cal would get there first and get himself a shot at a real Boone and Crockett bull. However, if he pushed one into me in the process, I would certainly not hesitate to fill my tag. I knew he felt the same way.

An hour and a half later, I was getting close to the area Cal had described. I had encountered more fresh sign in the form of tracks and droppings and therefore had been moving considerably slower. There was obviously more than one boggy spot because I had already seen several. At the beginning and during the rutting season, the bulls do a lot of thrashing around in wet, muddy bogs, urinating all over themselves for no other reason than to make a hunters job more miserable. It is a chore to field dress an animal that size in the first place, but to do it with mud, urine, and fecal matter plastered all over the hide takes even more of the fun out of it. It is a lot more work to keep the meat clean and uncontaminated from all that mess. Some hunters refuse to hunt big game animals during the rut for that very reason.

I stopped to listen and checked my cell phone to see if I still had a signal. I did. Then I heard grunting. The forest was so silent that the mosquitoes sounded like F-18 fighter jets and my heart was now thumping like Cal's Bell Ranger the first time I heard it pounding its way up Alfred Creek, waking me from my afternoon nap. I froze where I was. I could see a small clearing a hundred yards ahead through the forest of scrub trees, so I kept my eye on that little patch. I knew if I could hear moose, the moose could hear me, and I only hoped they had not already.

Slowly, I retrieved my cell phone from my shirt pocket and sent Cal a brief text. "Am wtchg a clrg, hear grntg, hldg here, whr r u?"

Within three minutes, my shirt pocket began to buzz. "Yur clrg is 1 of mny. I am nnwst wtchg three mdm sz bulls. Styg put 4 now."

Carefully, I worked my way into a better position where I could see more of the clearing with less interference from limbs in the event that I might get a shot. I was still hearing occasional grunting from the northwest, and it seemed to be getting closer.

Suddenly from my ten-o'clock position, southwest of the direction I had been moving I heard the labored breathing and grunting from what sounded like a good-sized bull moving in the direction of the original grunting sounds. Closer and closer it came until, finally, the biggest bull I had ever seen in my life, alive or dead, stepped into the clearing, directly in front of me not fifty yards away. Shaking his massive head on which were mounted a spread of antlers at least nine feet from tip to tip. He grunted and bawled his challenge to any other bulls that might be interested in any of his girlfriends. I completely forgot about how I wanted Cal to get the big trophy. This was a once-in-a-lifetime moment, and in one second the .300 Weatherby exploded. Without even thinking about it, I had placed the crosshairs just behind and slightly below the bull's right ear.

The great animals head reeled to the left, spinning counterclockwise and upward, slamming the ground in a thunderous cloud of dirt, grass, mud and pine needles. The echo of the rifle shot reverberated off the great wall of the Alaska Range and then fell silent. Moments later, an eerie kind of quiet returned to the forest, as if nothing had even happened.

I sat waiting, expecting that my shot may have moved some animals in Cal's direction and hoping he too would score a big one. I was shaking with excitement and adrenaline, but knew better than to rush over to the huge bull moose I had just put down. That could be dangerous. Suddenly, Cal appeared at the edge of the clearing, motioning for me to come out.

"You scored big, pilgrim. That will go into the book for sure. Let's get to work."

"How many bulls did you see? I was expecting you to get first shot," I said.

"I saw six. There was a couple really nice ones, but this is the biggest I've seen so far this morning. We'll get this one dressed and hung and then concentrate on mine. As a matter of fact, you could take off now and get the four-wheeler and come back for a load of meat while I keep dressing this animal out."

"No, I don't want to do that," I'm not leaving you here alone. We'll do this job together then I can go while you get back to hunting." Cal could tell from my voice that it was non-negotiable, so he let it go.

We took a thirty-minute break, during which time we traded granola bars and other energy-packed chewables, washing them down with water in preparation of the hard work that awaited us. Next, we constructed a meat pole, strong enough and high enough to keep the cooling game meat away from the local varmints. We knew that if a grizzly came by he would have his way with it no matter how high we hung it. Neither Cal nor I expected there to be any griz around because of the concentration of bull moose in the area. Normally, the bears will stay away from the humungous, angry, crazy, and rutting beasts. However, we also knew the hanging meat could be smelled by the rest of the herd, and they would be moving away from it. Which way and how far we were not sure.

"Lou, we're almost done here why don't you go back to camp and get your machine and wagon so we can at least get this meat out of the hunting area." We had the four quarters bagged and hung and was working on the back-straps.

"I can do that," I said. "Let me help you get those straps and the head off, and then I'll get going."

I wanted Cal to get back out there before the moose were plum out of the territory, but he did not seem that concerned and stayed until the chore was completed. Shouldering my rifle, I headed to camp. Arriving in less than an hour, I grabbed some additional cheesecloth meat bags, replenished my snack supply and water, fired up the four wheeler with its meat wagon, and headed back leaving the hunting rifle in camp taking with me the ten-gage.

When I returned, Cal was gone. I did not bother to call or text him, not wanting to interrupt his hunting. I already felt bad enough for shooting what in all probability would be the biggest bull taken that year. I really did want him to score the biggest, but as I stood there staring at that monster moose's head and nine-foot antler spread, it seemed a bit unlikely that he would.

I had brought provisions for us to stay the night in the event that Cal found what he was looking for. I knew he would want to get it hung up and cooling as soon as possible, however long it would take. Leaning my ten-gage against a tree, I stretched out within reach of it and with my head resting against the daypack, I soon fell asleep.

Like a movie trailer, the scene of the big bull biting the dust played and replayed itself in my dreams. Over and over again, in slow motion, he would step into my crosshairs. And each time, the scene would again play itself out like a silent movie. Until in the last scene as I pulled the trigger. *BOOOOM!*. A shot startled me awake, and my heart almost burst out of my chest.

"What was that?" I shouted. In that moment, I detected a blur from off to my right twenty yards away and moving my way while uttering a deep-throated, "GRRRRRAAAW." I spun toward my ten-gage, pumped a .400-grain cartridge into the chamber and fired at the massive wall of fur that was suddenly no more than twenty feet away. In an instant, the second of the first two .400-grain balls of lead had found its mark between the two front shoulders of the charging grizzly bear slowing him considerably as I twisted and turned to get away from the vicious, gnashing teeth. As the bear arrived at the tree I had retreated to and was less than two feet away from, the ten-gage let go two more rounds of number-eight buckshot full in the face of the furious grizzly. The three remaining .400-grain slugs went straight into his mouth.

I stood over the dead bear, frantically trying to reload the shotgun I had just emptied into the enormous beast. The first two slugs had taken him directly between the shoulders and the buckshot had taken out his face. The three remaining slugs that I put into his mouth, had blew out his spine at the base of his head. I had made it to another tree six-foot behind me and watched the bear take out his dying wish on the tree where I had just been sleeping.

Looking up, I saw Cal coming toward me.

"This is a good stand you got here, Lou. That's twice in one day. The trouble is, you are plum out of tags."

I was still shaking and was not feeling much like laughing at Cal's stand-up comedy act. As soon as he realized it, he crouched down beside me and put his hand on my shoulder.

"Criminy Christmas, Lou. You are shaking like a leaf."

"I ... I know. I was asleep when I thought I heard a shot and it woke me up. Then, all of a sudden, this bear was on me and ..." I paused. "My God, I think I messed my pants."

"Well, all I have to say is, between the big bull and this bear and the mess you made in your pants, the smell around here is enough to run-off every moose in the Range, so it's a good thing I already got my bull."

"So that *was* you who fired a shot? Let's go see it!"

"You're not going anywhere until you get cleaned up. Grab something to change into and follow me. I know where there is a creek."

I had not brought a change of clothes with me from camp, so while I washed in the frigid creek that I am sure was every bit of two degrees below freezing, Cal built a fire. Finally, much cleaner and dryer, we set about to field dress Cal's bull. He seemed pleased with himself about filling his tag, and I figured it was because he knew he would make it back to work in plenty of time. Cal lived for only one purpose and that was to manage the Alaska wildlife. Everything else took second stage. He still had not said anything about my bear. I had killed the grizzly legally because it was in self-defense, but that did not mean I had any right to it. I could only hope that I would be permitted to have it mounted and put it in the lodge. However, that decision was not mine to make. In the scheme of things it really did not matter. I had once again survived; that was the important thing.

We took with us on the four-wheeler what we needed to field dress Cal's moose, and he drove. About five hundred yards from where I had shot my trophy bull, we emerged into a small clearing, There laying on the ground (unbeknown to either of us at the time) lay the new world record of bull moose, taken by Calvin Trent, the game warden from Wasilla, Alaska. The last time I sucked air like that I was staring at a shiny, yellow substance on the end of my military spade thirteen years earlier at Alfred Creek.

"Cal, I think this one is bigger than mine."

Cal did not say anything; he just went to work.

It was almost dark by the time we had all the meat hung and the wagon loaded. We made our way back to camp for some much-needed sleep.

Three hours later, we were back on our machines headed to the killing field. I had unhooked my wagon to follow Cal. Before long, we had his wagon loaded and were on our way to the lodge, stopping by camp to hook to my already-loaded wagon. We each had the hindquarters and head to our own kills all tagged and tied down. I wondered why Cal was so by the book when there was no one to check the tags but him.

It took three more trips to get the bear plus the rest of our moose meat, and camp back to the lodge. We had field dressed the bear and brought out the head and hide, but it was two more days before we returned to finish the job.

"Cal," I said, "what are the chances I could have that bear hide made into a rug to keep at the lodge?"

"I'll have to talk to the superintendant about that. First, I will file a report and will need a written statement from you. Then it will be up to Arnold Bradley."

"How soon do you need the statement?" I asked.

"The sooner the better. You should do it while it is still a clear memory. I can corroborate the fact that it was self-defense, and you could add the request for the mount, if you like. Usually, a donation to the game management fund would help a request like that go through, but with all that you have done for Alaska's game resources, I don't think that will be necessary."

"Okay, Cal. I will get on that right away. Congratulations on your trophy. Only you could have done that."

CHAPTER 31

Between the two of us, Cal and I managed to get our game loaded into our aircraft. But my bear was going for a helicopter ride instead of an airplane ride. I waved as Cal lifted the Bell Ranger into the air and turned eastbound to Wasilla. I knew I needed to get going too because the meat needed to be cut and wrapped and put into a meat locker as soon as possible.

With the four-wheelers put away and the Skywagon loaded and back on the water, I took a last look around the lodge before leaving. Satisfied that all was well, I untied the line and stepped out onto the pontoon. Quickly climbing into the driver's seat, I carefully went through the start-up checklist, flipped on the fuel pump and fired the big Continental. It instantly came alive, propelling the floatplane through the calm lake water. With the power set to slightly above an idle, I slowly maneuvered the floatplane in a full circle water taxi around the lake, checking for logs and letting the new engine warm sufficiently as I performed the run-up. All systems were in the green, and beginning from the north end of the lake, I smoothly but with authority increased the throttle to full power. The cowl rose up into a steep climbing attitude and the floats plowed furiously through the calm lake water as the triple-bladed fan clawed at the morning air. In only a moment, the water gave up its grip on the pontoons. Seconds later, the floatplane, moose, and I were climbing high above the tree line at a rate of two thousand feet per minute. I almost felt a bit glad that my Skywagon had sunk up at Glacial Lake. Were it not for that, I may never have had it refurbished, and I could not even imagine trading my new 475-horsepower IO550 for the 300 horsepower IO470 power plant that had previously powered the airplane. I couldn't help but reflect on the spiritual lessons associated with the whole experience. It seemed that for God to work in humanity to make a situation better, He must first, completely destroy the original situation. Kind of like, before one can become a new man, the old man must be crucified. I remembered when I first bought our home from Arthur Bold, before we could live in it we had to clean it, and before we could clean it we had to completely remove everything that was in the way. It is no wonder that the apostle Paul said to 'Glory in tribulation.' I had not been a Christian very long but it was becoming increasingly clear to me that God was in the business of restoring. Whenever He takes something, He always replaces it with something better.

Mike Paulson owned Paulson Cold Storage in Palmer and was the best butcher around. He knew exactly how I liked my meat and had butchered, cut, and wrapped a couple dozen animals for different members of our family over the years. I had called him, and he sent his driver to meet me at my hangar with his butcher truck. Mikes driver was running a bit late so while waiting for him I unloaded my hunting gear from the Skywagon stowing it in the new hangar.

My next stop was Anchorage. I still kept the old 4Runner at Merrill Field, but the huge antlers of the moose seemed too much for that little car, so I dialed up the taxidermist that Cal had recommended and made arrangements for him to meet me at Merrill field. As I taxied up to the FBO, I saw a man in a silver and black Chevrolet Eldorado pickup truck waiting outside the fence.

"Mr. Sinclair?" I asked.

"That's right. Henry Sinclair. You must be Lou Worley."

"I am. Let me get someone to open that gate for you. I will need you to back that truck a little closer to the airplane." The moose, head, antlers, and cape were all still attached and tied securely to the float framework. It would be a two-man job loading it in the truck.

"I will need to see your tag and license," Henry said.

"That's fine. I would like to go with you to your shop, if you don't mind. Can you bring me back?"

"Sure, no problem. We can fill out the paper work when we get there. I will need fifty percent up front. Will that be a problem?"

"No problem at all, Henry."

Henry was about my age and had been working in the taxidermy trade for almost fifty years. He had begun working with his father in the same shop that he had taken over from him when his father had passed on thirty years earlier.

"We should take this to the sportsmen's show after the antlers cure, you definitely found a place in the Boone and Crocket book with this one. Are you the one who went hunting with the game warden?"

"Yes, sir. That's me. I suspect his might have measured a little more, am I right?'

"I haven't seen it yet. He called me, but still hasn't brought it in. If it is bigger than yours, it might well take the all-time record."

What luck. I shoot a moose that quite possibly is the biggest on record and four hours later Cal shoots a bigger one. I guess you could say that I hold the record for holding the record the shortest length of time.

I pulled the wheel chocks away from the amphibious floats and climbed up the ladder and into the cabin of the Skywagon. The weather was below VFR minimums and rain had moved into the area. With only an eight-hundred foot cloud ceiling and two miles visibility which is less than the one-thousand-foot ceiling and three-miles of visibility required for a normal VFR departure, I requested a special VFR clearance from Merrill tower and taxied out to the ramp. Shortly, I was in the air and crossing the knick arm. Ten minutes later, I was on short final to my home field.

At the far end of the landing strip, next to the old hangar that came with the place, sat a strange airplane parked in a position facing toward me with engines still running. Standing next to the gray-and-white Skymaster push/pull, twin-engine, high-wing Cessna were three men and a woman. Shortly after touchdown, even in the reduced visibility, I could see that the woman was Kati. Something did not look right about this picture.

As I made contact with the turf, two of the men started pulling and pushing on Kati, apparently trying to get her into the Skymaster. I had only moments to figure out that someone was trying to kidnap my wife right in front of my eyes. Reaching into the flight bag, I retrieved my .45 Glock and, pouring the power to the big Continental, headed straight for the churning prop of the twin Cessna's forward engine. All three men took off in different directions, and Kati disappeared toward the equipment shed. I opened the pilot-side door and bailed out of the floatplane about five seconds before impact.

The Skywagon hit the Cessna Skymaster at nearly thirty miles an hour and about eighteen hundred RPM. After the initial impact, which shredded the front of the 180's float framework and tore the forward engine completely off the Skymaster, I thought my airplane might once again still be salvageable. However, within seven seconds or less, the ruptured fuel lines ignited, and both airplanes erupted in flames followed by a one-two punch of first and secondary explosions, that completely destroyed both aircraft.

I had hit the ground with my knees tucked and in a roll, trying to pay attention to the four different directions everybody headed. The last I had seen of Kati was the instant before I bailed, and she was hoofing it southbound toward the east end of the equipment shed. I felt a stabbing pain in my hip, but managed to get to my feet and run for the shed. A shot rang out from over by the hangar just as the two airplanes burst into flames, giving me a little more time to get to Kati. Rounding the corner of the shed, I briefly saw my wife as she swung a stick at my head. Fortunately, she realized who it was in time to divert her swing to a glancing blow off my shoulder. I grabbed her and turned her in the direction of the big D-9 Caterpillar parked at the end of the equipment shed. Placing her behind me, we crouched low in the tall grass and made our way to the dozer. She did not have a coat, so I gave her mine and stuffed her under the big machine, handing her my Glock .45.

"If they come near you, baby, you shoot to kill, understand?" She nodded her head, her beautiful eyes as big as dinner plates. "Take my phone and send a text to Cal." I gave her a squeeze and disappeared back toward the equipment shed.

I had no idea where they were. I wished I could have gotten a shot off before the explosion so they would know I was armed. If I had maybe they would be a little more reluctant to come out of hiding, giving Cal a little more time to arrive. I had given Kati the only side-arm I had with me, which left me unarmed. I knew I had to be careful not to become a target. I worked my way through the tall grass westward on the south side of the long shed, listening for any indication that one of the would-be kidnappers may be nearby. Unable to see a thing and not caring to get too far from Kati, I finally laid still and waited.

Then a man shouted, "I found her! Come here, you little ..." CRRRAAAKKK. I heard the distinct report of my .45 Glock, which left one of the abductor's last words on earth as an incomplete sentence.

"Good job, Kati," I whispered to myself. Wow, I didn't know she had it in her. "Good job."

The distraction was just what I needed to get out of that grass without getting my head blown off. Assuming the deceased man had a gun with him, I knew I needed to get to it before someone else did. Bursting out of the grass, I slammed straight into a large man I didn't even realize was there, crouching on his haunches with his back to me, looking in the direction of the dozer. Somewhat stunned by the sudden encounter, I almost failed to realize the idiot had dropped his weapon and was about to pick it back up. I quickly planted my boot in his kisser and grabbed his gun, popping a cap into one of his knees, and putting him to sleep with a solid whack on the head with the barrel of his own gun.

Making a mad dash toward the D-9, I rounded the corner, expecting to find a dead man, but instead meeting my wife with her pointing my own gun at me.

"Where's the one you shot?" I held my breath, hoping she was not squeezing that trigger too hard in her excitement.

"On the other side of the bulldozer, I think he's dead."

"Good job, baby. Now get back under that dozer and stay there. There is still one left."

I found the dead man just where Kati had dropped him with one straight into his heart. I grabbed the .40 caliber semi-auto from his lifeless hand and placed it under my belt in the small of my back while moving to the front of the dozer, staying low behind the blade. I wanted to draw the fire from the remaining kidnapper and had a plan for accomplishing that, but did not want to do it where Kati was hiding for fear she might get hit from a ricocheting bullet.

I had a feeling he might be in the equipment shed where there was plenty of cover around all the machinery. A mad dash toward the still-burning aircraft would bring his fire down on me for sure, but with my bad hip slowing me down, it might also mean my demise. I decided to inch my way inside the shed and silently hunt him down.

Slowly crawling through the huge arms of the Caterpillar blade, I worked my way to the front corner of the shed. Crouching low and sneaking a peek around the corner at ground level, I searched every opening looking for a foot, leg, or any other body part that he may have left unconcealed. Failing to see any thing, I continued to crawl my way around the corner and alongside one of the old sluice boxes. Carefully, inch by inch on my belly, I moved toward the rear of the shed where I finally reached the darkened corner. There I waited, giving my eyes a chance to adjust to the darkness.

Suddenly, I heard the state police helicopter coming from the east. With gun in hand, I jumped to a standing position, my eyes frantically searching between every piece of equipment. Then I saw him. He was kneeling on the other side of the D-6 by the blade, peering toward the corner I had just come from. I waited to see what he would do as the chopper came closer.

Spinning around only thirty feet above the turf and on the far side of the burning aircraft, the chopper went into a hover. I watched as ropes came flying out of the far side door followed by five troopers dressed in SWAT uniforms. The blades of the helicopter had dispersed the smoke from the fire, creating a smoke screen for the team as they transitioned to the ground. I knew that was Cal's idea.

Kati's one remaining abductor threw his gun to the ground, shaking his head and cursing. I stepped up behind him.

"Good choice," I said. "Now, I want your hands on your head and lace your fingers together. We are going to head toward that chopper and say hello to those guys."

I stepped forward, grabbed his laced fingers, and pressed the barrel of his friend's .357 magnum against the back of his neck. Suddenly, six state police cruisers came screaming down the road to the airstrip with lights flashing and sirens screaming. Then one of the SWAT team members who had arrived in the helicopter yelled at me.

"Drop the weapon, sir. Drop the weapon now, sir. Put the weapon on the ground now."

I pointed the weapon toward the ground, still holding onto my prisoner with my left hand. The members of the SWAT team were now approaching with their assault rifles aimed directly at both of us. I dropped the weapon on the ground and raised my right hand.

"I am Lou Worley. This man is my prisoner. There is another one around back still alive. I think he is unarmed, but I'm not for sure, and I have another weapon in my back under my belt."

One of the team took my prisoner and threw him to the ground, another one said to me:

"Turn around, place your hands on the hood of that tractor, and spread your legs, sir." The other three made their way around behind the shed.

"Let this one go. He is one of us," a familiar voice said. I turned my head just enough to see Cal approaching and speaking to the team member who was still checking me for more weapons.

"Cal," I said, "Kati is under the D-9 at the other end of the shed. There is a dead man over there with her."

Finally standing upright, I was in position to retrieve my wallet and ID, showing them my State Police badge.

Satisfied, the SWAT team member followed Cal and me over to where Kati was crawling out from under the D-9.

"Are you okay, sweetie?" I asked, helping her up and embracing her.

"I am fine, Lou." She said quivering, and then, bursting into tears, she went completely limp in my arms. I scooped her up and carried her to the Bell Ranger where I laid her on a gurney.

The rest of the SWAT team members were coming back from the far side of the equipment shed carrying the remaining survivor of the three kidnappers.

In thirty minutes from the time I landed, it was all over. Six state police officers searched the entire grounds, including the house. Moments later, the NTSB arrived along with the FBI.

I had placed Kati on a gurney, propping her head up with my coat until she recovered enough to sit up and talk to the investigators. An aid vehicle arrived to transport the kidnapper whose left kneecap was missing, and the would-be person snatcher I apprehended was sitting in an FBI vehicle with his hands cuffed behind him. Two men in suits approached Kati and me as we sat on the edge of the Bell Ranger's floor. I had not had a chance to get any information from Kati on what happened. I assumed she must have said something over the phone about a kidnapping when she sent the text.

"I am special agent Singer, and this is my partner, special agent Travis. We are with the FBI and would like to ask this lady a few questions."

"How do you do? I'm Lou Worley. This is my wife, Kati." Just for the heck of it, I showed him my badge in reciprocation. "My wife is kind of upset right now. She actually collapsed a few moments ago, so she needs to get some rest for awhile. Can this wait until tomorrow?"

"I understand completely, Mr. Worley, I really do, but there may be more involved in this attempted kidnapping then just these three, and we need a head start finding whoever else that might be. So if you don't mind, Mrs. Worley, can you tell us what happened here?"

"It's all right dear. I'm okay," Kati said, placing her shaking hand on my arm. "I had just returned from the grocery store, parked the car, and brought a few things into the house. I turned around to shut the slider door when a man stepped through and grabbed me. I tried to get away, but he was too strong."

"Which man was it?" Singer asked.

"The one they took away in the aid car," Kati replied. Agent Travis asked, "Then what happened?"

"The other two men entered behind him, and the one called Jake ..."

"Which one was Jake?" Singer interrupted. Kati began to cry again.

"The ... one ... I shot," she answered in a choked voice. Overcome with distress, she buried her face in her hands.

"Okay, that's enough for now, gents. This is going to have to go on hold until she has a chance to deal with what just happened to her," I said in unmistakably non-negotiable terms.

Singer and Travis looked at each other with an obvious reluctance to concede the interview, but backed away as Cal approached.

"You gentlemen will get your chance again, but right now, this lady is going to the hospital to get checked out and then home for some rest. In the meantime, it all goes on time-out."

The two agents did not question Cal's orders and turned their attention to the suspect sitting in the back of their car. Ten minutes later, they drove away.

CHAPTER 32

C al and I, accompanied by one of the state troopers, took Kati
to the hospital for a physical and emotional evaluation. On the
way, I called Rusty. He had already left several messages on
my phone after having seen and heard of the incident live on the local
television news channel. Working our way through that same wall of
cameras and reporters, cordoned off from the scene by the local and state
law enforcement agencies, we made our way under heavy police escort to
the hospital. Rusty and the rest of the family were on their way to meet
us there.

The whole ordeal—the attempted kidnapping, taking the life of another
human being, the crash of the airplanes, and especially pointing a gun at
her own husband and very nearly pulling the trigger—traumatized my
precious Kati. Physically, she had checked out fine with the exception of
some bruises from the manhandling she endured at the hands of her would-
be abductors. The physician referred her to a psychiatrist for evaluation—
Erika Miley, a psychotherapist who specialized in trauma cases— penciled
Kati in for an appointment once a week. With a prescription meant to
reduce her anxiety and another one to help her sleep, she gave her an
appointment for the following week and sent her home for some much-
needed rest and recuperation.

The next day, all three of our daughters and their families were with
us in the big house. Keera, Kathy, and Kelly were smothering Kati with so

much love that she refused to take her prescription for fear it would make her drowsy and she would miss the attention.

"Dad," Rusty said to me. "I think we need to have a meeting and talk about putting in place some safety nets for our family."

"I know. I should have seen this coming. Go get Mitchell and Richard; we can talk down at the big hangar."

An hour later, we gathered around a wood stove in the far back corner, listening to a blazing fire rapidly bring warmth to the cold hangar.

"Every one of us is a target, Dad," Rusty began. "I think we need to reduce our exposure to the public and look at hiring bodyguards or something."

"What do you and Richard think?" I asked, addressing Mitchell.

"I think bodyguards would become complicated. The thing of it is, everyone knows where you live and where we all work, Maybe we should hire people to do our jobs and move our families to undisclosed locations and, like Rusty said, reduce our public exposure."

"How about you Richard, what suggestions do you have?"

Richard squirmed around in his chair, not completely sure of himself.

"I think we should fence the place and all live here together with guards at the gates, completely isolating our families from the public. We fly to work anyway, so why not fence in our perimeter."

We all sat staring at Richard, wondering why we had not paid more attention to his opinions in the past.

"We only have the one house," I said. "Should we divide the property into parcels, get permits, and build new houses for you boys and your families?" I addressed Richard again.

"Dad," Mitchell broke in," there are some really nice homes adjacent to yours and mom's property in the northeast corner. Maybe we could make them an offer they couldn't refuse, and we could all be in one place a lot sooner rather than later. Then we could fence the whole thing with a huge electric fence."

"I'd rather build a solid fence that no one could see through. I am sure the women would also," Rusty said.

"How about this?" I said. "A fourteen-foot-high concrete wall like they place alongside freeways as sound barriers to residential areas, and then an electric fence on the other side of that with gated entrances, complete with manned guard shacks. We could design it so that the perimeter guards would walk the outside of the concrete wall between it and the electric fence, and where we would never see the guards or they us, except when we go in and out in our vehicles."

"That sounds secure and while maintaining our privacy still allows us our freedom to come and go at will," Mitchell said. "Also, there is at least a mile and a half of undeveloped land between here and the town limit. We could buy it all up."

"I don't want to get greedy," I interjected. "The town will want to grow this way a little more. We should leave them some room to do that, but we could get half of it if it is available.

"Dad," Richard spoke up, "the kidnappers didn't drive in, they flew in. How will we secure the place from that?" "Good point Richard." I said. "We will look into that, but you are right we are still vulnerable from the top."

"Dad, we could have underground tunnels built from the hangars to the house and build a much larger garage that would accommodate more cars than the two car garage that you and mom use. With automatic garage door openers to close behind us when we come home we would add to the security.

I looked at Rusty and asked.

How is the hard-rock mining coming along?"

"Really good, Dad, we have gotten into several large veins that are producing really nice."

"When are you boys going to hire people to take over your responsibilities up there and just oversee the operation from a distance?"

Rusty paused and glanced at Richard and Mitchell.

"I think the time has come for us do that right now," Mitchell said.

"Dad, what are you going to do for another airplane? The 180 is definitely beyond restoration this time." Richard said.

"It is, and I am really depressed about that. But I have already turned the page. I ordered a Quest Kodiak two years ago from the Quest Aircraft manufacturing plant in Sandpoint, Idaho, and they have informed me that I can expect delivery early this fall. In addition, the Citation CJ4 personal jet I ordered a year ago is in a hangar at the Wasilla airport. Eric delivered it while Cal and I were hunting. So as soon as your mom is well enough, I will take her with me when I go to Aurora Oregon for my turbo-jet training, and when we return, the Kodiak should be here. I want your mom to turn the Foundation over to someone else so we can do some traveling together. I think that will be just what the doctor ordered."

"Who is going to supervise the security installation?" Rusty asked.

"I will get Leo Gerard to design it and hire the contractors. But, Rusty, you could get with him on the ideas we just discussed and get him moving in the right direction. I don't want to get involved in any project that would take me away from spending time with my wife."

"I can do that, Dad," Rusty replied.

"In the meantime, let's just all stay together and never leave anyone alone, especially the grandkids. We will need to provide some security for them at their schools immediately. I'll leave that with you, Rusty. You might even want to get Kevin and Brenda involved in that."

"I will deal with that, Dad. You and Mom just enjoy yourselves, and take good care of her."

The NTSB wanted to know what caused the two airplanes to crash. I told them I had crashed them on purpose in response to the imminent danger my wife was facing. They threatened to suspend my pilot certificate for six months during their investigation, but my lawyers managed to get it all worked out.

Both Kati and I prepared an in-depth statement of events from our individual perspectives and never saw the two FBI agents, Singer or Travis, again. The FBI never did charge or apprehend anyone else in the plot to kidnap Kati and hold her for ransom..

We managed to buy out the only five homes that were nearby and secured all the land from our property line to within a mile of the city limits. With the ninety acres that included the airstrip and hangars along with the twenty acres our home sat on, the total size of our commune had increased to six hundred acres, which is just short of a section.

The construction of a fourteen-foot-high concrete wall surrounded by a twelve-foot electric fence was underway around the entire four-mile perimeter, along with a gate and guard shack for the east entrance. Armed guards were already on the premises. Also under construction was a large underground shelter with underground access to both the house and the big hangar, complete with all the comforts of home and stocked with food and water provisions. Also, new parking garages were added along with additional security installation for the existing garages.

We remodeled every home with new security doors, windows, and alarms. The upgrade to the airstrip included an additional security fence around the perimeter of the runway with a high security gate next to the big hangar. This permitted us to come and go underground from the house to the hangar and out onto a secured runway using electric golf karts. We also had a jet fuel tank installed underground next to the 100LL (low lead) tank already in place.

I had been foolish assuming that we were immune to the evils of the world because of our faith or the work we had done for other people. It is true that only divine intervention brought me home that day in time to save Kati from some horrible experience. I believe God timed it all for her and for our whole family's welfare. Normally, I would just thank the Lord for His mercy and grace and not even look back. However, when it comes to my family, I feel a responsibility to not only protect them but also provide them a sense of security and sanctuary. If I had not been in a financial position to provide the security systems that I did, I would have done whatever I could afford to do and left the rest with the Lord's protecting angels. However, I could afford it, and so I did it. My only regret was that I had not done it much sooner.

Winter seemingly, came rather quickly. Our entire family was together. Too close together, in some opinions. All of us bumping into each other for the next three months was a challenge. However, much of the time, including Thanksgiving and Christmas, was spent at the lodge. It all took care of itself, though, so that we were all dreading going to our separate homes when the remodeling was finished.

The Cessna Citation CJ4 locked in a hangar at the Wasilla airport would need a bit more runway than we had, so we hired another construction crew that was already at work adding to the length of the runway. The extension project added 3,200 feet to the existing 2,800 that had, until now, been more than adequate. The CJ4 at maximum gross weight would need 3,100 hundred feet for takeoff and, at the same weight, 2,800 for landing. The new six-thousand-foot, paved runway would provide an extra buffer for a green jet pilot like me. Rated for single pilot operation, the small jet would be perfect for what I was planning to do, but I had some flight school training to go through before I would be qualified to fly it.

Kati spent three months faithfully making the weekly visit to her therapist and gradually weaning herself off the medications. I often wondered if it was really accomplishing that much, but as time went on, I saw her gradually return to her usual self. I knew it was up to me to protect her from ever fearing for her life again. For me, the good news was that she was ready to leave the safety net of home to venture out in public and do some traveling with me, somewhere we were not likely to be recognized. Her therapist gave permission for Kati to travel under certain circumstances. I was never to leave her alone and must always provide a secure place for her to live in.

Expecting that it would take at least six months to complete the work on the homes and security fences, I decided to get started on the Citation training. There was a Cessna jet flight school in Aurora, Oregon, where I could get the multi-engine and ATP ratings as well as my turbo-jet type rating. I needed a pilot who could fly for us until I finished.

Searching on the internet, I found a website called *homesitting dot something* and made arrangements to house-sit a small but secure mansion located on a golf course just outside the city limits of Aurora, Oregon. Leaving in less than ten days to go to China on a two-year construction project, the homeowner was desperate to find a reliable house sitter and relieved that we had responded to his ad. Of course, we would need to find someone to take over when we were ready to leave, and I assured him I would take full responsibility for his premises until he and his wife returned. Richard and Kathy, whose children were away at school anyway, agreed to go along.

I had bought the Citation from a Cessna dealer in Anchorage. The pilot who had delivered it to Wasilla agreed to fly us to Aurora. A quick call to the flight school, and I was registered for the training, which would begin the following week. We quickly packed, said good-bye to the kids, and on New Year's day, we were on our way nonstop to Aurora.

I wanted to be in the copilot's seat, but I wanted to share the ride with my dear Kati even more. I knew I would get plenty of seat time during my training. The CJ4 Citation shot into the air like an F-15 from a carrier deck. I was thoroughly impressed. Climbing to 41,000 feet in less than eleven minutes, cruising at 453ktas. (knots-true-airspeed) and helped along with a substantial tailwind, in three and a half hours we were shooting the RNAV GPS (radio navigation, global position satellite) approach to runway 35 at Aurora, Oregon. The 1,380 nautical mile trip had taken no longer then it would take to drive to Anchorage, go shopping, and return home.

"This is the way to do it," I thought to myself. I was definitely pumped and ready to get started on my training immediately. We landed, parked the jet, and while I checked in at the flight center, Kelly and Kati went with Richard to the FBO where he contacted a car rental agency, securing for us a GMC Suburban, which we would use for the next three months.

From the airport, we headed to the home of Mr. Phillip Gentry, a nuclear physicist, who evidently was some kind of a genius and had designed the development and construction of a miniature nuclear power plant for the exclusive use of developing local power to rural communities. Mr. Gentry could build a dozen of these facilities at a fraction of the cost of the nuclear power plants the US had used for decades (at great risk to humanity) and provide power to three times as many consumers at a fraction of the risk. It would be the first of its kind and would serve as a model to the world. If successful, the entire world's approach to nuclear power would revolutionize the risks of disaster associated with present day nuclear power technology.

Arriving at the huge electronically controlled gate, I gave Mr. Gentry a call. He seemed excited that we had come. The large gate swung open without as much as a squeak. I drove counterclockwise around a circular drive constituting the perimeter of a beautifully manicured garden of flowers and vine-covered lattice walkways to a drive-through portico, the main entrance to the mansion. A casually dressed man in his late forties stepped from the huge double doors and approached the Suburban as we stepped out.

"Good morning," he said cordially, extending his hand in greeting. "I am Phillip Gentry."

"Good morning, sir," I responded, shaking his hand firmly. "I'm Lou Worley, and this is my wife Kati, my daughter Kathy, and son-in-law Richard."

"How do you do, folks? It is so nice to meet all of you. I am very glad you responded to my internet ad. Please come inside and meet my wife."

We followed Mr. Gentry up the portico steps and through the double doors into a magnificent foyer at the base of a spiral staircase, leading to another level of rooms and doors. It all reminded me of a scene in the movie *Gone With the Wind*, where Clark Gable spoke the most infamous line in the history of moviemaking to Vivien Leigh, "Frankly, my dear, I don't give a—"

"Lou," Kati interrupted my daydream. "Watch where you're going." Lost in thought I had almost collided with one of the columns holding up the portico.

From a sitting room on the left as we entered the foyer, an elegant, refined woman, also in her early forties, approached us with a welcoming smile.

"Hello, I am Jan. Please come this way. I have prepared a brunch for us all. I am sure you must be starving," Jan led us into the parlor from which she had just emerged and seated us at a very beautiful dinner table loaded with everything from fruit and pastries to roast beef, turkey, scrambled eggs, and biscuits and gravy.

At the conclusion of our meal and conversation, Jan stood up as did the rest of us.

"Let me show you to your rooms." Turning to Richard and me, she continued, "Phillip will show you the grounds and how to operate the electronic security system after you get settled. We won't be leaving for three more days, so you will have time to ask any questions before we go."

Jan put Kati and I in a huge bedroom downstairs that looked more like a small condominium than a bedroom, and Richard and Kathy went upstairs to a guest room that was still bigger than our family room at home. Both had master bathrooms and small kitchenettes.

"One more thing," Phillip said just before they drove away three days later, "you can take that rented truck back and use our cars in the garage. The keys are in them." We thanked them, but decided against it. Both cars were brand-new Cadillac Escalades.

My training went well, and flying had become exciting again. Three different instructors were involved. A young man named Gerald Thompson worked with me on my turbo-type and multi-engine ratings, Ken Gilmore was in charge of my airline transport (ATP) license requirements, and Steve Smith was my cross-country instructor. Steve either had no brains or fear, I am not sure which. We would file for a cross-country to LA or Denver and, on the way home, he would have me descend to below ten thousand feet and fly slow-flight into high country airstrips at just above a stall—something I was very familiar with in my Skywagon, but in the small jet it was a bit scary. The training was top-notch, and when I finished, I was confident that my skill level was adequate to continue expanding my experience on my own without risking my life or the lives of my passengers.

It was getting close to spring, and I had finished my training three weeks earlier than anticipated. Kati and I were ready to go, but Richard and Kathy agreed to stay.

"If you two decide you want to come home, just let me know. You're only three and a half hours away," I said, "and when the kids get out of school for vacation, I will bring them down."

"Okay, Dad. Thank you. We love you both, and take good care of Mom."

We kissed our kids and climbed aboard the Citation. But before I left, I purchased a car for Richard and Kelly. They drove the Gentry's Escalades on occasion to keep them in running order, but we did not feel right about putting too many miles on them.

I was finally on my own in the CJ4. I had spent about two hundred hours in the jet during my training, not because that much was required, but because I wanted as much dual-instruction and experience as I could get. I had logged at least a hundred hours as solo time and my confidence level was high. I was absolutely in love with the airplane.

During training, I had made several solo cross-country trips to Sandpoint, Idaho, doing a checkout in the Kodiak with its 750 horsepower, four-bladed, turbo-prop Pratt and Whitney. I had ordered the amphibious float kit that had only recently become available as an option, which the factory installed for me, as part of the buyers package. When it was finished, their chief test pilot delivered it to my hangar in Wasilla where my instructor, Steve, and I were waiting for him in the CJ4 to fly him back to Sandpoint.

I knew I would always miss the 180, but it was time to move on. The Kodiak was more than I ever imagined, and its bush-flying capabilities would soon prove to be not only superior, but life-saving.

CHAPTER 33

K ati was excited with the the progress of the construction, which suggested to me that it was already giving her a greater sense of security.

The security measures were taking shape, but it would still be several months until they would be complete. It could get a little noisy at times, so I asked Kati if she would like to go to Loon Lake for a few weeks. She started rubbing her hands together, and I began packing.

Henry Sinclair had left a message informing me that I could pick up the moose head. I put that on my "to do" list, and then I called Cal to see if he and Nanci could get away.

I was anxious to get that Kodiak into the air and did not need much of an excuse, so I moved the moose head to the top of the list. The Kodiak flew behind a PT6A-34 750-horsepower Pratt and Whitney turbo-charged power plant, cruising at 134 ktas at an altitude of 12,000 feet. Fuel consumption was expected to be around 34 gallons per hour, averaging 1,113 nm over 8.1 hours. Its rate of climb from sea level at maximum gross weight and standard temperature was 1,371 feet per minute. With full fuel (320 gallons), it, theoretically, could lift over 1800lbs of payload into the air in eight hundred feet of takeoff roll. With dual Garmin G-1000 heads-up displays and a full IFR database with the latest in anti-icing technology, the Kodiak fit my every desire for a bush plane.

The whine of the turbo sounded like choir music to my ears, and the smell of the jet fuel sent a thrill through my soul. Pitching the feathered prop for taxi, I turned the yellow-and-black floatplane to the west and set the brake. Carefully, I went through the checklist, recycling the propeller several times. Satisfied and confident that I had completed every check, and setting the throttle to full power, I pitched the propeller for maximum performance takeoff, released the brake and pulled the empty Kodiak into the air. It easily climbed empty at over 2,700 feet per minute. I turned to the north toward the Eva Creek mine, basking in the feel and performance of the new machine. I wanted to fly the airplane forever, but a nice little vacation awaited us at Loon Lake. And I needed to get my mounted moose head.

I called flight service and filed a pop-up IFR flight plan into Anchorage and requested the RNAV-A approach. Receiving my clearance, I then climbed up into the overcast on a heading that would take me to the initial approach fix from which I flew the published approach. Soon I emerged from the overcast layer at 750 msl, at which time Merrill tower cleared me for a "circle to land" on runway one-six. The old days of NDB and VOR approaches were rapidly becoming a side note in history behind the new generation of GPS heads-up displays. I was glad I had lived to experience it.

Henry met me at Merrill field to pick me up. Together, we loaded and tied down the gigantic moose trophy I had bagged just the year before. It had placed second behind the new world record taken four hours later by Calvin Trent, which we also secured to the amphibious float framework of the Kodiak. Both moose heads were too huge to fit inside the airplane.

"Mr. Worley, the game warden wanted you to have this." I turned around to see Henry pointing to a huge grizzly bear rug, complete with head and claws attached.

My mouth fell open. "Is that the one I shot?"

"Trent said you would pay for it. I sure hope he was right."

"Absolutely, I will. How did you manage to fix his face? There wasn't much left of it."

"I used pieces from a couple of remnant hides left by customers who never picked up their orders. Cal said that bear almost got you, is that right?"

"Almost," I said. "Almost." My voice trailed off a bit as the memories of that day returned to my frontal lobe.

I thanked Henry and paid him for my moose and bear, as well as Cal's and the two other orders he had used to repair the face of the grizzly.

With the attempted abduction of Kati, I had completely forgotten to write Cal a statement in regard to the bear attack, and he had never mentioned it to me again. Evidently, he managed to get the authorization without it and probably figured I had enough on my plate at the time. I really considered him a true friend. There are not many like him in this world, sad to say.

Cal and Nanci with their son, Anthony, and all of our kids and grandkids joined Kati and me at Loon Lake. The weather was cold but clear, for the most part. The snow was three foot deep, but the lake was frozen solid underneath it, so there was more than enough runway for our airplanes, which were all on skis by that time of the year.. Even the Kodiak had been refitted with it's landing gear and was wearing a set of skis. I had brought in a dozen snowmobiles that were going constantly as we enjoyed the winter wilderness.

A few of us, Cal, myself, Richard and Rusty ice fished a little but mostly played bridge, enjoying the fireplace, the quiet, and the view, while the rest of the family played on the machines. It was a place we were always anxious to go to and never anxious to leave.

Two new world record B&C moose mounts hung on the largest wall with the most light. We spread the bear rug out on the floor between the couches in front of the fireplace.

The memory of Kati's attempted kidnapping was a constant reminder of the potential threat that existed. No matter how unlikely it seemed, we kept a twenty-four-hour vigil. Four off-duty state patrol officers had accepted invitations to attend our family vacation gathering, for which I rewarded them handsomely. All four were single and more than happy to make a few extra bucks. Two worked a twelve-hour day shift and the other two worked the night shift. Fortunately for the night shift, the rooms in the lodge were totally soundproof from the constant roar of the snowmobiles during the day.

With spring fast approaching, the uncompleted projects that had gone on hold for the winter would soon begin again. One of those projects—and one the entire family was looking forward to seeing completed—was an additional row of enclosed hangars at the home airfield. With everyone in the family now flying their own airplane to and from work every day, we had run out of places to park. Keera, Kathy, and Kelly until recently stayed all week at the learning center in Bettles, usually coming home only for weekends. Both Kathy and Kelly were flying Cessna 206s, and Kathy's straight tail that I had flown to Alaska fifteen years before, along with Kelly's Piper Clipper that had once belonged to William Shearer, were kept in the old hangar under a cloth cover. All the grandkids, still at boarding school, would sooner or later learn to fly in one or both of those airplanes.

Spring break-up had arrived and the snow was melting away in the lower elevations. I had already removed the skis from the Kodiak and expected to re-install the pontoons in the next couple of weeks.

It was late in the day on a Thursday afternoon and I was sorting through a mass of surplus army-navy gear and emergency equipment; putting together a survival pack for the new Kodiak. I had just gone through this chore with the 180 after its last refurbishing, and the emergency pack that had burned up with the airplane was one of the most complete I had ever put together. However, I still had the list, and after several stops at various surplus outlets, I had just about replaced it all. That completed and the 150 pounds of survival gear stowed in the back of the number two baggage compartment, I was about to close the door to the hangar office when the phone rang. It was Arnold Bradley, the Superintendant of Public Safety.

"Hello, this is Lou Worley."

"Lou, this is Arnold Bradley. Have you heard from Calvin Trent?" I sensed an urgency in his voice.

"No, I haven't. Why? Is something wrong?"

"Cal went out on a call two days ago. We expected him back yesterday afternoon sometime, but he hasn't returned, and I haven't been able to find anyone who has heard from him."

"Where did he go on the call?" I asked, reaching for a pen and paper.

"He never said. He goes all over the place and then fills out trip reports after he returns, usually within twenty-four hours. I have notified SAR, and they are going to start a search first thing in the morning. Would you like to join in?"

"Absolutely. Where do you want me to start?" I asked.

"Maybe you could check out the Denali area. That was where he had written several citations last winter for illegal trapping. I will try to get some help headed your way as soon as we can get everyone briefed in the morning."

"Okay, Mr. Bradley, I will get started at first light."

I immediately felt anxious, fearing the worst, so before calling Rusty, I bowed my head and prayed. "God in heaven, I know that Cal has never expressed faith in Jesus as his personal Savior, at least not publicly, so just in case he has not called on you in his own behalf, I am doing it for him. Please keep him safe from all potential harm, and lead me to him or him to me. Thank you, Sir. Amen."

I knew I needed Rusty's help, so I scrolled up his name on my cell phone and mashed on the green button."

"Hello, Dad."

"Rusty, Cal has gone missing. I just received a call from Arnold Bradley, and I am going to join in the search in the morning. Can you come along?"

"Sure, do you want me to come over tonight and look at maps with you?"

"That would be great, son, and I will throw a couple of mattresses in the Kodiak in case we have to sleep in it a few nights."

Rusty and I spread out the north Anchorage and north McGrath aviation sectional maps on the dining room table and studied the Denali northwest slope, a prime hunting and trapping area that Cal often patrolled, especially in the winter, and an area extremely popular to poachers due to its close proximity to the Denali National Park and Preserve. The deep snow and harsh weather of the Alaska Range drove the wildlife farther down to the lower elevations where they fought four-legged and two-legged predators for survival.

The poachers had taken a huge hit during our undercover operations and the outfitting and guided hunt industry was thriving once again, legally. But, as long as someone was willing to pay cash for trophy size bear rugs or wall mount antlers—and Alaska was still teeming with both—there would always be plenty of wannabe trophy hunters with deep pockets willing to pay for bragging rights. That is exactly why Calvin Trent had dedicated his life to game management and law enforcement for the future of those resources.

"Dad, there is a lot of country out there. Do you know where you want begin?"

"I think to start with we should pay a visit to every airport and airstrip we come to and nose around, ask a few questions, and look for anything that might be out of the ordinary."

"Did Arnold say if Cal had any special interest he might have been pursuing?"

"No, but he may still have more to say about that as the investigation gets going and information starts coming in. I am sure they are going over all of his current files for any clue. In the meantime, we'll just keep an eye out for his helicopter and talk to as many people as we can."

Kati prepared us a crate of food, anticipating that we might be gone a few days. The next morning, by the time it was light enough to see the windsock at midfield, we were on our way.

It was Rusty's first time in the Kodiak.

"Wow, Dad, this is a sweet airplane. I can see why you wanted it. The visibility and performance are off the charts."

"It is really great," I said. Totally preoccupied with Cal and his whereabouts, I was not much good for conversation on any other topic. Rusty soon realized that and started looking for anything that might look like a downed helicopter.

Our first stop was Talkeetna where we inquired in the FBO if they had seen Cal as of late. None had. Moving on and keeping low, barely above five hundred feet msl and with a constant eye on the terrain, we passed over the Summit NDB (non directional beacon) at the Summit airport, and then over Cantwell through Windy Pass, past the Denali Highway, and on to the Healy River airport.

Notorious for wind shear and sudden gusts, Healy River was famous for having humbled even the best of pilots. Rusty and I decided to take our chances and visit the local Box Cart Café located two miles from the airport.

"Dad, are you going to pack?" Rusty asked.

"Absolutely!" I said. "We have no way of knowing if Cal's helicopter went down or if there is foul play involved. I think it would be smart to play it safe."

Rusty reached into one of his bags and retrieved his .45 S&W and strapped it to his side. I had already done so with my .45 Glock when I got dressed that morning.

The wind was not that bad at Healy River but as we walked into town we could tell that it was building in strength and by the end of the day, landing anywhere along the Range could turn out to be a challenge.

We entered the roadside café with the morning rush in full swing, pausing at the door briefly to search for an available table. One of the waitresses saw us.

"You fellows want breakfast or just coffee?" She hollered above the drone of conversations.

"Breakfast," I hollered back. The conversation buzz had significantly diminished as most of the patrons immediately recognized Rusty and me. The Eva Creek mine was not that far from Healy River, and Rusty and his crew had patronized the diner occasionally over the years.

"Good morning, Mr. German," the waitress said to Rusty.

"Good morning, Alice. This is my father in law, Lou Worley."

"Hello, Alice. Nice to meet you. Has the game warden Cal Trent been through here lately?" I asked. At that moment, you could have heard a pin drop. Gradually, within a minute or so, conversation in the diner returned to normal.

"Not for awhile. I think he was in here about a month ago. Anything wrong?"

"No, just asking." I said.

Rusty and I had breakfast and returned to the Kodiak. The winds coming off the slopes of the Alaska Range were treacherous in the spring of the year and had already picked up considerably since we had landed. I expected the conditions to get even worse as the day progressed. It was unlikely we would be able to fly into the canyons without risking disaster, so we decided to keep looking along the perimeter of the foothills and southwest toward Farewell Lake and the Revelation Mountains.

"Let's stop at Stampede," Rusty suggested.

"The wind is going to be kind of rough in there. Are you sure?"

"I trust you."

We stopped at both Stampede and Kantishna, which was located directly at the foot of Mount McKinley. Kantishna had been a favorite landing spot for the famous mountain pilot Don Sheldon during the twenty-plus years he had dropped off climbers destined to leave their fingers and toes high up on the mountains of ice. We walked the length of each airstrip, looking for any sign that Cal might have landed in the recent hours or days. It seemed like a long shot, as it would only take one night of rain to erase any such trace.

We knew if it continued to rain, our chances of finding any of those traces grew less likely. Back in the airplane, we placed ourselves once again in the hands of God and launched into an ever-increasing wind. The Kodiak felt much more secure in strong wind conditions than any other airplane I had ever flown. Although a tricycle gear, it had a massively strong nose gear designed for extremely rough terrain, so it was much easier to control and much more forgiving. If Rusty and I had been flying the 180, we would not have even attempted to land in the winds we were encountering in our search for Calvin Trent.

The four-bladed, turbo-powered fan tore at the forty-mile-per-hour side wind cascading off the northwestern slopes of the mountain range. As the Kodiak lifted into the air, I banked sharply toward the rising terrain and into the wind, climbing in excess of three thousand feet per minute. Soon, we were high above the rocky ridges. I turned back toward the southwest and continued on to Purkeypile, the next airstrip.

CHAPTER 34

Purkeypile airstrip sat at the foot of 11,670-foot Mount Russell, often used by aspiring mountain climbers in preparation for the big climb up Mount McKinley.

At an elevation of two thousand feet msl, the eleven-hundred-foot long runway could be a handful in windy conditions. Rusty and I decided to do a flyby and check the surface of the runway and wind direction before committing to a landing. The airstrip was practically invisible to anyone who had never seen it before. The only time I had ever had occasion to land on it was with Cal in the Bell Ranger. This would be my first time in an airplane, a strange one at that, and in more than just a little wind.

"Rusty, I am going to carry a lot of power in this wind and just concentrate on flying the airplane. You will have to do all the looking," I said.

"I got it covered," Rusty said. "Just don't get too low and get caught in a downdraft that you can't pull out of."

The airstrip lay almost east and west with runway headings of 08/26 degrees magnetic. We needed the blinding afternoon sun behind us. Turning out to the west and circling back around, I approached the airstrip from the southwest with the sun to our back and at a forty-five-degree angle to the lay of the mountains on the far side of the strip rising abruptly out of the vast expanse of sparse timber and tundra. The idea was that if the wind proved to be more than I could deal with, I would be able to make a quick exit with a forty-five-degree turn to the west and live to try again another day. Turning toward the airstrip from a distance of two miles, I pulled in twenty degrees of flap, slowing the Kodiak and straining my eyes to makes sense of the landscape. It was like looking for the proverbial needle in the haystack.

"There it is, Dad! There's the Bell Ranger!"

I felt both excited optimism at the sight of Cal's helicopter and a sense of dread at the thought of having to land in that treacherous wind. I completed the flyby, turning back out toward the west once again and re-entered the landing pattern, setting up for a simulated approach in one of the most ferocious winds I had ever encountered in an airplane. With the power set to climb, I fought for control of airspeed and rate of descent with constant manipulation of the prop pitch. Lower and lower we descended; the increasing strength of the wind tearing more violently at the airplane the closer we came to the ground. It was so strong that at a reduced prop pitch we were actually in a hover over the airstrip when I finally managed to set the bush plane on the turf.

Although now on the ground, I remained in the airplane with the turbo still at full power manipulating prop pitch settings and maneuvering the ailerons and elevator in every conceivable attempt to keep the wind from getting under the wings and flipping the Kodiak upside down.

"Rusty, you will have to go check out that chopper. If I let go of this yoke, the airplane will go over."

"Okay, Dad." He scurried from the passenger-side door and ran toward the Ranger.

I felt like I was still flying as I continued the fight to keep the airplane fastened to the ground. Again and again it rose into the air as the wind repeatedly achieved speeds that produced the lift required to make the airplane fly.

The Bell Ranger sat at the far-east end of the airstrip, and I had set the Kodiak on the ground at approximately midfield. It seemed like it took a long time for Rusty to return, although it was more like only ten minutes.

"Dad," Rusty panted, "the Bell Ranger is all shot up. Cal is nowhere around, and there is blood on the collective."

"Oh, Lord! Then I guess we have ourselves a crime scene. Can you dig two trenches and bury a couple of tie-down logs? I'll get back in the air and contact SAR. You better get the shovel and some overnight gear in case I can't make it back in tonight."

"Okay, Dad. Hang onto that thing a little longer, and I will get everything I need. Don't worry about coming back. I will be all right."

"I will fly around and give you time to dig in those logs. I'll be back, son. You can count on it. See you later." I was not nearly as sure of myself as I sounded.

I continued to hang onto the dancing airplane while Rusty retrieved everything he would need in the event I could not make it back in. The biggest problem was getting back out. The power was still set to climb, and I knew that as soon as I pitched the prop for takeoff and brought the yoke back toward my chest a few inches, the airplane was going to go straight up like a helicopter.

With Rusty out of the way, I twisted the prop-pitch control to climb and let the airplane fly. I kept the nose low while still fighting to maintain level wings as the airplane immediately went airborne, elevating like a helium balloon. In seconds, the airspeed quickly increased to VXY (best rate of climb). A moment later, I was well away from the ground where the flying became somewhat easier. I could almost breathe again.

While fighting the wind, another fight was taking place in my mind—the possibility that Cal had met some horrible end. The good news, I kept telling myself, was that there was no body, at least not in the immediate vicinity of the helicopter. I climbed as high as the nine-thousand-foot overcast stacked up against the foothills would allow me to go and checked my cell phone for a signal. Rather than calling SAR, I decided—if I had any coverage—to first call Arnold Bradley. Finally, two little bars popped up; maybe that would be enough. I scrolled up Arnold's name on the call list and mashed on the green button.

"Bradley speaking."

"Arnold, this is Lou. Rusty and I found the Bell Ranger. It's at Purkeypile, and it's all shot up. Rusty said there is blood on the collective handle. You might want to wait till morning, the wind is really bad. I mean way past nasty."

"Is there any sign of Cal other than that?'

"I don't know yet. I left Rusty there. The wind is so bad I had to hold the airplane on the ground with control inputs while Rusty checked out the helicopter. I am going back. I have a weak signal, so I will see you when you get here."

The dinging in my ear told me I had lost the signal and that Arnold may not have heard everything I told him, but I figured he had heard enough. With still another forty minutes to an hour before Rusty would have the tie-downs in place, I decided I would check the surrounding area. Expecting the wind to get worse before it got better, I was relieved that it actually had let up some as I returned to a lower altitude and the foothills near the airstrip. By the time Rusty had finished, I had passed over the airstrip at least ten times. I hoped he had not gotten the impression I was trying to hurry him up. Finally on the ground, I had no difficulty in maneuvering the airplane directly over the new tie-downs, each buried four feet in the ground under each wing. I feathered the prop, closed the throttle, and climbed down from the pilot's seat where we quickly secured the Kodiak.

"Were you able to contact anyone?" Rusty asked.

"I got a hold of Arnold and told him he better wait till morning when the wind has quieted down a little."

"I am sure they will. By the time they get a team together it will be dark."

"I want to go see the Ranger." I said as I grabbed the ten-gage.

Rusty went with me back to where the Bell Ranger sat. I approached the helicopter carefully, taking care not to disturb any potential evidence. Whoever shot up the chopper had definitely done so with an attitude, for even the instrument panel had been shot to pieces. At least two hundred spent cartridges from three different calibers lay scattered both inside and outside of the helicopter along with a mass of broken glass from the shot-up windows.

As I stared at the ghostly remains of the Bell Ranger that I had come to associate with Cal's commanding presence, it was difficult to comprehend that he was in some kind of trouble. He was either taken captive, hurt, or the other, unthinkable possibility. I could hardly wrap my mind around it. There was only one thing to do, only one choice to make. I would choose one of the above and refuse any other consideration no matter what anyone else said or what conclusions they might suggest. I chose to believe that Cal was still alive, although probably held captive against his will and, more than likely, injured, and would survive long enough to make his escape or for me to find him. I would not consider any other option.

Rusty had picked up three of the spent casings, one of each caliber.

"Most of these are nine millimeter handgun, a few are from a .458 magnum handgun, and the rifle casings are .338 magnum caliber."

"Let's just take one of each. The investigators will want to check them all for prints ... hey, I found one that's not .338." Using a twig inserted into a very large rifle casing, I picked it up and checked the caliber stamped on the rear of the brass. "This one is .30 caliber/.378 Weatherby magnum. Whoever fired this one is in the money. Those rifles go for over three thousand bucks apiece and would drop a raging rhino at three hundred yards"

"How many of those are lying around?" Rusty asked.

"I just see the one for now. Whoever fired it may have fired more than once, but picked up his spent casings. Except he overlooked one."

"We better leave it for the investigators."

"Where do you think the blood came from on the collective?" I asked. "Did Cal get shot before he landed the Ranger, or did they shoot at him and he cut his hand on some of the broken glass, or what?"

"It could have been either one of those scenarios," Rusty answered. "I think it is more than likely that he happened on them as they were involved in some illegal activity, moved in on top of them, and one of them shot him while he was in the hover. Unfortunately, the fact that he landed instead of flying away suggests he might have been hit pretty hard."

"Maybe he didn't get shot until after he landed. He might have seen something that he wanted to investigate and landed to check it out, when they shot and only wounded him. Then maybe he got back in the helicopter to try to get back into the air when they surrounded him, which would explain why there is blood on the collective but not anywhere else. It seems to me that if he was hit vary hard there would be a lot more blood."

"Good point, Dad. One thing is for certain: They took him with them when they left, and it is a good bet they are far away from here now."

"What do you think they were flying?" I asked.

"Probably a helicopter. I don't see any wheel tracks from an airplane landing gear other than the Kodiak, so I would guess probably a Robinson."

"Why do you suppose Cal landed in the first place?"

"My guess is, he saw the helicopter—or whatever it was—and landed to check it out."

"That is what I think, too. So, he see's a helicopter, lands to check it out, gets out of the idling Bell Ranger, and starts walking toward the helicopter. Cal is left-handed. So did someone shoot him in the left arm and the blood ran down his sleeve onto the collective? Or was he shot in the right arm and used his left hand to grab the wound, thereby getting blood on his left hand, which he then transferred to the collective when he tried to leave?"

"Wow, Dad. You should have been a private detective. I could have used you back there in Spanaway. Actually, the latter scenario sounds the most likely."

Rusty and I investigated the area until it was too dark to see and then retreated from the crime scene.

The mattresses I had brought were only two and a half feet wide and six feet long, which left our feet hanging over the ends. With Rusty, who stood six foot four, the disparity was more apparent. I, on the other hand, found the mattress to be head and shoulders above the one-half-inch foam roll-up pad I had used for many years. Rifling through the food box that Kati had prepared, we soon satisfied our hunger and retired for the night. I did not sleep well and awoke at least five times. Each time, the scene of Cal's capture shot a dose of adrenalin through my veins, and I lay awake for another hour before drifting back to sleep.

Morning finally arrived. I crawled from my bed, shaking the airplane and waking Rusty. With my forty-four magnum holstered and the belt slung over my shoulder, I stepped from the Kodiak to pay nature a visit. The wind was still pouring off the side of the Alaska Range like a gigantic invisible waterfall.

"Here they come," Rusty said, stepping from the airplane and pointing toward the north. He had heard the other state police Bell Ranger coming at least ten seconds before I did. I returned to the cockpit, flipped on the master switch, and tuned the VHF (vary high frequency) radio to the CTAF (common traffic advisory frequency) 122.9 to listen for the pilot of the incoming aircraft. Seconds later, he made his first call.

"Purkeypile traffic, helicopter N … 27V three-north-inbound, landing Purkeypile."

"Two seven Victor, this is Lou Worley. You have an aircraft parked at midfield, should be no factor. The crime scene is located at the far west end. Be prepared for strong wind conditions including downdrafts."

"Roger that. Hello, Mr. Worley. This is Officer Daily."

"I hear you're a lieutenant now. Congratulations. Did Mr. Bradley come along?"

"No, sir. I have three other investigators and an NTSB inspector."

"The wind on the other end is a bit squirrely," I cautioned. "Be careful."

I had not seen much of Daily since the Alfred Creek investigation. Cal had informed me that he had risen to the top of the Crime Scene Investigation Department. I was hoping he was right because Cal needed him to be on top of his game on this one.

I was impressed with the way Daily handled the Ranger in that wind and would have told him so, but as soon as he was on the ground and had closed the throttle, matters of greater importance occupied our attention. As Daily and his team exited the helicopter, Rusty and I approached them, greeting each one as the lieutenant introduced us to his team members.

"Officer Billings, Officer Grant, and Corporal Lisa Finely, this is Lou Worley and his son-in-law, Rusty German. Lou is a long-time friend of the department and a retired officer, so to speak."

The NTSB inspector, whose name I learned later was Willford Flaggerty, immediately started walking toward Cal's Ranger, ignoring any introductions. I detected a note of concern on Lieutenant Daily's face and suspected that there might be a turf dispute over jurisdiction. Daily told his people to wait at the still-whining Bell Ranger as he turned to follow Flaggerty.

"Mr. Flaggerty, I don't want anyone entering this area until my team and I have had a chance to collect all the evidence."

"Lieutenant Daily, it has not yet been established that this is a crime scene. I am here to determine if it might possibly be a crash site, in which case, this scene belongs to the NTSB. Don't worry. I won't destroy any evidence."

Lieutenant Daily stayed with Flaggerty while he checked the shot-up Ranger for any indication that it may have crashed. Determining that it had not, he turned to the lieutenant.

"I'm satisfied. It's your scene, lieutenant. But I need to get back now."

"I will see if Mr. Worley can take you back," Daily responded, obviously relieved. "Mr. Worley, could I impose upon you to give Mr. Flaggerty a ride back to Wasilla?"

"I am sorry, but a friend of mine has been wounded and taken captive by criminals. I won't be doing any taxi service until I find him. Rusty and I are going to be searching every town and airstrip in this country for however long it takes." Then I added, "Doesn't the NTSB have there own airplanes?"

"He said it's in the shop getting an annual," Daily replied. He knew before he asked the question what my response would be. A slight grin came across his face as he nodded.

The NTSB inspector was not happy about it, but there was nothing he could do except wait for the team to finish collecting their evidence and documenting the scene, which took most of the day.

"Lieutenant Daily," I said, "Rusty and I have determined that there were three men involved in this kidnapping and also have come to the conclusion that Cal was shot on the right side of his body after he was on the ground. One of the men was shooting a Weatherby .30caliber/.378magnum, another a .458 magnum handgun and the happiest shooter was firing a nine-millimeter semi-auto. The one with the .378 Weatherby is probably the one who owns the helicopter, and I think we may be looking for a Robinson R66 Turbine. It is the most popular and economical personal helicopter and seats up to five people."

"You figured all that out before we arrived this morning?" Daily asked.

"Actually, it was last night," I said. "Rusty and I are going to take off and start looking. We want to check all the old mines, airstrips, and cabins we can find. I think they might be holding Cal somewhere they feel safe and are in the habit of going. Also, it might be a good idea if you try to get a list of all the Robinson owners who live in Alaska.

"That's a good idea Lou, we will do that."

Will you keep me abreast of anything you learn here that we might need to know?" I asked.

"I sure will, Mr. Worley, but I want you to promise me you will not move in on anyone until you have backup. I want you to call us as soon as you find anything. Do I make myself clear?"

"You bet, Lieutenant. See ya."

CHAPTER 35

I hollered to Rusty and waved at him, indicating that it was time to go. The turbo whined its way to full power as I went through the checklist, and Rusty climbed aboard and seat-belted himself into the copilot seat. We taxied to the east end and made our departure from runway two-six.

The next destination on our list was a very old prospector's gold claim that had played out so long ago the airstrip was barely even usable. Tin Creek was located about four miles upstream from where the Dillinger river spills into the Kuskokwim river forty-four miles southwest of Purkeypile. Like Purkeypile, it too was tucked tight up against the foothills of the Alaska Range and roughly eighteen miles east of Farwell Lake.

The vicious wind of the day before had significantly subsided and as the overgrown Tin Creek airstrip came into view we descended flying low and slow, searching the ground for anything unusual. Tin Creek sat at the top of the heel of a group of mountains referred to by the locals as the Grizzly Paw Mountains, a portion of the Alaska Range and the Revelation Mountains west of 11,258-foot Mount Gerdine. Evidently, someone's keen eye picked out the likeness of a grizzly paw print in the lay of the mountains. I am sure that, along with a vivid imagination, their altimeter must have been reading about twenty thousand feet mean sea level for them to see it.

I circled the area several times, checking the conditions and looking for any sign of life. There was nothing there.

"I don't see anything, Dad," Rusty said. "If you want to land anyway, we could check for tracks."

"Let's do that," I said. "We can walk down to the lake and see if there has been any activity there recently."

The bush plane settled into the overgrown grass and onto the soggy mud/turf runway, which only a short time before had been covered in snow. I quickly reversed the prop to stop as short as possible in an effort to keep the mud off the underside of the wings. As I climbed down from the cockpit my eye immediately noticed foot prints in the mud.

"This is a soupy mess," Rusty commented.

"Rusty look over here, we got grizzly tracks in the mud. They look fresh to." Rusty stepped around to my side of the airplane.

"Now, I understand why they call these the, grizzly paw mountains."

"I want to have a look at that lodge down by the lake. Would you mind staying with the airplane? I will be back in a half/hour or so. If I'm not, come looking for me."

"Okay, Pop. Be careful. I'll look around up here."

Armed with the .44 magnum and my ten-gage, I started down the path to the old deserted lodge some four-hundred yards away. I made my way slowly, looking for everything from gum wrappers to spent casings even tobacco chew that someone might have discarded—anything that would suggest human presence or activity.

The old lodge had sat vacant for over twenty years, and the path that led to it, along with the airstrip, had overgrown with grass and brush from lack of maintenance. I mounted the steps to the large porch and peered through the boarded-up windows to see inside. It was pitch black. Prying one of the boards loose, I held my flashlight against the smoke-stained glass. I saw nothing but a disheveled mess of plywood broken tables, chairs, and cobwebs. There was no sign of any recent activity. I walked around back where I found steps leading down to a fruit cellar with a door that was partially open. I filled my hand with the Desert Eagle and flipped off the safety. Carefully, I made my way down the rotted wood steps to the bottom where I pushed open the door in a sudden move. There facing me, sitting on his butt with his hands in his lap and legs outstretched, were the decomposing remains of an old man.

When I returned to the airstrip and told Rusty what I had found, he wanted to see the body. So we returned to the root cellar. Rusty moved in closer to study the remains.

"He was an old prospector, looks like he might have been in his seventies. He's been shot in the chest and it does not appear to be self inflicted. Someone murdered this old guy dad."

"What do you want to bet it was a nine iron?" I said.

"You are probably right about that."

"How long do you think he has been here?"

"I would say about nine months. There is not much smell right now; probably been frozen all winter, which explains why the critters haven't gotten to him yet."

"Well, I guess we ought to tell the lieutenant." I turned back up the trail to the airstrip.

I didn't try to taxi in the sloppy mud and slush that we had used as a landing strip. I just spooled up and cranked the prop to climb and let it go. I reefed back on the yoke at about a hundred feet, and the bush plane left the ground.

"We are already here, and that guy isn't going to get any deader, so we may as well have a look around."

I had initially planned to have a look at Farwell Lake, but I then remembered another little emergency airstrip sixteen miles up the Kuskokwim River called Tatitna. Already pointed in that direction, I just kept going. In only minutes, the airstrip came into view. The airstrip did not appear to be something that I really cared to land on. It was too overgrown and brushy, much worse than Tin Creek. Turning a counterclockwise standard rate turn around the landing strip, I noticed an old cabin at the confluence of two tributaries where they emptied into the Kuskokwim River. Slowing the airplane, I studied the landing zone, noticing that the far west end was partially clear of brush. Someone had apparently hacked out a spot for landing a helicopter. During the next pass, I concentrated on the cabin. It looked like there was a path leading from the cleared area straight up to the door.

"Rusty, someone has been using that cabin, and they have cleared a spot to land a helicopter. Maybe Cal is down there. Look for a place where I can set down."

"I don't see any place other than the runway that you can set this tricycle gear. Are you sure you want to try that?"

"This tri-gear is as tough as a cowcatcher on an old locomotive. I'm not worried about that as long as I don't dig into something soft and have room to takeoff."

"You could do a low pass over the airstrip and get a closer look at how deep that brush is. Maybe the prop would clear it. If the front gear is as tough as you say it is, it might plow through it."

I came in low and slow on the last pass. Evidently, I had sufficiently convinced Rusty, but, once again, was not so sure I had convinced myself. I guess there was only one way to find out. I was pumped with adrenalin at the prospect of maybe finding Cal and knew that time was critical. If the same people who took Cal had murdered the old trapper we had just found down at Tin Creek, landing in a thicket was a risk I was going to have to take. Slowly, I let the Kodiak settle onto the brushy runway. I could feel it snagging and tugging at the main gear. I kept the tail low, the nose gear high, and out of the brush as much as possible by using more power to apply extra air over the elevator of the rapidly slowing airplane, literally plunking the Kodiak onto its main gear.

As soon as the main gear was firmly on the ground, I reversed the prop and brought the Kodiak to an immediate stop. With one last burst of thrust, I spun the tail around like a tail dragger and let the nose gear come down. We had landed, and the front gear had barely even touched the brush.

"Nice job, Dad. If you can blast that elevator with enough air on takeoff to get it down when we leave, the nose gear will not even be in the brush."

"That's what I was thinking. How far is it down to that cabin?"

"Maybe a quarter of a mile. Do you want me to stay with the airplane?"

"I think I would rather you come with me. There is plenty of cover along that path, so if we hear a helicopter, we can run back up here within a hundred yards of the airstrip without detection. Let's grab all our weapons. We don't want to leave anything for someone to use against us."

Rusty still carried his .45 S&W along with a .300 Weatherby Mag. This time, I carried my .45 Glock, 44 magnum, and ten-gage shotgun. I had learned something in my incident with the grizzly bear that attacked me when Cal and I were hunting moose together. Since then, I always loaded the ten-gage with seven .400-grain lead slugs. On a big bear, take out the front shoulders first. If it gets to within twenty feet, put them in his mouth, one right after the other, right down the throat.

We left the airplane unlocked, but I took the key with me. In the event we needed to get going in a hurry, I did not want to be fumbling around trying to unlock a door. From the airstrip, or more appropriately, the bush-strip, Rusty and I headed down the path to the cabin. Carefully and quietly, we made our way across the tributary and through the shoulder-high vine-maple that concealed most of the pathway to the cabin. Stopping briefly where the brush cover ended, we studied the cabin for any sign of activity. Built on a side hill, the front portion of the log cabin protruded out of the hillside like a locomotive sticking out of a collapsed railway tunnel. It was at least eighty years old and the bleached white fifteen-inch diameter logs showed signs of decay from lack of care. I guessed that it was much larger inside, but how far back it went into the mountainside we had no way of knowing.

"Rusty, we need to split up. I will go to the right and approach the cabin from the side. Maybe you could work your way around and come at it from the left side. We can join up at the two front corners."

"Okay, Dad. But let me go first, and you wait until I am in position before you start up. That way, you can cover me, and I can cover you."

"Good idea."

I waited and watched Rusty work his way in and around the rocks and trees leading to the far side of the entrance. Ten minutes later, he was in position, and I began to move. Within forty feet of the south sidewall, I stopped to listen. The sound of the Kuskokwim River in the distance along with the fifteen-knot breeze flowing out of the Ptarmigan Pass sufficiently drowned out almost every other sound. Aware that my hearing was not quite what it used to be, I concentrated even more in an attempt to hear any sound that might be coming from within the cabin. I moved up to the log house, placing my hand on the wall and inching my way to the front corner.

Carefully peeking around the corner, I saw Rusty looking directly at me from the other far corner. I tried to whisper, but the wind muffled my words, so I just acted. Moving toward the door, shotgun leveled, I lifted the old iron latch, and Rusty kicked open the door. In a flash, both of us were inside. I instantly moved to the right, getting out of the lighted doorway, as Rusty did the same to the left. There we stood, waiting for our eyes to adjust to the darkness and listening for any sound. There was nothing. I turned on my pocket flashlight and began searching the inside of the dark cabin. Clearly, someone was using the place on a frequent basis. There were boxes of canned goods and staple items, such as flour, lard, coffee, and potatoes, with table and chair accommodations for at least ten or more.

"Dad, it looks like someone uses this place occasionally. Could be the guys that shot up the Ranger, don't you think?"

"Could be, looks like there is a lantern on the table, lets look for some matches."

"Here they are." Rusty handed me a box of wooden stick matches. I lit the lantern, which quickly brought light to the dark room. There was a wood stove in the far back corner with several makeshift shelves on the wall stocked with kitchen paraphernalia, under which, from nails driven into the log wall, hung an assortment of pots, pans, and Dutch ovens. Against the front wall was a stack of split wood for the stove upon which lay a khaki game warden uniform shirt with the right upper side stained with blood.

"There is Cal's shirt," I said, excited and alarmed at the same time. "He has either been here or is still here."

"There is a door into another room over there." Rusty pointed at a wood door on the back wall.

I raised the shotgun to my shoulder as Rusty quickly swung the door wide open, and we entered the dark room. It appeared to be a sleeping quarters. The room had a low ceiling and was approximately fourteen feet wide and twenty feet long with another wooden door beyond on the far end. Two army cots lay along the left wall and one on the right, where musty blankets and old clothing lay strewn about.

"I think someone actually lives here," Rusty said.

"I expect you are right, and some of this stuff probably belonged to the old prospector sitting on his butt down there at that broken-down lodge."

"I wonder how far back into the mountain this goes?"

"Let's keep going and find out," I said. "I am wondering if maybe Cal got away. Maybe they left him here and he escaped."

"He may have taken off that shirt and put on some of these warmer old clothes he found laying around here."

Through the next door we entered into another room not as wide but much longer, at least forty feet in length. The roof was no longer log and thatch, but timbers supported with huge six-by-eight cross-member beams that held the mountainside from caving in.

Along the walls on each side, stacked from floor to ceiling, were animal hides of every description. Moose, black bear, grizzly bear, Dall sheep, wolf, bobcat, lynx, beaver, even muskoxen were only some of the more than forty illegal game species stockpiled. Stacked alongside the hides was a huge pile of trophy antlers from moose, caribou and elk, even Dall sheep.

"It looks like Cal stumbled onto a good-sized poaching operation." Rusty said.

"He sure did, I think they brought him here and left someone to watch him. It may be that Cal overpowered his captor and took him prisoner. We may have flown over the both of them on our way in here."

"That's exactly what I'm thinking," Rusty said. "Let's go find them."

"There is still another door on the other end. Let's look in there first."

We worked our way to the far end of the long storage room to another door that opened into a mineshaft about eight foot high and ten foot wide. Rusty and I followed it for a hundred yards or so until it started down a steep incline and began a gradual turn to the left.

"Kind of unlikely this has an outlet, and the air is getting real bad," I said.

"Not only that, but the place gives me the jitters. There are no timbers supporting the roof anymore, so who knows when it might come down?"

"Well, it doesn't look like there is any more to see back here anyway. As I said, I think that old guy scratched a living from this place, trapping in the winter and picking out a few nuggets from this old mine. Good, honest, hardworking man, and then along comes an illegal poaching operation and they take it all away from him. We have to stop these guys, that's for sure. But first, we've got to find Cal."

Working our way back through the mineshaft and cache of hides, pelts, and antlers, we turned off the kerosene lantern and left it on the table. Slowly opening the door, Rusty cautiously peered outside, first checking the airstrip for any additional aircraft that might have landed while we were inside.

"You better get out of that doorway." Rusty quickly ducked back inside. "There is no telling who may have showed up while we were in the back." I added.

"I didn't see a helicopter on the pad, so unless they dropped someone off and left him, it should be all clear."

"Just in case, lets wrap Cal's shirt around a pillow from one of those cots in the other room and see if it will draw any fire."

I retrieved a pillow and draped the shirt around it. Poking a hole in the bottom of the pillow, I inserted a shovel handle into it and placed a hat on the top of it.

"Someone would have to be kind of dumb to fall for this, but I guess it is worth a try," I said. Crouching on my knees and holding the shovel man vertically, I leaned it into the dimly lit doorway where Rusty had stood only moments before.

BOOOOOM. The pillow disintegrated, and the end of the shovel disappeared along with a large portion of Cal's shirt.

"That would be that .378 Weatherby," I surmised.

"You just saved my life dad."

"I think the only reason you didn't get your head shot off when you first peered out was because he wasn't expecting it, and by the time he got his rifle to his shoulder, you were back inside.

Rusty said to me. "Someone must have dropped him off while we were in the back."

"I think that is exactly what happened. Furthermore, I bet when they seen the Kodiak they dropped him off and went for some help. We should have gone on to Farewell Lake they were probably there while we were nosing around at Tin Creek."

"Well that means that they now know that Cal and his captor or prisoner, whichever, are no longer here which means that they intend to come back in force. I wonder which one stayed with Cal The nine-millimeter guy or the .458 magnum guy?"

Rusty answered. "I figure it was the nine-millimeter guy. I bet the .458 magnum guy is the pilot, but the rifle man is the ringleader, and he owns the helicopter."

"You still think the nine-iron man killed the trapper?" I asked.

"I am sure he did. That's why they left him to watch Cal. They may have had plans for Cal before they killed him, though. Otherwise they would have already done it. I just don't know what it could be."

CHAPTER 36

"Rusty, we need to make a couple holes in this wall to shoot through. Look for something to dig with," I glanced around the windowless cabin.

"I have a little Swiss Army knife," Rusty volunteered.

The building was constructed with logs averaging about ten-inches in diameter. The narrow area where the logs were stacked on top of each other had been chinked with a mortar substance that over the years had dried and in many places was cracked and flaking away.

Rusty worked on digging through the old mortar where he could start carving a hole in the wall with his little Swiss pocketknife. I continued searching for something that would be a little more effective. Lying on the floor under some newspaper and trash, I found an ax with a short handle that for some reason was missing about six inches off its end. Lighting the kerosene lantern again, I began chopping at the narrowest point between two logs the closest to chest high. Rusty gave up his pocketknife endeavor, and we traded off hacking a three-inch slit through several of the log chinks.

"I wish I could get to the airplane," I said. "It is still four hours until dark, but the problem is it doesn't even get all the way dark. We could still get our heads shot off if the rifleman sees us."

"Yeah, but it if we are lucky it might get dark enough that he won't be able to see us in the scope, and I think he might be one of those guys who can't shoot without crosshairs," "Why do you say that? I asked. "Well why else would he own a Weatherby rifle, it doesn't have any sights mounted on the rifle itself, just the scope which makes quick shooting a lot more difficult.

"I hope you are right," I said. "Do you think if Cal was hiking out of here with his prisoner, and he saw us come in, that he may have turned around to come back?"

"If he did, he would have also seen the helicopter that brought the rifleman back in and might anticipate that we may need some help."

"It's a long shot, and long shots are good to hope for, but I am not going to bet my longevity on it. We will have to come up with something on our own."

I finished hacking a couple of shooting holes in the wall.

"Rusty, since that rifle is not a Weatherby and you have open sights under your scope, can you shoot through those holes?"

"I sure can, hey, listen." Rusty put his ear to one of the openings. "I hear the helicopter."

"Oh, great. He is probably coming back with reinforcements," I said, "We have to get out of here, they might even have rocket propelled grenades or something. I have an idea. As soon as the helicopter comes around the bend in the river in sight of the airstrip, that rifleman is going to be distracted. Maybe we can make a dash for it."

"Which way do you want me to dash, Dad?"

"Duck around the corner on your side and cover me. I am going to wait to see what that helicopter is going to do. If you happen to see the rifleman, go ahead and take him out. Oh, and when you go move fast."

Suddenly, appearing around the river bend and heading straight to the cabin, came the maroon–and–gray Robinson R66.

"I think he is going to try to land in front of the cabin, Dad."

"Its not level enough for that. He is planning on hovering low enough for his people to get out and then he'll land at the pad. As soon as the door opens and the first one gets out, I am going to put them and their whole helicopter out of business. You get around that corner. Find that rifleman and make sure he doesn't get me."

"Okay, Dad. Here I go." Rusty disappeared out of the door and around the corner of the cabin. I held my breath, waiting for a shot to ring out. Thank-fully, there was none.

The R66 came in clockwise, quickly setting down on the steep incline only fifty feet away and slightly below the entrance to the cabin. The pilot held the helicopter's left skid on the ground on the uphill side with the right one suspended in the air, keeping the craft level, which was now facing toward the airstrip and positioned directly between the front door of the cabin and the rifleman's position. The sliding door of the R66 opened, revealing three men besides the pilot armed with AK-47s. Instantly, I burst through the door, lunging toward the helicopter. I waited until I was within ten yards of it before I began blasting away.

The first of the three men saw me running toward him while he was only halfway out of the front passenger door when a slug from my ten-gauge took him in the chest, slamming his body back into the hovering chopper. The first of the two men in the backseat, surprised and off balance, frantically attempted to exit the rear door. As he raised his automatic weapon at me, a second slug caught him in the midsection. The third man shouldered his weapon from where he still sat in the rear seat, but before he could start shooting, the pilot tried to turn the helicopter in a clockwise direction and down the hill. His effort to get away proved futile as I managed to put three more of those four-hundred grain slugs into the cockpit, blowing out his windshield, instrument panel, and the pilots rib cage, in that order.

The Robinson R66 continued its turn to the right, rotating into a tail-up, clockwise spin, somersaulting upside down with its blades whacking the rocky hillside until they broke into a million pieces as the chopper exploded into flames. Expecting to hear the report of that Weatherby magnum any second I quickly retreated to where Rusty had made it around the corner of the cabin on the uphill side and from where he had witnessed the demise of the helicopter.

For several minutes, we waited for any secondary explosions. Still not sure what had become of the rifleman, we hesitated venturing out. I had not heard Rusty fire his rifle, so I assumed that the rifleman must still be a potential threat.

"Are you all right, Rusty?"

"I'm fine, Dad. I can hardly believe you did all that with only five shots."

"I can."

Rusty and I looked at each other, surprised that we were not alone. Together, we stepped from around the corner of the building. Stepping from around the opposite corner where I had originally approached the cabin, came Officer Calvin Trent.

"Cal! It's ... you!" I exclaimed.

"It *is* me."

"You ... son-of-a-gun. Are you okay? You had better get inside, there is still one left out there. Rusty, did you get a shot at that rifleman?"

"No, I never did see him. The helicopter was in the way."

"I took care of that," Cal said. "I also have a prisoner bound and gagged and waiting for us in your new Kodiak. Are you going to be able to get that tricycle in the air in all that brush?"

"You don't worry about that tricycle gear. That Kodiak is a whole new breed of bush plane, you'll see," I said as I wrapped my arms around my good friend, slapping him on the back.

"Oh, oh, easy there, Lou. I took a bullet in there."

"Oh, my God, Cal. I am sorry. I forgot all about that. Let's get you to a doctor."

Officer Calvin Trent looked more like a mountain man than a game warden. Disheveled and dirty from three days away from a shower or shave and wearing a dead man's clothes—that probably hadn't been washed in twenty years—caked in dried blood that also still painted his face and neck from the bullet wound in his lower shoulder. It was a miracle that he was still alive, not to mention being on his feet. I knew he had lost a lot of blood and had been through a frightening ordeal, but before we could take the time to hear the story, we needed to get in the air.

The Robinson R66 was smoldering with a dozen small fires still burning in the debris area, but none of them near enough to any trees or foliage that posed any danger of forest fire. We returned to the Kodiak where Rusty sat in the back with the prisoner, and Cal belted himself into the copilot seat next to me.

The whine of the turbo was a welcome sound as I once again went through the pre-takeoff checklist. With the brakes applied and the manifold pressure set for full power, I twisted the prop for maximum performance climb and hauled back on the yoke. The air from the four-blade propeller provided the elevator I needed to bring the nose up and away from the majority of the brush. I released the brakes, and the bush plane lunged forward. Within one hundred feet, we were airborne. I lowered the nose, and we headed to Purkeypile. I pointed out the Tin Creek lodge to Cal as we passed over it.

"Rusty and I found a dead man down there in that lodge in the root cellar. We think those clothes you have on and that cabin belonged to him. I reckon he refused to cooperate with the poaching ring, and they eliminated him. I am going to need to get Daily on it as soon as we get back. I have a feeling it might be your prisoner's doing. It looks like he was shot in the chest with a nine-millimeter."

"Well, I have his gun right here," Cal said, pulling a nine-millimeter Beretta from his waistband. "I will give it to the Lieutenant, and he can check the ballistics and see if they match the bullet from the body."

We could see that Lieutenant Daily and his investigation team were gone from Purkeypile as we approached the now-deserted airstrip. Cal was silent as he stared out of the window at the dead helicopter that he had flown for more than fifteen years.

"What happened down there, Cal?" I asked as we passed over the Bell Ranger.

"I had received at least a dozen complaints from trappers that the R66 was involved in illegal activities, but no one had any proof or pictures. Therefore, I had been looking for it off and on all winter. An old native trapper by the name of Benson Goodnight called me that morning and said he saw the R66 heading south from Tanana. I dropped everything and came over as fast as I could. As soon as the Purkeypile airstrip came into view, I saw the maroon-and-gray helicopter sitting between midfield and the west end of the airstrip. Three men were on the ground and had two dead wolves laid out alongside one another as I came over the ridge. Of course, they wasted no time in throwing the dead animals into the R66, and all of them piled into the helicopter.

"Before they could get spooled up, however, I came in above them and hovered over the top of the Robinson. Turning on the megaphone, I ordered them out of the chopper and onto the ground. Surprisingly, they initially complied, at which time I started to land the Bell Ranger. I was less than a foot away from setting the Ranger on the ground when that little creep in the back—who goes by the name of Possum—jumped up and popped off three rounds at me with this nine iron." Cal patted the side of the nine-millimeter Beretta.

"The windscreen shattered, and one of the rounds hit me as I spun the Ranger 180 degrees to get the chopper between the shooter and me and set it on the ground as quickly as possible. I would have gone airborne from there, but I knew I was hit and wasn't sure how hard. So afraid that I might lose consciousness I set it on the ground.

At that point, all three of them began to shoot at the Ranger while I bailed and took off running into the brush. I was bleeding a lot, and soon enough, I was down and everything was spinning around in circles. The next thing I knew, the other two fellows found me and dragged me back to the Robinson where they continued to shoot my Bell Ranger all to pieces. The only one who bothered to pick up any of his brass was the big one, who the other two called Victor and who I shot back there at the cabin because he had that big .378 Weatherby magnum pointed at you and was about to pull the trigger when you were busy taking down the Robinson. I thought it would only be a matter of time before they killed me. Otherwise, he wouldn't have bothered picking up the spent cartridges from that big Weatherby."

"Why did they leave you alone with Possum? And how did you manage to get his gun?" I asked.

Cal looked reluctant to answer my question. "Lou, first of all, I am going to make sure that this whole operation is completely shutdown. Secondly, we are going to call in the FBI to investigate another aspect of this case."

"Why is it taking you so long to answer my question?"

"Because evidently there has been a contract put out on you from some organized crime operation. When Victor—the one you called the rifleman—caught up to me, I heard him tell his pilot, who he referred to as Flyboy, not to kill me. His exact words were, 'We need him to get to Worley. Without Worley, we don't get paid.'

"That is when they took me back to the old trapper's cabin where they left Possum to watch me. I knew I had to do something while the other two were gone. I thought about waiting until he fell asleep, but figured it would be me that passed out before him so I—"

"You what?" I asked, leaning closer to Calvin for fear I might miss some of the story.

"I wet myself," Calvin confessed.

"You wet yourself on *purpose*?"

"Yeah ... and that's not all."

"What do you mean, 'that's not all'? You mean you ...?"

"Uh, huh," Cal said, obviously embarrassed.

"You did all that on *purpose?*" I asked again, totally, flabbergasted.

By now, Cal was completely red-faced and Rusty, who had been listening to the story, was in stitches.

"Okay, so keep going. Did you think you could knock him out with the smell or something?" I asked, my sides aching from laughter. Rusty was laughing so hard that he was sucking air like a Tim Taylor shop vac. I glanced back at Possum; even *he* was cracking up.

"I was taking a chance that he would want me to clean up as bad as I wanted him to let me clean up. I talked him into untying my hands so I could do just that and change into some of the old clothes that were lying around. With only the lantern going, visibility wasn't too good, so he didn't notice my picking up one of the dirty rags. When I tossed it at his face, he ducked and turned giving me the opportunity that I needed to overpower him and get his gun."

"Cal, in a million years, I don't think I would have ever thought to do that, and if I did think of it, I still don't believe I would have. But obviously it worked because you're here and he's there. So good job, Officer," I said. "Tell us what happened next."

"Well, after I got the gun, I grabbed these clothes I have on and a bar of soap, and we made a trip down to the creek where I was able to do a proper job of washing. Then Mr. Possum and I started to walk out. We made it about five miles on our way to Tin Creek, where I planned to go on to Purkeypile. Then we heard an airplane. Somehow, I knew it would be you. You have no idea how glad I was to see a tricycle gear."

"You just wait. This tri-gear is a real bush plane. You should—"

Rusty and Cal started rolling on the floor they were laughing so hard. "Cal, Dad is a little touchy when it comes to his new tricycle. Can you tell?"

"I see that. Well, anyway, we turned around and started back. I was not sure if we would make it before you left or not and half-expected that you might not even land once you saw the overgrown runway. This trike must be some super bush plane to get in and out of that place."

"It sure is," I shot back, "It surely is, and don't you forget it."

Rusty and Cal looked at each other, still grinning.

"Cal, tell me more about the hit that is out on me."

"I wasn't able to get a whole lot out of the Possum back there," Cal said in a low voice. "He did tell me that Victor Tortellini was the guy they worked for, but they didn't know who Victor worked for. We know it is an organization called Tourism International, Inc. They supposedly book tourists to see Alaska and then take them on illegal trophy hunts or sell them trophies from the stack of illegal kills back at that cabin. I have been after them for years, so I was surprised that they grew so careless all of a sudden. I think their carelessness was intentional so that I would catch them and they could get to me at a place where I would be alone."

"Whoever is behind this operation is the one who has the most to gain from Dad's demise." Rusty added.

"Actually, I am not convinced that enough of the public knew it was Lou who funded the poaching covert operations of a few years ago. Like I say, we are going to get the FBI involved and see what else is under the covers."

"The FBI investigated Kati's attempted kidnapping and that never went anywhere." I said. "I question whether they are competent enough to do any better now than they did then. But I know someone I can ask."

"Who is that?" Cal quickly asked.

"Gino Pastelli," I said. If someone has a hit out on me he would know about it."

"You killed his son, Deano. Do you really think he will tell you anything?" Rusty asked.

"Maybe, maybe not, but it might be worth asking. For that matter, maybe he is the one who has hired the hit. Cal, what would it take for me to get authorization to see him?"

"We will run it by the Lieutenant. He will be able to get us in."

"What do you mean us? You have to stay here and heal up," I said.

"I don't think you will get the authorization before then," Cal said, grinning. Rusty chuckled and shaking his head, then sat back in his seat.

As soon as I had acquired a cell phone signal, I called Arnold Bradley to report that we had rescued his game warden. As I turned to final, and sat the Kodiak on the ground at Bold's there were a half dozen cop cars waiting along with an aid car from Medic One.

Calvin Trent was very lucky. At the time he took the bullet, he had his right arm above his head. The bullet had arrived at a thirty-degree angle from Cal's right side as he sat at the controls of the Bell Ranger, barely missing his rib cage but destroying the latissimus dorsi muscle just below his shoulder socket and armpit. The injury required reconstructive surgery to repair the muscle. The surgeon warned that the damage would result in a substantial loss in range of motion to his right arm. I immediately became concerned for Cal's future as a commercial helicopter pilot. Nonetheless, I expected he would be back to work long before the doctors wanted him to because he was Calvin Trent. I also knew that he was ready for some rest and recuperation until then. As soon as he felt able, we would head straight to the lodge at Loon Lake to do some very important fishing. I mean resting.

CHAPTER 37

Lieutenant Daily and his investigating team had barely begun processing the evidence from the Purkeypile crime scene when Rusty and I came home with the long-lost game warden. Their elation at seeing Calvin Trent alive and somewhat in one piece eclipsed any disappointment they may have felt for not being involved in his rescue. However, their criminal investigation expertise would more than make up for it as they went about systematically connecting the chain of evidence recovered at the crime scene and identifying the many individuals involved as well as their connection with one another and the case.

Kati went with me when I took Cal to the hospital, where, together with his wife, Nanci, their son, Anthony, and Arnold Bradley, we remained during his surgery and throughout the night. Cal awoke briefly in the recovery room just long enough to acknowledge that we were there. Then, exhausted from his ordeal and with the help of the pain medication, he slept through the remainder of the night.

"Mr. Worley, you have done this department a huge service," Mr. Bradley began. "Cal may very well have not come back from that alive if it had not been for your quick thinking and action. I wish I knew how to thank you."

"That goes for me too, Lou," Nanci added, giving me a big hug. "Thank you so much."

"You all don't need to make a big fuss about it," I said. "Cal would have done the same for me. Besides, I will probably be regretting it in a month or so when we are up at the lodge and he catches the world record lake trout or something."

Nanci, Arnold, and Kati got a big laugh out of that one, as they were fully aware of the short time I held the unofficial world record for moose until Cal filled his tag no more than four hours later. Just the same, I was thankful that my efforts in diverting the course of the conversation had proved successful.

I would like to report that Calvin Trent fully recovered from his wound, but such was not the case. The damage to the latissimus dorsi muscle that wraps around the ribs and connects to the back muscles left Cal without the adequate range of motion in his right arm to satisfy the FAA requirements for the commercial pilot helicopter medical examination, therefore costing him his commercial flying privileges and forcing him into an early retirement.

Actually, he was not really forced. Arnold Bradley offered him a desk job with the intimation that he would be in line for the superintendant's chair when Arnold retired, but Cal was not interested. Fortunately, he could still fly helicopters as a private pilot, so I bought a brand-new Bell 407 with his name stenciled on the door, since it was obvious the four of us would be doing a lot more fishing and hunting.

Cal, Nanci, Kati, and I spent a few more weeks at our lodge on Loon Lake. The fishing was so good it almost got boring. (*Almost.*) The first day of moose season, we once again filled our tags this time, from the front porch of the lodge.

Shortly after returning home to Wasilla, a registered letter arrived in the mail from a law firm in Chicago, Illinois. I was stunned after reading it and handed the letter to Kati as I sat down, attempting to wrap my mind around another new development. The family of Victor Tortellini had named me in a wrongful death lawsuit for my part in his demise. I scrolled up Cal's name on my list of contacts and mashed on the green button.

"Good morning, Lou. What's up?"

"Cal, you are never going to believe this. I killed four guys up there at Tatitna, and I am being sued for wrongful death of the one guy I didn't even shoot."

"You mean Victor Tortellini?" Cal asked.

"Uh huh. His family filed suit with a law firm in Chicago."

"Don't worry about that. I was the one who took Victor down. I'll give Lieutenant Daily a call; he will get this straightened out."

Later the same day, Cal called me back.

"Lou," he said, "Daily wants to see you and Rusty. Let me know when you can go up there, and I will go with you."

I called Rusty, and we met Cal at the diner in Wasilla before going to see the Lieutenant.

"Daily wants to confirm my account and report of everything that happened at Tatitna," Cal said, "and he is going to suggest you retain an attorney to handle the wrongful death lawsuit. It has nothing to do with the criminal investigation or its findings. Anyone can file any kind of suit any time they want."

"Rusty, do you want to handle this for me?"

"Absolutely not, Dad. I will be to busy being your body guard, you need a trial lawyer who specializes in wrongful death suits to deal with this. However, I can do some investigating for you and find out who all is involved in this. I am sure it must be connected to the contract that is out on you. Don't you agree, Cal?"

"I would just about guarantee it," Cal answered. "In addition, I don't think that either you or Lou should go anywhere near Chicago because that is exactly why this suit has been filed—to draw you out there on their turf where they can get to you. I think someone is offering some big money for Lou to be dead."

"We better get going or the Lieutenant might think we are not coming," I said.

Lieutenant Daily heard us coming down the hall and ushered us into his office. "Have a seat, gentlemen. First of all, Mr. Worley, let me express the department's gratitude for your and Rusty's great work in finding and saving our beloved Officer Trent.

We have discovered a few things during our investigation that we think you should know. First, a corporation named Tourism International, Inc., or TII, owned the helicopter that Lou shot down and is nothing more than a front for illegal poaching among other things."

"Yes, sir. Cal already briefed us on all of that," I said.

Daily looked at Cal and then back at me before continuing. "The man who Cal shot—who, according to Cal's statement and report, was about to shoot you—was a man from Chicago by the name of Victor Tortellini."

"Yes, sir. Cal—"

Cal kicked me in the leg and shot me a look. Daily paused momentarily, without looking up, and then continued. "The two men who were with Tortellini when they abducted Calvin worked for him, but both of them had connections with the mafia in Chicago. The man flying the airplane— the one they called Flyboy—his name was Jeeter Pastelli, the nephew of Gino Pastelli and cousin of Deano Pastelli, who Mr. Worley killed almost seven years ago. We still have the third man they call Possum in custody, and he has proven very helpful in our investigation in this matter."

"Lieutenant, did he say anything about a mafia hit or contract that may be out on me?"

"I am getting to that," Daily said, glancing up from his file folder. "Possum's real name is Billy Bob Bower. His connections with Chicago organized crime go all the way back to when he was a kid, shining Gino Pastelli's shoes on the corner of thirty-fifth and Manhattan where Gino owned a nightclub called The Manhattan Club. Gino, of course, is still in prison at Leavenworth and will be for the rest of his natural life. However, he still holds control of his organizations from the inside. Lou, it is clear to the department that you and your family may be in very grave danger. The problem is this: This whole thing is out of our jurisdiction, and the only way we have of handling it is to turn it over to the FBI." "Lieutenant, do you believe that Gino has ordered this hit on me?" I asked.

"Yes, I do," Daily answered. "I also believe that the attempted abduction of Kati was the beginning of several planned plots to get to you or your family, including the abduction and attempted murder of Cal and the wrongful death lawsuit that has been filed against you. We see this as an attempt to get you to go to Chicago where they can make you pay for your crimes against Gino's family.

"I suggest that you retain an attorney who can fight this lawsuit for you. I also recommend that you stay away from Chicago and keep your family away from public places as much as possible. In the meantime, I will turn this investigation over to the FBI."

"Lieutenant, can you do something for me?" I asked abruptly.

"Sure, Mr. Worley. What is it?"

"I need credentials and authorization to get into Leavenworth to see Gino."

Daily's mouth fell open. "Lou, I just told you. If you go back there, it is very unlikely you will come back alive."

"It appears to me that if I stay here it will be just as unlikely that I stay alive. At least I will be doing something to eliminate the threat. Oh, and please do not say a word to the FBI. Heck, they probably used to wash his car or something."

Daily grinned ever so slightly. Picking up his office phone, he punched one of the interoffice connection lines. A secretary answered. "Florence, would you tell my two guests they can come in now?"

I turned to Cal, but he was avoiding my eyes. Rusty had as big a question mark on his brow as I did on mine. We could hear footsteps walking down the hall, approaching the office.

"Come in, gentlemen. I'm sure you remember Mr. Lou Worley," Daily said.

Turning to see the two men who were coming through the door, I was not pleasantly surprised to see special agents Singer and Travis of the FBI. I had not seen either of them since the day Kati killed one of her would-be abductors.

Both agents extended their hands in greeting, as did Rusty and I, putting forth an effort to conceal our lack of respect for their mediocre investigation into the attempted kidnapping, which amounted to basically, doing nothing about it.

"How ya doin'?" I said and sat down.

"Lou and Rusty, I have asked Agents Singer and Travis to join us to bring you two up to date on their conclusions. It has been determined that Dale Stanley was the brains behind Kati's attempted abduction and there is also a connection between Dale Stanley and Gino Pastelli."

Suddenly, Lieutenant Daily had my attention. I sat up in my chair and looked intently at Agent Singer, eager to hear more.

"The FBI and our investigation team," Daily continued, "anticipated that you would want to pay Mr. Pastelli a visit, so Agents Singer and Travis are going to see to it that you get to do just that."

I was all ears. I had to reconsider my opinion of Agent Singer and Agent Travis. Actually, they were a little more on top of their game than I gave them credit for.

"You have been keeping all of this a secret?" I asked.

"Yes, sir, Mr. Worley. We had to make it appear that we were unable to pursue the case any further due to lack of evidence, while at the same time establishing the connection between Dale Stanley, who, by the way, is Gino's sister's son, and organized crime." Singer answered.

"So Stanley was a brother to the other nephew, Judo that I shot and killed during the drug war?" I asked.

"No, that was Gino's brother's boy. Gino had a half-brother named Frankie Markin, who died of cancer twenty years ago, and Gino raised his son Terry, aka Judo, and taught him to fly as he did his own son, Deano."

"No wonder they call themselves 'the family,' " I muttered.

"Mr. Worley," Singer continued, "we want to help you get this contract taken down, and you are the only one who can do it. We have some ideas that you might be able to use to persuade Gino to take it down. Until he does, sooner or later, someone will get the job done. You have done too much for your country and the state of Alaska for us to leave you hanging."

"I appreciate that, Singer, but I just want to get in there to see him. I already know what I am going to say. You can believe me when I get done talking to him he will be left with little choice but to take it down," I said.

"So what is it you plan on saying to him?" Travis asked.

"That is between him and me and only him and me. I just need you guys to get me in there."

"Okay, that's fine. But for your safety, we want to fill you in on our plan for getting you in and back out of there alive."

"That I am interested in, as well as grateful for."

"We think that for you to go there as Lou Worley, you would be at a greater risk of detection than if you were disguised as an FBI agent under an assumed name. So, here is our plan.

"First, we will contact Gino and let him know that you want to talk to him. Then, we will set up a date and time for your visit, maybe a month from now. That will give him time to make whatever arrangements he wants to make to have you ambushed, either while coming or going from the prison. Then we will move you in several weeks earlier, disguised as an FBI agent and not even the guards will be any the wiser. Besides, we assume that most of them are spending Gino's money anyway. At that point, you can say whatever you want to him, but I would suggest you make it convincing. If Gino still hates you when you leave, sooner or later you will be a dead man."

"Don't worry. I will be convincing. You can count on it. When do we leave?"

"Let's plan on meeting with him in three days. We can either fly commercially or, if you prefer, we can go in your personal jet," Singer said.

"Be at my gate at five a.m. the day after tomorrow," I said. "Are you coming, Cal?"

"I wouldn't miss it for the world, Lou."

"How about you, Rusty? Are you coming?"

"Absolutely, Dad. Keera would skin me if I didn't."

"One more thing, Mr. Worley," Singer said. "Here is your FBI identification and shield. Rusty and Cal will only accompany you from where you all will be staying to the parking area and back. You will only be accompanied by Travis and me when we go to the prison. That will be the most vulnerable time, but anything we do to add security at that point may tip our hand.

"I need the N number (FAA registered ID number for all US registered aircraft) of your private jet. We will deny all access to that number via the FAA website. The designation in the remarks section of your flight plan shall be 'military business.' Any questions?"

I looked at Singer and Travis with a completely new respect for the thought they had put into the plan. I was suddenly more than willing to cooperate with them.

"No. I think I got it. Just be there at five a.m. I'll provide the food for the flight. We are flying into Kansas City International, is that right?"

"No, we will be flying into the 'Sherman Army Airfield'," Travis answered. "Agent Clarence Fynn from the Kansas City FBI field office will pick us up and brief us on when we go in to the prison and the procedures. We will call him today, and they will set up our phone conversation with Gino."

"What if that doesn't go well?" Rusty asked.

"We are the FBI. He will see us. Remember, he will not be expecting a visit from you," Singer added.

"What are the chances he would say no?" I asked.

"The more he wants to see you dead, the greater the chance he will agree to the interview. He would expect the interview to be next month and would also expect you to be dead before you ever make it to the interview room. He certainly won't be expecting you to show up disguised as an FBI agent."

"I do have a question," I said. "How much is Gino worth in liquid assets?"

Singer and Travis paused for a moment as I looked first to them and then to Daily and Cal.

"Close to a billion, I'd say," Singer conjectured, looking at Travis. "Why? Are you thinking about buying him off to get him to take down the contract?"

"Absolutely not, never in a million years." I said.

I called a local catering service and placed an order for sandwiches and pasta salads to be delivered to my airplane by three a.m. the morning of our departure. Then, I began preparing my IFR flight plan. By six a.m. the morning of our planned departure, we were pulling the nose of the Cessna Citation CJ4 off the new asphalt runway on our way to the Glasgow airport at Billings, Montana, our one and only fuel stop.

The flight to Glasgow some 1,646 miles away took four hours and fifty-three minutes. The next stop was Sherman Army Airfield, which is actually an uncontrolled general aviation community airport on the south runway and military base runway on the north. The FBI had made previous arrangements with a military flying club for the use of one of their old World War II hangars where we parked the CJ4.

Agent Clarence Fynn met us at the parking ramp, where we transferred our belongings into his limousine. From there, he took us to a field office located in a house in the town of Leavenworth, Kansas, a short distance from the prison. It was a large, six-bedroom, three-bath home owned at one time by a wealthy railroad tycoon. This would be our home until we finished our business in Leavenworth.

"Dad," Rusty called from his bedroom.

I paused, just inside the doorway.

"What do you plan to say to Gino to get him to take down the contract?"

"I have no idea, I am waiting for the Lord to give it to me before the time comes."

I returned to my bedroom and shut the door to pray. It went something like this:

"Father in heaven, I would very much like to see Gino Pastelli saved into the kingdom of God. I know that is your will too. However, it seems like such a long shot from a human perspective, but my experience with you so far, has convinced me that long-shots do not exist when it comes to the will of God. I pray that you will find a way that Gino can get past his pride and hatred long enough for him to realize the love of God through Jesus Christ His Son. I also pray that the Spirit of God will move upon him to do the right thing as far as the contract is concerned and for the honor and Glory of God. Amen."

CHAPTER 38

D ressed in a Jack Victor two-piece gray suit with white shirt, tie, and a gray Peter Grimm houndstooth fedora, the last thing I felt like was an FBI field agent. But when I stepped in front of the mirror, I had to admit that I actually did resemble one. My new undercover name was Special Agent David Myer.

"How do I look, boys?" I asked, approaching Agents Singer and Travis as they were having coffee in the kitchen.

"Wow!" Travis exclaimed. "Just like a real G-man. If I didn't know better, I would think you were part of the detail."

"Mr. Worley," Singer spoke up. "The guards may ask you what we are wanting with Mr. Pastelli. Just tell them we have news about his late nephew. Do *not* say we have questions. We don't want him requesting that his attorney be present. That could take two weeks."

Singer and Travis had provided small arms and ammunition—several Glock-nines and four AR-15s in case our little surprise for Gino blew up in our faces. Cal and Rusty were searching through it all, checking and rechecking to make sure everything was functional and ready to fire. There really was no way of knowing who was on what side. When it comes right down to it, very few people are not for sale. Sometimes I wonder if there will be any functional honest citizens left in America beyond the next few generations.

A nondescript, tan Crown Victoria pulled into the driveway. Two men looking like FBI clones emerged, dressed almost precisely as me.

How are you supposed to tell these guys apart? I thought to myself. *It is like a uniform.*

Agent Travis looked out the window for anything strange in the vicinity. Moving to the front door, he unlocked three deadbolts and let the two men inside.

Agent Fynn was the first through the door. Neither Singer nor Travis had ever seen the other man and had not expected anyone else to be with him.

Fynn flashed his credentials. "This is Warden Gilley," he said introducing the new man, "and this is Agent Singer, Agent Travis, and Mr. Lou Worley. These other two men are with the Alaska State Police and have come along as bodyguards for Mr. Worley."

We all greeted the warden cordially.

"We weren't expecting anyone to be with you or to know about this other than ourselves," Singer said.

"Nothing goes on in my house that I don't know about, gentleman," Warden Gilley said. "Those are the conditions. You need not worry; your secret is safe with me. I am well aware of Gino Pastelli's operations, that he still has control of even from the inside, and we are trying to sever his outside connections. That is why I insisted on briefing you men personally. If I wanted you exposed, I would have had you come to my office where you would be more at risk of exposure, but I came to you to help you do this without all of that. Today, we are having a surprise lockdown. All the guards except for a chosen few I have selected will be involved in an in-house sweep for contraband. The normal procedures for visitation will be modified somewhat, and I will accompany you personally to the interview room along with my people. If you gentlemen are agreeable to those conditions, we can move forward from here. Otherwise, the deal is off."

I immediately liked the warden. He was a no-nonsense leader who drew an unmistakable line in the sand.

The warden and Fynn came with us in the limo, and Singer drove us to the prison. We entered through a private entrance used only by the warden himself and his immediate staff. The first set of sliding bars let us into a control room that I am sure was usually well staffed. However, for our visit, only those members of the warden's elite, which he had brought along, operated it. Seven electronic, sliding, solid-steel doors later, we stepped into a room approximately thirty-feet square with one poker-sized square steel table with two chairs, all of which were bolted to the floor. Seated at the far side of the table, facing us, was Gino Pastelli.

There was no evidence that Gino recognized me when I came through the door. Actually, he seemed a little baffled.

"Sir, I was under the impression I would be able to speak to him alone," I said to the warden, under my breath.

"You can, Mr. Worley. We just want to make sure that he is completely secure. How long will you be?"

"I really have no idea. Is there a time limit?"

"No, but if it goes over thirty minutes, he could start getting restless and uncooperative."

"I will remember that."

"We are going to walk over with you and introduce you so he knows that I have sanctioned this meeting."

The five of us walked toward Gino, who was briefly distracted by Singer and Travis checking his security shackles and bracelets.

"Gino," the warden began, "do you remember Lou Worley?"

I stepped forward and looked Gino in the eye from five feet away. At first, he just sneered at me, but then started squirming in his seat.

"I thought yuz wazn't comin' for annutha month? I had a little surprise party planned for yuz."

"Gino, Mr. Worley wants to have a chat with you, so we are going to step out of the room for awhile. But we will be watching through the one-way glass, you be a good boy, okay?" With that, the warden turned and, followed by Fynn, Singer, and Travi,s stepped out of the room, leaving me alone with Gino.

Neither of us spoke for at least two minutes. I stood looking at him with my hands in my pockets before sitting in the chair four feet across from him.

"Yuz killed my zon and iz juz a matter of time till yuz and yuz whole famileez, diez for it," Gino said through clenched teeth.

I did not answer. I just sat looking at a very small, shriveled, sad, and bitter old man who had lost his one and only son. I could hardly imagine how he must have felt. I could see the hatred in his eyes and face. If he could get free and get his hands on a gun or knife, he would fill me with bullets and cut me into a million pieces, not so much to kill me, but to express the grief that he felt over losing his only son.

"What about Jeeter and Judo. I killed them too," I said, watching Gino's reaction.

"Themz wazn't my zonz," Gino said turning his head away. "Yuz are going to die becauze yuz killed my zon. Is thatz what yuz come here for, to see why I wantz yuz dead? If it iz, now yuz knowz, and yuz can go." For the first time, Gino appeared a little agitated. I waited a minute before answering.

"Jeeter and Judo was part of your family too. Not only that, but I am responsible for shutting down your drug and poaching operations in Alaska and have killed several of your major players. Why is this just about Deano?"

Gino's face turned red and his eyes narrowed, glistening with emotion. *"He waz my zon."* The emotion was coming to the surface, and I was hoping it would make it all the way to the top. I knew he needed to get it out of his system or there would be no chance that he would ever get past his hatred, no matter how unreasonable it was.

Gino picked at his fingers and looked at the one-way window, regaining his composure.

"I can only imagine what that must have felt like," I said. "I wish for your sake there could have been some other way."

"Why aren't yuz defending yuzelf?" Gino asked. "Doezn't yuz have zome story to tell me about how Deano wuz juz about to kill yuz or zumething, and you had no choice but to kill my zon." Again, the pain came into Gino's eyes, and he had to look away.

I kept silent, seeing deeper into the man. I had made it past the mafia persona, past the organized crime boss, and was now looking right into the heart of a father. For the first time, I felt compassion for the man. My God, if anyone killed one of my family members, especially my wife or daughters, I would pay a million dollars to every hit man in the world to get even, right or wrong, legal or not. Gino was growing more and more curious.

"Soez whutz are yuz doin here?" he asked. "Did yuz come to try to threaten me to take down the contract. Iz that what yuz came for?"

I looked him square in the eyes for a long moment.

"I am a father too, Gino, and have a rather large family that I will do anything to protect. So, yes, that is what I came hoping for except I was not planning to threaten you in any way. I really wasn't sure how to go about it because I thought I would be asking a convicted mafia crime boss. I don't know what makes you guys tick. I cannot understand why a father who claims to love his son as much as you obviously did would put him in harm's way by raising him to walk a path that leads to only one end—destruction and death. Did you think there would be no consequences for that lifestyle?

"Gino, I can feel your hurt. I see it in your face. There is no question that you loved your son, but it wasn't I who killed him. It was you. You are the one who raised him to take a road that leads only to death. And look at where your choices have landed you. You and Deano should be fishing on a lake somewhere in Michigan or Alaska, enjoying the God-given camaraderie of a father and son. The only thing that comes close to that is the relationship of father and daughter. I trained my children to reason from cause to effect and to put their decisions on fast-forward before they make them. Then take full responsibility, without making excuses or blaming someone else for the outcome. I feel horrible that it was me who handed Deano the inevitable effect of his lifetime of choices, but if it had not have been me, it would have been someone else. The Bible says in Proverbs 26:2, "As the bird by wandering, as the swallow by flying, so the curse causeless shall not come."

"My prayers are with you Gino, but I will continue to fight to protect my family, no matter what you choose to do. It is just a shame that others have to die so you can continue to hate everyone else for what you have brought on yourself."

With that, I stood, turned toward the door, and motioned at the one-way window that I was finished.

"Worley," Gino called after me. He paused. "Yuz are a brave man for coming here today. Yuz iz right, if I could do it over ... well, whuz eh the point. I will take it down."

Slowly I turned back around and took one long, last look at Gino.

"Thank you, Mr. Pastelli," I said. I turned once more toward the door, my footsteps echoing on the concrete floor.

"Worley," Gino said again. My heart stopped at the thought that he might have already changed his mind. "Whatever happened to that kid that worked for Deano? Whutz-eh his name, the one that wuz in the plane crazh?"

"Beltray," I said.

"Thaz it, Beltray Gibbons. I heard he went to work for yuz. Iz that right?"

"He is working for God now," I said. "Would you like him to come and see you?"

Gino's gaze fell toward the floor for a long moment before he answered. "Yeah. I think I would like that."

The steel door to the interview room opened, and Warden Gilley, with Singer and Travis in the background, ushered me through.

Rusty and Cal were waiting in the car. After Singer Travis, and I thanked Warden Gilley for his cooperation, we climbed into the limo.

"How did it go, Dad?"

"He said he would take it down," I said. "I'll tell you all about it later."

Cal squeezed my shoulder as if to say *thank God*, which I immediately did.

Over the next year, I took Beltray Gibbons to see Gino seven times. The threat of assassination no longer hung over my head, and Beltray had no fear or concerns about it at all.

Seven times he went in to meet with the crime boss and seven times he came out alive and praising God for the miracle that had taken place in another human heart. Like seven washings or purifications, seven Bible studies took place between two career criminals inside a federal penitentiary.

One year later, Gino Pastelli passed away, succumbing to the cancer he had battled for the last ten years.

Cal, Beltray, and I made one last trip to Leavenworth. Gino was laid to rest in the prison cemetery with no friends, family, or business associates present except the three of us and a few inmates and guards.

Beltray gave the final eulogy. "A life on this earth, three-score and ten-years of time, is given to a man that he might have time and opportunity for *choosing* eternal life. Some make that choice sooner, some make it later, and some—sadly—never make it at all. Today, in the halls of heaven, there is joy and rejoicing, not over a life of bad choices and crime, not over a life of dysfunctional behavior and sin, but over the choice Gino Pastelli made that decided his eternal destiny. The one choice in his entire life that he finally got right was the decision to accept Jesus Christ as his personal Lord and Savior. Our Father who art in heaven, into thy hands we commend his spirit. Amen."

Another long winter reluctantly gave way to warmer weather, longer days, and liquid lakes. Kati, Nanci, Cal, and I prepared to spend another summer and fall at the lodge.

The international investigation into Jay Bold's activities during and after the Second World War had taken awhile and cost a lot, but had answered many questions. I had received the final determination of the investigation in the mail. Genneta was right; indeed, it was a love story of grand proportions, and much more than that. In fact, I may write a book about it someday.

I had just finished annualing the Kodiak when I got a call from Rusty.

"Dad, I just remembered that if we are going to hang onto that Alfred Creek claim, we need to go up there and work it again sometime this summer."

"Do you really want to go through all of that again?" I asked.

"All we need to do is work the claim. It doesn't have to be on a large scale."

"Okay. Let's wait till things dry up a little more and go up there and have a look at the place. Gee whiz, I haven't been there in over ten years. Cal and Nanci are going with Kati and me to the lodge for the summer. Why don't you guys come up and, the first chance we get, we can take off and run over to Alfred Creek one day," I said. "And don't forget to bring Mitchell along.

"Sounds great, Dad. See ya."

The boys and I had cut and cleared by hand a two-thousand by one-hundred-foot patch of ground behind the lodge designed to suit our need for a landing strip—more than adequate for the Kodiak, but we needed it to be long enough for the grandkids who were flying the old Cessna straight tail and Piper Clipper. We needed a small dozer for grading off the layer of tundra and sod and preparing the surface of the airstrip for the base course, which would consist of four hundred tons of quarry spalls, topped with another 240 tons of a special mixture of topsoil and crushed rock.

I arranged with the Air National Guard out of Anchorage to pick up some equipment from our home base and deliver it to the lodge: a little D-4 Caterpillar, a roller, and a John Deere tractor with backhoe and front-end loader. The equipment would arrive one at a time slung from a Boeing CH-46 helicopter. We were expecting the deliveries any day. The daily delivery of the rock would begin as soon as the dozer arrived and we could begin clearing.

Jason Sorenson (the chopper pilot who rescued my Skywagon from Glacial Lake) with his Sikorsky logging helicopter—capable of carrying three tons of payload—would make ten round trips a day from the Willow Lake quarry thirty-seven miles east of the lodge. The suspended hopper, with a remote-operated bottom gate, could be opened in motion less than ten feet above the ground and somewhat spread the load of rock along the graded portion of the airstrip. It would take Jason a total of sixty-four fifteen-hour days to transport the 640 tons of rock needed to build the runway. It was imperative that he got started as soon as possible.

Richard and Kelly were back from Aurora, Oregon. Unfortunately, Mr. Phillip Gentry had failed to survive a heart attack suffered in China in a remote area where little medical attention was available. His family had brought his remains home and no longer needed the house sitting services of my youngest daughter and her husband, who happened to also be my favorite dozer operator. Soon Richard and Kelly joined us at the lodge.

CHAPTER 39

The little D-4 needed some help, so I asked the army if they could transport our D-6 from our equipment yard at Bolds. I think they called it a CH-2000 or something. Whatever it was, it filled the sky with iron and sat the D-6 Caterpillar on our runway. Richard ran the D-6, and I ran the D-4.

The project progressed beautifully, and by summer's end, we had a high and dry turf runway. Well, more compact dirt than turf, at least until the grass grew in, which in Alaska could take a while. It didn't matter to us; we used it anyway. The mixture of compactable dirt and the two-inch ballast, when rolled and compacted on top of the three-foot-deep quarry rock for a base, provided a solid surface that left no ruts or loose sand or rock that could get sucked up into the propellers and potentially cause prop damage during takeoff.

Mitchell and Rusty wanted to work the Alfred Creek claim again to satisfy the claim laws and ensure that we preserved our mining rights. We decided to make that a project for the following summer season. However, while the runway project was still in full swing, the three of us along with Cal decided to have a look at it. We never did pursue our search for gold any further than the excavation site where we unearthed the mother lode, even though we still suspected that there might be more treasure yet to discover on the other side of the creek downstream.

Leaving Richard to run the dozer while Jason continued his grueling fifteen-hour days delivering the big rock, the three of us piled into the 407

Bell Ranger with our own private chopper pilot Calvin Trent and headed for Alfred Creek.

On the way, I nostalgically recounted all the experiences the boys and I had during the five years we mined over seven billion dollars of gold from the Alfred Creek claim. The memory of the vacation I had taken when I lived in Darington Washington—the flying trip to Alaska in the old straight tail—and my very first landing at the Alfred Creek airstrip became more and more vivid in my mind the closer we came to the Caribou Creek drainage.

If I was looking for an adventure when I left on that trip, I certainly found it and more. Moreover, I found what I was really in search of but did not even know it: identity, purpose, and God.

Somehow, when a person is born into this world, without even knowing it, their life becomes a quest of the discovery or who they really are and what their purpose is for being on this earth. I have come to understand that apart from God, who is our Father, our desire will always be to find our divine parentage. As Beltray and his mother Lorraine, although separated for all those years and having never met, still felt the desire and need through those years to make that paternal connection to their identity. I remember Beltray describing it as: "The blood crying out."

We have no say in the matter of who our parents are, and no say in what we inherit from them, physically or materially. The only say or responsibility we have is what we do with the hand we have been dealt, the life we have been given. The wasted years of searching no longer matter when once our parentage is discovered. Beltray found it, Gino found it and I found it. I believe it is the longing of every human heart. It is true. The blood indeed cries out.

I sat in the copilot's seat of the Bell 407 next to Cal, eyes glued to the open hillsides as we passed by the north side of Sheep Mountain. There on the high altitude meadows, grazing in the lush green grass pastures was the familiar picture of the herds of Dall sheep. Frozen in time, virtually unchanged for thousands of years, the magnificent scene was breathtaking.

Cal began his descent into the Caribou drainage, watching the lush vegetation along the swollen creek for evidence of wind direction and velocity. Mitchell and Rusty were straining to see out of the side windows as we approached the airstrip. Carefully, Cal set the helicopter down in precisely the same spot he did the first time he and I met.

Although the construction of the cook shack and other buildings during our mining operations had changed a great deal of the landscape, I could still make out the spot where I had taken my afternoon nap while shoveling the gumbo from the runway that had stranded me and was preventing my departure from Alfred Creek. Moreover, I could still remember the elation I experienced when I found that stash of gold. Just thinking of it rekindled the gold fever we had all fallen victim to.

There have been times when I have thought, *what if*: What if I had never thought to reinvent the privy? What if the pasty gumbo had not been on the surface of the airstrip? What if I had never met William Shearer, or found Beltray, or prayed that prayer to God that was the precursor to my rescue?

I looked at Cal. "Do you remember the first day we met?"

Cal grinned and said, "Yeh, I was just thinking about that."

We walked around a bit, looking at the area where the lower end of the great vein had ended next to the east bank of Caribou Creek.

"Where do you want to work the claim, Mitchell? Everything on this side of the creek is all played out."

"Rusty and I were thinking that we should look into getting a permit to divert the creek. The last time our permit would not allow us to excavate into the creek bed, and we feel that there might be some money laying in there."

"I seriously doubt they will give us a permit to do that because of the effect it would have on the Salmon run," I said, "but it would be nice to dig around on the other side of the creek and see if we can find anything interesting over there." I turned to Cal. "Do you see any place on the other side of the creek where you could set us down?"

"Sure, no problem. I'm sure we can find a spot. Climb aboard."

The turbo wound back to life, and soon we were hovering above the swollen banks of the confluence of Alfred and Caribou Creeks as Mitchell and Rusty decided on a spot that might have the most potential.

"Cal," Mitchell called out, "there is a gravel bar protrusion where the creek separates and then dead-ends. Can you set us on that?"

"I see it." Cal said.

Moments later, we were again on the ground. Mitchell and Rusty began searching and probing for any sign of sand that might have some color in it, while Cal and I strolled around, reminiscing the early days of our acquaintance. Suddenly, something caught my eye. Only twenty feet away and at the water's edge, something lay glistening just under the surface. I knelt down and, with Cal looking over my shoulder, used my hands to scratch away some of the mud and sand that all but completely obscured the submerged shiny rock. Quickly, we realized that it was indeed gold.

"Rusty! Mitchell!" I hollered. "Come here quick!"

Seconds later, they were beside me with their shovels, carefully digging away the gravel, mud, and sand. We all stared in disbelief. The more of the sand and gravel the boys shoveled away, the larger the boulder of solid gold grew in size.

"Stop!" Mitchell yelled. "Cover it back up. We don't want anyone seeing it until we can get some equipment in here and excavate it. It will have to wait until next spring."

"Mitch is right," Cal, said. "It is way too big to deal with without equipment."

Then, Rusty verbalizing what each one of us was already thinking. "Dad, I think maybe we are back in the mining business. This might be our sequel."

"Hey Lou. You should write that book you told me you were researching," Cal said with a facetious grin. "You could call it—"

"*The Sequel to Alfred Creek.*"

Conclusion

What may seem fantastic or improbable to some are often normal fortuity for those whose experiences have conditioned them to expect nothing less.

The adventures of Lou Worley along with his friends and family are only a stage that I have constructed to demonstrate the good fortune that is nothing more than normality for the functional way of life.

In the story, Worley had spent many years toiling at his trade, living paycheck to paycheck as a loving husband and father, providing for his family. The Worley family's lifestyle epitomized functional living. Lou Worley's commitment to his family, community, and country brought him great respect and honor.

Although his wife and children held to the Christian faith, Lou Worley himself had never acknowledged the Lord Jesus Christ as his personal Savior. Nonetheless, good fortune attended him throughout his life. Even after his experience at Glacial Lake where his life was in grave peril and he sought the Lord for help and salvation, his success and prosperity remained uninterrupted.

Two paths, or two ways of life, are set before every man, woman, and child. Whether they understand or not, whether they believe or not, does not matter. It is entirely a cause-and-effect issue; a law of the universe.

The Bible describes the two paths as "blessings" and "curses"; one path will profit a man, and the other path will surely destine his every endeavor to failure. Prosperity, or fortuity, has nothing to do with spirituality; they are a way of life, the result of proper choices and behavior. Spirituality is: Jesus Christ; the Holy Spirit of God in dwelling in humanity.

The path that Beltray Gibbons had initially chosen was rapidly leading him to inevitable ruin and certain death. When Lou Worley presented him with an opportunity to take his life in a different direction, for the first time, Beltray realized that he held his destiny in his own hands. Opportunities like that often come but once in an individual's lifetime.

Beltray caught a glimpse of the eternal salvation of God through Jesus Christ, and the Lord employed him in His work. However, regardless of the vocation Beltray chose, his life was destined to become a positive contribution to society by virtue of the new road he had chosen to travel—that of functional living. The cause-and-effect relationship to choices and behavior, once again, are the issue.

Many people for many different reasons have no interest in eternal life provided through the Lord Jesus Christ. It may be that they only care to live their "three-score-and-ten" on this earth. That is of course, each individual's prerogative. Eternal life, though provided to all of humanity through Jesus Christ, may not be something all of humanity chooses to believe, receive, or for that matter, even want. Nonetheless, the cause and effect of everyone's thoughts, choices, and behavior is as certain as the law of gravity.

A few characters in the story met with the inevitable fruit of their way at the hands of Lou Worley and his ten-gage-shotgun. It may seem strange that a man who had entered the "born again" experience of a Christian would still take up arms in defense of himself and his community. But it is God who had His hand in the provisions of the constitution and amendments that guarantee every citizens the right to protect, their person, family, homes, and property. This part of the story illustrates that not only does the path of dysfunction end in destruction but the functional peoples of the earth, both Christian and non-Christian alike, are ultimately responsible for the protection and defense of their country and communities in which they live and raise their families. It was not Lou Worley who killed those men; it was the life *they* chose that dictated their end.

On the other hand, Lou Worley was not perfect. He had the same nature as the rest of the human race. In spite of that fallen sinful nature he inherited through the first Adam, he still made choices that resulted in prosperity and success in all of his endeavors. You could say it was the fruit of integrity. The only difference between his pre-Glacial Lake experience and his post-Glacial Lake experience was his choice to receive the Lord Jesus Christ as his Lord and Savior. That was a spiritual experience that took place in his heart. At *that* moment, *God,* became his life. A dependency and reliance on God replaced his self-sufficiency. There were no major changes in his behavior because he was already living a functional life; no major changes in his lifestyle because it was already reputable.

Few--even of professed Christians--live as pious a life as Lou Worley and yet he did not initially lay claim to a faith in Jesus Christ. The prosperity of his life was the result of the choices that he made. Then he encountered God. In that encounter, he realized that the "God of Bill Shearer" had heard his prayer and answered it in a most remarkable way. That was enough for Lou Worley. He was convinced that the God who answered his prayer as he lay dying from injury and exposure in that landslide of rocks at Glacial Lake, who also had performed such a miracle in Beltray Gibbons, was more than worthy of his worship, honor, and service for the rest of his life on this earth and for eternity.

When humanity considers one another, we see many differences: The rich and poor, the Christian and non-Christian, black and white, good and bad. But in God's eyes, there is no difference between the good person and the bad person, or their status, religion, creed, or color, not even saved or unsaved. God only sees man as encapsulated into His Son, therefore saved. On the cross of Christ, God incorporated all of humanity from every age, past, present and future, into His Son. The Lord Jesus Christ lived, bled, and died on the cross as the divine substitute for human kind. To understand what shall become of you, simply consider what become of Christ.

In God's eyes, salvation through Jesus Christ, His Son, is a reality for all humanity. The choice that any man ultimately makes regarding that fact will be the final say that shall override the declaration of God concerning that mans destiny. It is simply a matter of coming into agreement with God.

Let faith comprehend the invisible reality and your mouth—by faith-- speak the fact: that, "For me to live is Christ ..." (Philippians 1:21).

CPSIA information can be obtained at www.ICGtesting.com
Printed in the USA
BVOW07s2047200713

326384BV00001B/5/P

9 781462 713110